Clear Lake Dark Lies

Clear Lake Dark Lies

Jeff McClelland

Writers Club Press
San Jose New York Lincoln Shanghai

Clear Lake Dark Lies

Writers Club Press
an imprint of iUniverse.com, Inc.

For information address:
iUniverse.com, Inc.
620 North 48th Street, Suite 201
Lincoln, NE 68504-3467
www.iuniverse.com

This novel is a work of fiction. Any resemblence or references
to real events, businesses, organizations, and locales are intended
only to give the fiction a sense of reality and authenticity.
Any resemblance to actual persons, living or dead,
is entirely coincidental.

ISBN: 0-595-14676-7

Printed in the United States of America

To my children whom I love deeply, and to all those children, young and old whose voices will never be heard.

CHAPTER ONE

"Never have I seen such beauty. Mountains and trees that reach the sky surround the lake. I can think of no other place to make a home for my children."

From the diary of June Pringle
July 1883

"This is a horrible crime! This is one of the most detestable acts against another person that I have ever seen as a judge. In all my 21 years on this bench I have never passed judgment on a man as disgusting and evil as you. It's with great sorrow that I can not go beyond the law and add a hundred years to your sentence. If it were up to me, you would never see the light of day again. You're sentenced to seven years in the state prison without the option for parole." The sound of the gavel hit the wood. It was finally the end, or was it?

As I heard those words I felt as if some justice had been served, but another part of me cried for the people that were damaged. There were people whose lives had been changed, and how many more would come to feel the effects of all the evil that had taken place. The phrase, "sins of the fathers to the third and fourth generations," kept running through my mind. I wondered how long this evil had been passed from generation to generation. I was thirty years old and wondered if I would ever come to find the truth about all the things that had brought me to this place. As I sat in the courthouse, thoughts about my life, my childhood, things I had long forgotten, dreams, started to come back to mind. What was real? What was my imagination? There were doors I had closed and never wanted to open until now.

I grew up in a small town in the Pacific Northwest called Clear Lake. Clear Lake I felt was the safest place on earth most of the time. Growing up, I believed that everyone should have the chance to live here. About 500 people lived in town and the surrounding countryside. There were three grocery stores in Clear Lake. A Texaco station at the north end, a Shell station at the south end, and one right downtown called Meekers. Clear Lake had a Post Office and a jewelry store. There were two churches, one on the hill on Mud Street, and one on the main highway that ran through the middle of town. There was one tavern right in the center of town called Ellens. There was one barbershop next to the Odd Fellows Hall. A lot of odd people went to that hall. Clear Lake had a grade school but the older kids were shipped north to the town a few miles across the river to attend middle and high school. There was a wood mill on the west side of town, west of the lake, near where the old mill used to stand.

The town was among four hills, between two lakes, one being Clear Lake and the other being Mud Lake. It was strange to me that lakes being so close could be so different. One lake so clear you could see to the depths of the bottom, and the other one so muddy you couldn't even see one foot down through the water. It was as if nature had planned for the countryside to mirror the town that was to grow up between the two lakes. The town of Clear Lake, at times, probably should have been called the town of Mud Lake. This small rural village was the center of the world, as I knew it. It was like the television town of Mayberry. All that was needed was Sheriff Andy, but that wasn't reality. The reality is what happened to me and the people I knew.

I knew almost all the people in town and countryside. In and around town lived three kinds of people, those who knew nothing, those who knew some of the things, and those who knew and did the things. I believed I knew everything. I thought I was the only one who really knew about the things. To me life was about knowing. If you knew the right things the least likely you were to get hurt.

Most people in town believed I was slow and dumb, and I played along letting them believe what they wanted. Because of this belief they talked freely not realizing I was listening and understanding all along. It hurt me to be thought of as dumb, but I knew I would prove them all wrong some day. I thought life was pretty normal and that most people around town were as normal. It was only at certain times that I saw things were not right in Clear Lake.

I knew they would be coming tonight. It was something I could feel. Sometimes they would come many nights in a row. Other times not at all. Yet, tonight I knew they would come. I lay in my bed with the lights off hoping that they couldn't see me. Who was I trying to fool? They lived in the dark and could see best when the lights were off. I was afraid to fall asleep but my eyes grew heavy and I drifted off to a land of dreams.

I felt a presence in my room and awoke to see them floating towards me. My body is stiff and tense and I can not move. They are here to hurt me again. Maybe this time they will take me away for good. I close my eyes and wish them away.

That morning I woke up and looked out my bedroom window. What I saw terrified me! They had let me see them in the light. In the sky were witches, demons, ghosts, and many other creatures of evil. The sky was on fire and all these spirits seemed to be in their finest day. I screamed to my brother Collin, "quick, come to the window and look!" Collin replied, "are you seeing things again Luke?"

"No, come look, the sky if full of evil things."

"OK—I will—just wait a minute."

As Collin got out of bed and made his way to the window, our sister Liz came running into the bedroom. I told them both to look outside at the sky. As they did I wanted to hear the words of confirmation on what I saw. Collin said, "so what is it you see again?"

"Witches, demons, and such."

"I see no such things, you must still be sleeping or dreaming." I asked Liz what she saw? She said, "nothing but sky."

I wondered to myself if I was crazy or gifted to see such things? They were as real as my brother or sister. With disappointment I let go and shut the curtain and headed off for breakfast.

As mom made me a bowl of cold cereal I asked, "mom do you believe in demons and witches?"

"No silly boy," she replied.

"Well, I saw the sky full of them and I know they were there mom, but Collin and Liz couldn't see any."

"They don't exist Luke so don't worry." I knew better because I had seen them.

I don't know why my mom didn't know the demons? They were the ones that always made her sick. She would be in and out of the hospital, and I spent a lot of time living with other people because dad had to work so much of the time. I was never close to my mom; I didn't like her in my personal space, because to be in that space you had to be invited. I continued my talk with mom.

"Mom, if demons and witches do not exist than why do they have names?" Mom sighed really deep—as if I was asking too many questions.

"Luke they are things that men have made up to scare little boys."

"OK," I responded not believing a word mom had said. I knew full well that what I saw was real and not something made up in my mind. It did seem to my brother that being so young and worried about such things was a waste of time. I didn't really know why the demons and ghost had let me see them. I thought maybe they didn't want to be seen by me and that was the reason they were after me.

"Why do you worry so much about these things?" Collin asked with milk dripping down his cheek.

"Don't you care, that they could take us away at any time?"

"No, " he responded.

"Well I do! And I want to know about them to beat them before they get me."

"Just like mom says, 'silly boy that you're.'" Collin was laughing as he walked off to go outside as I followed behind. Collin was a year older than I was, and I felt it was my job to watch out for him because no one else did.

Now our little sister was different. I really didn't trust her at all. She would tell on us all the time, and in my mind she was our parent's favorite child. She seemed to always get her way. I could never understand her.

While camping up at Baker Lake one day, Collin and I were standing on the shore of the lake. We were watching dad and Liz in the boat. Dad was throwing the dog in the lake and making him swim back to the boat. When the dog got back to the boat he would throw him again and again. I asked, "Collin, why is dad throwing our dog in the lake?"

"I don't know. We should find out when dad and Liz get back in, "

"Sure makes me mad that they are doing that to my dog!" I said with anger.

As dad and Liz made their way back to the shore, Collin and I ran to meet them to find out why they had thrown Cumpy in the lake. I asked, "dad why did you throw Cumpy in the lake?"

"Because your sister thought it was funny to watch him swim."

"Liz it's not funny to see my dog almost drown!" I screamed.

Liz started to respond but dad jumped in and said, "Luke you let your sister alone, she was having fun."

It seemed to be that way all the time. Liz getting her way and Collin and I getting in trouble for trying to defend ourselves and the things we loved. When it came right down to it, I loved my sister and if anyone ever tried to hurt her I would defend her and keep her safe. Even at such a young age I felt I was the defender of the family.

Sometimes at night when the whole house was asleep I would hear Liz crying. I would get out of my bed and go sleep at the foot of her bed. I would say, "Liz I am here, the bad things won't get you."

"I am really scared Luke."

"What is it you're scared of?"

She couldn't tell me, but I knew it was the demons and witches that had made their way into the community of Clear Lake. I would wonder when the rest of the people were going to see what I saw and help me chase them away.

One morning I woke up and went outside. I fed my ducks and chickens and came back inside to eat breakfast. Every morning I would eat cold cereal. My mom was in the kitchen washing dishes. The house I lived in wasn't very big, only about 800 square feet. It had three small bedrooms, a kitchen, living room, bathroom, and a porch. It was heated with a wood stove. There was an old barn and a garage where dad stored his tools. It wasn't the nicest house in town, better than some, worse than others. Yet it was my home and I liked it. At breakfast I would always ask mom questions that I had been thinking of during the night.

"Mom, if there are no such things as ghosts, why does Liz cry sometimes at night?"

"Silly boy, your sister gets so tired she cries in her sleep."

Mom had an answer for every thing. It was usually wrong but she gave it anyway. She believed what people said about me, that I was dumb. I couldn't talk all that well, for my mouth wouldn't work right. That was why she called me silly boy. Always having dreams, chasing fantasies, and coming up with what she thought were elaborate tales, and always asking too many questions. Most of the time people didn't understand me because of my speech. They would have to listen very closely to what I said in order to understand.

I left the table and wandered up the road to the frog pond. I would go there often to catch frogs, and think about things. It was near the place where dad had taken me hunting once. While hunting dad had me lie down behind this old Douglas fir log. I stood up and looked over the log and there were a thousand rabbits. Dad had a gun with him and he was going to shoot the rabbits but I yelled and scared them and they all ran to safety. What I did made my dad mad, and when he was mad, things were not pleasant.

It was deep in the woods up on the hill where I met Mr. Woodchopper. He looked to be an old man of about 60 or 70. He had gray hair and always looked like he needed a shave. He was tall and always had overalls on with a flannel shirt. He had the biggest pair of logging boots of anyone in town. I came across him chopping wood up by the frog pond. I watched him awhile then went up to him and asked him, "what is your name mister?"

He smiled at me and said, "I don't have a name little boy."

I looked at him kind of confused—everyone had a name I thought. I said, "my name is Luke, and since you don't have a name I will give you one."

He let out a laugh and kept on chopping his wood. "I know what I will call you—Mr. Woodchopper. Yep, that is what your name will be. You chop wood and you're good at it—so that's your name."

He started laughing hard and put his ax aside and sat down and said, "I like that name, Mr. Woodchopper shall be my name."

From then on, not only me, but also everyone else started calling him Mr. Woodchopper. I would visit Mr. Woodchopper often and we became good friends. Mr. Woodchopper would always smile whenever I would call him by that name. He lived in a small cabin up the road from my place, and my mom and dad always told me to stay away from the old man. I didn't really know why, and I didn't listen to them for I could clearly see that Mr. Woodchopper was no demon or witch.

Mr. Woodchopper was up by his house when I walked by, so I thought I would ask him about the things I had been seeing. "Mr. Woodchopper, do you think there are demons and witches?"

"Before I answer that question why don't we go sit down in the cabin and I will make you a cup of coffee."

I thought about going into his house and decided that it couldn't hurt any—so in I went. His house was really small, for it had no indoor plumbing and consisted of a kitchen and bedroom. It had a dirt floor and only one window. It smelled very musty but when the coffee started to perk the smell filled the whole house. The coffee made a nice smell as it finished perking. He gave me a cup and as I looked at it I said, "my mom says I am not old enough to drink coffee."

"How old are you?"

I held up my hand and said, "only five."

"Old enough in my book. So do you want some sugar with that coffee?"

"Sure would Mr. Woodchopper, thanks."

"So why are you asking about demons and things for?"

"I saw some a while back in the sky and they looked so real, but my brother and sister couldn't see them at all."

"Let me tell you, there are such things but it's not what you think."

"What do you mean?" I asked with a puzzled look on my face.

"Demons are what bad men become. They do terrible things to people."

"I know, they make my sister cry almost every night."

He was thinking and had a serious look on his face as I said that to him. He said, "now why would they do that?"

"I don't know. They also make my mom sick."

"Some day you will find out what those demons are—some day you will know all you need to know."

"I want to know right now."

He sighed as he said, "I don't have all the answers. But some day you will find the answers you're looking for."

I drank his coffee and continued to talk to Mr. Woodchopper. I think I was the only friend he had. I never saw any of the other kids talk to him, and never any of the adults. When I spoke to him he would listen real hard to make sure to understand me. He never thought I was dumb as others did. We always talked a lot when we were together, and I always had coffee when I was at his house. If my mom would have known how much time I spent there I think she would have beaten me. I never wanted to ware out my welcome so I said, "thanks for the coffee."

"You're welcome, and come visit again sometime."

I headed up the road to Brian's house. The Marks family was different from others. Mr. Marks never worked anymore. They said he was hurt in a logging accident. I always thought it was strange, it seemed he had no problem doing anything around his house that he wanted to do, and he was really good at yelling a lot. I thought he should have been a boss. Mrs. Marks worked all the time, and when she got home she would yell a lot also. Brian and his brothers didn't mind all the yelling. It made me very thankful that I had a dad who worked, and a mom who was always home except when she was in the hospital. Yet I liked going to their house. They always had hamburgers for dinner and ran to the big town at least four times a day.

All the neighbors talked about them, but very seldom talked to them. Mr. Marks coached little league baseball. He was a good coach. He would yell at us kids and yell at the umpire and yell and fight with all the parents, but we played well for him and won games. I think I lived there more sometimes than at my house. It was always exciting, a fight every minute. The three oldest boys were thin and fit. The youngest was fat.

They would always fight over who was eating too much and what they were going to watch on television. Sometimes the other neighbors would sit out on the street and listen to the fights. "Kind of good entertainment," Mr. Buntz would say. I thought it odd that people would take pleasure in a family fighting, but I did hang around to watch myself.

Mr. Buntz lived a little farther up the road. His house is where my brother and sister and I would go when the bad guys came to our house. My mom would send us up there every time the bad guys were coming. The bad guys seemed to come every time my dad was working nights. I thought maybe the bad guys were working for the demons, but no one would ever talk about that. Mom would get really scared at night when the phone would ring. She would round us up and drive us up the road and sometimes she would leave us, and sometimes she would stay with us. After the bad guys had come and gone mom would take us home. I didn't understand why mom never called the sheriff.

When I got to Brian's house no one was home. They must have run to town. Walking back home I had forgotten about going to the frog pond. As I made my way through the yard to the house I thought I would ask my mom who the bad guys were. "Mom, who are the bad guys that come here?" I asked walking through the door.

"You won't understand."

I already understood more than she thought I did. "I understand that they scare you really bad."

"Yes they do, and I hope some day it will end."

"Why don't you call the sheriff mom?"

"Because it's none of their business."

"Why not?"

"Luke will you stop asking so many questions!"

"Well, I want to know mom."

"Drop it now!" She yelled.

I hated to hear those words. I wanted to know what was happening. I had this belief that it was my job to protect the family, and how could I do that without knowing everything? The demons had hidden themselves well in the town of Clear Lake.

I was in my first year of school. Kindergarten was a lot of fun. I loved show and tell time. A lot of kids would bring things that they had received as gifts from their parents, all kinds of neat toys and things I didn't have.

So when it was my turn to show or tell, I never had anything to show, but I sure did have something to tell them. I would tell them of the great adventures I would have, whether I was eating with the three bears or exploring deep caves. I would tell them about the demons and witches that lived in town. I knew it was my job to warn them of the dangers. I always kept them entertained. My teacher would always smile and remind the class that not every thing I said was true. My report card said, "Luke rarely does his work, but he has a very good imagination, though it does get out of control sometimes." I wonder why my teacher never told me she didn't believe me.

One day after school I wasn't paying attention to what bus I was getting on. I got on the wrong bus and ended up at the high school. I knew I was on the wrong bus and I was becoming scared. I got off and started walking and looking for my older cousin Lynn, because I knew she would be somewhere around there. She spotted me and asked, "Luke are you lost? What are you doing here?"

"Yes, I got on the wrong bus and I don't know how to get home."

"You had better come home with me and I will make sure you get home."

"Thank you Lynn." She was a lot older than me but always treated me nice.

When we got on the bus to go to her house the bus driver said that the buses were not going anywhere until someone confessed to setting the fire alarm off. I became fearful, and I didn't think I would ever get home. I started to cry and Lynn was getting mad at me.

"Luke will you stop crying."

"I can't, I am afraid I will not get home."

"You will, it might be a while. So don't worry." She said trying to comfort me.

I tried to hold my tears back—the bus driver told me to come up to the front.

"Did you set the alarm off boy?"

I stood there and look at him and I didn't reply.

"I am asking you a question boy, now answer me."

I didn't know what to say to the man. I was afraid and crying even more.

"Damn it, will you stop crying and answer my question or am I going to have to beat it out of you, cry baby!"

Lynn jumped out of her seat and yelled, "leave him a lone!"

"Shut your mouth girl or I may have to slap it."

"Your not going to hurt him at all, now let him be." She said.

"Sit down and shut up now!"

Lynn sat back down and I looked at the bus driver and said, "you're a mean man, and I think that demons are in you."

"You shut up boy, and answer me, did you pull the alarm?"

"No."

"I think you're lying, so one more time, tell me the truth."

"No!" I said in a firm voice.

With that he grabbed me and pushed me off the bus—another man came running over and asked, "what are you doing?"

"This boy is the one who pulled the alarm."

"Did he tell you this?"

"No, but he is crying and that tells me that he is guilty."

The other man took me by the arm and led me to the main office in the school. I was scared and I thought I was going to have to go to jail for something I didn't do. Demons did things like this I thought.

He asked, "what is your name?"

"Luke Mills."

"Did you pull the alarm?"

"No."

"I am going to have to call your parents, is your dad Carl Mills?"

"Yes."

I wondered how he knew who my dad was. My dad was very smart so maybe he remembered him from school way back when.

"OK, I will call him to come get you, and you had better not be lying to me."

I didn't know what to think of all this—I get on a wrong bus, and blamed for something I didn't do, and now I am going to have to face my dad and try to explain everything to him. It was confusing to me. I should've walked home.

When my dad arrived I was sent out to wait in the hall as they talked. My dad came out and told me to get in the car. I did, and waited to be yelled at. On the way home not a word was said—I thought maybe my dad believed I didn't have anything to do with what happened. I got out of the car to go inside the house and dad said, "why were you at the high school in town?"

"I got on the wrong bus."

"Likely story. You went there to cause trouble didn't you?"

"No, I am telling the truth dad—I got on the wrong bus."

"I am not going to argue with you. You did a very bad thing and I have to punish you."

My dad took off his belt and started hitting me. It hurt so I started running and he started chasing me. He caught me and threw me to the ground. I must have been knocked out because I don't remember what happened next. I woke up in my bed and I was hurting all over my back, my head, and my butt. I started to cry and was wishing that someone would come make things better.

As I fell back a sleep. I dreamt that I was on an island paradise. There were lots of friendly animals in the green grass, and there were water-falls and lakes. The water was so clear. It was a place that I would want to live in forever. I saw this girl who was my friend. It was Marie. We were laughing and having a good time. It was as Heaven should be I thought. I asked Marie, "what are you doing here Marie?"

"I am in Heaven now Luke, it's much better than home."

"Don't you miss your family?"

"Yes, but I like it here, it's safe, and no one hurts me."

I watched as she walked away in to what seemed like big clouds. I wanted to follow but my legs wouldn't work. I started to cry as she faded away into the mist. I woke up, it was morning, and that dream was firmly planted in my mind.

CHAPTER TWO

"The local Indians will not venture up on Cultas Mountain. They believe that evil spirits make their home there. I do find it interesting that the Indian word for bad is Cultas.

Journal of Victoria Southerland
May 1892

As a little kid, things replace other things in your mind so fast that some things are quickly forgotten. As time moves from day to day, things change as to importance. Whether swimming at the lake, fishing at the creek, catching frogs at the frog pond, running through fields of hay, or hiking in the mountains, life sometimes felt so care-free. That is the way it should always be for little kids growing up. I felt sorry for the kids that didn't have the life that I did. In my mind I had everything that a child could want. It wasn't toys or things like that—I had freedom and a great place to express it.

My first job came when I was seven years old. I was picking strawberries for twenty-five cents a flat. I would pick about three flats a day. I knew right away that this wasn't for me. Besides, I didn't like the older kids who rode the berry bus. They were a mean bunch—the Moss brothers and the Small brothers. One day after picking berries they stopped me and said, "Luke come here."

"Why?" I asked—I knew they were looking for trouble.

"Because if you don't we will kill you." I had no choice—I was dead if I went or not.

"OK, but don't hurt me."

They took me to this barn by the bus stop at the north end of town. I was really scared. I was trying to find a way out of this problem. Then one of them said, "Luke take off your clothes."

"Why?" I asked.

"Because we are going to make you do the elephant walk."

I thought to myself, what is the elephant walk? I also thought, where is Batman when you need him? I asked, "what is the elephant walk?"

Dan Small the oldest and meanest of them said, "every time you take a step put your thumb in your butt and on the next step stick it in your mouth."

Now in my mind I was beating these wicked people up and running out of there to a safe place. "Get going," Dan said.

"No I am not going to do that!" I was starting to cry.

I was in fear for my life. I thought what is going to happen to me. Why did the demons hate me so much? I stood my ground and waited for the beating I thought I was about to receive.

"Turn around Luke." Dan said in a mean wicked voice.

"We are going to cut off your dick." Troy Moss said.

They were all laughing. I thought I was going to die right there. I heard them whispering to each other.

"If we make him do this and beat him we may get caught." Troy said to Dan.

"Yes, let's take his clothes and let him walk home naked."

Then Dan said, "take off your clothes now Luke. You're retarded and retards shouldn't have any clothes."

"No, I am not going to do that and I am not retarded!" I screamed.

"If you don't we will beat the crap out of you and take your clothes anyway."

They pushed me down and started ripping at my clothes like wild animals. They took my clothes and left me there in the barn. I was lying on the hay naked, crying, wishing I were dead. I thought to myself, what would make these people do this kind of thing? Maybe the demons had them in their control? I waited till night when it was dark to make my way home. I was glad that no one saw me. When I got home I crawled through my bedroom window. I was too scared to tell anyone—I didn't want people to know how much of a chicken I was. I stayed away from those mean boys as much as possible. The two youngest of the brother's were in the same class as I. The two others were 4 years older. Someday I would make them pay.

When bad things would happen like that I would head to the frog pond. I was usually the only one up there except for Mr. Woodchopper and he was usually chopping wood. He saw me by the pond and came over and asked, "what is going on Luke?"

"Oh just thinking."

"Do you want to talk about it?" He asked.

"You told me once that demons make men do bad things to people."

"Yes Luke they do, and sometimes there isn't anything you or I can do about it."

"Is there anyone that can help us?"

"I don't know Luke—maybe you could ask the preacher. He is one who should know how to deal with this sort of thing."

"Why? Do you go to church Mr. Woodchopper?"

"No, I don't Luke."

"Why not Mr. Woodchopper?"

"Don't belong in one. I live a wrong life—so it's best that I stay away from church. Besides people would never accept me."

"What do you do that is so bad Mr. Woodchopper? You seem really nice to me."

He smiled and said, "come to my house and I will show you."

We headed off to his cabin down the trail. I was excited about finding out what he did that was so bad. In my mind I could find no fault with the man. He was nice and minded his own business, and never seemed to hurt anyone. I followed behind him as we entered his cabin. He said, "sit at the table Luke."

That was the only place to sit, so I did. "So you going to show me?" I impatiently asked.

"Yes, " he said.

He went in to the other room and brought out a scrapbook and a big jar of some sort. He said, "now you can't tell a soul, do you promise?"

"Yes I do."

"Me telling you could get me into a lot of trouble."

"I promise, I won't tell a soul."

He took a deep breath and said, "I rob banks for a living."

I was thinking I was in the house with a man who was telling me he robbed banks for a living, but I still thought he was a nice man.

He pulled out a couple of newspaper clippings that mentioned banks being robbed. The banks were in Seattle and Everett. Then he opened the jar and pulled out lots of money—more than I had ever seen. I was amazed. I was wishing that I had that much money. I could have lots of things with that kind of money. He said, "I live this way because people will not think about me being one who has money."

"Why don't you buy a nice new truck?" I asked.

"People would think where did he get the money to buy that? So I won't get a new truck until I have enough money to leave and head to Mexico."

"When will that be?"

"Someday soon, I can't do this kind of thing forever," he replied.

I didn't think much about Mr. Woodchopper being a bank robber. He was poor and I was sure he could use the money—besides banks have lots of money. I was wondering why he had told me? So I asked, "Mr. Woodchopper why are you telling me all of this?"

"Because I trust you. You're the only friend I have."

"When I grow up I want to be like you."

He got a real serious look on his face and said, "no you don't Luke, no you don't."

"Why not?"

"Because it's not the best life. I believe there are good things in store for you."

"What do you mean?"

"You're a good kid, kind of special, different from other kids."

"I know they say I am different—slow and dumb."

"Luke you're not, and never believe that about yourself."

This man was the nicest man I had ever met. He would always have something nice to say to me. We had many great conversations over coffee. He was my best friend.

When I left his house I knew in my mind I wouldn't tell a soul until he was long gone. It was kind of strange that I never saw anything wrong with him robbing banks. To steal was something I felt was terribly wrong—yet I thought that every neighborhood had a bank robber living in it. It was a part of normal life even for a small town. It seemed every time I went to Mr. Woodchopper's house I went away having forgotten what I was going there for. He always had a way of doing that.

There were lots of poor people in town. It seemed to me that we always had lots of things and plenty of food. I felt sorry for the people who had less than I did.

Sometimes I would take meat out of our freezer and leave it on the front porch of people who had little. It was like being Robinhood to me. I always thought we should share more than we did as a family. I guess that was kind of like stealing—taking meat from my family to give to others. Even though I was stealing—I never saw myself as a thief.

There was a really poor family that lived down on the road across the field from our house. They were a Mexican family. I was never allowed to go into their house. One of the kids was a girl the same age as I. I really liked her. She had dark skin with wavy long black hair. Her eyes were dark brown, almost chocolate in color, and she had the cutest smile when she would laugh. She was real short. I think I was a full foot taller than she was. We would always play and talk, but I had to always be careful that her dad wouldn't see me with her. I would leave meat and vegetables on their porch quite often. No one in town really seemed to talk to them much or invite them over. Most of the kids teased Marie and her family. Call her names because she was different. I would take time to talk and play with her. She was the first girl I thought I loved.

Some people in town were mean to her and she was afraid of them. One day while playing she told me, "sometimes bad things happen to me."

"What kind of things?" I would ask.

"Men that scare my family—come and touch me and do bad things."

"Well let's run away to the frog pond. I will take care of you."

"Oh I wish I could, but they will find me and hurt me."

"I will tell my mom and dad, and they will be able to get help for you."

"No! If someone finds out they will surely hurt me."

She had fear in her eyes and voice, a fear that no child should have. I wanted her to know she was safe with me. "OK, I will pray for you, I am sure it's the demons and witches that are doing these bad things."

"I wish it would end. I am so afraid sometimes."

I was wishing it would end for her also. It made me mad that bad things would happen to her. I was wondering how many other kids in the town of Clear Lake were getting the same treatment. I was wishing that I could do something to make the demons leave. I went home after playing with Marie. Walking in to the kitchen I asked, "mom can we help Marie? Some bad things are happening to her."

"And what would that be silly boy?"

"There are bad people being mean to her."

"Oh, she is just like other kids in this town—upset because her parents make her do work she doesn't want to do."

"No! This is different!" I was getting mad.

"Don't yell at me Luke."

"I want to tell you—you don't understand mom."

"Drop it Luke, this isn't good talk, drop it."

I went to my room and slammed the door. I was unhappy that I couldn't get anyone to believe me. I could see deep in Marie's eyes, as she would tell me things that were happening. I had vowed to myself that someday I would take her away from this place so she could be safe.

In the summer Marie and her parents would leave to go to work the fields in the eastern part of the state. Summers were long without her around. It was in the summer of 1967 that I heard that Marie died. I cried for a long time. It was ruled as an accidental death, because they say she suffocated in some hops. I didn't believe this was the case, because she was 7 years old and could fight her way out of many things. I was sure that the demons had killed her. Being seven who would believe me? I would never have the chance to take her to a safe place. I went to her funeral and watched her be put in the grave in the cemetery in Clear Lake. There were not many people there. I thought that every one in the whole town should have been there. It was a sad time.

The summer lingered on and I was spending time at the beach, swimming, boating and fishing. When I wasn't at the beach I was playing in the fields and in the mountains. At night I would sometimes sleep outside and watch the stars. I would wish that I could take a trip and visit them all. Sometimes late at night you could hear the train whistle blowing way out in the valley. The sound would be carried over the hills by a warm summer wind. The wind would move through the trees and make music in the leaves.

Life seemed so carefree and any thoughts of bad things were far from my mind. In the morning I would get up and take my trip around the town and say hi to all the people I knew. I would listen to every word and hear all the local gossip. Sometimes I would do some odd jobs for the older folks in town. I enjoyed the work, and they all trusted me to do a good job. I was well liked by most people. I was destined to be a gardener for life.

Later that summer the whole county was distraught over the events in Clear Lake. We had a girl that would come and watch us when my parents would go away. Her name was Sharon. She was a teenager who was about 19 years old. She was a nice girl. She had the bluest eyes I had ever seen. She was the lifeguard at the beach and every one liked looking at her because she was so beautiful. I would go to the beach and sit and stare at her for hours. I'd sometimes do something wrong so she would have me sit by her for punishment. It sure was some kind of punishment. Just to have her say any word to me sent my heart into a rush. I can still see her long brown hair blowing in the wind, and her tan body swaying to the music as she watched the water. It was a beautiful sight. I liked her smile, and she was always nice to me.

She would come in my room when I went to bed and we would talk about many things. She would tell me her dreams of being a movie star, being rich, and getting out of this town. She wanted to meet a really nice man who would treat her right.

One night when she was watching me, she came in and started to ask me questions. "Luke are you scared of the dark?"

"Yes I am. Why do you ask?"

"And what are you afraid of?"

"There are demons and witches who might get me in the dark."

"I don't know about that, but I know that bad things are happening here in this town."

"Yes I know, but I really don't know what it all is yet."

"Evil men have done things to me for years, and I know they are doing things to others in this community this very day. I don't like it and I'm not going to sit back and let them do these bad things anymore. I'm going to turn them into the sheriff."

"Who are they?" I was wondering if I knew any of them?

"I only know a couple of them, they will be so scared that they will rat on the rest."

"Can you tell me their names?"

"No I can't. Some of their names I don't know. If word gets out that I am going to the sheriff they may try to harm me."

"I will protect you Sharon." I wasn't going to let anyone get the one I loved.

She smiled and said, "I know you would if you could, but they are very evil men and a lot of children are being hurt—so I must do what I have to."

"What have they been doing to you?"

A very sad expression came over her face and anger showed in her eyes. "It's things that little boys shouldn't hear or even know. Now go to sleep and dream of sweet things."

I looked into her eyes, they were beautiful, and saw a sadness I had never seen before. I wished I was older and could help Sharon get the bad guys put in jail, and I wished I could chase the demons away for her. In my heart I loved her, and wished that she could see that I did. As she walked out of the bedroom I stole one last look of her. I thought to myself that I would do what I could to help her. As the wind slowly moved the curtains back and forth, I saw the first star of the night and made my wish for her to be safe. I wished that she would be able to fulfill her dreams in life.

In the morning I got up and made my way to the kitchen to get my Wheaties. I was a champion so I needed to start my day off like the rest of the champions. Mom came into the kitchen and started doing the dishes. I started to tell her about what Sharon and I had talked about the night before—knowing she would be able to help Sharon.

"Mom, Sharon needs our help." I said while slurping up my Wheaties and milk.

"And why is that silly boy?"

"There are bad guys doing evil things to her and to other kids in town, she says."

"Now don't be telling stories."

"I'm not! She is going to tell the sheriff about them. Maybe they are the same bad men that come here."

"Oh if they're doing those things the sheriff will take care of it."

My voice was rising as I said, "the sheriff doesn't help us when the bad guys come here!"

"Luke you're too little to understand."

"Well we need to help her. If they find out she is going to tell the sheriff they might hurt her like they hurt Marie!"

"Luke enough of this talk now. Marie died an accidental death, and nothing is going to happen to Sharon."

"I don't believe that mom. I don't believe that!"

"That is why you're a silly boy."

I hated to hear those words. It was true that I was silly sometimes, but this was very serious. The thought of no one helping really annoyed me. I left the house and started off for the other end of town. I was going to go to the lake and do some fishing and thinking.

Even though I was young I had lots of freedom to do what I wanted. I really didn't have any best friends my age. I had lots of friends. It never bothered me that a lot of my friends were older people that I would stop by and visit often.

One old man that I talked to often lived up the road from my house. He was considered the town drunk. He was always fishing during the morning hours at my favorite hole. We called it the A-frame hole. There used to be a big old A-frame that lifted logs out of the lake. The hole was deep and it was good fishing. Nearby were old concrete structures that were the only remnants of the big lumber mill that had burned. It was a fun place to play and run around. Sometimes you had to be careful at the A-frame because of some bad kids who were mean that would also hang out down there.

When I arrived at the fishing hole Mr. Banks was there and he already had a string full of fish. "How are you?" He asked.

"Just fine today. Is the fishing any good?"

"Yes it is. Now don't get too close to me and invade my hole." He thought he owned the whole lake at times.

"I won't, but can you tell me what kind of bait you're using?"

"Do you think I am going to give you my secret? Well I'm not, so don't ask again."

I was trying to see what kind of bait he was using. He always caught a lot of big fish. Sometimes Mr. Banks was crabby. I thought it was because he drank too much. I felt sorry for him. He had lost his wife to a sickness and he seemed to have no one around his house much. After fishing all morning, he would go sit at Ellens Tavern till they closed the doors, then he would drive his old truck home. It was the same routine every night, drive home, stumble across the bridge over the creek, and slam his door as he walked into his house. We could count on him like clockwork.

I fished awhile and caught a few and threw them back. It was nice to sit in the sun and think about things. Thinking was a pastime I enjoyed very much. I knew I had the answers to many problems of the world. People just wouldn't listen to my ideas. As I thought about things I would ask questions to try to understand people.

"Mr. Banks why do you get drunk so much?"

"Why do you ask so many questions?"

"I want to know about things."

He looked at me, tears starting to well up in his eyes. I think that he had already been drinking and that would make him sad and mean. He said, "I miss my wife, and maybe if I had done things right she would still be here, and than I don't think I'd drink."

"She died of a sickness people say—how could you have changed that?"

"She died of cancer. We both were doing things that we ought not to have been doing, and there's nothing that can change that."

"What kind of things? Were you eating bad food that made you sick?"

"I can 't go into it. It's not for little boys."

I'm tired of being called a little boy!"

He laughed and said, "well, you're a little boy."

"I don't want to be a little boy."

"Just watch yourself and don't become one of us. In many ways a lot of people in Clear Lake are sick."

"What do you mean everyone is sick?" Most of the people I knew were well. What he said didn't make much sense to me.

"Inside of us we all have a dark side, and some people do not keep the dark side in check."

"Are you talking about demons?"

"If the darkness is demons, than yes I am."

"Have you seen them before?"

"They are inside men you can't see them."

"Well, I've seen them many times before, and I'll find a way to chase them away someday."

"I hope you do—I really hope you do."

For a man that was drunk most of the time he sure knew a lot of things. He picked up his tackle box and pole, grabbed his fish, and headed back to the road where his old truck was parked. I knew he was heading for Ellens where he would spend the rest of his day until they closed.

I picked up my pole and started off to the swimming area. It was there that I spent most of my time growing up during the summer, swimming all day. Well, I would stop to eat once in a while. It was there that my thoughts about bad things would vanish, and thoughts that this was the dream life would abound in me. Playing with friends, chasing girls, eating potato chips, and drinking pop all day, what a life and who could ask for more? After swimming I went home and showed up in time for dinner.

Sitting at the table I brought up the subject of Sharon again. Thinking maybe my dad would listen to me.

"Mom did you tell dad about the bad guys that are going to hurt Sharon?"

"No I didn't. Why don't you tell him? I'm sure he'll get a kick of it." My mom was mocking me and I didn't like it.

"Dad, some bad things are happening to Sharon and she's going to tell the sheriff."

"Oh she is?" He had a curious look on his face.

"Yes, and I think she needs our help. She says if they find out she will be killed."

"Luke stop this talk. Ever since Marie died, you have been thinking about people dying. Accidents happen, and nothing is going to happen to Sharon, so stop talking that way. Do you understand me?"

"Yes sir, I understand."

I had learned early on not to argue with my dad. If I did argue with him, it would upset him and I would be punished.

I was shot down again. It wasn't new to me. Maybe they were right. Maybe I was over reacting. After dinner dad went and grabbed some things and said he was off to college. My dad was smart and he was a good man. He said he was going to school to give us kids a better life. I was so proud of him. I wanted so much to grow up and be like him. The only thing I didn't like was that he was gone a lot.

Most nights and holidays he had to work, and the nights he didn't work he was at college. It was on these nights that the bad guys somehow would know that he was gone. Maybe they watched the house. Maybe the demons would tell them my dad was gone. My mom would get real nervous and take us kids up to the Buntz house. We would stay awhile, and then mom would come back up and get us. Kind of strange how we thought it was part of normal life.

A couple of weeks later I got out of bed in the morning and ate my cold cereal and headed off to make my morning rounds through town.

When I arrived at the highway I saw sheriff cars all over town. I knew something big was happening. I didn't know what. I went to the store on the main highway and asked, "what's going on?"

Mr. Meeker looked at me and said, "there has been a murder." My heart fell a mile. I was afraid to ask who it was for fear that it might be one of my friends.

"Who was murdered?" I asked.

"It was Sharon Holms. She was stabbed to death up on the hill last night. Someone stabbed her twenty times and slit her throat from ear to ear."

I turned and ran, screaming and crying, not wanting it to be true. It was as if a part of me had died. I needed to find someone to talk too. I needed to know if they knew who had killed Sharon. I wanted answers. I was mad that no one had helped her. For not even the sheriff had kept her from being killed. I was hoping this was all a bad dream. I decided to head up to Arlene Gates house. She was the town gossip and surely she would know what happened. She had a police and fire radio of some sort and was on the phone constantly, finding out everything, and talking about everybody.

When I arrived at Arlene's house, she was on the phone. She moved the phone away from her ear and asked, "Luke, what's wrong?"

"Have you heard what happened?"

"Yes I have—I'm on the phone about it right now."

I listened as she talked. She was saying, "yes—she was stabbed—that's what is coming across on the radio. I knew it would be someone like the Barker boy! He has always been on drugs and in various kinds of trouble."

I wanted her to get off the phone and talk with me, and tell me all the things she knew about how Sharon was killed and who had done it. I was dying listening to her talk on the phone. She finally hung up and turned towards me.

"Luke, these are things that little boys shouldn't concern themselves with."

"I am not that little!"

"These are horrible things, and I don't know if you should hear them."

"I am old enough to know how Sharon died and who did it."

Arlene paused for a moment and said, "you heard what I said on the phone. It was Ron Barker who killed Sharon—they say he was down at the tavern drinking all night and taking some kind of drugs."

"Did he do it alone?"

"Why yes he did, why do you ask such a question?"

"Because she told me that bad men were doing things to her, and she was going to the sheriff with their names."

"And when did she tell you this?"

"A couple of weeks ago when she was baby sitting at my house."

"We all know that she used to date Ron a couple of years back—so maybe it was Ron that she was referring to."

"I don't think so—she was really worried about a group of men— not just one."

"I think that you're really upset and are stretching things a little."

"No! I am not! I know what she said!" I yelled.

"Give it some time, and the whole thing will be better—let it rest."

"Don't you think that there is more to it than what you have heard so far?"

Arlene was becoming frustrated with me. "No I don't Luke. Ron was drunk, and on drugs, and jealous that she wouldn't see him anymore. That is why he killed her. Now let it rest. Little boys shouldn't be concerned with such things. Now run along and play."

I left there confused and not believing that it was because Ron had been jealous. Yes, I did think that he was drunk, and on drugs. The summer before he had killed a lady on the main highway while driving drunk. It was during the first week of July. He never served any time behind bars for that murder. He got a slap on the hand and was turned back loose. I knew from talking to Sharon that she wasn't afraid of Ron. She didn't like his drinking and drug taking. Besides the drugs and drinking, Ron was always nice.

Sharon always told me she wanted more out of life, to be a movie star, to travel, and to meet the man of her dreams. I had always dreamed about that man being me—even though I was several years younger. It's funny how when you're young you fall in love with older girls. I felt sad and alone, for she would never live her dreams and I knew I could never convince any one of the things I knew to be true.

Everyone was talking about the murder as I walked through town. I would stop by people and say hi, and stand around listening to try to find out anything else, but they all seemed to be saying the same things that I'd heard from Arlene. I wanted to think by myself so I headed up to the frog pond.

I don't know why other kids never went there. Maybe it was because they were afraid of Mr. Woodchopper. When I got there, I sat down and watched the frogs all head for deeper water afraid that I might catch them. Tears began to flow from my eyes as I wept for Sharon. I asked God, why Sharon, why not evil men? I wanted to hurt something myself to try to make me feel better. I was there for a good hour when I heard someone coming up the trail. It was Mr. Woodchopper coming up to see me. He walked up to me and said, "why are you crying Luke? I saw you walking by my house and you looked really sad. So tell me, what is wrong?"

"I am sad because of what happened to Sharon."

He sat down next to me and put his arm around me as he talked to me. "Yes, I have heard the rumors flying around."

"Have you heard what really happened?"

"No, I haven't, but I think there is more to it than most people think."

"Why do you think that? Do you know something I don't know?"

"I think there is more to it than the sheriff and the people in this town believe."

"I think it was a group of bad men that were in on this killing all together. That is what I think Mr. Woodchopper."

"Be careful with what you say."

"Why do you say that?"

"Because if what you say is true they may want to hurt you. I don't want to scare you but I want you to be safe."

"I don't like that thought at all"

"If you're ever in trouble you can always come to my house."

"Thank you—you're a nice man—even if you do rob banks."

He let out a laugh when I said that. It made me feel better inside that someone who was old believed what I had to say. As he started to walk away he said, "be careful and don't talk too much to anyone."

"OK, I won't." I yelled out to him as he walked away. I watched him walk down the trail and decided that it was time to head back home.

The leaves were turning color and starting to fall, reminding me that summer would soon be over and it would be time to go back to school. If I had my way summer would never end. Even after all the horrible things that had happened, I still felt I was safe in Clear Lake. I always found the good things to dwell on, my family, my friends, and all the things that a boy could find to do in the great Northwest. It's interesting that I always thought that it was everyone else who had problems. I would put bad things out of my mind and enjoy life.

It was a couple of weeks after Sharon was killed that one night my dad said, "let's go for a drive."

We all loaded into the car and drove to the other side of the lake and headed up the hill. I asked, "dad, where are we going?"

"Up on the hill to see where Sharon was killed."

"Why are we going there?"

"Just to see what it looks like now."

I thought to myself that it's dark out how are we going to see anything? Asking that kind of question would get the whole car in an uproar—so I kept quiet. We turned off the pavement on to an old dirt road. The hill where the murder took place was thick with trees, which made it even darker. The wind was blowing the leaves down the dirt road, and the clouds were covering the moon and stars.

When we arrived at the place where Sharon was stabbed, dad got out and looked around. By the look on his face, I could see it bothered him being here. He was looking intently at everything—probably trying to figure out what happened. I knew he liked Sharon. My mom told us kids to stay in the car. I had no real desire to get out. I thought there might be demons waiting in that place. My dad wasn't outside long before he was back in the car and we were heading off the hill.

That place gave me the chills. Even to this day I hate going near that place. It's as if a spirit of death hangs over the site warning all to stay away. Right at the end of the dirt road, before the pavement, I saw a man walking on the side of the road. He looked intently into the car and scared us all. He had evil eyes. They were like the eyes of the devil. I knew I had seen those eyes before, but couldn't remember where. The only one who wasn't scared was my dad, for he was brave. I knew by the look on that man's face that he had something to do with the murder of Sharon.

When we got home we all went to bed. I started to dream that I saw Sharon being carried off up to the top of the hill by demons and witches. The sky was red in color and I could see her mouth moving saying help, but I couldn't hear her, for no words were spoken. The demons put her down in a clearing on the hill, and out of the woods came bad men carrying knives. They tied Sharon up so she couldn't run. I was there but I couldn't speak or help, for my legs wouldn't work and I had no sound. The evil men stabbed her, and one man took his knife and cut her throat spilling her blood on the ground. He was speaking of sacrifice but I didn't understand what he meant.

Sharon's beautiful body lay there, lifeless, and I saw her spirit leave heading for heaven. The men took up their knives again and came after me. I tried to run but my legs wouldn't work. I was screaming and crying but no sound would come out of my mouth. They were closing in on me, grabbing at my clothes, catching me. I woke up screaming, crying for help. My brother woke up and told me to go back to sleep. He said everything was going to be all right. Even to this day that dream sticks in my mind.

The rest of the summer was uneventful. I swam, played with friends, and dreamed of things that I was going to do someday. The thought of going back to school was usually exciting. It was nice seeing kids that I hadn't seen all summer. Not everyone was as fortunate as I to be able to fish and swim all day at the lake.

On the first day of school I saw Jimmy Samuel. I asked him why I never saw him down at the beach all summer? He said his mom wouldn't let him go swimming until he learned how to swim. I always thought it was strange that an adult would think that way. How can someone learn to swim unless he gets in the water? It never made any sense to me. I thought swimming was like life—some drown—some tread water—and some swim the ocean. It depended on what you wanted I always thought. I wasn't the brightest kid in school and it didn't bother me all that much. I was a dreamer. Dreaming was easy to do and bookwork took effort.

During the first week back to school I was on the playground playing and talking to Rueben. He was Marie's brother. He was always cold to me and I never knew why? I asked, "Rueben did Marie ever talk to you about me?"

"Just that you were a good friend of hers."

"I miss her being here and playing with us all, I wish she was still here."

Rueben looked at me as if I had said something bad. He said, "let me tell you—she didn't want to come back to this town. My dad and her had an argument before she died. It wasn't a good thing."

"What did they fight about?"

"She said she didn't want to come back to Clear Lake because she wasn't going to do what those men wanted her to do."

"Did she say what they were doing?"

"No, but dad said he had no choice because if he tried to fight them they would kill him, and the rest of our family."

"What are you saying?"

"I'm telling you what I heard—that's all I'm saying."

"Were you scared?"

"Yes, and so was my dad—scared of the same thing that Marie was scared of. The morning after the fight we found Marie dead in the hop bin."

"Do you think it was an accident?"

"No Luke, I think that she killed herself, or was killed. But I don't tell anyone because they won't believe me. I want to move from this place."

"Why not tell someone? Someone will believe you. I do."

"No one will and that is the way it is."

"What does your dad and mom say about this?"

"They just keep silent, they don't even say Marie's name. I heard my dad tell my mom that he was thinking of moving to the east side of the state and leaving this wicked place. I sure hope we do move."

The bell rang telling us it was time to get back to class. A few months after our talk Rueben and his family packed up and moved away. It was sad that no one in town came to help them, or even to say good-bye. I waved to them as they drove off, but they didn't wave back. I thought to myself, why didn't they wave? I never did anything bad to them. I guess they were mad at the whole world. I felt that way sometimes. I hoped that somehow they knew it was me who had often left meat on their porch. I hoped that their life would be better wherever they ended up.

I knew for sure that I would never know what really happened to Marie. I decided it was time to let it rest. I went down to the cemetery that same day that Marie's parents left. I went to her grave and told her I would always come and visit her whenever I walked by. I told her that her parents had moved and I would be her family now. I often picked flowers in the spring and summer and put them on her headstone. I did the same for Sharon—left her flowers and talked with her. After her death her parents had moved away also. Maybe they couldn't live in the town where their daughter was killed, or maybe they wanted to get away from whoever they thought might do this horrible thing again. Maybe they knew the demons and wanted to avoid them.

That winter when it snowed I went down and built a snowman for Marie, as we use to do when she was alive. Even to this day, whenever I drive by the cemetery, I think of Marie and Sharon, how beautiful they were and how I wish they could have lived their lives out to the fullest.

CHAPTER THREE

A few items were stole from the mill shop on Monday night. It was believed that the Negro miner is the thief. He was found with Caleb Cultas who defended this Negro he called his friend. No items were found on his person or at Caleb's house. The Negro was beat and told never to come back to town again. Caleb was warned to watch who he kept as friends.

Clear Lake News

My schoolwork was lacking in the fall. I had no desire to do any of it. I would sit and stare out the window at the mountains. I would think of being up there, fishing, exploring, and hiking. It seemed my life could be so simple, why did I need to know all of this stuff anyway? It never made much sense to me. My teachers worried about me. I knew they thought I was slow, but what they said kind of upset me. They sent a letter home for my parents. I read it before I got home.

Dear Mr. and Mrs. Mills,

Your son Luke is falling further behind in class. He hasn't finished any work this entire year. We feel that he may be retarded and would like to have some tests run on him at the University of Washington. We know this may be a shock to you, but we feel this would be in the best interest of Luke and this school. Please call to set up an appointment to meet after school someday soon.

I read that with disbelief. How could they say such a thing about me? It was true that I couldn't talk all that well, I had to go to speech therapy twice a week, but that didn't mean I was retarded. I could see in my mind what they were trying to do. If they could put me away in some institution I wouldn't be able to tell anyone what I had seen, or heard, or knew. I thought for sure that demons had a hold of my teachers. The demons feared me because I knew the truth, and they would do anything to keep me quiet. I decided it was time for me to run away from home. I knew that my parents would believe the teachers and have me sent away to this university place. I wasn't going to let that happen.

When I got home I didn't show my mom the letter. I went straight to my room and grabbed a few things and put them in a bag. I crawled out my bedroom window and made my way to the frog pond. It was there that I was going to spend the rest of my life. I could eat berries, fish, and frogs. I would hunt and trap and live off the land. I didn't need anybody. I could stand-alone and defeat the demons myself—well—at least as long as it was daylight. I knew I would be very scared when darkness came. The demons would always show themselves in the dark. I wondered when I would be able to overcome my fear of the dark.

I started to cry as I usually did when I felt alone. I wanted to be normal, to be like the other kids in my class, to have school work come easy. I wished that I would somehow become the smartest person in the world. If I was the smartest person in the world, I could make everyone love everyone, and everyone would have all the things they needed and wanted, and no child would ever go hungry or cry again. If I were the smartest person in the world I would create a pill to make everyone live forever so we could be with the ones we love forever. I would often dream that I would become the smartest person in the world.

I heard a noise that brought me out of my daydream. It was my good friend Mr. Woodchopper walking up the trail. "Luke, are you OK?"

I kept looking at the ground and said, "no."

He got closer to me and saw that I had been crying. "Tell me son, what's wrong?"

"My teachers think I am retarded and want to send me away from here."

"Now who in the world told you that?" I could see in his eyes that he cared for me very much.

"It's right here in this letter I was to take to my parents."

"Can I read it?"

"Sure you can. It says they want to send me to some university. What is a university?"

I sat and waited for his answer as he read the letter. When he finished reading it, he looked at me and smiled saying, "first of all don't believe a thing they say. Second thing is they want to test you, not send you away. And third thing Luke, you're one of the brightest boys I have ever met, and please never forget that."

"But what are they going to do to me down there? I heard that they give you electric shocks and things like that—like they do at Northern State Hospital."

"That place is for the mentally insane, people who have gone crazy and lost their minds, believe me, your mind is well in place."

"Are you sure?"

"Yes I'm sure. The University is a place they call higher learning. I don't know if it is, but they call it that. It's not a place to torture little boys. You will go down there and they will find out that there isn't anything wrong with you."

"Well I know that, and you know that, but my teachers don't know that."

"Trust me, they will find out soon."

"Some kids say I am retarded because I have to go to speech class."

"Luke, we're not all perfect, some of us have to work harder for things. Do you mind going to speech class?"

"No, I like my speech teacher. She is beautiful."

"Luke, don't let yourself fall in love with her, those older women will break your heart." He left laughing, walking down to his house. He knew me too well.

I don't know if my speech teacher thought I was dumb or retarded, but she knew that I liked her very much. She always wore a mini skirt and lots of makeup over her eyes. It was a dark color, almost dark blue with sparkles, like little stars. She would be giving the lesson and I would sit there and stare, with my mouth wide open, with a big dumb look on my face, wishing that I were going home with her after school. I don't know if I ever passed a test, I don't remember ever taking a test. I just remember what she looked like. She looked like no other teacher I ever had before. I imagined that she wore that dress to keep my mind on her. Funny thing is I don't even remember her name.

It was starting to get dark out and I was hungry. I knew that I had to go face my punishment, so I decided to make my way back home. Besides my mom and dad loved me, and they would want the best for me. I wasn't looking forward to giving them the letter, but I knew there was no way around it. I knew I would probably be yelled at, and my dad might get mad and spank me. Sometimes my dad would be upset that I wasn't doing well in school. I knew he was a very smart man. He had lots of awards for doing math and science, and I knew it bothered him that his son wasn't all that good at math or science. He would always ask me, "are you going to be anything other than a bum when you grow up?" I thought being a bum would be a nice job sometimes.

When I arrived home, I crawled in my bedroom window—I didn't want them to see the things I had with me, for it would get me in more trouble. I put my things away, walked into the kitchen, and sat at the table. My mom said, "you almost missed dinner."

"I have been up at the frog pond."

"Yeah, we know, the neighbors saw you headed that way with some of your things." Mom didn't seem that mad at me.

I said, "I was thinking of running away." That didn't faze her at all as she started in on me about Mr. Woodchopper.

"The neighbors also tell me that you've been visiting that dirty old man that lives up by the frog pond."

I didn't know what to say—what did that have to do with me running away? Not only was I going to get in trouble for the letter from my teachers, I was going to get in trouble for being friends with Mr. Woodchopper. "Yes I talk to him every once in a while, and he is a nice man mom."

"Stay away from him, he might hurt you."

I would have to lie and tell her what she wanted to hear—I knew he would never hurt me. So I told her what she wanted to hear. "OK, I will be careful mom." I could see it eased her.

"So tell me why you wanted to run away."

"Because I have this note for you from my teachers."

I gave her the note and sat in silence while she read it. I was watching her eyes to see if there was any reaction. She started to get upset about the letter. "Luke, why have you not been doing your work?"

"Just don't feel like it. It's not important to me."

"That is no excuse—I'll be making an appointment with your teachers to discuss the problem."

I tried to reason with my mom saying, "I am not retarded like they say."

"We'll have to let the experts decide that."

Those words cut to my heart. Not even my mom believed that I was normal. I didn't say a word as I got up and went to my room. I cried awhile, and thought to myself that I would prove to all these people that I was normal and smart. I dreamed of that day when I would be justified, and wished that it would come soon. I would see myself as the President of the United States that would show them all I wasn't dumb.

I would take all these people and send them to Russia and see how they like it there. The thought made me smile.

A few days later my mom told me, "Luke we will be going to Seattle for a few days next week."

"Why? Is that where the University is?" I couldn't even say that big word let alone read it.

"Yes, it's all right, nothing is going to hurt you. They want to help you with your problem."

I looked at her and said in a calm voice, "I don't have a problem."

"Now Luke, try to be sensible here. It's the best thing."

"Well, I don't want to go."

"You have no choice, both your father and I think it best, and so do your teachers."

I knew it was no use arguing. I would go down there and have a good time. Maybe they would believe me about the demons I had seen. "OK mom, I will go and I won't fight you."

"Thanks. You'll be OK."

I headed outside to play; I was going to forget things. I was walking up the street when I saw Roger Shaw and Rich Leader. They were in the same class as I, but I never played with them much. They were not very nice boys. They were always in trouble and most of the time they were very mean. They walked up to me and said, "hi Luke."

I said, "Hi."

Roger asked, "would you like to come up and play with us?"

I thought, this could be a trap, but maybe they had changed their ways and were going to be nice. So I said, "yes, I will for a while."

Walking up to Rogers place I began thinking that maybe I had judged these boys wrong. We were laughing and talking boy things—I was having a good time. We arrived at his house and went on down to the barn. When we got inside, I started to feel that something bad was going to happen. Roger and Rich were acting strange. Roger said, "Rich, get the books out."

I watched as Rich made his way to a covered box in the corner. "What kind of books are they?" I asked.

"You'll see." He looked over at Rich and asked, "are they there Rich?"

"Yes they are."

They brought the books over to a table and opened them. The books were Sears and Penneys catalogs. Rich said, "we have a surprise for you Luke."

"And what is that?"

"Just take a look." He said with excitement.

I looked at the page in the book where they had it opened. All I saw were people in underwear. It was no big deal I had seen people in underwear before. I asked, "what is so big about people wearing underwear?"

"It helps us get ready for what we're going to do."

"And what is that?"

"We are going to screw each other in the butt."

I couldn't believe this was happening to me. I was thinking, why did I let myself get into this. I started looking for a way out without them being able to catch me and hurt me. I said, "I don't think that is something I want to do."

Roger looked at me and asked, "why not Luke? It's fun. We do it all the time."

By the way those two acted I could understand why they did it all the time. No one else wanted to be with them, and I knew no girls wanted to be with them. "Well I don't, and I am not going to."

Roger pulled his pants down and so did Rich. I started to back towards the door. I was scared. Roger bent over and Rich got on him from behind. I thought why are they doing this? I had never heard of this thing—let alone seen it. I thought this is something little boys shouldn't see or know. I came to the conclusion that demons had gotten to Roger and Rich, and that's why they were not nice boys. I left running for my house—I felt as if I set a speed record for the half mile. I never went around those boys again, and I avoided them like the plague. I never told anyone what happened. I was afraid that people might think that I did those kinds of things. I always felt sorry for them. I didn't know how to help them or what to say to them, because they wouldn't have listened to me anyway.

On the day I was to head off to Seattle, it was raining. My dad took my mom and me to the bus station. It was about an hour and a half drive to Seattle. We were going to stay at some friend's house. My dad said they lived near the University. It was exciting, because this was going to be much better than sitting in class all day. I wasn't scared about going to be tested. I felt I was on a mission to prove to everyone I wasn't retarded; I had a peace about me that they would prove that I wasn't. It was going to be my first bus trip and I was looking forward to it.

There were lots of weird people standing in line to get on the bus. I wondered if they thought I was weird? The bus was really full. I was making my way down the isle, looking for a place to sit. After mom found a seat—the seats were full except one. My mom looked at the man sitting in the seat that was next to the empty one, and said that I could sit on her lap. That's the last place I wanted to be. I liked my mom but not enough to sit on her lap. The man next to the empty seat was the first black man I had seen up close—all the others were on television. He was sitting in the very back of the bus. I walked back and sat next to him. I wasn't nervous at all. I couldn't help staring at him—I was looking intently at his skin and his hair. I knew he could tell I was amazed with him but he wouldn't make eye contact with me. Maybe I looked scary to him? We both sat there for what seemed like the longest time without saying a word. I decided to talk to him.

"Hi, my name is Luke, what is your Name?

He looked at me and smiled. I thought that maybe he couldn't talk. Then he said, "Hello, my name is Walter, Walter Smith."

"Nice to meet you Walter."

"Yeah, same to you."

"Where are you from?" I asked.

"I'm from Oakland, California. How about you?"

"I live about 15 miles from where I got on the bus. Its called Clear Lake."

It was strange talking to a black man for he sounded like me. He was nice, different from the things that I had heard some kids say. Growing up in Clear Lake I heard the term "nigger" used all the time, but my dad said he never wanted to hear me use those kinds of words. A lot of the people I knew really didn't like black people, and it never really made any sense to me. I would ask them why? They would say because they were black. It was so stupid I thought.

He asked, "so where are you going Luke?"

"To the University in Seattle, to be tested to see if I have a brain."

He was laughing, "you have a brain or you wouldn't be here."

"Well, some people think I am retarded or something like that."

"Are you scared about the test?" He asked.

"No, I know I am not retarded, but they just can't figure it out without an expert."

"I can see you're not retarded." At least someone knew besides Mr. Woodchopper and myself that I wasn't retarded. I was starting to like this Walter.

"Thank you. So why are you on this bus?" I asked.

"It's a long story."

"It's a long trip and I like stories, so please tell me." I sat back in my seat and smiled at Walter.

"I guess it won't hurt to tell you. I came up here to try to get into Canada. I don't want to go to Vietnam."

"Where is Vietnam?" I couldn't even say the word but he knew what I was asking.

"It's a country faraway, where we are fighting a war right now."

"So you don't want to go fight a war? Are you scared?"

"Yes, I'm more scared now, more than I was before I left to try to get into Canada."

"Why is that?"

"Because I have to go back home now and show up to the draft board, because Canada won't let me in."

"Why won't they let you in?"

"Look at me, what do you see?"

"A man, a black man."

"Yes, and that's why they won't let me cross the border. If I were white and rich they would let me into their country in a heartbeat. But they don't want anymore black people there than they already have—it's not fair."

"Mr. Woodchopper says that it's up to men to make things fair for others, maybe you should work on making Canada fair."

"Oh I wish it was that easy, it will never be fair for my people."

I had seen black people on television being sprayed with water and mean things like that. So I could understand why he felt his people would never be treated fair. I remember a song that I had heard in Sunday school. "Jesus loves the little children all the children of the world. Red and yellow, black and white they are precious in his sight."

Yet, some of the same people who lead Sunday school would use the term nigger and say other bad things about people. I did believe that God loved every one the same. So I thought I would tell Walter.

"God loves everyone and he doesn't care what color you are. I learned that in Sunday school."

Walter said, "that is—if you believe in God."

"I do. I have seen the cloud he lives on in the sky when I was four."

"I'm glad for you, I hope you always will believe."

I shook my head yes that I would and asked, "what are you going to do when you get home?"

"I have to report to the draft board, and they will send me off to Vietnam."

I didn't understand everything he was talking about but I was trying. I could see in his eyes that he was scared, scared of dying, scared that he would never be treated fair. I thought, this is the first black man I have ever seen up close, and I have even gotten to talk to him, and he is just like me. I started to daydream that if I was the smartest person in the world I would make everyone the same color, so no one would ever feel out of place and people wouldn't hate others because of their skin color. I was feeling for him, about how he wanted to go to Canada and they wouldn't let him enter. I thought that when I become president, I would take over Canada and that way anyone could get in if they wanted. If the Canadians didn't like it, I would ship them to Russia. I was wishing I could understand all this talk about the war, I had seen some pictures on the news but it wasn't real to me. I had other battles I had to fight.

I continued talking to him. "So are you in trouble when you get back?"

"No, I haven't missed my sign-in date."

"Well, I have something for you."

I reached in my pocket and took out one of my lucky rabbit's feet. "Here Walter, I want you to take this with you. It's my lucky rabbit foot. It will help keep you safe. It will also help make your wishes come true."

"I can't take that from you Luke, you need it for your testing."

"I have many more where that came from, and besides, I have three with me, Mr. Woodchopper always says more is better."

"Who is this Mr. Woodchopper?"

"He is a friend of mine."

"Thank you very much. I'll keep it with me at all times."

"Maybe it will help you get a girl friend also."

"I already have one, she is sad that I have been drafted and she doesn't want me to go to Vietnam."

"Do you love her Walter?"

"Yes I do, and I don't want to leave her here alone. If I had made it into Canada, she was going to move up there."

"Is she going to go to Vietnam with you?"

"No, just people in the army go there to fight the war."

I didn't understand it, I knew he didn't want to go, and he was going. I didn't like the idea of forcing people to do things that they didn't want to do. I couldn't think of why the army wanted to make people go and be killed.

We talked about many different things on the way to Seattle, how he grew up, his dreams, and his fear of dying. I told him about my life, how great it was, about my friends, and about the demons that he should avoid. He said, "I know about demons—I have mine own that I have to defeat." It was nice that he knew about demons. I didn't feel all that alone in my battle. I told him I knew he would return safely. Before the bus pulled up to the station in Seattle, he asked, "Luke, is it all right if I write you?"

"Yes, I would like that very much."

I watched the news more after I got home, because I was always hoping to see Walter. I often wondered what happened to him in Vietnam. One day, about six years after we first met, I received a letter from him. It was addressed to Luke in Clear Lake, and the postmaster knew it was for me. It said he was married and had two boys, he also said that he was attending church with his family for he had found faith in God. He thanked me for the rabbit's foot. He said it gave him faith to stay alive and make it home. It was nice to hear that he didn't die in that war. I always wondered if he still wanted to go to Canada.

I remember when I was young, going to some type of Sunday school. It must have been when I was about four years old. At that time my parents attended church, but for some reason we stopped going. I didn't mind going, I remember that my parents would pick up these girls that didn't have a dad and take them to church with us. One time I was called into the front of the church with my family and the minister took some water and splashed it on my brother. I looked at him and thought, in no way are you getting me wet. So I took off running down the isle. I made it outside and hid in the big bushes by the front door. My dad came looking for me and found me and gave me a spanking—I don't know if it would have been better to be splashed with the water.

Besides the baptism, people at that church would sing a song about cheese. The piano would play and everyone would start singing, "bringing in the cheese, bringing in the cheese, we will come rejoicing bringing in the cheese." It was strange how cheese excited these people, yet there was no cheese in the whole church. God and Jesus must have really liked cheese. We sat behind a couple of old people that could cut the cheese—they did every Sunday. I often wondered why we stopped going to church? I knew there was a God, but I thought he lived on some distant cloud someplace.

We arrived in Seattle in the afternoon. It was my first trip to a big city. There was so much to see—it was so exciting—all of it. Mrs. Garret and Lisa, friends of my parents, were at the bus station to pick us up to take us to their house. I had only seen them a couple of times. Mr. Garret had recently married this new woman. I had heard Mr. Garret say he married this woman because his first wife had left him. I was thinking maybe there was something wrong with him. I later learned that it was his second wife who had left him, the first one had left years before. I knew for sure that something was wrong with him.

On the way to their house Lisa was telling me all of the rules for living in the city, where to go and not go, whom to talk with and not talk with. It was different from Clear Lake, where you could go anywhere and talk to anybody. I asked Lisa, "do you like your new mom?"

"No, she is very mean sometimes."

"How is she mean to you?"

"She locks me in my room for hours and threatens to beat me if I tell my dad."

Mrs. Garret asked, "what are you two talking about?" We both looked at her and she looked really mean—she had evil eyes. It was enough to scare the devil himself. I leaned over and whispered in Lisa's ear, "I would still tell your dad if I were you."

"No, he's not all that nice to me either, he says he loves me and wants to show me all the time, and I don't like the way he tries to show me."

I thought it was very sad that she didn't have a father like mine. "Why did your old mom leave Lisa?"

"My dad says she couldn't handle life, so she left." She was talking as though she didn't care that she was gone.

"Do you still see her at times?"

"No, I haven't seen her in a long time."

I asked, "do you miss her?"

"Sometimes I do. But most of the time I don't think about her."

I was feeling kind of sorry for her. I wouldn't want to grow up in a house with a new mom every once in a while, and I wouldn't want to live in the city. I was thinking maybe she should come and live with us, but I knew it would never happen. Later in her life she would move in and live with her grandma. Her new mom didn't want her around anymore. She said she didn't like the competition. My mind went back to the testing that I would be going through in the morning at the University. I didn't eat much at dinner, which was unusual. I wanted this to be over.

My mom told me I must get some good sleep because of the big day I was going to have. Lisa showed me where I was going to sleep. The house she lived in was really big and old. Walking down the hall of her house, I asked, "what is in this room?"

"It's not a good room Luke."

"Why not?"

"Because it's full of bad things, very bad spirits, there is a hole in the floor and if you're not careful they will pull you down into it and you will never come back."

"How do you know all of this?"

"My dad tells me. He tells me I am not to go in that room."

"So you believe in demons and ghosts and witches?"

"Yes, but I've never seen them, my dad says if I don't do things right and the things he tells me to do they will get me."

I got to the room where I was going to sleep and there were two beds in the room. I was glad to see that, because after what Lisa had told me I was afraid to sleep in that house by myself. I asked, "Lisa, are you going to sleep in here?"

"Yes, this is my room."

She turned off the lights and I got in bed. It was kind of fun, and I knew we were going to talk about everything that night. Lisa was two years older than I was, and I was looking forward to learning more things about the city, her life, and what she liked to do. We were talking about lots of things then she asked me a question that surprised me.

"Luke, have you ever seen a girls private parts?" "No, I haven't."

"Would you like too?"

I thought for a little than said, "I don't know. Is it right?"

"Yes, everyone does it. Its called sex."

I thought this is really weird, why would everyone be doing this? Did the demons have everyone but me? It was strange. As she was talking I remembered playing with a girl that lived down the street from me. One day she had gone to the bathroom in the woods. I looked at her and saw that she didn't have a penis. I was about four or five. I thought that maybe she had gotten her penis cut off, so when I got back to her house I went to the garbage can and looked inside to see if I could find her penis. I was sure she had one, and thought maybe her dad or mom had cut it off. I didn't find her penis and I went and asked her mom what she did with Cindy's penis? She let out a laugh and said, "little girls don't have a penis." I never thought much about it after that. I didn't know girls and boys were different back then. Now here I was, being asked if I wanted to see the private area of a girl.

"Well—if you think it's OK—go ahead and show me." She got out of her bed and said, "OK, just wait a minute."

Lisa walked over to the window and opened the curtains to let some light in the room. She walked over to my bed and lifted up her nitie and pulled her panties down and stood there for a couple of seconds—then she pulled her panties back up and went back to her bed. We didn't say another word all night.

All night long I heard noises outside, sirens, yelling, cars going bye. It was very noisy and I wished I were back at home in the country. I lay there in bed and thought about why Lisa had shown me her private area. What would make her want to do that? What was so great about seeing it anyway? I thought that mine looked better than hers did. Why had I gotten a weird feeling inside me, one that I had never felt before? I wondered how many other boys had seen her that way? Did her dad and mom know she was doing these things? I fell asleep wishing tomorrow would come and be over.

The University was a big place. There were lots of hippies and weird looking people there. Many of them were holding signs—I guess they were trying to tell us all something. We made our way to the hospital area and met Dr. Johnson. He seemed like a nice man. He led us down a long hall and into this room with about 11 people inside. They were all wearing white overcoats. I thought that everything looked really clean. They had my mom and me sit at a table and started to ask questions about me. They were general questions, like, how old is he? Does he misbehave often? I was wondering why my mom had to be there. Maybe they thought I couldn't answer those questions myself. I sat there and acted totally bored. They finished asking their questions and asked my mom to leave. Dr. Johnson said, "Luke, we are going to do a few tests on you, and none of them are going to hurt you."

"Are you sure?"

"Yes. The first one will be what we call an EEG test. We measure the amount of electrical activity in your brain."

"My brain has lots of activity. I am thinking all the time."

"I know you are." Dr. Johnson said smiling.

I didn't know what to think of all of this. First, I thought they should have some of those people that were going to school up here doing testing on them. I was very normal compared to them. Second, I wondered why all these doctors. Do they think I'm a dangerous person? Then I thought I was special, as Mr. Woodchopper said, and I was someone that needed to be studied, so all my fears about being tested were slowly fading away.

They took me up to a room with lots of computer looking machines inside. They took some wires and hooked them up to my head. They used some type of glue to keep them on—it seemed kind of weird. After they had the wires on my head, they asked me many questions. All the questions were easy. When they were all done, they took me to another room and had me read a story from a book. I read it—it was simple. I asked them why they had me read it, I thought maybe they couldn't read it for themselves. They said they wanted to know if I could read. I said, "I can."

We spent most of the day doing various tests. Most of them were very boring. At the end of the day I was taken to a big room. There were lots of doctors in the room—I felt pretty important. Being eight years old and being the center of attention to all these adults was most impressive to me. I thought I was smarter than they all were. I thought maybe they were going to ask me if I was from another planet, or something like that. My mom and dad often said they found me on the beach under a rock. I sat there in the center of the room, with a big smile on my face; ready to tell them anything they wanted to hear.

"We are going to ask you a few questions about your life, and how you see things."

I thought that finally someone is going to know about everything, about the demons, the truth about the deaths. It was exciting.

"Do you understand what we are going to do?"

"Yes, I do."

"OK, lets start. I'm going to introduce all the doctors here, then I want you to repeat all their names, as best as you can, back to me."

After he said all their names, I repeated them all back to him.

"Very good, how did you remember all of their names?"

"I remembered the first letter of each name, that is how."

"Why do your teachers say you have great trouble reading? When tested down here, you read at a higher level than at your school."

"I know I can read—I don't have to prove that to my teachers every day do I?"

I heard in a low voice, "we're dealing with a smart ass, not a retard."

I said, "I am not trying to be smart—I see no use in being made fun of every time I read out loud in front of my class."

Dr. Johnson asked the others to hold their comments. Then he asked, "do you feel there is anything special about you?"

"Yes, I can see things that others can not."

They asked, "what things do you see?"

"Oh, I can see witches and demons, and things like that."

"Now we are being serious here."

I looked at him and said, "so am I, I do see these things!"

Dr. Johnson sighed and said, "OK, is there anything else?"

I was frustrated with all of this. I was really thinking I was way smarter than any of these doctors could ever be. I wanted this to be over so I thought I would have some fun with them.

"Yes, there is something else, when something bad is about to happen, a little bell goes off inside my head and warns me to stop doing what I am doing."

The whole room sat in silence, I looked and I really believed that they had swallowed what I said. I was amazed, tell them the truth and they don't believe—tell them a lie and they take it as the truth. It all seemed kind of odd to me, but the world seemed that way most of the time.

The rest of the day I told them stories, I made them laugh, and made them sad and we all had a good time. They asked many more questions and I did my best to answer them, when all was said and done I was very glad I had come down to this University.

They took me back to the main office where we had first arrived. They told me to wait outside while they had a talk with my mom. I wanted to hear what they were talking about but no matter how hard I strained my ears I couldn't hear. After about thirty minutes, my mom came out smiling and said, "let's go home."

"Why? I thought we had to be down here two or three days."

"No, the doctors said all the testing is done."

"Well what did they say? Am I dumb or what?"

"No, you're not dumb, maybe a little silly sometimes but not dumb at all."

"Good, because I know I'm not. I want others to know I'm not."

"You need to work harder at school."

"Is that what the doctors said?"

"Yes. And a few other things that I can not tell you about right now."

I wanted to know. It really didn't matter to me at all because the experts had spoken, I was justified, maybe it would change the way kids treated me at home.

I couldn't wait to get back to school and have my teachers know that I wasn't dumb. I wanted to see the look on their faces and hear them apologize to me—it never happened.

Despite all that, I still had a good time in school. My report card from the second grade is one I still keep and look at every once in a while. It says, "Luke will never amount to anything in life. He is constantly day-dreaming and never finishes any of his work. He is a student who shouldn't be in this school system." I always wondered why that teacher hated me so much. I did learn, despite what others believed, and it was a lot of fun.

As usual, time moves fast and so does the thoughts of a little boy. It wasn't long before I had forgotten the whole thing and was on to other things. During the school year I always looked forward to the weekends. I could make my rounds around town on Saturday mornings and talk to everyone. I could play with some of my friends and sometimes I would spend the night at a friend's house.

CHAPTER FOUR

My husband has taken to drinking spirits. He won't talk to me, but only mumbles that things are not right. The long hours in the woods and seeing men die in logging accidents are taking a toll on my dear love. I fear that he may die from too much spirits.

Letter from Lula Jackson to her sister in New York.
October 1897

It was on the weekends that my parents would go out dancing, and sometimes we would stay with my grandma and grandpa. Grandma and grandpa would always watch Lawrence Whelk on Saturday nights, and it drove Collin and me nuts. Just a bunch of bubbles and old people singing, yet when I see reruns of that show, it brings back fond memories of both my grandparents sitting in their chairs staring at the television.

Sometimes our Uncle Ted would watch us. He wasn't very nice except to my sister. He would take Collin and me outside and beat us. He would knock us down and when we went to get back up he would hit us again. We would be crying and he would say mean things and keep hitting us. I never told dad because I always thought dad would kill him. I always prayed when Saturday night rolled around that we would be watched by anyone but Uncle Ted.

One Saturday when I was with my grandma she told me to get my things together because we were going to take Uncle Ted to town. On the way to town there were lots of young men walking towards the train depot. I asked, "grandma, where are all these men going?"

"They have been drafted to go to war."

"I know someone who was going to war, someone that I met on the bus."

My grandmother looked really sad as she said, "I wish no one had to go to war. Your Uncle Ted is joining the Air Force so he doesn't have to fight in the trenches."

I thought maybe that is why he always beat us up, to learn how to fight. "Is he going to fly a jet?"

"I don't know Luke, I just hope he comes back safe."

I watched as uncle Ted got out of the truck; he walked over and gave grandma a kiss on the cheek and a hug. I was happy he was going away, I didn't want him to get hurt, but I wanted him to leave Collin and me alone. He got on the train, and grandma was crying almost all the way home. I was quiet, but very happy, for I knew I wouldn't have to be beat up by him again.

When mom and dad came back from dancing, they would come get us kids and take us home, which was always a relief to me because I didn't like sleeping overnight at my grandma's house. Sometimes my mom was drunk, she didn't think I could tell but I could. She would do stupid things when she was, and my dad would always be real quiet and not say much. I could never tell if he was drunk or not. I worried about men drinking, because, when they did, they did bad things. I believed that there were demons in the drinks, as Mr. Woodchopper had told me.

Ellens tavern was busy every Friday and Saturday night, with lots of people drinking and playing pool. It seemed that people came from miles around, to be there until it closed early in the morning. For entertainment a few of us kids would sit across from the tavern on the railroad tracks and watch the people coming and going.

Sometimes it was pretty exciting when there was a fight and the sheriff would come and haul some men away. I was glad that my dad didn't do things like that. A few times when things were boring we went to the pay phone and called the sheriff's office and told them there was a big fight at Ellens. When the sheriff showed up, people would start running and hiding. It was funny to see people running to hide. They must have been doing something wrong to be afraid like that.

One night after watching people at the tavern, I was walking home and Mr. Banks passed me on his way to his house. I thought it would maybe be a nice time to try to talk to him, because he was going home real early. I made my way up to his house and crossed the bridge over the creek, and walked up to his door and knocked on it.

"Who's there?"

"It's me, Luke."

"Wait a minute, I'll be right there."

I waited for what seemed an eternity—I finally heard him coming to the door.

"So what do you want?" He said in a grumpy voice.

"Oh, I wanted to know if you wanted to visit for a while."

"Are you trying to find out my favorite fishing bait?"

"Well, if you want to tell me, I would like to know"

"I don't think you're here for that Luke."

"I want to know why you look so sad and mean most of the time."

"Why do you want to know that? You sure are a curious little boy."

He was starting to get comfortable with me. He invited me in his house. I could see that he was drunk by the way he was walking. I knew he would talk to me. So I asked, "I want to know what would make you happy, or do you think you will ever be happy?"

He took a deep breath as he started to talk. "There have been too many things that have happened. I don't know if I could ever make things right, it would be better if I was to pass on in this life." His eyes were motionless as he spoke.

I asked, "what do you mean by that?" I could tell he had been drinking more than usual because of the smell of his breath as he talked.

"Oh, I guess it won't hurt to tell you. I know you will know all of it someday, you might as well learn now."

My heart went up into my throat, I thought I was about to hear things I had been waiting to hear.

"It's OK, Mr. Woodchopper tells me lots of things."

His demeanor changed when I had said something about Mr. Woodchopper.

"He isn't one of us. He is a stranger, he should have never moved here, and you shouldn't listen to him at all."

I was shaking my head and said, "he is a very nice man."

He shrugged his shoulders and said, "I was nice once, it was a long time ago though."

"When did you stop being nice?"

"I don't really know. I was a very nice man, and now look at me."

I saw tears starting to well up in his eyes. I really wanted to know what could have been so bad? "You can always be nice again, if you wanted."

"It's too late for me, I have done so much wrong that I could never make up for it." I was thinking it was never too late.

"Are you one of the bad guys, that comes to our house sometimes?"

"No, I am not, they are a mean bunch of men, mean and nasty. Stay away from them—stay away from them."

"Can you tell me who they are?"

"If I do, they might kill me, you have to forget they exist for they will do anything to keep themselves from being found out."

"Well, you can call the sheriff, he might be able to help you from being killed."

I think I was starting to make him mad, and I wondered why whenever I talked about the sheriff people became upset?

"No! Enough of this talk, you need to go home now."

"All I want to know is if you knew what really happened to Sharon?"

"Listen to me, I already feel bad about the things that have happened. There isn't anything I can do to change that."

"Well I thought you would know something because you're always at Ellens."

He sighed a deep breath and looked at me as he was going to do me harm and said, "one thing I will tell you is the night Sharon was killed, Ron was in the tavern and some men were around him buying him drinks. I was close by listening to the conversation, and they were telling him he should go get Sharon and make her be his wife. They said if she left for college she would never come back, she'd marry some rich man from the city. He drank and became mad and angry as the night went on. Not long after that Ron left."

"Who were the men? And why didn't you tell the sheriff this?"

"Because I am afraid of them—oh—what have I done? I am not a man at all."

Tears were streaming down his face, and I felt so bad for him. I wanted to reach out and heal his broken heart. He broke down, fell to his knees and started shaking and sobbing out loud. I didn't know what to do but stand and stare at him. I started to cry for him. He reached out and grabbed my arm; he looked intently in my eyes and said, "don't tell a soul I have told you these things, if they find out, I will die."

Staring back at him I saw fear as I had never seen before. It scared me. He continued to say, "if they know of the things I have told you, and find out that you know them, they will kill you also. Promise me that you will not tell anyone, I mean not even your brother or mom or dad, Please!"

I stood in silence, not knowing what to say about all this. I was scared, confused, and I wanted this to all be a dream. "I promise not to tell a soul."

"Now go, before anyone sees you have been here. And please don't come back here any more, it's not safe for you."

I left running for home and I was sure that the dark was full of evil things chasing me all the way down the road to home. My heart was racing when I ran through the door. My mom and dad were sitting there staring at me. "What is wrong, Luke?"

"Just afraid of things in the dark, so I ran home."

"And where were you? I saw you walk by the house headed up to Brian Mark's house."

"Yes, I went up to see if I could spend the night, but their mom said, not tonight, so I visited them awhile, then came home."

They were content with my answer. I was afraid they knew whose house I had really been at, and that they would tell someone and I would die. The thought of being told you might be killed for something you knew was hard to handle as a little kid. I would often try to put it out of my mind. It was from then on that I started having fears of being killed by someone, even though most of the time I thought I was safe. For a couple of months after that, I was real quiet and played with my friends close to home.

It's amazing how fast things disappear in a little boy's mind. Fun and laughter bring peace and joy, even in the saddest of times. Not wanting to wander far from the house didn't keep me from daydreaming. I would dream of things I would do and be when I grew up. I was going to be a football player, and build a big house up on Cultas Mountain and over look the lake and the whole valley. I would become king of the county and make sure every one was treated fair and right. I would dream that everyone in the world would want to live in the city I would build. It was great fun to dream like that, and I believed that it would someday become reality.

It would soon be Christmas, which was one of the best times of the year, yet also one of the saddest times for many people. The week before Christmas we would go and sing Christmas carols for people all over town. There would be my brother, sister, a few of my cousins, and a few friends. Our last stop would always be Ellens tavern.

We would sing about three or four songs and the drunks would start coming out giving us money; we got as much as a hundred dollars. We would take the money and decide who needed it the most in our community. We would leave it on their porch, hoping that the parents would make sure their kids would have a good Christmas. I received joy from doing that, because I thought we were making a difference in the world.

A couple of days before Christmas, we would usually go to the big town, and hopefully see Santa Claus. My list for Santa Claus was very long, and I hoped that I would have time to tell him everything so I would get the things I wanted.

When we arrived in town, we parked outside Sears. I got out and ran straight for the toy department. It was amazing there wasn't a very long line of kids waiting to see Santa. I waited for about five minutes and finally got my chance to sit on Santa Claus' lap. He said, "what is your name little boy?"

"Luke."

"What do you want for Christmas?"

"Well, I want a Tonka dump truck, a new football, and a BB gun, and most of all I want the bad guys to go away and the demons also."

"OK, be good and you will get what you want."

He gave me a candy cane, and I jumped off his lap and started to run to find mom to tell her she would never have to worry about the bad men again. I tripped and fell and broke my candy cane, it made me mad and I decided I wanted a new one. I thought about how I was going to get another candy cane. I got back in line and when I got to Santa Claus he said, "weren't you just up here?"

"No, that must have been my twin brother."

"Oh, what is your name?"

"John."

"And what do you want for Christmas?"

"A Lego set, a baseball bat, and a new bike."

Santa gave me another candy cane. I jumped down again and started running and fell and broke the second candy cane. I was really upset. I couldn't go back up again, or could I? I thought Santa fell for the twin thing once, why not twice? I got back in line and when I got up to Santa I said, "hi, I am Mark."

"What do you want for Christmas?"

I had done it, I had fooled Santa twice, and this was too good to be true, I was thinking of all the things I was going to get for Christmas. He gave me another candy cane and this time I walked, I didn't think Santa could be fooled three times. Then I thought Santa was supposed to know every thing—it sent doubt into my mind.

I went looking for my mom and the rest of the family. I had to tell them the news that Santa was going to make the bad guys go away. I looked all over the store for them and didn't find them. I went to the Montgomery store and started to look for them there, I walked in to the toy section, and it was amazing, I saw Santa Claus in this store. I thought that he could move really fast for a big old fat man.

My family wasn't there so I went to JC Penneys and started to look for them there. What I saw made me start to wonder even more about Santa Claus. He was at Penneys also. I ran out the door as fast as I could to Sears, and—yes—Santa was still there. I decided to go back to Penneys and take a close look at Santa. I watched awhile and I saw that he had a fake beard. I went and looked at the other Santa and saw he had a fake beard also. I was really upset that my older cousins were right; there was no such thing as a real Santa Claus. I knew that the bad guys wouldn't be going away. I was upset and started to cry—was there anything true in the world?

I walked towards the door, looking for my family. As I was walking, a strange man came up and asked me if I was lost. I looked in his eyes and saw evil—he tried to grab my hand and told me to come with him. I was scared and ran to hide. I ran to the end of the store and decided not to go outside, because the man might get me easier out there. I climbed under a bed display by the front window, thinking that maybe I could see my family walk by. I stayed under there, scared, and crying softy so no one would hear me. After a while of watching and waiting for my family to walk bye, I was tired and fell asleep.

When I woke up it was dark and there was no one in the store. The lights were off and the streets were empty except for a few policemen. I was scared and wanted to be home. I climbed up on the bed and crawled under the covers and fell back asleep. I heard a loud knocking noise that awoke me from my sleep. It was snowing hard and there were a few inches on the ground. A policeman and another couple were looking though the window. They were pointing their fingers and laughing; it was nice to see smiling faces. It was still dark outside and I was wondering where my parents were? The policeman was talking loudly to me through the window. He said, "don't move, we will be in to get you out in a second. Your parents are being notified that you have been found."

I was so glad to hear that; I never liked sleeping by myself. The lights went on and two policemen came walking over to the bed. One said, "we are so glad we found you. People have been looking for you for hours. Some thought you might have wandered over to the river and fallen in. Your mom and dad thought you might have been kidnapped. You're one lucky boy."

"I want to go home." I said.

"Your mom and dad are going to be here in a few minutes, they are worried about you."

It was nice to hear that my mom and dad cared so much for me, but I knew that I would be in deep trouble for falling asleep and making them worry about me. My parents arrived and thanked the police for finding me.

It was taking forever to get home, because the snow made the roads bad, and there were lots of cars in the ditches. My dad was concentrating on driving so he didn't say very much about what had happened. When we got to the bottom of the hill where we lived, dad tried to make a run up it, but he didn't make it, the car slid back down to the bottom, so he ended up parking the car, and we started walking to the house.

It was a fun walk as the snow was covering everything making it white. The snow was falling so hard you could hear it hit the ground, it gave me a strange peace inside, one that I will never forget. I felt like no matter what would happen in my life things would turn out all right. My mom and dad didn't say a word as we walked, I knew that to them this was all work, and not very fun. I arrived at home and went straight to bed; it was much nicer than the one in the store. I fell right asleep and dreamed of things to come at Christmas time. I didn't get punished for what happened that night, I knew my mom and dad were happy that I was safe.

It was Christmas Eve, and as usual my dad had to work, so we couldn't open presents until he came home on Christmas day. I wished that my dad could be like other dads who were home for the holidays, but I knew he had to make enough money to keep the family housed, clothed, and fed. It was a big job.

I loved to listen to Christmas music all night. I turned on the radio, and as I fell asleep, I could hear the story of the birth of Jesus being sung all around the world. I wondered if Santa Claus isn't real, maybe the story of Jesus isn't real. Why would adults want you to believe in something that didn't exist? It was real confusing to me.

On Christmas morning, I got up early and had to wait before opening presents. After opening presents, I started to make my rounds around town to see what every one else had received for Christmas. I walked to the Marks house and saw all the things they had received. From there I walked over to the Clarks house. They were my cousins, and they lived across the field from our house. It was always a scary time crossing the field, there was an old house in some trees that everyone said was haunted. I usually ran to the Clarks house as fast as I could, hoping the ghosts or evil things wouldn't get me.

The Clarks were different people. Mrs. Clark had been married many times. She had one son by her first husband, six kids by one of the other men, and none by the man that was living with her at the time. It was a fun place to visit, for there were people coming and going all the time. If any kid didn't have a place to stay or sleep, they were always welcome at the Clarks house. You could even get a good meal there every night. Mrs. Clark liked having people around all the time I guess. They never did have much money but they had the biggest hearts in town. Mrs. Clark would help anyone who needed it. She could also put you in your place when you needed it.

Tim was my age and we played together often. Joe was about 6 years older than me, Mark was 5 years older, Lindsey was 4 years older, Dan was 8 years older, Sis was 9 years older, Cal was 10 years older, and June was 2 years younger. They never had much money but they always had a good Christmas. It was fun to see everything all over the place, paper, gifts, and candies canes; it was a real mess. Their house was always a mess, and you never had to worry about damaging anything, for it was already done. Mrs. Clark was a screamer, she was constantly yelling at everyone, but no one seemed to pay attention to her. When she got really mad, she would start throwing things, and that got everyone's attention.

From there I made my way back across the field, running like lighting, to go see what Mr. Woodchopper had received. As I approached his house, I could smell the smoke coming from his wood cook-stove. I knocked on his door and heard him walking over to open it. "Come on in Luke, Merry Christmas to you son." He said with a happy smiling face.

"Merry Christmas to you."

"Sit down and I'll pour you some coffee." He gave me the same cup every time.

As he poured the coffee I asked, "what did you get for Christmas?"

"Nothing, I have no family, besides I don't need anything now that you're here."

"Why not? It's nice to get gifts from people that love you."

"I wouldn't know Luke, I was raised in an orphanage, and never had much growing up."

He didn't seem all that upset as he talked about these things. "So you have never been married, or had kids?"

He sat down at the table and thought deeply and started to talk. "No, I was in love one time, but her parents didn't approve of me, so she said she couldn't marry me. She had such beauty. I love watching her walk down the road when we would go out. I loved her very much; I cried and cried when she told me that she wasn't going to marry me. I begged and pleaded with her to run away with me, but she didn't want to upset her parents."

He was almost crying as he told me his life story. It was making me sad. "Why did her parents not approve of you?"

"Because I didn't have any standing in the community. Her father was a banker, very wealthy, a real snob. Her mom would always watch everything I did, as if I was going to steal something."

"Well that wasn't nice of them, I bet you have more money than they have now."

Mr. Woodchopper was laughing, "yes Luke, I have his money now, and I'm going to get more of his money."

I was happy for him, for Mr. Woodchopper should have all of his money I thought. "What are you having for Christmas dinner?"

"Some fried potatoes, and coffee, that's what I'm having for Christmas dinner."

"Are you having some friends over?"

"No Luke, you're the only friend I have, and you're here now. I do enjoy your company very much. A man couldn't ask for a better friend."

What he said made me feel good inside. I wanted to do something special for him. "This isn't good Mr. Woodchopper, I will be right back."

I jumped up out of my chair and ran out the door and headed for home. I was going to go ask mom if we could have Mr. Woodchopper over for Christmas dinner. I thought maybe that was the best gift he could get from anyone. My mom was in the kitchen when I got home. She said, "did you get to see what everyone got?"

"Yes I did. Mom can we have Mr. Woodchopper over for Christmas dinner?"

"I don't know. We don't even know the man."

"I know him. He is nice mom."

"I have told you not to visit him."

"Mom, he is all by himself, he has no family."

"You just don't understand, Christmas is time for family, not strangers."

I thought she must have never been alone before. "Well, can we mom? It won't hurt anything, and we have enough food to feed an army."

Mom was getting upset with me and said, "listen to me Luke, it's his own fault he has no family, not ours. We're not going to have him over."

"Mom, why not? He is lonely, and has no one, and it's Christmas!"

"Luke, drop it now."

I left feeling sad that we were not going to have Mr. Woodchopper over for dinner, because it didn't make any sense to me. If it were my house I would invite everyone in the whole town, and have one big feast and lots of fun for everyone.

Dinner was almost ready and the smell of fresh cooked turkey throughout the whole house made me real hungry. My grandparents were over and dad was home. We sat down and enjoyed the dinner. It was customary to go and sit in the living room to rest and talk after dinner. When everything was cleared off the table and put away and everyone was in the living room, I went back into the kitchen and took a bunch of leftovers and put them on a plate. I wrapped the plate in foil and put it out on the porch. I went back into the living room and told my mom I was going up to the Marks house to play awhile. Out the door I went and took the plate with me. I went straight to Mr. Woodchopper's house and knocked on his door. "Hi Luke." I could tell he was very happy to see me back. "I didn't think I would see you again today."

"Well I have something for you. It's Christmas dinner."

He smiled and I could see by his eyes that he was very pleased. "Thank you. I haven't had a turkey dinner in a long time. Does your mom and dad know you brought me this food?"

"No, they think I am up at the Marks house playing there."

"This is very nice of you Luke, you're the best friend I've ever had, I hope that you will always remember that."

"I will—I will never forget you."

I sat and watched him eat the dinner. I drank his coffee and we talked for what seemed like hours. He told me about growing up in the orphanage, how he was hungry a lot, how they used to beat him if they were mad at him. He told me about trying to run away many times, that he wasn't any good in school, how they all thought he was dumb. He laughed and even had a few tears. It was one of the best visits I've had.

He told me stories of robbing banks and being chased though the city streets. It was all very exciting. I knew that if my mom and dad ever found out how much time I was spending up there they would beat me to death, but I never feared enough to stop visiting. It was getting dark so I decided it was best I be getting home before my parents figured out I wasn't at the Marks.

CHAPTER FIVE

"Some of the people around town stop talking whenever I walk by. They seem to have secrets and I am determined to find out what they are."

Letter from Olive Johnsen to her mother in Ohio
January 1902

It was the New Year and things seemed to be pretty normal around town. Winter time in Clear Lake was almost as fun as the summers. When it snowed we would sled down the hills, and there were lots of them. If it was cold enough the lake would freeze over, then we would go out and play on the ice, skating, or playing hockey, or chasing each other, it was fun. The snow would come and go—it would never stick around for long. The only thing I didn't like was the fog. It would sometimes stay for days and I wouldn't be able to see the sky or the sun. It made me feel as if I was in a box and couldn't escape. I liked the feeling of being free and having open spaces, to be able to see forever.

Once every couple of months my mom would give me a few dollars to get my hair cut. I would walk down the hill to the highway to the town barbershop. The barber was Mr. Anderson. I thought he was a little strange. Sometimes I would see him out in his boat fly-fishing on the lake, drinking his whiskey, enjoying life. He would catch lots of big fish, and when he came to shore I would walk over to his boat to see the fish and try to see what he was using. He never showed me what he was using, he always said it was his secret. Everyone in Clear Lake it seemed had secrets.

All the boys liked getting their hair cut by him because he would let them look at some books with pictures of naked girls. He would always ask me if I wanted to look, but I always said no. It wasn't because I didn't want to, just because I didn't want anyone to see me doing that kind of thing. Other than that he was a nice man, never said a mean thing to anyone. The only bad thing I heard said about Mr. Anderson was that he had to have a couple of drinks to be able to give a good hair cut.

When I walked in the door of the shop Mr. Woodchopper was there, he was getting his weekly shave. They both turned towards me and Mr. Woodchopper said, "Luke, we were just talking about you."

"Am I in trouble?" They both started to laugh.

"No, you're not in trouble, we were talking about how you seem to ask so many questions about everything and everybody."

"Well I want to know about things."

Mr. Woodchopper got up out of the chair, walked over to the cash register and paid Mr. Anderson. As he walked out the door he dropped some papers out of his wallet. Mr. Anderson went to wash his hands and Mr. Woodchopper motioned threw the window with his hand over his mouth. It looked as if he was trying to tell me not to talk too much. Mr. Anderson walked back in the room and asked, "Luke, are you ready for your hair cut?"

"Yes, my mom says I am looking like a hippie."

"Have you ever seen hippies before?"

"Yes, down at the University, and I know there are some living up on the hill."

"How do you know that?"

"Well, Tony and I were up there playing one day and way back in the woods we found a whole hippie camp. There were almost a hundred hippies up there. They were living in tents and looked like they haven't had a bath in years. Some of them run around naked."

"Oh, I don't think that many people would be up there."

"Well there were lots of them, and I think they are really weird."

"And why do you think that?"

"Because they dress different and live in tents and things like that."

"Luke, do you think Mr. Woodchopper is weird?"

"No, I think he is a very nice man."

"How well do you know him?"

"My mom says I am not supposed to talk to him, she thinks he is a dirty old man, but he has clean clothes on every time that I see him."

"So you visit with him often?"

"Once in a while. When I am up by the frog pond, me and him will talk for a bit."

I thought he was asking too many questions that were not right. So I was only going to tell him what he needed to know.

"Do you know what he does to make his money?"

"I think he chops wood and sells it. He is always doing that when I am up in the woods. And I know he can peal cascara trees for the bark."

"Has he any family that you know of?"

"Not that I know of. He hasn't told me anything about a family."

I could smell whiskey on his breath as he was talking to me. I wondered why he drank. It seemed awfully early to be drinking. Even though he drank I had never seen him down at Ellens tavern.

"A lot of people are talking about your friend Mr. Woodchopper, they say that lots of bad things have happened since he came to town a few years ago."

"Oh, he isn't bad. I think he is one of the nicest people in town."

"Be careful Luke, no one wants you to get hurt."

"OK. I am always careful Mr. Anderson."

I was wondering why he was telling me to be careful. It wasn't Mr. Woodchopper I was worried about, it was the bad men whom I didn't know, they were the ones people needed to worry about, and the demons. Instead, they worried about Mr. Woodchopper because they didn't know anything about him and were afraid to ask. I thought life was like that—people fear others because they are different. Mr. Anderson finished cutting my hair. "There you go. Now you will have the girls chasing you all over town."

"I sure hope they don't. I would get too tired running all the time."

I paid him for cutting my hair and headed for the school to see if anyone was down there that wanted to play. At the school, a bunch of older kids were playing football in the field. Even though they were older, they usually let me play with them. I was always nice to these older kids, but it seemed that being nice landed me in trouble most of the time.

After one such game my cousin Dan Clark asked, "Luke, do you want a ride home?" I thought about it. I had played hard and I was tired and my house was up hill from the school, so why not? "Yes, I would like that. I am really tired."

"Get in Steve's truck and we'll take you home."

I didn't really know this Steve person, and he looked like someone you wouldn't trust. I should've trusted my judgment. I got in the truck anyway. He started it up and said, "hang on boys, we're going to have some fun."

I was in the middle of the two, wishing I were walking home. He put it in gear and did a donut in the school parking lot, straightened his truck out and headed across the blacktop into the school field doing donuts and tearing it apart. I didn't understand what enjoyment Steve and Dan were getting out of tearing up the yard, but they were yelling and screaming and laughing and acting like they had won the Super Bowl. They were acting crazy and looked like demons had a hold of them. I was scared, and started to cry. I said, "I think this is enough, take me home now please."

Dan said, "there is no need to cry. You're going to be OK, no one is going to hurt you."

Steve turned his truck around and headed for the road. He stopped and told Dan, "let this cry baby out. He can walk home. I'm not going to have a cry baby in my truck."

Dan opened the door and told me, "get out!"

I did and was glad. I felt a lot safer walking home than riding in that truck, even though Dan was a relative I didn't trust him.

The first day back to school I was sitting in class and my teacher asked me to take a note down to Mr. Jobson, the Principal of the school. I always hated the way teachers in grade school would try to make you think you were doing them a favor. I knew that anytime you had to take a note to the principal's office it was a death sentence. I was trying to think of what I had done wrong? I had been nice to the other students, I hadn't mouthed off to the teachers, I couldn't think of what I had done to be sent down to Mr. Jobsons office. I walked into his office and handed him the note. He looked at me and said, "so tell me Luke, what did you do this weekend?"

I knew I was dead. I was in the truck and I was going to be blamed for what had happened to the schoolyard. The demons were trying to get me again.

"I played football and got my hair cut this weekend."

"What else did you do Luke?"

"Nothing."

"Luke are you lying to me? Someone said they saw you in a truck tearing up the school yard."

"Who told you that?"

"That has nothing to do with you. Just tell me. Did you tear up the school yard?"

"No, the truck I was in did—I was sitting in the truck."

Mr. Jobson didn't think what I said was funny, it made him angry. "That makes you as guilty as the other two that were with you. Can you tell me who they were?"

"Why don't you ask whoever told you I was in the truck?"

"Luke you're making me really angry! The people who saw you don't know who they were."

I was thinking that if I tell on them they might kill me. If I don't tell on them I will get the blame for the whole thing. I was trying to decide the lesser of two evils, and decided it was better to be alive and in jail than to be dead. I knew the demons wanted to get rid of me somehow. "I don't know who they were Mr. Jobson."

"Are you sure about that?"

"Yes. I wanted a ride home, and they decided to tear apart the yard first."

"If you're not going to tell, I'm going to have to punish you and tell your parents, and you're in big trouble."

I stood there in front of his desk trying to hold back tears; I didn't want to give him the satisfaction of seeing me cry. He said, "go back to your class and I will deal with you later, after I talk to your parents."

I walked toward my class but decided to leave. The demons had a hold of Mr. Jobson and he was going to have me sent to jail. I thought I might as well go home and gather up my things and head to the frog pond. On my way home I stopped to see my other grandmother and grandfather. They lived in a log house behind the post office. I could always get something to eat at their house. Grandma was in the house working on her fishing pole. She saw me walk in and said, "Luke what are you doing out of school?"

"Not going to go anymore. They are out to send me to jail for being in a truck at the wrong time."

"Now they wouldn't send you to jail for that."

"Well if they don't, my dad is going to beat me to death."

"Your dad isn't going to beat you to death." She said shaking her head.

"Well I don't care, I want to go away and hunt and fish and live off the land, and never go to school again."

"Luke you have to go to school, you will like school in a few more years and you will wish you could go to school forever."

"I don't think so grandma, I wish I were all grown up right now."

"Don't wish your life away son, it will come all too soon. It was the other day that I was a little girl, oh I wish I was young again. Enjoy being a child, grown up things come so fast."

I understood what she was saying, but I felt as if I was a grown up already, in a little body, and no one treated me like a grown up except for Mr. Woodchopper. I grabbed some cookies and headed for the door.

"Thanks for the cookies Grandma, I will talk to you later."

"Remember what I told you, think and stay young."

"I will." I knew I would be young forever.

I was back on the road, heading for home, thinking about what my grandmother had told me. It was hard to think young when there were so many grown up things happening all around me. I started to think about why I always thought I was going to jail.

It all started one day back when I was four years old, playing in my other grandpa's barn. Earlier that day, when grandma took us to town, I found a book of matches on the dash of the truck. It was a 1963 Ford, kind of light green, and to me it seemed so big. I took the matches and put them in my pocket.

Later when I was in the barn with my brother Collin, we were in the hayloft building forts and tunnels. I had often seen my older cousins in there and they said that there were demons and evil things in the barn that would get us if we were bad. My brother always told me, "they say those things so we don't go in there and ruin their stuff."

Well, I wasn't so sure if there was or wasn't, but I wasn't going to take any chances with them getting me. I decided to make a fire, knowing that bad things were afraid of fire. The only thing I didn't think of was that we were playing on 12 tons of dry hay and building a fire on top of that wasn't so smart. I took a match and lit it, and put it to the little pile of hay that we had made. It started up, and in less than thirty seconds about four bales were on fire. I took off to the house to tell grandpa that the barn was on fire, and Collin took off for the milk house to get the water hose. I reached the house and said, "grandma, grandpa the barn is on fire!"

"Now don't be telling stories like that." My grandpa said.

"I am not! It's on fire for real."

Just then grandma said, "grandpa the barn is on fire! Call the fire department! Luke, where is Collin?"

"He is trying to put the fire out."

Grandma took off running for the barn and grandpa called the fire department. I was scared that Collin would burn, because the whole barn looked as if it was on fire.

Standing there watching the barn burn seemed like forever. Grandpa said, "Luke come with me. We have to get the boat and truck out of the barn."

When we got down to the barn, grandma came running out with Collin and they helped grandpa and I get the boat out. The fire was so fast and hot that we couldn't get the truck out. The barn was really big, at that time one of the biggest barns in the county. My grandfather's business was in it. The whole bottom floor of the barn was a big walk in cooler, with a milk house on one side, storage to another side, and a big loft for hay.

It took forever for the volunteer fire department to get there. Once the fire department arrived, Collin and I took off for the woods, we knew we were in big trouble and decided that the best thing we could do was hide until everything calmed down.

The fire took a very long time to fight. Clear Lake firefighters had to call for help from Mount Vernon because there were no fire hydrants close. When the fire departments gave up and said, "let it burn to the ground," my dad was there and everyone realized that Collin and I were not around. We heard them yelling for us to get to the house, so we decided that we should go face them and receive our punishment.

My dad was really mad and started yelling and screaming and trying to hit us. It was probably funny seeing him chasing us around the house with his belt off, swinging wildly and cursing us. I was afraid this would be the end of my life. Collin and I stopped running and were whipped for a while, then dad asked, "which one of you set the barn on fire?"

Collin said, "Luke did. He is the one who got the matches."

Well, so much for my brother sticking up for me. I had taken the matches, and I guess at four years old I should have known better. Dad said, "Collin, get in the house. Luke, head down to the barn."

"Dad, the barn ain't there any more, it burned up."

"Don't be smart with me boy, get down to the barn!"

As I started to walk to the pile of ashes dad took after me with his belt. He was hitting me as my aunt and uncles were cheering him on. It made my heart hurt that they were all laughing at the thing my dad was doing to me. Even though it was the middle of November the barn was still burning, it would burn for at least three days. It was nice because I didn't have a coat on and the fire made me warm.

Dad went and got a chair and said, "sit in this chair."

I sat in the chair and was wondering why my dad wanted me to sit here?

"You're going to sit here all night and think about what you did. I should have you taken to jail. You're one bad boy, and sometimes I wish you were never born. If you would be good like your brother you would be OK. Look what you have done, you have destroyed your grandfather's business, I hope you're satisfied with yourself. You will not come up to the house and you will not get dinner, sit here by yourself and think about what you did."

"But dad, I didn't mean to do that, and I don't want to stay here in the dark by myself, I am afraid dad."

"Just grow up you cry baby, nothing is going to get you in the dark, except the demons that get bad little boys."

"But dad…"

"Shut up and stay put or I will beat you within an inch of your life."

I was crying as my dad walked off. I deserved what I was getting—I had done a terrible thing. It was the first time that I wished I was dead, that like my dad said, "that I was never born." Maybe he could take me back to the rock he and mom had found me under on the beach. With tears falling out of my eyes I watched the remains of the barn burn. The fire made images like ghosts and demons, like faces howling and crying in pain, thousands of them screaming and wailing, turning into smoke and vanishing into thin air. As the night wore on, I grew tired and was afraid to fall asleep for fear that somehow I would burn with the rest of the barn and fade away like the demons that disappeared into the night. I kept staring at the fire and thinking of keeping myself awake.

Sometime during the night I fell asleep, someone had come and took me home and put me in my bed. Those images are something I would never forget.

About a week after the fire my mom and dad came and told me, "Luke a man is coming to talk to you about the fire, you have to tell him the truth about what happened. If you don't, you will go to jail."

I was scared, because I didn't want to go to jail. I was wondering why did my parents have to tell me to tell the truth? I didn't think they had ever caught me in a lie, though I had seen both of my parents lie at various times. I had already told them that I had taken the matches and started the fire. When the man came to the house I got really scared and hid in the top of my closet. I could hear dad and mom asking Collin where I was hiding?

"Luke get in here now or I will spank you."

I climbed out of the closet and walked into the living room and saw this big man in a suit. I asked, "are you going to take me to jail?"

He started to laugh. "No, I am not going to take you to jail, I'm here to ask you a few questions."

"OK, I can do that for you."

He had my parents leave the room, and proceeded to ask me about what happened the day I set the barn on fire.

"Luke, on the day that you set the barn on fire, where was your grandpa?"

"He was in the house."

"Did he give you the matches?"

"No, he didn't. I took them out of the truck."

"Did your grandpa ask you to set the barn on fire?"

"No. Why would he want me to do that?"

"Are you telling me the truth?"

"Yes, my dad said if I didn't tell the truth I would go to jail."

"So as I understand things, you took the matches and did this thing all by yourself with no help from anyone. Is that right?"

"Yes, the only person there, besides me, was my brother."

He talked a lot about things and asked many more questions. I didn't really know what he wanted, he kept asking the same questions over and over again and I kept telling him the truth. After about an hour, it seemed like all day, he said, "thank you, you have been very helpful."

"Do I have to go to jail now?"

He looked at me straight in the eye and said, "as long as you keep telling the truth, you will not have to go to jail." I was happy to hear that.

About fifteen years later I learned the circumstances surrounding the burning of the barn. My grandfather had insured his barn for a bunch of money. The man who came out to my house was from the insurance company and he was convinced that my grandfather had put me up to burning the barn down, to collect the money. My grandparents received the money after it was concluded that I had set the fire on my own. Life sure makes some strange turns on people when they least expect it.

It seemed to me that whenever I got into some type of trouble, I was worried about going to jail, maybe it was something I didn't have to really worry about anymore, maybe I was being lied to.

I walked into my house and tried to sneak into my bedroom without my mom hearing me, but I wasn't quiet enough. "Luke is that you?"

"Yes it is."

"School called and said you had left. Do you want to tell me why?"

"You know why, I am sure they told you."

"Yes, now go to your room, you're grounded and wait till your father gets home."

I could wait a lifetime for that. Funny thing about my mom was she would never take after us kids, just always yell that dad was going to deal with us when he got home. The problem was my dad was really crabby if he had been working nights. I am sure the last thing he wanted to hear when he got home was how bad us kids were. So when mom would start in on him about us, I think he was mad at her, but took it out on my brother and me.

CHAPTER SIX

"I have not seen Olive for two weeks. I fear that something bad has overcome her. It wasn't her nature to leave and not say good-bye."

Journal of Victoria Southerland
April 1903

In the winter Clear Lake smelled like burning wood. The mill would have its burner going all day. A lot of people used wood as their main source of heat, and you could smell all the smoke drifting through town.

I was afraid of the dark, but I believed that if I was in it enough I would over come that fear. It was always at night that the demons would come. I would sometimes go for walks in the middle of night. When it was clear out, the air seemed so crisp and clean and the stars looked so close. A rising moon would broadcast its light on the water of the lake. If someone was out fishing on the lake, their sound would travel to the shores, and you could easily hear them, as if you were sitting next to them.

It was on such a night that I was sitting on the edge of the lake, down by the A-frame, watching the ducks swim in the light of the moon. I saw a boat moving slowly across the lake. It was evening and the moon was full and the stars were shining, almost as if it was day light. I could see three men in the boat. I hid myself in the brush so they couldn't see me, since they were heading my way. I listened as they talked, "OK, this looks good, we can dump the body right here."

"What if someone sees that we have taken the boat out, and they find his body?"

"No one will see us you fool, so shut your mouth."

My heart was racing fast as I was trying to see, lying on the cold ground, trying to not make a sound, but my heart sounded as if you could have heard it on Mars.

"This will teach this old man to talk too much; he should have kept his mouth quiet.

"What if they find his body?"

"You idiots, the sheriff is so stupid, people will think he came down fishing and was drunk and fell in and drowned."

"Yeah right, no one will ever know."

I heard a splash in the water and the sound of men rowing the boat towards shore. I was so scared that I couldn't stay there anymore, I jumped up and started running to the road, which was about a quarter mile from the A-frame. The men started to shout, "hey boy stop! Stop now!"

I wasn't stupid—I kept running—fearing that if they caught me they would throw me in the lake. I made it to the road and decided to walk. Then I heard the sound of someone running up the dirt path that came from the A-frame, and I knew I couldn't outrun an older man. The closest thing to me was Meekers store. I made my way to the back of the store and climbed in the garbage bin and buried myself under some cardboard. I thought to myself—this is dumb—Meekers is right next to Ellens tavern. What if the men come down here to drink? I was wishing I had run the other way and hid in someone's back yard, or run all the way home.

I waited for what seemed like a year, then climbed out of the garbage bin and made my way across the road, and headed through a patch of woods. I didn't want to be on the road if a car came by. I made it to my house and when I walked inside my mom asked, "Luke where have you been?"

"Out in the back field watching the stars."

"You don't usually spend that much time in the back field. Are you lying to me?"

"No mom, I was playing in the back field and thinking of what I wanted to be when I grow up."

I knew that would end the conversation, mom was interested in what I was doing at the present time. Anytime I talked about the future she would stop asking questions. I went to bed and thought about what I had heard and seen earlier. I was afraid to tell anyone for fear that those men would find out and come after me. I knew I could talk to Mr. Woodchopper about it, so I planned to head up and see him in the morning to tell him what I had seen and heard.

It was Saturday and I was eager to get up to Mr. Woodchopper's house. I ate my cold cereal and grabbed my coat and headed up to his house. The weather had changed over night. It was raining hard and the clouds were low, making it foggy. I knocked on Mr. Woodchopper's door and he opened it and told me to come in. He already had coffee on the wood cook stove and the smell was filling his small house. His table was just big enough to fit two plates and a few condiments. It never had a tablecloth but always looked clean. He always had sugar out for me when I showed up, he drank his coffee black, but I needed sugar for mine. Even to this day I have to have sugar in my coffee.

"So tell me Luke, what is on your mind?"

"How do you know something is on my mind?"

"I can tell, you seem like you have something very important to tell me."

"Yes. I saw some men last night on the lake and I think they were throwing a body in the water, some man, I heard them say."

"Did you see who the men were?"

"No. It was too dark, and I was scared and ran as they chased me, I don't think they knew who I was."

"Luke you have to stop being so nosy, it's going to get you into trouble, or maybe even hurt."

"I know, but I didn't go down there to see them do that—I was watching the ducks, and thinking about things."

"I don't want you to tell anyone about this. I'll see what I can find out. If these men find out, they might hurt you."

"I know, but they don't know who I am."

Mr. Woodchopper poured me another cup of coffee. He sat back down and said, "I have something to tell you, you have to keep it a secret."

"OK, I can keep your secret. Is it something bad?"

"It might be to you, it makes me sad, because we have become good friends, but I might have to be moving on soon."

"Why? Are the bad guys after you now?"

He started to laugh with a big smile on his face. He said, "no, the bad guys are not trying to get me. I have to move on soon or the good guys might get me."

"I don't understand what you mean."

"Luke, the good guys are the police, and I don't expect you to understand."

"OK, I got it now. When are you going?"

"I will tell you before I leave. Now don't tell anyone, OK?"

"I won't, not even my mom or dad."

I finished my coffee and said good-bye and headed up to the Marks house.

Whenever I went to play with my friends, I would forget the bad things in town and the demons. It's then that I would be the little boy that I should have always been. I loved all kinds of sports and loved playing football or baseball with my friends. The Marks boys all loved sports also, except the youngest one. Mr. Marks was an expert at any sport.

He would watch games on television and tell everyone from the coach to the players how to play the game. If the team he was hoping to win would lose, he would get mad and break things and yell at his kids and wife. It was interesting because his boys would do the same thing when playing any kind of game. They would get mad if they didn't win. They'd cuss and yell, and sometimes leave and go in the house. I never really understood their thinking, for I wanted to have fun, win or lose. I knew that if I asked the boys to come outside to play they would say it was raining too hard. So we sat inside and watched television. I made the comment to Mrs. Marks that I had not seen Mr. Banks drive by today. She said, "no, I don't think he came home last night, usually I hear his old truck making so much noise, and him cussing and yelling at things he thinks he sees when it's dark, but last night was quiet."

I started to wonder if—my mind was really running—no, they wouldn't! I started to put things together. I told the Marks's good-bye and headed downtown hoping to find Mr. Banks truck. I was sure it was at the tavern and he would be inside.

It took me about 15 minuets to make it down town. I found Mr. Bank's truck parked outside Ellens Tavern. I sat outside, across the road on the railroad tracks, waiting to see if Mr. Banks was inside or not. I didn't want to wait so I thought I would go in and check and see if he was there. I knew that you had to be old to go into the tavern, because I never saw any kids going in and out, just adults. I walked to the front door of the tavern and opened it, and walked right in up to the big bar. I could hardly see over it. The man behind the bar asked, "can I help you with something boy?"

"Yes, I would like a pop please."

The whole place burst into laughter. I started to look around at the men to see if I could see if Mr. Banks was sitting someplace, but the room was full of cigarette smoke and for some reason they had the lights basically turned off. I wondered why men had to drink in the dark. It was that way with my grandfathers, they both drank, but they kept their bottles of whiskey in the cellar where it was dark. I never understood why.

The man behind the bar said, "you're going to have to go get your pop at the store down the road, this place is for adults only."

Then I heard a couple of men say, "let him have a pop Joe, this is the Mills kid. He's one of us."

"Yeah Joe, no state people are going to find out he's in here, give him a pop, I'll buy it for him."

I was still trying to see if I could find Mr. Banks, but I saw no sign of him. I said, "well thanks for the offer, but I will go to the store and buy a pop."

I started to walk out but a man stood up and said, "not so fast boy. You just sit here and have a pop with us."

"I have to go. The man behind the bar said I am not to be in here."

He grabbed me and sat me in the chair at the table with two other men; men I had seen before but I didn't know their names. I had a pop set in front of me and the man told me to drink. He then asked, "so tell us little Mills kid, is it you that we see running all over town late at night? And be sure to speak slow so we can understand you."

"Maybe during the day, but never late at night."

I was lying, but I thought maybe these men were up to no good, and I didn't want them to think that maybe I saw something I shouldn't have seen.

"Have you ever had a drink of beer before?" One of the men asked. "If you were a man you would be drinking beer with us." One of the men said to the man at the bar, "Joe bring this young man a beer."

"Now you know I can't serve beer to a minor."

"If you know what is best for you Joe, you had better bring a beer over here now!"

I was becoming scared, because these men seemed really rough. The man behind the bar brought over a glass of beer and set it next to my pop. I think he was afraid of those men, just as I was. "I have never had a beer before. But I have been drunk once, my mom and dad say."

"Oh, you have been drunk, and how did that happen? Drinking your pop?"

The men in the tavern all started laughing, they must have thought it was funny what this man had said. I didn't think it was so funny. "No, I thought I was drinking pop, but it was my grandfathers whiskey, he thought it was funny, and it burned my throat, so I am not going to ever drink again."

Since I was serious about what I was saying the man started to ask questions. "How did you know you were drunk?"

"I was five and I remember trying to walk up the steps to my grandpa's house, then I fell asleep and missed dinner, that is all I remember."

"You're experienced at drinking, so join us by drinking this beer we bought you."

I looked at the beer and looked at the man, and picked the glass up and took a sip and spit it all over the table on their drinks and hands. I thought I was going to die, because it was the worst tasting thing in the world. I thought the men would be mad but they all started laughing again. I stood up and said thanks for the drinks and took a quick look around to make sure I didn't see Mr. Banks, then headed for the door.

I could still hear them laughing as I walked down the street towards Meekers store to get some gum, to get rid of the taste in my mouth. I was thinking, if Mr. Banks truck was parked at the tavern and he wasn't in there, than where could he be? I started to fear the worse. Maybe it was his body that those men were throwing in the lake the night before? I opened up the door to go into the store and Mr. Banks almost ran into me. It kind of shocked me. "Mr. Banks, I thought you were dead."

"Now why would you think that Luke?"

"Mrs. Marks said you didn't come home last night. That is why."

"Is it everyone's business whether I am home at night or not?"

"No—I was worried about you."

"No need to worry about me. I can take care of myself. You watch yourself." He barked.

I could see that Mr. Banks was being his own crabby self, he headed back down to Ellens tavern.

It left me thinking that I would never know whom those men had thrown into the lake the night before. I went into the store and bought a piece of bubble gum for a penny. I often found pennies and nickels, and saved them to spend at the store. Mr. Meeker was always nice to us, even though we didn't spend lots of money. I paid him the money and he asked, "so why did you think that Mr. Banks was dead?"

"Oh, I know that he drinks a lot and I was wondering if he had gotten in a car accident, because he didn't drive by last night."

"That's very thoughtful of you. You're a good boy, stay that way."

"I will, I like being good." I was thinking that if he really knew how much I lied he would never let me in his store again. I was getting too good at lying and deceiving people.

I was thinking that I had better stop all this lying I was doing. I didn't know how much longer I could keep lying and not be found out. I thought about what would happen if I told all these people the truth about things. Some wouldn't believe me, and others would want me dead. All these things were getting very confusing to me. I found it strange that it was good to tell a lie.

I decided to go on down to the school and see if any of my friends were down there playing basketball. I walked back past Ellens, then past the barber shop and jewelry store. I noticed a sign on the door of the barbershop. It read, "gone to Texas on vacation. Be back in three weeks. Thanks, Mr. Anderson."

I thought it was nice that he was going to warm weather instead of this cold weather we were having. I wish I was going to Texas, I would like it there I thought.

I made my way down the only sidewalk in Clear Lake, past the oldest house in town. I had never talked to the old lady that lived there, because she looked mean and would stare at me whenever I walked by. I don't think she had any friends. I heard a lot of the people in town call her the white witch. She always wore black coveralls and she had the whitest hair I had ever seen. I never saw a smile on her face. I think she must have been at least a hundred years old. People said she had been born the same time the town started. I had no doubt in my mind that she was a witch. All you had to do was look at her house. She had one hand missing, replaced by a hook, as the older kids would say, "it's easy for her to grab little boys. With that hook she can reach over the fence in her front yard and take them and cook them in one of the many stoves she has in her house." After hearing that story I would usually run by her house as fast as I could, so I wouldn't become her dinner.

Walking by the stores and the tavern that were before her house, I would see my reflection in the windows and I would think, I sure would make someone a good meal, not too fat, not too skinny, umm just right. I couldn't stop thinking of having an apple in my mouth, in a big pot, on the stove. Maybe my mom was right—maybe I was watching too much Bugs Bunny on television. As far as I know the white witch never ate any of my friends. There were a few kids in town she could have eaten, and it wouldn't have bothered me at all. I thought she probably didn't want to eat them because they were not sweet, they were a bunch of sour kids.

I made it to the schoolyard and no one was there. I didn't want to hang around and wait for anyone in case something happened and I get blamed for it. I started walking home, ran past the white witch's house, and continued walking home. I got home and mom said, "Luke your dad and I are going out tonight and you and your brother are going to be baby-sat over at the Steens house."

"Where is Liz going to be?"

"She is going to be watched with the girls at some other house. We think that is best."

I was happy to hear this and was eager to tell Collin that Liz wasn't going to be around to annoy us all night. "OK mom, hope you and dad have a good time."

I ran to find Collin. He was in our bedroom reading. My brother was very smart, but lacked common sense. I hated following in his footsteps, because all the teachers thought that I should be like him. One time a teacher said to me, "Luke, why can't you be like your brother?"

I got mad and made a smart remark back, "because I have a different dad than him, he was born, and I was found under a rock, that is why!"

The teacher didn't have a thing to say after that. She left me alone and let me do my work my way.

I knew not to annoy my brother when he was reading, if I did he would get mad, and that would be asking him to come and pound on me. I was tired so I took a nap.

Latter that evening mom and dad loaded us into the car. It was always a fight to see who got to sit by the windows. I got a window about half the time. We arrived at the Steens house and went inside. It was great—just a bunch of us boys there with no girls—it was going to be a fun night. We wouldn't have to argue over what we were going to watch on television, and there was no one to tell on us, just one older boy to make sure we were safe.

This started happening on a regular basis, almost every Friday or Saturday night the boys went to one house and the girls at another house. The older boy who watched us was a little weird, because he would always ask, "Luke are you a playboy?"

I would say, "sometimes, but I work a lot also, but I prefer play, it's a lot more fun."

He would laugh when I would give him that answer. I didn't know what he meant. I don't know if he ever asked any of the other boys. There were eleven of us from seven different families. It was apparent that our parents all were out together. One time Len the boy who watched us asked, "Luke have you ever sucked a boys penis?"

I knew right then that the demons had control of him also. "No! I have not, and never will!"

"Do you know who Lee Walker is?"

"Yes he is a weird kid who I am afraid of."

"Him and I take turns on each other and it's fun, do you want to try?"

"No, No, No!"

I jumped up and ran to find the other boys. I wasn't going to stay near this boy, and when my mom and dad came to get us I was going to tell on him. I didn't want to have him watch me or any of the other boys again.

I told my parents when they were taking me home, "mom, dad, Len is saying bad things to me when he watches us. I think he is a demon or one of the bad guys."

"What is he saying?"

"He is talking about his penis, and things that are not right."

"That is the way boys talk. It's nothing to worry about."

"Well, I don't want him to watch me anymore."

"Forget it, your father and I need to go out, and you're going to have to accept him watching you. It saves us a lot of money."

"I don't like it, and I think he is thinking of hurting me."

"Drop it now Luke."

I heard those famous words again. I knew not to continue because then dad would get mad. I just didn't understand how my parents didn't see the things I saw.

From that time on I tried to keep my distance from Len, and never said much to him. He just became mean and nasty. I knew he didn't like me anymore, one time when he gave us ice cream, he put a whole cup of salt on mine, and made me eat it. I was mad, I was crying and I swore that one day I would make him pay. I wanted to get bigger so I could tell him, no, and that I am not going to do things I don't want to do. It was sad to me that people forced others to do things that they didn't want to do. But from watching television that was what demons did to people all the time.

I wanted to be bigger, but I wasn't growing up as fast as I wanted too. I decided to ask my grandpa how he got so big. He was a big man over six feet tall and I knew he had to know the secrets of how to get big. So one day I went to ask him how to get big. "Grandpa how did you get so big?"

"Let me tell you, when I was your age, I would go stand barefoot in the cow manure. Yep, just stand there and feel myself grow." He had a real serious look on his face so I knew he was telling the truth.

"How does that make you bigger?" I asked.

"Look at the garden, put cow manure on the beans and they grow tall. Put cow manure on the corn and it grows tall. It's the way cow manure works."

I thought for a little bit and said, "well if it makes those things grow big, it must be able to make me grow big."

"Yes it will, but you have to stand in it every day for a week for it to do any good."

"OK, thanks for the advice, talk to you later grandpa."

I ran back to my house and went out to the barn. I took my shoes off, and than my socks, and planted my feet deep in the cow manure. It was cold and very stinky, but I was already feeling myself growing standing there. My brother came out to feed the cows and pigs and saw me standing in the cow manure. He said, "what are you doing, standing barefoot in that stuff, are you retarded?"

"Grandpa said it would make me grow."

"You're a fool. Do you believe everything someone tells you?"

"No, but whatever Grandpa says I do. He makes a lot of sense."

He shook his head as he finished his chores. I was done standing in the manure for the day and went and washed my feet off and put my socks and shoes back on. I did it for a whole week. Even my mom said it wouldn't help and that Grandpa was telling me a tale. I knew it was helping—I could feel it. The cow manure had even made my hair grow faster.

It had been sometime since my last hair cut, I thought as I walked to school one day. As I passed the barbershop, the note that Mr. Anderson had left on the door was still there, it was getting a little old and faded. It had been more than four weeks and he still wasn't back. I thought he must be having a good time. I felt that way sometimes—I sometimes wanted to leave this place and never come back. A couple of weeks later, when walking by the barbershop, I saw the sign again and wondered if maybe something had happened to Mr. Anderson. Maybe he was in a car accident, or he decided not to come back. It was strange no one around town seemed to notice that he had not come back, at least no one was talking about it.

I began checking almost every day, and every time the sign was still there. One night after some hard winds the sign blew off the door. I stopped and wiped the dust off the window and looked inside the shop. It was getting dirty and nothing seemed different, because every thing was in place. It looked as though he had disappeared. Maybe the demons had got him.

It was springtime and I love smelling the fresh cut grass, it is so sweet. Spring has a pleasant smell. Everything is blooming, with the rain constantly refreshing it. It is always beautiful. It seemed everything was calm in Clear Lake. The bad guys were not calling the house, and no one was disappearing. Everyone around town seemed to be in good moods, and spring always meant fishing season.

Every April the Lake would be full of boats, and people trying to catch fish. The resort down at the lake was always full at this time of year. Some people would stay the entire fishing season. I often visited people at the resort to see if they were catching any fish, and if so, what they were using. I met a lot of nice people. I think they looked forward to me coming around, asking them all kinds of questions, and eating their food.

I kept the boat that my grandpa gave me at the resort. I would get out of school and head straight for the lake and get in my boat and fish until dark. I usually did this by myself because I didn't know any other kids that liked to fish as I did. Mr. Hollis owned the resort. He had three kids, Denise was my age, Randy was two years younger, and Teri was 5 years younger than I was. Denise would see me come back in from fishing and would come down and meet me at my boat. One day she asked, "how many fish did you catch today?"

"I caught my limit, but they are all small."

Denise always acted a lot older than she was. It seemed to me that my business was her business. She would always tell me that. So it wasn't long before she asked, "Luke, don't your mom and dad care that you're always out on the lake by yourself?"

"They don't care, they know I can swim really good, and besides they like eating the fish I catch. And it's a lot better thing to do than most kids do in town."

"My mom says you're an accident waiting to happen. She says that boys like you grow up to be trouble makers. She says that you should go to church like we do on Sundays instead of being out on the lake fishing."

"Why would I want to go to church?"

"Because that is what good people do."

"Does that mean I am not good people?"

"My mom says that bad people don't go to church, so if you don't go I guess that kind of makes you bad."

"I think your mom is wrong Denise. I am not bad, I work at being good all the time."

"That is what my mom says."

I knew there was no use arguing with her, so I told her, "maybe I will go to your church someday."

She smiled and walked back to her house. I grabbed my fish and headed home. It was close too dark and I was hungry for dinner. When I got home my mom had dinner made and I sat down to eat and asked, "mom is dad working tonight again?"

"Yes, he had to go in because someone called in sick."

Not long after talking to mom the phone rang and mom answered it. I could see by the expression on her face that it wasn't a good call. Mom got off the phone and told me to grab a few toys because the bad guys were on their way and she had to get us up to the Bunts house. Whenever this happened, my sister Liz would start to cry and Collin and I would be afraid that the bad guys would get to our house before we made it up to Bunt's.

Mr. and Mrs. Buntz would never ask any questions, they would give us treats and let us watch their television until it was time to go home. Once, while in their house, I saw a picture of two kids, I asked, "Mrs. Buntz who are these kids? I have never seen them around town before."

She started to cry as she walked over to me. She picked up the picture and said, "that boy is my son, and the girl is my daughter."

"Where are they now? Why are they never around here?"

Mr. Buntz walked over to Mrs. Buntz and put his arm around her. He said, "our son Dean killed himself five years ago."

"Where is the girl?" I should have shut up but I wanted to know.

"We don't know. She ran away three years ago, and we have not seen her since."

I felt bad for asking them about the kids. Mrs. Buntz was crying with her hands over her eyes and Mr. Buntz was looking angry. I didn't know what to say. I went and sat down in the living room and Collin said, "way to go, you really know how to upset people. You should stop asking so many questions."

I didn't say another thing all night. I sat and waited for the time we could go back to our house. I was wondering why their boy had killed himself? What would make their daughter run away? The Bunt's didn't seem like mean people, for they were always nice to my brother and sister. Maybe they missed their kids so much that they liked having us around to make up for their loss? It didn't make any sense to me at all.

Whenever mom said it was safe to come back home we would go, and I never knew if she was certain that the bad guys wouldn't come back. It would scare me and when I got home I wouldn't be able to sleep. I would lie awake wondering about why the bad guys came, I wondered who they were, and what they wanted. Of all the kids I knew no one else ever talked about any bad guys.

That night when I finally fell asleep I had a dream. I was in my house, which was alone on a hill. The sky was dark and a foreign army was marching all around my house looking for me. I was running trying to hide inside but they tore everything apart inside my house, so I ran up to the barn and hid under the floorboards. I could see them walking by, their calf high black boots coming within inches of my body. They couldn't find me so they started searching the whole town. I could still see them from under my barn and I could hear them marching in step, looking for me to kill me. I made a sound when I moved and they heard it and started marching right for me. I couldn't move I started to fight, they were closer—legs won't work—can't run—screaming.

I woke up with sweat running off my forehead. I sat up in my bed and my brother looked over at me and said, "go back to sleep, it was another one of your crazy dreams."

"Collin, do you know who the bad guys are?"

"No, I don't, but I sure wish they would go away."

"So do I—I think that next time they come I will get super powers and beat them up. And I will chase them out of this town."

"Go back to sleep Luke, and stop dreaming."

I lay in my bed thinking of the day when the bad guys would come no more. I hated that they scared my mom and made her cry. I hated that they made my sister and Collin and myself afraid. I hated that my dad wasn't home to protect us. I knew it had to be someone who knew my dad had to work at night—it had to be one of our neighbors. I knew it was no use asking my mom who it was, she would get upset and tell me, "those are things silly little boys shouldn't know." I was trying to think why the bad guys would come? Maybe the demons would put them up to coming and trying to get me. If they could hurt my family, that would be a good way to get me. I knew they were afraid of my dad, because they never came when he was home. I never understood why the bad guys never came on Saturdays or Sundays. Maybe they were annoying other people on those days.

The next day, I went up to Mr. Woodchopper's to ask him if he knew who the bad men where. It was lightly raining. It made a wonderful sound as each raindrop would fall from leaf to leaf, ending when it hit the ground. It was like listening to music made by nature. I was getting close to his house and I could smell the smoke coming from his wood stove, and I could almost smell the coffee in the smoke. The rain was making a different sound as it hit on the cedar shakes on Mr. Woodchopper's house. I looked like a drowned rat when I arrived at his door. I knocked, and waited for him to come and answer the door.

"Come in Luke, are you ready for some coffee?"

"Yes, I am cold and wet. It will warm me up."

"So what brings you up here on this rainy day?"

"I was wondering if you knew who the bad guys were that come to my house and scare my mom and brother and sister?"

"No I don't Luke, do they harm you?"

"No, my mom takes us up to the Buntz house every time they call and say that they are coming."

"I haven't asked around much, most people consider me an outsider here, and the person I talked to and trusted in this town just disappeared off the face of the earth."

"Are you talking about Mr. Anderson?"

"Yes, something happened to him, he told me he was only going to be gone two weeks, not months."

"What do you think happened to him?"

"I don't know, but I think it is something bad."

"Maybe the bad guys got him?"

"Maybe they did, I don't know, but I don't dare go around this town asking too many questions about things."

"My brother thinks I ask too many questions. Do you think I do?"

He was laughing as he answered, "no Luke, I think asking questions is a good way to learn things." He had a way about him that made me feel comfortable, I always felt safe in his house, I couldn't see why my mom thought he was a dirty old man.

"Well thanks for helping me Mr. Woodchopper, see you around."

"Take care Luke, and be careful."

I closed the door as I headed down the road, heading for the school. It had stopped raining and I thought that maybe some kids might be playing baseball at the schoolyard. I passed my house and Collin was outside so I yelled, "hey Collin, want to go play some baseball down at the school?"

"Sure, let me grab my mitt and bat, and I'll go with you, wait for me."

"Be sure to grab my mitt also."

Collin came running out of the house and walked with me towards the school. At the bottom of the hill on the highway a car stopped, the driver rolled down his window and asked, "do you boys want a ride to the school?" Collin opened his mouth and said, "yes."

I couldn't believe what I heard. This man was a stranger. I looked into his eyes and saw that he had evil eyes. I said, "no mister, I don't need a ride, and neither does my brother, the school is right down the street, less than five minutes of walking."

"I don't mind giving you a ride for a ways."

"I said, no thank you!"

"What's your problem kid? I just wanted to give you a ride, now get in."

I looked at him, right in the eyes, keeping my distance from the car, and said, "Nothing is wrong with me, I like to walk."

He started cussing as he took off squealing the tires on the pavement. I watched him drive away and Collin started in on me, "why didn't you want to get a ride? It's a long ways to the school and we could be playing right now."

"Collin, think about it. Why would that man want to give us a ride? I think he was up to no good. He had bad intent in his eyes, I think he wanted to hurt us."

My brother was getting mad at me as I continued, "Collin if we would have got in that car we would end up in the river dead."

"What makes you say that?"

"He looked bad, maybe he is one of the bad men himself or a demon."

My brother's lack of commonsense sometimes amazed me. I always had to watch out for him and work on keeping him safe. It was my job for no one else was looking out for him.

We continued to walk on down to the school. Before we got to the white witch's house, I started to run fast. My brother was right behind me, when we got safely past her house we started walking again. Collin said, "I wonder when that old lady is going to die?"

"Why do you wonder that? Does she scare you like she does me?"

"She is so old. She has to be at least 100 years old now."

"Maybe witches don't die, maybe they live forever like vampires."

"Luke, she isn't a real witch, and there are no such things as vampires, you have to stop believing everyone is evil and that they are all out to get you."

"Yeah, that is what you think, I will prove it someday, you will see. Besides why do you run past her house?" He didn't answer me, I knew he was just as scared as I was.

We made it to the field and started to play baseball with a bunch of our friends. It was interesting that none of the bad kids that were mean and nasty played any sports. I figured they were too busy getting into trouble. My brother and I were good at sports and always liked playing together. It was these times that I cherish most.

CHAPTER SEVEN

When the men come to town on the weekends from camp they act like a bunch of wild animals. They drink spirits and make improper advances towards not just the women in town but also the children. I have asked the Reverend to address the subject this Sunday in Church.

NewsLetter of the Clear Lake Woman's Society
March 1907

It was my birthday and I had been waiting a long time to open the presents that my mom and dad had bought for me. After dinner dad stood up from the table and said, "everyone wait here, I have to get Luke his gift."

He walked away from the kitchen, as my heart was going a mile a minute. He came back with a big slender long box. Excitement ran though me, I had the biggest smile I think someone could have. He handed me the box and said, "here you go Luke, I think you're old enough to handle one of these now."

I opened the box end and saw the butt of a gun; it was the 12-gauge shotgun I had been wanting. I started jumping up and down, filled with joy. I loved to hunt with my dad in the fall. My brother really didn't like hunting as much as I did. "Luke, that isn't a toy, you handle it with respect at all times. Do you understand?"

"Yes I do."

"It can kill, always keep that in mind."

"Oh thank you dad, thank you mom for such a wonderful gift."

I thought I was the happiest eleven-year-old kid in the world. I couldn't wait to go hunting in the fall.

That summer, mom was sick. She was in and out of the hospital all the time. My dad didn't like the idea of paying someone to watch us, so he made Collin stay home and watch Liz and me. Like all brothers and sisters, we would often fight about anything, whose turn it was to wash the dishes, who is going to take out the garbage, what we were going to watch on television. Collin, being the oldest, usually got his way and Liz would always remind us that she was dad's favorite.

Dad was working a lot and he was hardly ever home. It was kind of nice because there wasn't anyone around to tell me what to do. I could come and go as I pleased. I hung out at the Clarks house a lot. I ended up spending the night there for five weeks straight. It was a real education for me. Beside myself, there were two brothers from New Mexico, and some other guy from I don't know where. His name was Frank, and I thought he was on the run from the law.

There were also a few strange girls, whom I didn't really pay attention too unless they were in their bathing suits. Come nighttime it was like a big hotel with people sleeping everywhere. I always wondered how Leanna could feed all of these people. One morning I woke up to hear Leanna yelling at Frank, "if she gets pregnant you're going to marry her!"

"I'm not going to do no such thing. She can have an abortion."

"The hell she will! She ain't going to no hole in the wall and get herself killed."

"I ain't going to be no dad." Frank yelled.

"You're going to do what I say, hell she's only 15, I could have you arrested for rape."

"You know we've been having sex all along, so don't play those games with me."

I could hear Lindsey crying in her room. I felt bad for her, I thought that if you were to have sex with someone, you were to be in love, and Frank wasn't being all that loving it seemed to me. Everyone knew that when Leanna was mad you just kept quiet. I got up and headed across the field to home. I walked in the back door and mom was up, working in the kitchen. She was always better when she came home from the hospital. She saw me walk in and said, "what brings you home to bless us with your presence?"

"Oh I was wanting to get some breakfast, what kind of cereal do we have?"

"The same kind we usually have."

"Why don't you buy some Captain Crunch, or Sugar Puffs, like the Clarks have?"

"Because they cost way too much money."

"The Marks's don't have much money and they have sweet cereal. All we have is plain stuff."

"Your father works hard to put food on this table so don't you be complaining, or you can go hungry."

I got out a bowl and the milk and grabbed my Wheaties and sat down at the table and started to eat. "Mom, what is an abortion?"

"Why do you ask that?"

"I heard it said, and I don't know what it is."

"When you're old enough to know I will tell you."

"I am old enough now."

"No, it's something that little boys shouldn't know."

I knew not to keep pressing. I decided who really cares about abortions anyway. I finished my cereal and headed off to the lake to do some fishing. I was walking through town looking at the big maples that lined the highway. I walked past the barbershop and there still was no sign of Mr. Anderson. I guess he was never going to come back. I wondered why anyone wouldn't want to live in this great place, with the green mountains, streams, open grass fields, and the lake itself that was so clear and clean. To me it was a big playground, a special kind of paradise. Get rid of the bad people, and demons, and other bad things, and it would be heaven.

While eating dinner, the phone rang. Mom picked it up and didn't say a word. I could see her face as the fear started to show in her eyes. She hung up the phone and said, "grab some toys and get in the car, we are going to visit the Bunt's again."

I knew the bad guys were on their way here. I was mad. Why did I have to leave my house? Why did dad always have to be gone? I grabbed a set of Legos and got in the car with Collin and Liz. When we arrived at the Buntz house they were getting ready to go see a movie at the drive-in theater and asked if we wanted to accompany them.

It was my first time at a drive-in theater, and it was fun. I got some popcorn and pop and settled into the car to watch the movie. The movie had something do with Moses. As I watched, I started to see myself in Moses. He was a great man, a man who wanted to have things fair and right for his family, friends, and his people. He didn't like the bad guys that wanted to hurt his people. He saw things that other people didn't see, like the bush that was on fire. He was a powerful man, because he was a man that stood a lone. I loved the movie, because it gave me hope that someday things in Clear Lake would be safe and fair and right for everyone.

On the drive home from the show I decided that I was the Moses of Clear Lake. I was the savior, and I was the one chosen to chase the evil men away. All I had to do was get the power and I could defeat the demons and the evil that was hurting the people in town. Like Moses, I knew that no one would believe I had the power to set them free.

When we returned home I went to bed. I dreamt that night that I was able to fly. I had been given super powers to use for the good of people. I was flying over Clear Lake and I tried to go down and land on the highway, but I couldn't get through some very thick dark clouds. I put my hands together as if I was diving into water, but still I couldn't break through. I could hear people crying and screaming for help but I couldn't see them because of the clouds. I was hitting and clawing at the clouds but they wouldn't budge. I heard my sister crying—I heard little kids screaming in pain—I had to help them. I started to fly to see if I could get around the clouds but I couldn't. I was getting mad, I started to fall from the sky, my powers had left me, I am falling, falling, I am going to hit the ground now, I can see the evil creatures, they are waiting for me, no, please no.

"Luke, wake up. It's OK, you were dreaming again."

"It was real Collin, what I saw was real."

"Go back to sleep. Everything will be all right in the morning."

My body felt tired, it seemed to me that what I had dreamt was so real. I was sweating as I got up to get a towel out of the bathroom. I walked by my sister's room and heard her softly crying. I went in and asked, "Liz why are you crying?"

"I am afraid that the bad guys will come back and get me. I don't want that to happen."

"It won't happen, I will make sure of it, no one is going to hurt you—ever."

I made a vow to myself that night. I wasn't going to let the bad men scare my brother or my sister or me any more. I was going to fight back. I was going to stand up to them as Moses had done to the Egyptians. They would scare my family no more! I went back to my bed and fell back asleep.

With everything that was going on around our place, mom was in the hospital even more. It seemed to me that she had so many things wrong with her. Dad would always be working or sleeping. My brother and sister and I had to make sure we were quiet. If we made too much noise it would wake up dad, it could mean quick and hard punishment. It was at this time that I started to have different opinions about my parents. I knew my dad worked hard and my mom did lots of things for us kids, but something in me told me things were amiss.

I knew my dad didn't like my mom always being sick. He never seemed to be happy, he never talked much, and he sat and read all the time. If he wasn't working, he was sleeping, if he wasn't sleeping he was reading. The only time he really talked to us kids is when something went wrong. Then he would be really mad and yell and cuss a lot. We learned not to make him upset.

I learned to cuss listening to my dad. I could stand on a stump and cuss for two hours and not same the same word twice. The neat thing about cuss words is that you don't even have to pronounce them right. They were all short and easy to spell and everyone understood them even when they were said wrong. Cussing was something I was good at.

One day Collin took a beer from the refrigerator and went into our room and drank it. I knew it was nothing but trouble. I told him, "Collin you shouldn't be doing that."

"Oh, it won't hurt a thing."

"If dad finds out he will be really mad at you."

"Oh, he won't care at all."

"Well, remember I told you so."

Later that day when dad went into the kitchen to get something to drink, I heard him mumbling to himself. I heard the refrigerator door slam and footsteps coming towards our room. I could tell by the way that his feet were hitting the floor that he was mad about something. He opened the door to our room and said, "OK, which one of you took and drank one of my beers?" I looked at Collin. I was about to say something but I held my tongue, he was getting a look in his eyes that I didn't like.

"Someone better tell me now who took my beer!"

There was silence. I was thinking that Collin should confess, or we would both be getting a good whipping. "Both of you, outside, now!"

Dad was really mad. I looked at Collin and got up and walked outside to the side of the barn. Collin was right behind me and took his place beside me. Dad came walking out with his belt. I was hoping this wouldn't last long. I said to Collin, "why don't you tell dad you took the beer?"

He looked at me as if he wanted to beat me to death. I knew I couldn't tell on him, if I did he would make me pay for weeks, so I braced myself for the lashes I was about to receive. Dad took his place behind us and said, "OK, one more chance to tell me who took the beer."

Collin didn't say a thing, I was thinking, dad should know I wasn't one to take a beer. Just then the first lash hit Collin on his butt. I saw a grimace on his face and his teeth clenched. I could hear the sound of the belt coming towards my butt. I let out a cry as it hit me. Then dad hit Collin again, then me. He hit us about ten times and said, "is any one ready to confess yet?"

I looked at Collin—his face was hard. I knew he wasn't going to own up to taking the beer. Just then the belt came down on Collin, then on me. I was crying, thinking to myself that dad would have made a good Gestapo for Hitler. I was innocent and being punished for something someone else had done. It was starting to get harder every time the belt came down on our butts. I took another look at Collin and I could see he was strong, he wasn't going to give in to the pain. I asked my dad to stop the hitting, "please dad, stop, please."

"Not until I get a confession."

I couldn't go on. This would last all day. I knew the only way out was to tell dad I was the one who took the beer. "OK dad, I took the beer. Please stop now."

He gave me one more whip. Then he sent me to my room. As I was walking he said I was grounded for two weeks and had to do all the chores. I was glad the punishment was over. Collin came into the room,

I looked at him, I could see that he was happy, he didn't have to take the blame. He didn't say a word as he grabbed a coat and left. I was breathing funny, the way you do when you've been crying too much. I lay on my bed and wished that my whole family were dead. I thought I could live by myself, and that I could take care of myself.

It didn't take me long to get over those feelings. I loved my family, but I didn't like to hurt, and I wanted things to be fair. I served out what I called my prison time, and was excited about getting to see some of my friends again.

One day I grabbed my fishing pole and some bait and headed down to the A-frame at the lake to catch some fish. When I arrived, Roy, Sue, and Carol were at the lake playing. I sat down and put my line in the water and enjoyed the sunshine. They came over and we all started talking. It was nice to see them all. Roy and Sue lived across town. Carol lived close to the school. Carol's brother was a mean person. He was older than we were; he was in high school. He would sometimes chase me and pick on me when he saw me around town.

Sue lived with her mom and a step dad, and Carol lived with her mom. Sue's step dad was always trying to touch her in her private areas all the time—she had told Roy and me one day. It was sad to me that he would do that, and I never understood why kids didn't have both parents at home. I was friendly with everyone so I didn't mind talking with them. Roy and his mom were a little different; she was always talking and driving around with other men who were not Roy's dad.

I was tired of fishing and so I asked, "do you all want to go swimming this afternoon?"

Roy said, "maybe. We were wondering if you wanted to go explore the woods and parts of the old mill with us?"

"Sure that sounds like fun."

I picked up my pole and hid it in some brush, and took off with the three of them. We walked around the lake and came to a clearing. It was a nice warm day. We all stopped and Roy grabbed Sue and started kissing her. Carol looked at me and said, "are you going to kiss me Luke?"

I was thinking, no, I haven't kissed a girl before, and I am not attracted to this girl at all. How could I tell her without hurting her feelings? I said, "I don't know how to kiss a girl Carol."

I started to feel funny about things. She looked at me and said, "just kiss like Roy and Sue are."

She stepped towards me and I backed up. Roy was starting to take Sues clothes off. I asked, "what are you doing Roy?"

"Sue and I are going to have sex, and so are you and Carol."

"I have never had sex before, and I don't want too."

Carol pulled a knife out of her shirt and pointed it at me. I started to get scared. She said, "I know how to use this, my brother taught me how. So take off your clothes."

She moved a little closer, and Roy and Sue were calling me chicken and saying it wouldn't hurt to have sex. Carol asked, "you don't like me, do you Luke?"

I wanted to say no, but I didn't have the guts to. I didn't want to hurt her feelings. "You're nice." I was shaking and my heart was racing fast.

"No, you don't think I am nice looking, you think I'm ugly. I don't care, you're going to screw me, so take your clothes off now."

I needed to get out of there fast. So I said, "OK I guess it can't hurt, but you take your clothes off first."

She said, "OK, I will, you will like it Luke."

She put the knife down and started to pull her pants down. I was watching, and I was full of fear. When she got her pants down to her knees I stepped forward and pushed her down and took off running. Roy and Sue had slipped behind a huge old stump. She screamed and pulled her pants back up and started chasing me. I ran towards the nearest road, which came out by the school. I was running fast. I made it to the road by the school, and ran past Carol's brother who was standing in his yard. I kept running. I could hear Carol in the woods, screaming and cussing me.

She came out of the woods and saw her brother and said, "help me Shane, get Mills, he hurt me."

When I heard that, I knew I was dead meat. I couldn't outrun him. I turned into a back alley and looked behind me and there he was on his bike chasing me down. I jumped over a fence into Mr. Jackson's yard and ran toward the road. My heart was telling me I couldn't keep running, but fear drove me on.

I started running toward home on the highway but Shane came riding around the corner, so I turned and ran back the other way. I ran into a yard and behind a house and back across the alley and into another yard and hid by a big old tree. I rested for a minute and then Shane and the mean Randahl kid saw me and started chasing me again. I was thinking that Bud Randahl must have seen Shane chasing me and decided to join in on the chase. Randahl never liked my brother or me, because he was a mean nasty kid.

I kept on running and avoiding them; it was getting to be a game of cat and mouse. Every time I thought I had a chance to break free and make it home they cut me off. I started running for the white witch's house because I was thinking that maybe they were afraid of her also and would stop chasing me. It was broad day light out and I wondered why no one had come out to help me. I knew they could see me running from these mean kids. I got close to the white witch's house and could see her working in her yard, so I kept on running by. She looked up and stared at me, and I thought she was sizing me up for dinner.

Shane and Bud were right behind me, they were close enough to grab me and I thought that they would, but they let me keep running. I turned down a side street and into the alley that ran behind the white witch's house. I was getting slower and slower I knew I couldn't keep going much longer. I was starting to get really scared; I didn't know what they were going to do with me when they caught me. I knew it was only a matter of time before they had their hands on me. They had finally gotten smart and spilt up, and now Bud was coming toward me down the alley and Shane was behind me. I stopped and waited for them to close in. I could see the white witch was watching us, she was probably thinking of how good a dinner I would be. Bud and Shane came up to me and stared at me with evil in their eyes.

They looked me up and down as I stood still, trying not to look scared. Shane grabbed my shirt and said, "come with me, we have to talk."

We started to walk towards Shane and Carol's house, when Carol came running towards us. She walked up and spit in my face, and said, "Shane, he thinks he is too good to have sex with me. He thinks I am ugly."

I started to tell her that I didn't say that, but Shane told me to shut up. He looked at Bud and Carol and said, "what should we do with someone that thinks he is better than us?"

Carol said, "you should beat him to death, that will teach him."

I saw Buds eyes light up, and I could see he was thinking bad things. He said, "if he thinks he is too good to have sex with Carol, than we should have sex with him, he's not too good for us Shane."

Before I could even start to cry or scream for help, Shane pushed me down and put his hand over my mouth. I started kicking and fighting, trying to get away. Bud and Carol started pulling at my pants. I heard them rip and then they pulled my underwear off. I looked up and saw the white witch watching from her yard. I was hoping she would come over and stop them for me. She turned and walked back to her house. I was crying and trying to fight myself free. Then Bud hit me in the face and said, "hope you don't like your pretty face Mills."

Shane told them to hold me down so I couldn't see what he was doing. I heard him undoing his zipper—fear was striking at my heart. I closed my eyes and felt the pain when he forced himself into me. I wondered where God was, why was he letting this happen to me? It was hurting and I wanted it to stop. Shane got off me and said, "I hope you liked that, I sure did."

They all were laughing. Shane spit on me and said, "OK Bud, it's your turn."

I heard a door open and they all took off running. I turned to look to see who was coming and saw the white witch standing on her back porch. I was whimpering and sobbing, feeling so dirty. She walked back in her house and closed the door. I put my pants back on and started to walk home. I could hardly move because it hurt so much to walk. When I got home, my mom was in the kitchen and asked, "what happened Luke? Why are you walking that way?"

"I fell down and hurt myself. I need to go take a hot bath and shower."

What was I going to tell her? Mom I got raped? She wouldn't believe me anyway. I took off my underwear and they were all bloody, so I threw them in the toilet and flushed them down. I felt the need to be clean, so I started a hot shower and climbed in and scrubbed and scrubbed to get the badness off me. I sat in there for what seemed like hours. I cried and thought of a day when I would make things right with those people. After my shower I crawled in bed and went to sleep.

Sometime during the night I had a dream about a big bull that was running over the hills around Clear Lake. It had big horns and I was with my brother and sister and it was trying to get us. The town wasn't the same, as I knew it. It had somehow changed. It was like it wasn't really there, almost invisible. The bull could see it all and he knew where everyone was hiding and who was talking. The bull was breaking lots of things and looking for my family and me. He was close to my house—close to getting me, then I woke up.

From then on I was always very careful where I went in town. I wasn't going to let that happen to me ever again. I would rather die than have someone force me to have sex with them. I thought when I grew up I would never force anyone to have sex with me. I would do anything

I could to stop it from happening to anyone. I would make things fair and right.

I stopped running past the white witch's house, I figured if she had really wanted to get me, she could have when I was lying on the ground after my incident. That's what I called it, and I tried to bury the hurt and pain deep inside me. I had fears that kids I knew would find out and make fun of me at school. The demons seemed to be winning and I didn't know what to do. I wanted to run away forever.

All through this time I still thought I was a normal boy growing up in a normal town. I had lots of fun, and not all of the kids were bad, because most of them were good like me. Sometimes I was bad. In the sixth grade during Valentines, Tim Jones and I played a mean trick on one of the girls in the class. It was mean, even though today everyone still laughs about it.

It was getting close to Valentines Day and Julie Macallister was being her own usual self. She was a very pretty girl, the best looking of any girls in town, long blonde hair, and blue eyes. She was always saying how good-looking she was, and always cutting down and saying mean things to the girls that were not that pretty. I didn't like the way she treated other girls and me. She always teased me about being dumb. She would tell other girls that they were ugly, and that on Valentines day they would get no cards from anyone, except from that stupid Mills kid. Kathy was one of those girls, she was very nice, and we would talk about what we liked and would spend time together after school. Julie was always teasing Kathy about being poor and not having nice clothes and being a little over weight.

One day Julie teased Kathy so much it made her cry. It made me so mad. Just because someone didn't have money to buy new clothes didn't make him or her any worse than any other. I couldn't stand what Julie was doing and neither could Tim. We decided to get Julie back in front of the whole class. We thought, and thought. We wanted to make Julie look funny in front of everyone. Walking down the street after school one day Tim and I saw some dog doo that had been turned white by the sun. Tim said, "too bad we can't get Julie to eat that somehow."

A light went on in my head. I said to Tim, "if we get a heart box of chocolates and eat the whole box, and buy some chocolate bars, and melt them down, and cut the dog doo into little pieces and dip it in the chocolate and put it back in the empty box, she would maybe eat them."

Tim got a big smile on his face, "lets do it!"

We bought the candy from Meekers store and ate it all. It kind of made us sick. We collected the dog doo, cut it into little pieces, and dipped it in melted chocolate. We had Mr. Meeker put new wrapping paper around the box for us. He thought I was buying the candy for my mom and had eaten a few. He said it was like me to do such a thing.

Our masterpiece was finished and on Monday, a couple of days before Valentines Day, we put the candy box in Julie's mailbox at school. Her box was almost full, but those of the other girls who were not as popular were almost empty. On Valentines Day Julie was telling us how popular she was, how every one loved her, especially the boys.

Tim and I were gagging and filled with excitement, waiting for the time to come to open our Valentine cards and gifts. When Julie got her gifts and cards, she said to everyone, "see, I got the biggest box of candies, everyone loves me."

Everyone was watching Julie open her box of candy. Tim and I were the only ones that knew what was really inside, and we were filled with anticipation. Julie slowly opened the box and pulled out a piece of candy. She stuck it in her mouth with a big smile, looking at everyone in the room, being the spoiled brat that she was. She bit down on the chocolate and started to chew, I couldn't contain myself any more, and neither could Tim. We both started to laugh hysterically, to the point of almost falling on the floor. All of a sudden Julie started to scream and yell at the top of her lungs, "oh no dog shit!"

She ran towards the door, spitting and hacking it out of her mouth. Everyone started to laugh and kept laughing; she looked so funny running trying to get the dog doo out of her mouth. A record player was playing a song by the Archies called "Sugar Sugar." From that time on a few of us called Julie our candy girl. I was especially happy for the girls she had said mean things to.

Our teacher Mr. Woods looked right at Tim and me and said, "come with me boys."

I wasn't scared, he knew we did it, but he was laughing also. He took us down to Mr. Jobsons office and told him what we had done. Mr. Jobson started laughing as he was telling Tim and me that this was no laughing matter. He made us both call our parents and tell them what we had done, and we had to call Julie's parents and apologize to them for having their daughter eat dog doo. We had to say we were sorry to the whole class, and last we had to say how sorry we were to Julie. It was so easy to lie to her face, I wasn't sorry; she got what she deserved. Anyway, she never would talk to me after that. She said her dad was going to come down and beat Tim and me up. He never came after us. Maybe he knew it was something his daughter needed. When I saw him in town all he would ever do is smile at me. I often wondered if his wife was just like his daughter.

CHAPTER EIGHT

Tom Bearskin stopped by our house last night all excited. He kept on saying, 'me kill him.' I told him it was not right to kill someone and that he should not do such a thing. He said, 'no, me kill him.' I understood by his tone that he had already killed a man. Later the next morning I learned that he had killed the son of a local chief of the Samish tribe. The chief's son had kidnapped Tom's wife and raped and killed her. Tom not only killed the man but also cut his body into a hundred pieces and left them on the main trail between the two tribes.

Recorded by Susan White in The History of Skagit County
November 1877

Life kept going on in Clear Lake, as always mixing the good with the bad. I learned to take life that way. I never figured it would be easy. I would take the sad days with the happy days, but it always seemed that the happy days far out-numbered the sad days. In the fall I played soccer and football at school. I loved football. School was fun most of the time.

We had a music teacher that would come in twice a week and have us sing songs. He was a hippie type of person and would have us singing protest songs about the war, songs like "Blowing in the Wind," and "Where Have All the Young Men Gone."

I thought it was kind of odd that he would want us to sing those songs, he would tell us that America was bad and wicked. I knew better; I knew that this music teacher was off his rocker. Now that I think about it he was smoking a little too much wacky tabacky. I thought if he didn't like America he should pack his bags and move to Russia, or someplace like that, and I took every opportunity to tell him. He said I was being brainwashed by the far right. All I knew that I was right and he was wrong.

I loved to hunt, and with fall arriving I was eager to use the new shotgun I had received for my birthday. I hunted in the lakes for ducks and in the mountains for grouse. I also hunted in the swamp for ducks; it was north of our house in the valley. It was a really eerie place. If you were by yourself and fell in a hole you could drown and never be found. The swamp was always dark and had ugly trees all over, kind of like what you would see in a scary movie. I could imagine the swamp thing coming up for me at any time. I wasn't scared because I had my new gun and I was ready to shoot whatever tried to hurt me.

One day hunting for ducks in the swamp I saw one of the biggest bucks I had ever seen. He had been eating in the cornfields all summer long, getting big and fat. He would hide in the swamp during the day. He was a smart deer. I decided I was going to get him before the season was over.

That night I told my dad about the deer I had seen and asked him if he could get me some big slugs for my shotgun. He said he would, because he thought if I could get that buck, it would make good deer jerky. I felt like I was doing my part for the family.

Dad and mom were ready to go out, and for the first time, left Collin and me at home by ourselves, but took Liz to be watched at some other person's house. I guess mom and dad didn't trust us to take care of Liz. We were told never to answer the phone when they were gone, which made me glad. I didn't want the bad guys to come, and they only came after they had called our house.

Collin and I watched television. Our favorite shows were Batman, and Gilligans Island. I wanted to be like Batman. I had a bat suit with the mask and everything. If I were Batman I would chase all the evil out of Clear Lake. I always thought it would be nice to be stranded on a deserted island. If I were Gilligan I would have been chasing Maryann, I liked her better than Ginger, and I would have never done anything for Mr. Howell. I wanted to have a paradise to live in, and my fantasies always took me to the places I wanted to be, and where I felt safe.

It was getting close to the end of hunting season and I still had not shot that big buck. I was in the swamp every day looking for him. I could find his tracks and where he was sleeping, but could never see him to have a shot at him. I was done hunting and I was headed back to the house. I was at the far end of the swamp and was taking a trail that wound back close to Mud Lake. It was a clear winter day, and the air felt clean and crisp. A slight breeze came from the North. It was one of those beautiful days in the Northwest. Trumpeter swans were flying overhead. They spent their winters in the valley, feeding in the farm fields. It was a beautiful sight to see them flying overhead, singing songs, talking to each other.

I was about in the middle of the swamp when I heard something walking close to me in the brush. I lowered my gun and pointed it in the direction of the noise. In my mind I was seeing that big buck walking right out in front of me. My heart was going a mile a minute as I started to shake with excitement. Then, Shane, Carol's brother, came walking out of the bush carrying a shotgun. I lowered my gun and waited for him to say something to me. He walked over by me and looked me up and down. He said, "seen any ducks?"

"No I haven't, not many flying today."

"I haven't seen many ducks either, but I shot one of those swans and killed it."

"That is against the law, Trumpeter swans are protected and you could go to jail for that."

"I just wanted something to shoot at, so don't be telling anyone I shot a swan or I will make you pay."

I wasn't going to say anything to make him mad and I sure wasn't going to tell him I was hunting for that big buck. Shane said, "if I am not suppose to shoot swans maybe I should shoot you."

He was laughing, as I was thinking—great—now I'm going to be shot by this mean kid. I said, "that wouldn't be nice, besides what have I ever done to you?"

"You don't like my sister, and you're right you have never done anything to me. But I sure did you. You're tighter than my sister."

He was laughing hard as he said those words to me, and I began to burn inside with hate and anger towards him. He kept laughing and said, "in fact you were so good, I think since I have nothing to do, I think I will do you again."

My heart fell as my whole body froze up like a pair of pants going threw a washing wringer. I could hardly move my hands let alone my feet. In my heart I felt utter contempt for him. My eyes became full of fire. Shane said, "put down your gun, and take off your pants."

I didn't say a thing as I stood there holding my gun looking at him. I clinched my teeth and started breathing really deep.

"I said put down your gun and take your pants off boy!"

I wasn't going to let him do that again. I wasn't going to feel dirty. I was ready to die to avoid it. I stood my ground, staring at him. He said, "damn it Mills! Do what I tell you to or I'll shoot your ass. I know you won't shoot me, besides, what are little Bb's going to do to me any way?"

I looked right at him and said with a deep strong voice, "no!"

"What the hell was that? Am I going to have to take your gun away from you? You will wish you were never born."

I stood there with tears starting to well up in my eyes. I didn't want to hurt—to be made a fool—I wasn't going to let him have his way with me. I was still all tensed up, like being in a dream when you can't run and your body won't work. Shane started to walk towards me. I raised my gun up and said, "I have a slug in my chamber, so leave me alone!"

"You liar, what are you hunting ducks with a slug for? You don't scare me Mills."

He was laughing as he took another step towards me. Time stood still it seemed as we looked at each other. He was less than three feet from the end of my barrel. I clenched my teeth and started to squeeze the trigger and it all happened in slow motion.

The gun went off and Shane started flying back with a terrified look on his face, like he couldn't believe I meant what I had said. The smoke from the gun cleared and I saw him falling to the ground and he was bleeding out of the big hole in his chest. I slowly walked over to him and looked in his lifeless eyes—they were empty—no more evil would he see or do.

I started to get scared because I had killed a human being, even though I felt no remorse. I was the judge and jury, and he was sentenced to death for the rape of a child. I needed to hide his body fast, before someone saw what I had done. I took the rope I had brought to drag the buck out and tied Shane to some rocks that were close by. I rolled his body into one of the deep holes in the swamp, and I knew no one would ever find him. I cleaned myself off and picked up his gun and started to make my way back home. I was nervous because maybe someone had seen me. I was hoping everyone would think that Shane ran away, he had done that once before.

I had only made it about 200 yards when the big buck came walking right out in front of me. I wasn't excited at all as I looked at him. He was looking back at me. His eyes looked like they could see right through me. He watched me walk across the meadow and into the woods before the road. I turned to see him standing there, watching me. I was wondering what was he thinking, did he know the wrong I had done? Was that deer watching me the whole time? Was his life spared because I had taken one life already?

I was starting to feel bad. I was starting to be scared. What was I going to do? I was hoping I could act cool like I had done nothing wrong. I knew it would be hard to do, because I was an easy person to read. I was scared I would be found out, but I needed someone to talk too, I wanted to be told I had done nothing wrong, that I was right in not letting him have his way with me. I knew he would never hurt any boys or girls again. It made me feel kind of good that there was one less evil person in Clear Lake. When I got to the road I threw his shotgun in the brush by the hill; I figured someone would find it and take it home with them.

I was smiling as I finished walking back home. I went in the house and started up some bath water for myself. My dad was home and he came in my room and asked, "did you see the big buck?"

I didn't feel like talking so I told him, "no."

"You can get him next time. He would make a nice trophy on your wall."

"No, I don't think I will shoot him if I see him, he has lived this long, I think I will let him live his life out in that old swamp."

I think I confused my dad. He knew I loved to hunt, and my wanting to let that buck live didn't make any sense to him. I put my gun away and didn't go hunting the rest of the year. I went and got in the bathtub and started to cry hoping that all the badness would be washed off me and out of me.

That week in school Carol was telling everyone that her brother had run away again, and that her mom was happy she had one less mouth to feed. It made me sad that no one missed Shane. I felt really bad that his mom felt that way. I knew if anything ever happened to me that my mom and dad would truly miss me. I didn't understand that some of the kids in town functionally didn't have a mom and a dad. It was strange to me.

I thought that someone would find out that I had shot Shane. I thought that maybe someone had seen me. It was a rainy Saturday and

I decided to go up to see Mr. Woodchopper. I walked up the road and knocked on his door. He had seen me coming so he was quick about letting me in. He looked like he had lost some weight, and he was acting really nervous. He served me some coffee and as always asked if I wanted sugar. "So what brings you up here today?"

"Oh, I was stopping bye to visit, I haven't seen you in a while."

"Yes, I have been out on the road. Tending business down south."

"Mr. Woodchopper, have you—umm—have you ever killed anyone?"

He looked at me with a puzzled look on his face. I could tell he was thinking, searching for the right words. Maybe he was hesitating to tell me because he had killed someone before. Maybe he was trying to understand why I was asking such a question.

"Now Luke why would you be asking a question like that?"

"I was wondering if you had."

"Tell me what you did."

When he asked that question I knew I was easy to read. How did he know I had done anything? Was I that obvious, that he could see through me? So I started to tell him what I had done. "A man was going to do something bad to me, and I shot him and he is dead."

He sat there silent for the longest time it seemed. He looked at me and started to shake his head. "Who knows this besides me?"

"No one that I know of—I have only told you."

"Where is the body—will it be found soon?"

"It's in the swamp, and I don't think anyone will find it soon, besides the fish and critters will eat it before anyone can find it."

"Luke, I don't know what happened, but I am sure you had reason to do what you did, just don't make a habit of killing people. It's not a good thing."

It amazed me that Mr. Woodchopper always believed me. He didn't doubt any of the things I told him, while my mom and dad didn't believe a thing I said.

"I won't, I don't want anything bad to happen to me."

"If you have any problems, or if men come around asking questions, just come up here to my house and I will make sure you will be safe. Do you understand what I am saying?"

"I think so."

"If the authorities come after you, you may have to leave, runaway, go someplace other than here. I can help you. They will put you in jail for a very long time, no matter if you were justified or not in killing that man."

"I understand. But I hope no one ever finds out."

"So do I Luke. So do I."

We talked for a while about other things and when I finished my coffee I got up to leave. Mr. Woodchopper said as I was leaving, "be careful Luke, always be careful."

I left there, heading for the lake. I was thinking about everything Mr. Woodchopper had said. I thought if the sheriff did find out, I would have to go to Mexico with Mr. Woodchopper. I was thinking that would be kind of fun, and I wouldn't have to go to school or do any work. I could lie on the beach and play in the warm water all day. The only thought I didn't like about going to Mexico was that I would miss my parents and family and friends. I was thinking maybe that was where Mr. Anderson went to live, I had heard it was kind of like paradise. I thought I could live down there, because it would be better than going to jail for a long time. Mr. Woodchopper had lots of money so we would never run out.

I decided to go fishing, so I grabbed my pole and tackle box at the house. It had stopped raining and fishing was always good right after a rain.

As I was heading out the door the sheriff pulled into my driveway. He got out and came to the front door. Mom and dad came to the door and the sheriff said that he had a few questions to ask of me. I was worried that he somehow knew what I had done. I was thinking of running but thought that would for sure give me away. I went in and sat down and waited for him to ask me whatever he wanted to know. He asked, "Luke before Shane ran away he had broken into a house and stole a pistol and a shotgun. His sister said he had hid them somewhere around Mud Lake. Town's people have told me that the last day that Shane was seen he was headed into Mud Lake with a shotgun. The same people say that they saw you heading down there hunting yourself. I was wondering if you saw Shane down there that day?"

I took a deep breath and said, "I saw Shane walk out of the swamp area and I thought I saw him throw something in the brush by the Baptist church. I can show you where—if you like."

"Sure I would like for you to show me."

He started to walk towards the door then stopped and asked, "if you saw him throw something in the brush, why didn't you go and see what it was?"

I was thinking fast and lying and trying not to show it. "Shane was always mean and I didn't even want to be close to him so I always tried to avoid him as much as possible."

That answer seemed to satisfy him, which I was glad of. I got in the Sheriff's car and he drove me down by the Baptist church. Both of us got out and walked over to the blackberry bushes. I said, "it's somewhere in there."

I was pointing to the middle of the brush. He looked at me and I knew he wanted me to crawl in there and look around. He was a big sheriff and I am sure he didn't want to get all dirty. I got on my knees and crawled into the middle of the briars and found the shotgun right where I had thrown it. I grabbed it and hauled it out to the sheriff. When I was back standing up I told him, "sorry for getting my finger prints on it."

I had seen that on the FBI show on television about fingerprints. He looked a little confused and said. "Yes, I guess I should've had you take a towel or something in with you to get it. I am sure you will find Shane's on there also."

We got back in his car and he drove me home and told me, "thanks for your help, if you ever need anything give me a call."

With that he drove away. I was glad he couldn't tell I was lying. I was scared and I hope I didn't show it too much. I hoped there would never be any more questions about Shane again.

I headed off fishing and was planning to enjoy the sun and the sound of the waves on the lake. I needed a good rest. When I arrived at the A-frame, I picked a nice place to put my line in the water. I was watching the water in the lake reflect the clouds as they passed by. It was like having two skies. I thought life was a lot like the reflection, sometimes I didn't know what was up or down. I sometimes wasn't sure of what was right or wrong. Some things were neither black nor white, only gray like rain clouds. It was a beautiful sight to watch, I thought that not everyone saw the things I did.

I heard some kids walking toward where I was fishing. It was a popular place for people to hang out. It was the Sather sisters—everyone said they were different. They were twins and they did everything together. They were always dressed in black, and people said that they were into weird things such as witchcraft and Satan worship; they never seemed to be all that clean. I wasn't really scared of them, but I kept my distance.

They came up and sat right down next to me. They sat there staring at me, and I started to get nervous. I was wondering what they were thinking about. They had a radio with them and were listening to KJR; it was a rock station. They pulled out some grass looking stuff and put it in some paper and took some matches and started smoking it. I was watching them, waiting for them to turn into something strange like a demon or a dog or a cat, I had seen that on television before. They started talking to me, "hey Mills, we heard you're stupid."

I sat there ignoring them, and I was thinking about leaving.

"Hey Mills, we are talking to you—are you deaf?"

They were laughing, thinking they were so funny. I turned my head towards them and said, "no, I am not stupid! And no, I am not deaf. I can hear you just fine."

"Oh! He can talk." They started laughing all the more. They said, "hey Mills, do you want to get high with us?"

"No, I don't even know what it is."

They started laughing again, and I didn't understand what they were laughing about. I was shaking my head, when one of them came close to me and said, "come on Mills, try it. It will make you feel so good, almost like having sex."

"I wouldn't know. I have never had sex before."

"That's not what we heard."

They were laughing so hard they rolled on the ground, grabbing at their stomachs. I smiled, but inside I was burning with anger. One of the sisters said, "before Shane ran away he said he had done you up the butt."

They were still laughing. "And if that isn't sex, than I don't know what it is."

I had tears starting to well up in my eyes. The whole town knew for sure. I wanted to tell them I had killed Shane, but I bit my tongue and said, "well maybe Shane lied to you?"

"Hey Mills, Shane wouldn't lie about that. Besides, we like it up the butt. Would you like to do us up our butts?"

I couldn't believe what I was hearing. I picked up my pole and tackle box and started for the road. I knew for sure that the demons had gotten to every kid in town. No one was safe. Was I the only normal one? Was I the only one seeing what was going on? I could hear them laughing and calling out my name as I walked away. The last thing I heard was, "Mills, we are going curse you tonight. You will be with us one of these days."

I kept walking, besides, I was getting big now and no one was going to hurt me anymore. Standing in the cow manure had paid off. I was starting to grow like a weed. I was getting bigger than my older brother. What was a curse anyway? They were just girls. What could they do to me? I made my way back up the hill towards home. It was starting to get dark, the day had gone by fast, and I had no fish to show my mom. The fish must have known the Sather girls were coming down to the lake, and swam and hid on the other side.

My mom was getting ready to put dinner on the table. When it came to cooking, my mom was the best. She could turn anything into a meal. Anything from baked beans to steak, it was always good. There was never a time that we went hungry at home.

Mom always made enough food for an army. It was like she was always feeding us our last meal. When dad was home we were one big happy family; we would laugh and talk and have a good time. Collin was always worried I was eating too much and not leaving enough for him. Liz never ate anything; she always picked at her food. It was always fun to see everyone happy. I thought our house was almost like the show "Leave it to Beaver, " just your normal American family in your normal American small town, although we rarely had any of the neighbors over for dinner. I would see families on television doing that, and I wondered why we didn't do that more.

One evening, I was playing in my room and I heard my mom running down the hall. She seemed to be in a panic, screaming for us kids to hide, that the bad guys were down at the bottom of the hill. My mom was crying and she looked very scared. My brother started to cry and Liz was hanging onto my mom's leg. I was wishing my dad were home. I saw the fear the bad guys were causing and I decided to take action. I wasn't going to let them hurt my family. I went into my closet and pulled out my shotgun and put three 6-shot shells in the holding chamber. I felt like John Wayne. Bring on the bad men.

I pulled the pump back and heard the first shell load into the barrel. It made the sound of power, a double click, enough to stop anyone in their tracks if they recognized the sound. Everyone was in a panic. I calmly walked towards the front door. Looking through the picture window in the front room I could see a car moving slowly on the road. It was pitch black outside and I couldn't make out what kind of car it was. I could hear my family crying and whimpering in the back of the house. I opened the front door, keeping the porch light off. My mom was screaming at me to get back inside. I stood on the porch not afraid because they couldn't see me standing in the dark.

I stood there and watched the car pull into the driveway. The doors of the car slowly opened, and four men got out and started walking towards the front door. They had only taken a couple of steps when I said, "what do you men want here?"

They stopped and one of them said, "look who is here. Do you think you're going to stop us from coming in Mills?"

"Yes I do!" I said with authority.

"Hell you can't even talk let alone stop us from coming in." One of the men said.

I was starting to shake, my hands were getting sweaty, and my heart was racing fast. The men were laughing and started to walk towards me. I raised my gun and pointed my bead right at the inside car light. I squeezed off a round and saw fire leave the end of the barrel and heard Bb's hitting flesh and metal. It made me feel good hearing and seeing that. The men started to scream in pain, and in about a second I had pulled the pump and squeezed off another round. The men were stumbling back inside the car when I squeezed off the third round with the Bb's hitting the car and breaking the side windows. The car started up and pulled out of the driveway and took off up the hill out of sight.

It happened so fast—smoke was still hanging in the air smelling like gunpowder. I lowered my gun and blew the smoke away from the barrel and walked back into the house like nothing had happened. It was that easy, bang, bang, bang, and no more bad guys. My mom and brother were looking at me like I had done the most horrible thing in the world. I was feeling like a million dollars. I had saved my family and I was a hero. John Wayne couldn't have done it any better. If I'd had a horse, I would have chased the bad guys all the way out of the county. I could see myself sitting high on a white horse like the Lone Ranger. I was the sheriff. I was right. I was the savior. My mom started in on me, "Luke you could have killed someone!"

"I was trying to mom. I wish they were all laying outside face down in the dirt."

"Do you know what your dad is going to do to you when he gets home?"

I was thinking that he would tell me what a great job I had done in protecting the family, maybe give me the first-born birthright? I had done a great thing. Maybe he would take me out for ice cream as a reward. I smiled and said, "no I don't know what dad is going to do."

"Now put that thing away before you hurt someone you love."

I was wondering if the sheriff was going to come out, if any of the neighbors had heard the shots and called. I knew the bad guys wouldn't be calling the sheriff, so the thought quickly left my mind.

I put my gun away and climbed into bed and fell asleep. Sometime during the night my dad woke me up. He pulled me out of my bed and started hitting me and yelling at me. I was trying to cover my head and face. He was spitting on me as he yelled at the top of his lungs. I could hear my mom crying in her room. My brother was hiding under his covers. It was the first time I remember not crying. I looked intently into my father's eyes and wondered why he was doing this to me? I had protected the family, I had kept them from being hurt and here I was being punished for doing right. I didn't understand. He went into my closet and took my gun and said, "you won't be needing this any more."

I watched him walk away. My dad always said that violence never solved any problems, I often wondered about that, he always hit Collin and me when we did something wrong. I didn't like violence either, but I was willing to use it to defend my family and myself. I knew my dad loved me, he was doing what he felt best to do. I was sure he didn't want me to get in trouble.

A few days after the bad guy incident, the paper reported that some men from the Clear Lake area were treated for shotgun wounds from a hunting accident. It said that one of their shotguns went off in the car, wounding all four of them. They were treated and released—no names were given. I was wondering if they were going to try to come and get me. I was a little afraid of them, but that didn't stop me from making my usual rounds through town. Besides, most people liked me, and I was nice most of the time. I think many of people thought of me as a perfect angel. Anyway, I did my best to not hurt anyone unless they deserved it. I was always taking the sides of the little people, at school I wouldn't let someone be picked on for fun. I would step in and tell whoever was doing the picking, to pick on me. I was getting bigger every day and they usually look up at me and backed off.

My school work still wasn't where my teachers thought it should be, so they asked for a conference with my parents to discuss sending me to a new kind of alternative school up at the hippie camp. I already knew a few of the kids that went to that school. Len was going there and so was Jeff Mays. They told me all the fun things they were doing. None of it sounded like work to me.

One day during school, a man came down from the hippie school to take me up to the school to visit. I thought I would see what it was about. Driving up to the school, I saw a bunch of kids running naked into a building. I thought this is strange. I got out of the car and walked up to the first building. Inside were some ladies who were dressed funny and they stank. They started telling me about the school. They said, "here we learn differently. You can do as you want, you can read or play, if you don't want to have your clothes on you can take them off, they are repressive anyway. If you want to sleep, find a place to sleep and when you want to eat, eat."

I asked them if there were any rules? They said, "no, just do what you want."

I was thinking this could be a nice place to go to school. They told me to go walk around and take a look at anything I wanted. I went outside and made my way to one of the buildings next to the woods. I went inside and there on the table were playboy and penthouse magazines. I saw Jeff Mays and asked him about the magazines; he said that he could look at them any time. He said he liked it better than comic books. I guess they needed books with pictures because I was sure they didn't learn how to read at this school.

I didn't know what to think of it all. I had heard that the kids that went to this school were retarded, but I knew Jeff and Len, and they were not retarded, they were very unhappy people. I looked at the faces of all the kids I saw there that day and I didn't see one happy child. To me they all looked lost, like they had nowhere to go. The demons had a hold of them all. I thought what a sad life they had. I looked at some adults that didn't seem to be teachers. They all looked sad also. A few of them were smoking out of the same pipe, passing it around and taking deep breaths, like the Sather sisters. Maybe they were the leaders of the demons. I thought this would be a good school for them—not me. I didn't see anyone learning anything.

I made my way back to the main building. Inside, the people asked me what I thought about their place? I told them it was nice and asked if they had any sport activities? They all looked at me kind of funny and one of them said, "no, we do not want to encourage aggressive capitalism. We all live here in peace and everything belongs to every one."

I didn't have the foggiest idea what he meant. What was aggressive capitalism? If everything belonged to everyone than could you wear your neighbor's underwear? It didn't make any sense. There were things we all had that were very personal, and didn't belong to anyone but ourselves. I was thinking that these people could learn a lot of things from me, that maybe I should start up the school of common sense and have all these people come and learn to get a grip on their lives. I smiled and asked if they would take me back to my other school. They took me back and I was wondering how I was going to tell my mom and dad that I didn't want to go to that school.

I spent the rest of the day at school working really hard on my assignments. I figured that if I showed them I could do my work they would let me stay. It was hard, I hated schoolwork, but in no way was I going to attend that special school. I was special but I didn't need to go to a school for people to know that. When I got home that day I told my mom that I wasn't going to go to that other school.

"Why not?" She asked.

"Because I feel if I work really hard, I can do my work, and I will pay attention like I am suppose to."

"Let me talk to your father, and if he agrees, we will think about it?"

"OK mom. I think I will do better where I am, not some new place."

I always had to get the last word in, I thought it helped me get my way if my thoughts were the last thing in other people's minds.

I didn't have to attend the hippie school, but I was reminded about it every once in a while. My dad and mom often told me I better behave or they would send me to the hippie school. I knew better, the kids that went there became worse than they were before they went to that school. None of the kids that went to that school ever made it into high school.

It was getting close to Halloween, and nobody could tell me what the purpose of that holiday was. Who wanted a trick? Just give me the treat any day. I was getting too old to go out and trick or treat, but I still wanted to be with my friends that night. All of the boys in the sixth grade class were invited to spend the night up at Robbie Burst's house. I thought it was nice that everyone was invited, rich or poor, cute or ugly. I was looking forward to being with all my friends even though there were some kids I didn't care for that would be there. It was a lot of fun and Mrs. Burst made us hamburgers and fries.

We watched the Rat Patrol on television and afterwards we went in to Robbie's room. We were all sitting around talking boy things—about what girls we liked, about fishing and hunting, about all kinds of sports. I don't know how we actually got to the next thing but we ended up there. Someone asked if we wanted to play spin the bottle or truth or dare. We all agreed that spin the bottle was out, so it was truth or dare. I was getting a little nervous.

We all started to play truth or dare and every one was picking truth. No serious questions were asked; just questions like have you ever kissed a girl? Have you ever seen a girl naked? We were at that age when all of us boys were starting to think about girls. It was my turn for truth or dare, so I prepared myself for an easy question. Greg Sather, the younger brother of the Sather sisters, asked if he could ask the question and Robbie said yes. He started to smile and asked, "Luke, have you ever been screwed in the butt?"

I didn't expect that question. I knew that he had heard that from his evil sisters. I also knew that he had already told everyone in my class. No one was laughing.

There was a silence that came over the room as a few of my friends hung their heads and looked at the floor. A couple of them looked at me, waiting to hear my answer. I took a quick look around the room and said, "no."

All at once Rich jumped up and said it was his turn for truth or dare. He said he had his own dare and went in the closet and shut the door. He was in there for a few minutes, and asked for someone to open the door.

Robbie opened up the door and Rich was naked, showing us his penis. I thought here we go again, the demons had gotten to him also. No one said anything. He stood there for a bit and pulled his pants back on. I thought, why are people like this? It would have been nice if it was a naked girl, but a boy, who could be excited about that? I was hoping that things wouldn't go any further. I asked, "why do you find that so fun Rich?"

"I like everything about sex, you're so square Mills."

"No, I am not! I don't understand why you would want to show us your penis?"

Robbie was getting uncomfortable with how I was talking. He jumped up and said, "let's all go outside."

I thought that was a good idea. We should all get out of there before Rich wanted to get on someone.

We put our shoes on and headed outside to play. It was dark and we were trying to decide what kind of game to play. Robbie and Rich were talking and they decided to play kick the can. They looked at me and Rich said, "Luke you're it."

I thought, OK. I can protect the can, and it would be fun. Everyone went out in the woods to hide and I started my search for them. Robbie lived up on the long hill, overlooking Clear Lake. The trees were tall and the hill was very steep, and it was very nice to look at. Towards the top of the hill was a rock face that had the letters CL painted on it. You could see the CL for miles, as you drove into Clear Lake.

I made my way into the woods, hoping I could hear one of my friends to catch him and beat him back to the can. I was walking real quiet when I heard Robbie and Rich behind me. I turned to start running back to the can but they didn't run. Robbie knocked me down and put a chokehold on my neck and started choking me. I was trying to fight to get away. Rich kicked me in the side of my ribs, then he kicked me in my testicles. I couldn't move—pain ran through my body. I had tears in my eyes thinking that they were going to kill me. Robbie let go of my neck and stood up. He looked at me and at Rich. He said, "we don't want you to tell anyone this happened to you."

I looked at him, not saying a word. I wanted so much to strike back, just him and me, without Rich there. I wanted him to feel the pain I felt inside.

"Are you going to speak? Or are you going to play dumb? You have to learn Mills that you either got to be part of us or be against us. Do you understand what I'm saying?"

"Yes I understand."

I was thinking I would never be like them. They let me up and Robbie said, "let's get back to the game."

By the time I got back to the can, everyone was there. I was wondering if they all knew what had happened to me. Someone said, "you lost Luke, it's your turn again."

They all took off for the woods again. I turned and went inside the house and got my sleeping bag and started off for home. These kids were not my friends. They teased me all the time, and beat me up sometimes, and called me stupid. I didn't need to have friends like them. I hated the darkness on that hill, and I wasn't all that far from where Sharon had been killed. I wondered if the demons had everyone on this whole hill in their hands. I was feeling sad and I was scared; I wanted to be safe at home.

The wind was picking up and it pushed clouds by the moon like waves of water rolling up on the beach. Stars would shine like bright flecks of sand being picked up and put back down. That was me I thought—someone who is picked up and put down like the sand on the beach. I was walking down the Old Hill Road hoping I would make it safely home. I was wondering if the boys would come looking for me. I was trying to walk as fast as I could.

I had to walk past the cemetery. When I got there I walked by Sharon's grave and said, "hi." I sat down and started talking like she could hear every word I was saying. I told her that I had shot Shane, told her if she saw him, to tell him I was sorry. I told her about how school was going for me. I told her about everything that was going on in the town. I told her, if she were still here, I would almost be old enough now to be her boyfriend, to take care of her. I told her she was the most beautiful girl I had ever seen. I sat there awhile hoping I could hear her voice telling me every thing was going to be OK.

I walked across the cemetery and stopped at the place where Marie was buried. I lay down on the grass and put my head on my sleeping bag. I was watching the sky, talking to Marie. I told her it was good that she wasn't here to see all the bad things that were going on. I told her I missed her smile, and missed playing with her. I sat awhile, remembering the fun we had. I told her it would be snowing soon and that I would come down and build a snowman to keep her company on the long cold winter nights.

I was lying there, feeling nice and warm as the south wind moved across my body. I was getting sleepy so I thought I would take a little nap by Marie's grave. I fell asleep and started to dream.

I dreamt it was winter and it was snowing big pure white flakes of snow, but each snowflake had a name of a child on it. It was a beautiful sight to see. There were thousands of kids falling softly to the earth from heaven. They were covering everything, making everything pure and clean. The snow looked so alive for it was living. Up from the evil hill came down demons of fire and they started to melt the snow. There wasn't a thing I could do to stop them. I was yelling and screaming for them to stop because the snowflakes were becoming children. They kept their fire going and melted all the snow. The snow turned into water and seeped into the ground. Out of the ground came trees—big cedar trees. The water made them grow fast and they reached their tops up into the sky. The cedar trees started to cone and drop their seeds and up sprung other trees.

The demons reappeared with fire and set the trees on fire. I was screaming and yelling for help, and I could hear the fire alarm sounding off. The firemen came and put out the fire, but the cedar trees were all dead. I saw loggers coming to saw them down. They took the trees to the mill and beautiful wood was cut from them.

I saw an old man taking the wood, and he sanded it and worked with it to make a music box. He gave the music box to me and said, "take it. Keep it safe. It's alive."

I opened the music box and saw Marie going around in circles, very quietly humming a song I had never heard before. She stopped and looked at me and said, "Luke, I fear for you! Run, Luke, Run!"

I looked at her and tried to touch her, but my hand wouldn't fit in the box.

"Hey Mills, wake up! Wake up!" I was startled to hear voices yelling at me. I was confused as to where I was. I sat up and saw the Sather sisters and a bunch of their friends. They were dressed in black, as usual, and they all seemed to be in good moods. One of them got down in my face and said, "so you have come down to join us tonight."

I didn't know what to think. I looked around and saw about 10 people all dressed in black. Some of them I knew, and some I didn't know.

"I was on my way home, thanks for waking me, I will be going now."

I was going to get up when I heard someone say, "let's have some fun with him."

I was thinking that I should have gone home, if I was home, I would be in my own bed, away from all these weirdoes. I thought I'm too tired to fight. I remembered something my dad had said, "fight by the sword, die by the sword."

I was preparing myself to be with Marie and Sharon. Then one of the Sather sisters said, "leave him alone. Let me talk to him awhile. You guys go get started and I'll be there in a little bit."

I watched as they moved to the middle of the cemetery and formed a circle. Shirley Sather looked at me and touched my face and said, "Luke do you want to know the greatest power of all?"

"I know the greatest power of all, it's God."

She let out a laugh, and reached for my face again and rubbed my cheek. She looked intently at my eyes and said, "did God stop Shane from hurting you? Does God do anything that you have seen? You don't have to answer that Luke, for I know that no God is as powerful as mine."

"I know there is a God, and I know there is a Devil and demons, but I don't know your god."

She smiled and said, "our god is what you call the Devil, he has more power than anything or anyone in the world. Come serve him and things will be much better for you."

I was wondering why I would want to serve such evil things, like the Devil, all I had ever heard about him was that he wanted to hurt everyone. "He is a bad guy, he wants to hurt everyone."

She looked at me with a frown on her face. She looked over at her friends and said, "watch this Luke, I will show you that you can use the power he gives to do anything you like, good or bad."

I watched her as she focused her eyes on a tombstone in the cemetery. It started to rise. I watched in amazement. Was what I seeing real? Or was my mind deceiving me?

I was scared and jumped up and ran. I ran as fast as I could, and I could hear her laughing as I ran away. I ran past the school, past the white witch's house, all the way home. Our doors were very seldom locked. I walked in, and made my way through the dark to my room and crawled in my bed. Running had made me tired and I wanted to sleep, and to wake up in the morning and have this all be a dream, and have everything be all right.

I thought I had a good grasp of right and wrong. It was right to treat people fair, to be nice, to do good things for them. I knew it was wrong to hurt people, and to take things from them, and it was wrong to kill. It seemed to me that doing wrong sometimes brought good things. Maybe there was something to what the Sather sisters were doing. I gave it a little more thought and put it to rest, for there were far more important things to be doing than staying up late being weird.

CHAPTER NINE

The young boys that I have met in this town know more about things they shouldn't, then things they should. I have brought this to the attention of the ladies society. We need to teach our sons to be gentlemen and not act out as wild dogs.

Diary of Mary Mundt
March 1909

I went to the post office one day to pick up the mail for my mom. I always took the time to look at the FBI's list of most wanted men. The postmaster would hang them on the wall of the post office. I often thought Clear Lake would be a good place for all the bad guys to hide, for there seemed to be plenty of bad people to keep them company. The postmaster came out and opened a big box and said, "here you go Luke, I received the new wanted posters this morning."

I took them from him and started to look at the bad men. I would always pretend I had seen them all. I was about half way through the pages when I saw the picture of a man that I really did know—it was Mr. Woodchopper.

It said he went by many different names, yet they didn't know his real name, and he was wanted for bank robberies in Washington and Oregon. They said he was armed and dangerous, I laughed at that, I knew Mr. Woodchopper would never hurt anyone. I looked around the post office to make sure I wasn't being watched. I stuffed the page in my pocket. I had to show Mr. Woodchopper.

I left the post office and ran straight up to Mr. Woodchopper's house. I was out of breath when I made it to his house. He was outside stacking wood, and looked at me and asked, "what's the big rush Luke?"

"I have something very important to show you." I walked up close to him and handed him the paper and said, "is this you?"

He stared at it, then put it in his pocket and looked at me with very discerning eyes and asked, "did anyone else see this besides you?"

"No, the Post Master said he received it in the mail this morning. So when I saw it I took it and brought it to you."

"Luke you're a good man, never forget that. I owe you my life. I have to be leaving now. I'll pack my things and leave. Would you like to go to Mexico?"

I had to think about that, I thought it would be fun, but I loved my mom and dad and brother and sister. I liked my home. I really didn't want to leave. "I am sorry Mr. Woodchopper, but I want to stay here with my family."

"I can understand that." He said with a sad look on his face. Then he said, "I want you to have something before I go."

He walked in the house and came back out with a gold pocket watch. He said, "here you go Luke, the first person that ever loved me gave this to me many years ago. I want the second person that loved me to have it. I hope you take care of it. It's something that is dear to my heart."

I said thanks as I took the watch and looked at it in amazement. I had never received such a gift. It was beautiful, it said on the back that it had seventeen jewels, and was made of real gold.

I watched him as he got his things packed and loaded them into his car. It didn't take long because he didn't own much. When he finished loading his car he came over to me and held out his hand. I reached out to shake his hand and he grabbed my hand really firmly. He looked me in the eyes and said, "work hard at doing right, stay out of trouble, because it's not a good life to be on the run from the law. Please never forget me, and remember everything I have told you. Someday you will come to understand your purpose in life. Never stop dreaming. And most of all Luke, don't let the demons get a hold of you."

He turned around and got in his car and drove down the hill. I smiled as he drove off, knowing he would have a good life, but something inside me told me I would never see him again. I was happy for him, because he was going to have a nice life in Mexico.

I walked over to the Marks house and walked inside. I always made myself welcome, and I never did knock. No one was home except the oldest boy and his friend, they were in his mom's room tearing things apart and I scared them. I saw something in their hands and knew they were up to no good. He looked at me and said, "why in the hell don't you knock, you don't walk into people's houses without knocking."

"Sorry, I have never had to knock before."

He shrugged his shoulders and asked me to come upstairs, so I did. I asked if they wanted to go play some football. He said they would after they took care of something first. They took some pot out and started smoking it. He said, "here, try this."

I took a puff of it and they looked at me and he said, "now how do you feel?"

"I feel normal."

I was thinking this has to be the stupidest thing in the world. I didn't take any more hits off the joint they had. I watched them get high and afterwards we went out to play football. I was 12 years old and they were 18, but I could outrun them and outplay them in football. They said they would play better by smoking their pot. I thought they played worse.

After playing awhile I went home, I was afraid to walk in the house because I felt bad about taking a puff of pot. I was worried that my mom and dad would smell it on me and I would be in big trouble.

When I finally went in, nothing happened and I decided I was never going to try any kinds of drugs again.

Things were different with Mr. Woodchopper gone. No one ever asked me where he went. No one seemed to notice he was gone. I was sad that I didn't have my friend around to talk to, so I thought I would have to find a new friend like him.

One day I saw Mr. Banks flying by in his old truck. He would never look at me; it was as if I didn't even exist. I was starting to think that I really didn't belong in this place. I seemed so different from most of the kids that I went to school with, and I knew I was different from all of the adults. I wanted to fit in and be accepted by everyone. My mom and dad often told me that they found me under a rock on the beach, so I thought that maybe aliens had left me there. Sometimes I went outside at night and looked at the stars and wished, and wondered if there was life out there, and if so, would they come get me and take me to a nice place.

One day looking for candy in the store I saw a magazine on UFO's. I picked it up and started reading about aliens and flying saucers. It fascinated me. I wanted to know more. Over the next few months I bought every magazine that I could find on the subject and I read them as fast as I could. My friends and teacher thought I was crazy, but I was quickly becoming a believer.

One article stood out in my mind. It was about what they called the mark of the beast, 666. The whole article was about how the beast would rule the world someday. I don't remember much about it, just that it started to make me think that maybe the Sather sisters were right. Maybe God wasn't as strong as the Devil. I was thinking of going and talking with them, but decided to wait awhile. I was thinking, if I can't chase the demons away, maybe I could join them to make them work for me.

That summer I took a real interest in the American Indians and how they lived. I was putting in hay for all the local farmers to make money, and in my spare time I did a lot of swimming at the lake and playing in the mountains. I wasn't home much. I was living the dream life.

It was time for my parents to take us on our annual vacation. This summer we were going to go to Disney Land. We were having dinner a few nights before we were to leave, and every one was talking about the trip. Collin said he was going to sit by a window on the trip, and Liz spoke up and said she was going to sit by the other window. I said that we should all take turns so we all had the same amount of time. Liz started complaining and asked dad to set the rules for the windows during the trip. He thought awhile, then said, "on the trip you kids will sit in the order you were born."

I asked, "well, I was born second, does that mean I sit in the middle?" He said, "yes, that is what that means."

I was thinking, how fair is that? So I asked him whether that arrangement was fair. He said, "Luke, you heard what I said. You will sit in the middle during the trip."

I started to argue with dad about it. He got mad and said, "if you don't like it, you can stay home."

"OK, I guess I will stay home."

Dad got mad. "Go to your room! Without finishing dinner!"

I didn't mind being sent to my room without dinner. It had happened before, so I always saved cookies and chips and other things, and hid them in my room. I had them fooled. I never thought it was a good punishment anyway, it seemed odd to me that parents would want to starve their children. I always ate well in my room. I knew I was smarter than they were.

The morning of the trip, I got up to get ready to go, but when I went to wake Collin he was already up. I went out to the kitchen and no one was there. I ran outside to see if the car was there and it was gone. I thought they were trying to prove a point with me so I went back inside and made some cold cereal and started to eat. I was looking around and saw a note on the refrigerator. I took it down and started reading it. It said, "Luke we decided to leave you home like you wished. There is plenty of food and you can make your own spending money. If you have any problems, go to your grandparent's house. We will be back in two weeks."

I still thought they had gone to the store and would be right back to pick me up. After a few hours I realized that they weren't coming back, I wasn't very sad. I thought it would be nice to be home by my self. That night I got angry and wished my parents would crash and die. I was scared of being by myself so I went and found my shotgun in my dads closet, and I kept it by my side as I fell asleep.

The next day I went down to the beach to go swimming, I thought it was nice not having anyone at home, and I looked forward to having my friends over without asking anyone for permission. It was a hot summer day and the beach was busy.

I always liked to hang out on the high dive and swim in the deep part of the lake. Sometimes I swam out to the float that was in the middle of the deep end of the swimming area. One day a few kids were at the lake that I hadn't seen before. Most of them were older than I was, and they were not being nice. I swam out to the float and I had crawled out of the water onto the float when I was pushed back off into the water. I looked up to see who had done such a thing. There was an older kid who had blonde hair and evil eyes. He looked at me and I said, "sorry, for what ever I did."

I tried to get up on the float again. He did the same thing, pushed me off, but this time he kicked me in the head as he did. I looked at him and asked, "why did you do that?"

"Because you're Luke Mills. And I have something for you."

He jumped in the water and started swimming towards me. I thought he was playing so I didn't swim away. He swam close to me and grabbed my neck with his hands and started choking me and pushing my head under water. I had no choice but to dive under the water to try to get away.

I was a better swimmer so I went down deep and swam under the water, and I surfaced and swam to the dock. He was right behind me. I jumped up on the dock and turned to face this boy who was trying to hurt me. He said I should run because he was going to hurt me when he got his hands on me. I figured I couldn't out run him, so when he put his hands on the dock to get out I stomped his fingers as hard as I could. He let go and screamed with pain. I took off running for the main office at the beach. I picked up my things and headed for home. I knew I was safe there.

The next day I went down to the beach again. I kept looking all day for the kid that was trying to harm me, but I didn't see him. I was wondering why he wanted to hurt me? The only thing I could think of was the demons had put him up to it. .

The two weeks that my family was on vacation I had mixed feelings about a lot of different things. I wondered if my mom and dad really did love me. I wondered if they would come back, maybe they were tired of all the bad things in Clear Lake. Maybe they didn't want me to be their son any more. Maybe I was the reason all the bad things happened in Clear Lake? Then I would forget those thoughts, and I would think that this was the best of times. I had no one to answer to, and I could go where I wanted.

I would hang out at the neighbor's houses and eat their food and watch their televisions. No one asked me where my family was. I would pretend they were gone awhile and would be home soon. In my heart I wished that they would never come back. I would think that and then I would feel bad. I was thinking I could find a girl to love, and spend the rest of my life with her. I wanted to have someone to love, but I thought if someone really knew me, they wouldn't love me. I thought maybe that was what my parents knew, they knew the real me and didn't like me anymore. My mind was all confused. I would lie in bed at night and think and think and cry myself to sleep. In the mornings, I was usually able to smile and be happy about every thing I was going to do during the day.

I wasn't at the house when they came back home. I was down swimming at the Lake. Walking up the hill, I could see that the car was home. I walked in the house and asked how the trip went. Mom said it went fine, and asked me how I was. "Fine," I said.

That became my answer for everything. Whenever someone would ask a question about how I felt, or things like that, I would tell them I was fine. I never did understand how I really felt about everything; I was slowly becoming more of a loner. I liked being by myself, yet there were times when I wanted people by me. What I really wanted was true love, yet I didn't know what true love was.

Summer came and went, just like the summer wind does. I was in junior high. It was a big school, with lots of kids from all over. In all the classes I had, there weren't any of the kids I had been in grade school with, so I had to make new friends. The second day of school they took us to a carnival. It was a fun day as I got to mingle with a lot of kids and became acquainted with a few of them.

Part of the day, I walked around by myself watching people and the things that were going on. As I was standing in line to get on a ride, a girl came up and asked if she could go on the ride with me. I said, "sure. I would like that."

We went on the ride, and on another one, and we went and had a coke together. We were having fun. Towards the end of the day I reached out to hold her hand and she took my hand in hers and it felt so good. A big smile was on my face. We talked about each other, where we lived, and what we wanted to be when we grew up. It was like a dream. Her name was Chris. She had brown eyes and brown hair and a big happy smile. She was nice and friendly, the kind of girl that I had dreamed of having someday.

The rest of the week at school we ate our lunches together, and between classes we talked and held hands. She lived up river, about 20 miles from me, so I didn't get to see her after school. That weekend was the first that I wished would hurry up and end. I wanted to get back to school to see Chris as soon as possible.

Monday morning I got up, took a shower, washed my hair, brushed my teeth, and slapped on some aftershave lotion, even though I didn't shave. I got on the bus and wished it would move faster, to get to school so I could see her. Her bus arrived before mine and I expected to see her standing, waiting for me to get off mine. She wasn't there. I got off and looked around, but I couldn't find her. I asked another kid that lived up by her if he had seen her. He looked at me and said, "she was killed in a traffic accident Friday night."

From deep down inside me, pain started to well up and surface as tears. I wanted to lie down right in the halls of school and sink into the ground. I was feeling so bad I couldn't go to school so I started walking home. It was a ten-mile walk for me. I was so sad. I knew for sure that the demons had killed another person close to me. I wanted to go away from this place for there was no comfort I could find here. I decided to take the railroad tracks towards home, no one would see me there, and no cars would try to run me over. I had tears in my eyes as I walked.

I was about half way home when I came to one of my biggest fears. It was the bridge over the Skagit River. It didn't mater which bridge it was over the river—I was terrified of them all. Even to this day I dream of that bridge, and in my dreams I am always falling in the river and drowning. I was scared of being thrown off the bridge into the rushing river. The river itself was over 100 yards wide, and very deep. The water was always green from the glaciers melting in the mountains. I often fished the river in September for summer run cutthroat, but when it came to walking over the river on a bridge, I feared for my life.

It was up from the railroad bridge that my friend, John Handover, had drowned. It was just another accident everyone said. He was only ten at the time he died. He would come to school sometimes with black eyes, and bruises all over his body. He would tell us he fell down, and we all believed him because he wasn't very coordinated. We heard that the night he died, he had done a bad thing at home. They lived right next to the river, and his dad took after him with a belt. Johnny ran towards the river and tripped and fell in and his dad couldn't save him. I always wondered why anyone would live by a river if they didn't know how to swim. His dad couldn't swim. It didn't make much sense to me.

I started across the bridge. With each step I took, I felt as though I was going to fall in the river. I was still crying over Chris. I was wondering why everyone I had ever loved died? Maybe I shouldn't like anyone any more, than they would stay alive. I started to become convinced that I was evil myself, why else would people die and disappear around me. As I continued to walk, I decided it was best not to go home because mom would be mad at me for not being in school, so I walked down to the A-frame. I thought it would be nice to hang out down there until school was out and afterwards I could go home and pretend that I came from school.

I was walking by the edge of the lake when I heard some noise in the brush. I walked towards the noise and saw the Sather sisters, with some other weird guy, having sex. Shirley Sather saw me and stood up and walked over to me. She reached out to touch me on the face and I stepped back. She was standing there totally naked. I slowly backed away from her as she kept walking towards me. She said, "Luke, come to me. I will show you feelings you have never experienced before."

"I feel all right the way I am." I said.

She reached and took my hand. I followed her as she walked me back to the other two. She put her clothes on and told me to follow her. I was curious to see where she was taking me, so I followed.

We ended up at the old concrete burner. It was a structure about a hundred feet around. It was full of black dirt and there was only one way into the center of it. The walls were about twelve feet tall and about five feet thick. It was part of the old sawmill that had burned. At one time the lumber mill was the biggest mill of its kind on the West Coast.

All that remained of the mill was the old burner and a couple of other concrete structures. We walked to the inside, and up to the center of the old burner. When we reached the center she told me to sit down and said, "do you believe in God?"

"Yes." I was thinking, where is this conversation going?

"Do you believe there is a devil?"

"Yes I do, and he is bad."

"If I could show you that it's he who is stronger, and cares more about how you feel, would you join us rather than follow God?"

"Maybe, I don't know for sure. Can he help people out of bad things?"

"Yes, he can help everyone, and if you serve him he can make you feel good."

I was wondering why she would want someone like me? I was young, and not really looking for anything like this. She kept looking at me with her dark eyes; she looked like she cared so much about me. She told me how she and a few other people came down to the old burner to have their meetings. She said that they had lots of fun, and no one got hurt, and that I could join her and her friends for their next meeting. I didn't know what to think about all of it. All I wanted was for people to be safe, for no kids to get hurt. Maybe this was what I was looking for. Maybe the answer was with what they believed.

I got up and she put her hand out for me to help her up. She reached for me and gave me a big hug, and said, "come here on Saturday night. I will show you what sex really should feel like."

I didn't respond, but just smiled and walked towards home. I walked by her sister and the man that was with them. I didn't know him. He smiled at me as I walked by; he gave me the creeps. He looked like what I thought the devil would look like, black hair, dark eyes, a beard, and awful teeth. He was ugly, and I wondered why the Sather sisters would want to have sex with an ugly man? It was all very strange to me.

On my way to the house I decided to go Saturday night, to meet with all those people. It couldn't hurt. Maybe everyone who believed the devil was bad were wrong, and if it was true that God could do everything, than why did He let the kids in Clear Lake suffer and die? I was willing to take a look at what this was all about. I didn't understand it, but I wanted to learn. Maybe if I could get the power that Shirley told me about, I could do many good things, for I thought there was no one more able to judge how to use that power than myself. Maybe I could even make people come back to life. I would go and have everyone I loved, that had died, come back to life and live with me forever. It seemed like a nice thought.

I was walking by Steve Mosers house he didn't go to school much and a lot of kids that were bad hung out there. His mom worked a lot and was never home all that much. He was the same age as me and he had a wooden leg, when he was three years old his dad ran him over with the lawn mower. He lived with his mom, because his dad had left many years before. Steve was a very bitter, mean boy, but I always tried to be friends with him. I figured he was mean because he wanted to be like everyone else and have two real legs. He would always ask me to smoke and drink and I always turned him down.

I knocked on the door and Lenny opened it up and told me to come in. I looked around the house and saw a bunch of kids that I had never seen before. The house was full of cigarette smoke, and they all were drinking beer. Steve's mom usually bought cigarettes and beer for him, I thought that was strange, since it was against the law to do such things. I said hi to Steve, and had a seat to watch and listen to what was going on. Steve asked, "why are you not in school today Luke?"

"Just don't feel like being there today."

"I feel that way every day." He said as he puffed on his cigarette.

In one corner was a rough looking kid. He had a cigarette in his mouth, and took it out and burned himself on his arm. He was telling everyone how tough he was. No one was really paying attention to him and he started to get mad. He jumped up on his feet and came over to me and said, "do you want to have a drag kid?"

I was thinking—what is a drag? I don't have a car, and if he wants to race, my bike is at home. I didn't understand what he meant. I said, "no, I don't want to race right now."

"No you retard, I mean do you want to have a smoke?"

"No, I don't smoke, but thanks for asking."

His face seemed to change in front of me and he started calling me names because I didn't want to smoke. To him I was a chicken, a mother's boy, a pussy, everything that kids can say to each other to be mean. He took the cigarette out of his mouth and said, "give me your arm. We will see how tough you are."

I didn't know what to do. I didn't want to make him mad and end up getting in a fight. I looked over at Steve to see what his reaction was. Steve saw that I was scared so he jumped to his feet and said to the kid, "so you think you're tough, how tough do you think you are?"

The kid that was smoking turned around to look at Steve and said, "I'll show you how tough I am."

He took a lighter out of his pocket and started it and held it under his arm, burning it. All I could think was that this kid wasn't tough—he was plain stupid. He took a deep breath and let out a soft moan of pain and looked at Steve and said, "I bet you can't even handle a little cigarette burn on your arm."

Steve was standing there thinking with his eyes going back and forth; it was a show down. He had to risk being called all the names that I was called, or do something that proved how tough he was. It was strange to me that boys had to act this way.

Steve started towards his bedroom with a big smile on his face. He returned with his 22-caliber rifle. I started to feel real uneasy about the situation. Steve looked at the kid who had burned his arm, and looked back at me and winked. I knew he was up to something but I didn't know what. He said to everyone, "I am the toughest boy in this whole town, in fact I am the toughest boy in the county."

He took the rifle and pointed it at his wooden foot. Apparently the kids that I had never seen before didn't know Steve had a wooden leg. Steve never wore shorts, not even in the summer. Steve pulled the trigger and the bullet went though his wooden foot. He looked at the kid who thought he was tough and said, "oh! That feels soooo good." The kid and his friends jumped up and said, "you're crazy, you're absolutely nuts! You're out of your mind!"

They grabbed their things and ran out the door. They were scared to death. They really thought he had shot himself in the foot. The rest of us were laughing to the point of almost crying. Steve put the gun down and went back to drinking his beer. I got up and told everyone I had other people to see and walked out the door.

I wondered why Steve, Lenny, Harry, Lloyd, and a few of the other kids that lived in town had to drink and smoke. I didn't like it at all. Melvin Dobson, who lived down the hill from me, started smoking at age five. He was kicked out of school in the first grade for smoking in the boys' room. I wondered why they thought that was so much fun. My mom and dad smoked and I hated it. I was walking around town and everyone was smoking. I didn't understand it, and for them at age 12 and 13 to be drinking beer and getting drunk didn't make much sense to me.

I knew for sure something was amiss in their lives, but for the first time I didn't blame it on the demons, it was the adults that were to blame. Maybe all the adults were the demons? I felt sorry for all of these kids. I knew that somewhere inside them was something good. I wanted to help them, but they didn't want my help. They wanted me to be like them, to drink and smoke, to do things that were not right. I wasn't going to have any part of it. I was going to learn the power, and do good.

CHAPTER TEN

"Last night I had to speak to my husband about an urgent matter. I stopped down at the club and the door was locked. I know that women are not part of the club, but to have the doors locked seemed odd to me. So I set about the building and saw the men inside engaged in some devilish activity. I am fearful to say anything to Andrew, because I know I should have not seen what I saw."

Letter from Elle Roberts to her sister in Seattle.
February 1905

It was Saturday afternoon and I was thinking of what was going to happen at the meeting. I grabbed my fishing pole and told mom I was going to be fishing late. I told her there was a big old catfish I wanted to catch, so I would be home sometime in the early morning. She never seemed to care too much, yet she told me to be careful. I went down to the A-Frame and started fishing. I was watching to see if anyone was coming early, but no one showed up while it was light. The sun was setting and the sky was clear with a full moon lighting the lake making flies look like dancing fairies on the water. A warm wind blew in from the West, bringing the smell of the cedar shakes that had been cut early in the day. It was a nice evening to be out and I was filled with excitement—yet feeling like I was about to partake in something very wrong.

About an hour after dark I heard some people walking down the path towards me. I was very nervous but I didn't run or hide—I sat there like I didn't hear them coming. When they got close, I turned around to see who it was. I couldn't tell if they were men or women. They were dressed in totally black clothes. They acted like they didn't see me and walked right past, towards the old concrete structure. I waited a while longer and more people began to show up. One of them came towards me and pulled their hood down so I could see their face—it was Shirley Sather. She didn't say anything, just motioned me to follow her. I walked right behind her, right up into the center of the old burner.

Someone had built three fires around the edges of the old burner and it looked really eerie. I was trying to recognize the people by how they walked and stood. I could tell that Mr. Johnston was here because of his limp. Mrs. Homer was there, and I could see her shoulders slouching like they did every time she stood at her kitchen sink. It struck me as odd that she was there, because she was always in church on Sunday morning with her husband. I was wondering why I didn't have a black robe on, they all could see that it was I, Luke Mills.

I started to think I had stepped into a trap. I began to wonder if I had been fooled and that I was about to be sacrificed to the devil. All kinds of crazy thoughts were running through my head. I should have brought a gun with me to be safe. I was looking over the wall to see if I could make a run for it. It didn't look like all that long of a fall. Then Shirley came over and took me by the hand and led me to the center of the circle that someone had drawn on the dirt ground. I looked closely at it and I could see the outline of a star with five points. Everyone began to close in around us and I was getting really scared. Shirley raised her hands towards the sky and everyone stopped and listened as she began to speak in words I didn't understand. After she said a few sentences she said in English, "you have been given as a gift to our god. He is the one who will give you the power you're looking for. Use it wisely and never betray your brothers or sisters, or surely death will come quickly to you."

With that, all the people began to chant, using strange words. It sounded like a lady who I heard in church once. She stood up and started speaking nonsense—strange it was. It was like demons trying to sing, and I was wishing they would stop. I didn't feel any different after everything was said, but maybe it was something that couldn't be felt. Shirley took me by my arm and led me out of the circle and everyone backed up and made some room in the middle. I watched as a small person came forward and stood in the middle of the circle and took their robe off. It was a girl I knew. Her name was Nikki, and she was 13, with light blonde hair, and very nice looking. It was strange that she was here. Maybe Shirley was right—maybe everyone knew that this was a stronger god than the One that people went to church to hear about. Was I the only one that was in the dark about this? Someone big came up towards Nikki and stood beside her and started to talk. "Are you ready to give yourself to darkness, to be a servant for all pleasure?"

She looked at him with dark cold eyes and said, "yes."

He took his robe off, laid it on the ground, and instructed her to lie down. When she did, he got on top of her and started having sex with her. I was watching, wondering why this was happening. The rest of the people began to cheer, as this was some kind of football game or boxing match on television. He didn't take long to do his thing and when he got off her another man came to take his place. I hadn't seen any thing like it before. It went on like this for over an hour, one man after the other, getting on her and than off. When I thought it was all over a couple of men came and said to me, "it's your turn, you get to be last, but it's probably your first."

They were laughing as they said this. I stood still, I wasn't going to have sex with her, and I wasn't even excited about what I'd seen. I did have a desire for sex, but I wanted it to be with someone I would love and be with the rest of my life. I didn't want to be part of every man in the town of Clear Lake. I felt sorry for Nikki. I was trying to figure out why she wanted to do this kind of thing. As I was thinking this I heard someone say, "are you going to do it or not?"

Then, Shirley Sather came near me and said so every one could hear, "he is going to be mine. I get to have him first."

That scared me even more. I had heard that she, at one time or the other, had sex with every man and boy in town. Even though I didn't know much about sex, I did know you could catch a disease by having sex with someone who had sex with too many people. Joe Clark had told me that. She came over and whispered in my ear and said, "when you're ready, I will show you every thing that is good about sex, watch what happens the rest of the night and you will soon want to be a part of it all."

She turned to the people and said some strange word that I didn't understand again, and every one took their robes off and started having sex—male with females, young with old, females with females, males and males, all having sex. I couldn't take it any more. I took off running for my house. I left my fishing pole and box where I had hid them and ran as fast as I could for the house. No one was chasing me. I guess they were too busy to notice. I was so confused inside. I didn't know what to think of all I'd seen. A part of me was excited by what I'd seen and a part of me told me that it was evil. I wondered what was right or wrong. Deep down I knew, but the wrong seemed so good.

I wanted to know more about those things, so I started looking for books to read on the subject. I thought the school library would be a good place to look for things on the occult. I looked during break but didn't find anything that really caught my eye. After school I went to a used bookstore in town and found a book called "The American Indian and the Occult." I took it to the check out stand and bought it. I couldn't wait to get home and read it. I had always wanted to live like the Indians. To live in the mountains, hunting, fishing, living a carefree life is what I dreamed.

What I read excited me. I knew I could find the truth about how to help people and learn the secrets of the power that I had longed for. I took my book to school and during free reading time I opened the book and started reading. It wasn't like me to read at school. Usually, in class, I would sit and stare out the window and dream of places, and of a girl I wanted to fall in love with. So when my substitute teacher saw me reading a book, it made her wonder what I was reading. She got up from her desk and came over and looked at the title of the book. I looked at her and tried to hide the book; I didn't want to get in trouble for reading a bad book. I figured she would probably freak out when she saw the title. She leaned over, and said in a quiet voice, "Luke, what are you reading?"

"Just a book on the Indians and the occult."

"Do you find those things interesting?"

"Yes I do."

"I want to see you after school, I expect you to be back in my room right after the last bell rings."

She walked back to her desk, and a couple of the other kids were laughing figuring I was in trouble. I knew it was going to be the death of me when my dad found out what I was reading. I could see it now—getting my butt beat for actually taking the time to read a book. My dad had always been after me to take an interest in reading, but I'm sure he wanted me to be reading about things he thought were good things. I was worried what my teacher was going to say. I wasn't a popular kid in my seventh grade class. I wasn't fitting into the social groups. I was a loner. I was sure she was going to lecture me about how I needed to take the upper hand and move along with the other kids and be a part of the group. I knew she was going to tell me I should be reading books like the Hardy Boys, and Huck Finn. I didn't need to read those books, from what I had heard about them, I was Huck Finn, and I did better work than the Hardy Boys. I had most of the day to think about all these things.

The last bell rang. I went to my locker, grabbed my things, and headed for Mrs. Cook's room. She was not our full time teacher but a substitute. I thought Mrs. Cook was about 27 years old. She looked good for being that old. She was fit and had brown hair and wore glasses. The glasses hid her eyes, so I could never tell what color they were. I walked down the hall getting nervous about what she was going to say, because I never liked getting in trouble. I knocked on her door and she motioned for me to come in. The room seemed so quiet without the kids there. She wasn't sitting behind her desk. She was sitting in a chair and told me to sit in the chair next to her. "So why don't you tell me why you were reading that book?"

"I am interested in the way the Indians lived."

"Don't play dumb with me, I have watched you the last few days I know you're a smart boy, you may fool others into thinking you're dumb, but I can see you're very bright. So tell me what you know about the occult."

What she said set me back. I didn't know what to think, but I sensed I wasn't going to get in trouble for what I was reading.

"I don't know very much about the occult. I want to learn more, so I am trying to find out all I can on it."

She looked at me intently, I could see it wasn't a look a teacher should have for a student. She reached out and took my hand and said, "if you're truly interested, I could teach you many things about what you're longing to know. I hope you won't be upset with me for what I am about to tell you, and please don't tell a soul. I am a practicing witch. I am very knowledgeable about Wicca and things people consider to be wrong in this community."

I sat in silence thinking that maybe everyone was a witch in this community. And if they were not witches, they were demons. I couldn't think straight so I smiled at her and asked her to tell me more. She told me that she met with a group of people once a month, to practice things, and to get more power for living her life. She asked me if I wanted to meet with her sometime so she could show me things that would change my life. We talked for about a half-hour. I said I had to get moving so I wouldn't miss the second bus that went to Clear Lake.

On my way home I did a lot of thinking about the things she had told me. I was almost convinced that I had been raised wrong, taught to believe in something that wasn't true. I was upset at the people who taught me these things, my parents, some of my friends. I suspected they had all of these rules to keep me in their control. I was finally learning what it was that most people wanted. They want to control the lives of others. I wasn't going to be controlled. I was going to commit myself to learning about the other side of things, the side that most people called the dark side. If I could break through the darkness, than I might be in the greatest light I had ever known. Maybe that is why people didn't talk much about the dark side, if everyone knew, than everyone would be free and happy, and control would be out of their hands.

I was 12 years old. I was glad I knew more about life than my teachers and most adults, and what I didn't know, I was going to learn. I wanted to know why Saturday was called Saturday. I wanted to know who named the months. Every little thing about how my world came to be, I wanted to know. I wanted to know if we were not alone in the universe, if Bigfoot really existed. Some of the kids at school laughed at me because I read books on all kinds of subjects that didn't mean anything to them at all. I wanted to understand everything that other people didn't give much thought too. I was going to understand, and use the knowledge to help others. I believed it was a good goal to have.

After school I had long talks with Mrs. Cook—she told me all about witchcraft and other related things. She asked me if I had experienced sex yet? I told her no. I didn't think she needed to know I had been raped. To me that wasn't sex. It was an act of violence against me. Mrs. Cook encouraged me to write down my feelings and thoughts and share

them with her. She said great things were in store for me if I would follow the ways of Wicca.

I wrote every day about many different subjects, but I never wanted
to show anyone, because I didn't want to be laughed at. I thought I was
in touch with how I felt about life—more than other kids did. I was
longing to be loved.

I was sitting on the bus, heading home after school. As always, the
bus stopped to pick up the kids from the high school. Shirley Sather was
there and got on the bus. I was wondering why she was at the high
school, I thought she had quit. She came towards the back of the bus
and asked if she could sit next to me. She looked at me and smiled and
leaned over to talk to me.

"Luke we are meeting again tomorrow night, you need to be there."

I was trying to think of how to tell her I wasn't going to be there. I
had decided that I was going to try meeting with the other people that
Mrs. Cook had told me about.

"I don't think I can make it Saturday."

"Luke this isn't an option. You have to be there. You made a pact and
now you have to keep it. Besides, it's time that you learn to have good
sex, and I want to show you."

I was thinking that I didn't want to have sex with her. It looked to me
like that was all her group was into, having sex—not wanting to help
people. It was strange to me. "No, I know I can't make it, maybe some
other time."

"Damn it Luke. You be there, or you will regret it for the rest of your
life. You don't know what you're really messing with."

She was looking really mad and jumped out of the seat and went up
and sat next to Nikki. I was glad that was over, because I didn't like dis-
appointing people.

When the bus finally arrived at Clear Lake, I got off down town and
so did Shirley and Nikki. I started to walk towards Meekers store when
Shirley came up to me and said, "Luke, you had better be there

Saturday. Right now Nikki and I are going down to the A-frame. Do you want to come down and have some fun with us?"

"No. I have to get a few things at the store and go to the Boy Scout meeting."

"OK. But don't miss on Saturday."

I smiled and started back on my way. I was wondering what made Nikki want to do the things she was doing. I thought she was a nice girl; she was always nice to me. I didn't understand why she felt like she had to have sex with all those people. Ever since that night a few weeks ago, rumors had been going around town that Nikki was having sex every day down at the A-frame. She would go down there and have sex with anyone that showed up. I felt really bad for her, but I didn't know what to say to help her. The demons had her, and the only thing I could do was learn about the demons.

I was finally old enough to join Boy Scouts. I was excited because I wanted to learn about the outdoors, and how to live off the land. I went to the meeting and listened to everything the Scout leader was saying. He said that the local grange had asked him if the Boy Scouts would take over mowing the cemetery, he said our Scout Troop would mow as one of our community service jobs. I thought that would be nice. Sometimes the lawn didn't get mowed in the summer, and I thought Marie and Sharon would like to have a nice looking resting-place.

After the meeting I decided to walk down to the A-frame to see what was going on. I came the back way, through the woods, so I wouldn't be noticed. As I came near the lake, I could hear people laughing and screaming. I walked quietly through the brush and stopped to see Nikki and Shirley surrounded by Lenny, Steve, and a few other guys. They were using things to have sex with the girls. Steve had his wooden leg off and was using that on Shirley. Two older men were holding Nikki down and she was screaming—it sounded a lot more like pain than pleasure. I didn't like what was happening so I stepped out of the brush and said in a loud voice, "Nikki, Shirley are you OK?"

It startled the guys that were around them. They lifted their eyes to look at me and seemed upset that I had interrupted their fun. Lenny said, "Luke this is none of your business, so if I were you I would be moving."

"I want to know if Nikki and Shirley are OK." No one said anything, but they looked mad. The girls were lying still but I could see by their eyes that they were a little scared. Steve said, "Luke, do you want to help us teach these two whores a lesson?"

"No I don't, I want you to stop hurting them now."

I was feeling pretty bold, and I was going to do what I could to stop these guys from doing bad things to Nikki and Shirley. Lenny said, "we're not going to give them sex from us, we're giving them sticks and whatever we can find, these two are trash."

"Well if you don't let them go, I am going to go tell someone to call the sheriff."

I left, running as fast as I could. I ran to the swimming area where there was a pay phone. I stood there awhile, wondering what to say when the sheriff answered the phone. I was about to pick up the phone when I saw all the guys that were at the A-frame walking out onto the road towards me. I waited for them to get close to me and said, "I didn't call the sheriff, I wanted you guys to stop. It's not right to do that to those girls."

Lenny looked angry and said, "Luke, it's none of your business. You had better watch what you do around here, something might happen to you."

It seemed to me that everyone was always full of threats, but nothing ever seemed to happen because of them. They all walked away to go smoke and drink. I watched as they walked off, wondering what made them want to hurt those girls, what possessed them to do those ugly things? Did the demons have a hold on everyone but me? I couldn't shake the image of what I had seen out of my mind. It was really bugging me. I made my way home and ate dinner. At dinner I wanted to ask my mom about some things, "mom why do some people call girls whores?"

"Where did you hear that?"

"I heard a couple of kids saying it to a friend of mine."

"It means that a girl is kind of loose."

"What do you mean by loose?"

"Luke it's something that you're not old enough to know about."

"Mom does it mean that they are having sex?"

I probably knew more about sex than my mom ever thought of knowing or at least I thought.

"That is something you can ask your father about when he gets home from work."

I knew I would never get a straight answer from my mom. It was a control thing again. She thought the longer she could keep me in the dark the longer she could keep me under her control. I wanted to tell her she had lost control of me when I was four years old; it was something I'll never forget.

I was going to the bathroom and my mom came in and asked if she could help me. I told her, "no, I can do it myself."

She kept insisting that I needed help. I finally got mad and said very loudly, "no! I don't need your help!"

She said OK and reached forward to hug me and I lifted my arms up and pushed her away from me. Ever since that time, I didn't let my mom hug me or come close to me. I never thought of it as strange, just a choice I had made.

I spent the rest of the night watching television. I finally went to bed and fell asleep. Sometime during the night I started to dream. I dreamt that I was walking through town and there were all these men working on digging a ditch between Clear Lake and Mud Lake. I stopped and asked them why they were making the ditch? They said, "so we can mix the water of the lakes."

I said, "but if you add muddy water to clear water, it all becomes muddy."

The man working in the ditch said, "yes, that's why we are doing it, so it all becomes dark."

I didn't like this so I ran to tell the people around town what was happening. I started knocking on doors and screaming for every one to come help me fill in the ditch. They said OK and the people went to get their tools to help me fill in the ditch. I was happy that the people were going to help me save the clear water from becoming muddy. As they came to the ditch they all started jumping in and helping the men who were digging it in the first place. I started getting mad and yelling at them that I didn't ask them to come here to help the bad guys, but to fill the ditch in.

As everyone was digging, bones started to appear in the soil. They were all little bones, bones of children from days long gone by. With each dig of the shovels, more and more bones would appear. Just when the ditch was almost finished, all the bones started to come together and make a dam to stop the waters from mixing. The people of the town didn't like it so they took their picks and shovels and started tearing at the bones, trying to tear them down. The bones were crying as they were being hit, and I could hear them speaking to me saying, "don't let us be forgotten!"

They were voices I had heard before. I was yelling at the people to stop, but no sound came out of my mouth. I went running over and tried to grab the shovels and picks out of the hands of the people, to stop them from tearing down the dam of bones. I slipped and fell in the mud, I was being sucked under, the dam was starting to give way, and water was leaking through. I was going to drown. I tried to fight my way out of the mud. I couldn't move—the water is rushing in around me turning black, blacker, I scream.

I woke up and I could hear the rain falling hard on the roof of the house. I listened to it awhile, trying to understand what I had dreamt. It didn't make all that much sense to me.

CHAPTER ELEVEN

"The Johnstone Children were found at home alone. Their ages being seven, five, and three. This is not the first time the Johnstones have left their children. The new minister and his wife are presently tending them. The state has been notified with a request that the Johnstones be found unfit to receive their children back."

Clear Lake News
September 1919

"The Johnstones returned back to Clear Lake this week. They packed up their belongings and left asking no one about their children."

Clear Lake News
November 1919

That fall, I spent most of my time fishing instead of hunting. The summer-run Cutthroat trout were thick in the river. I spent my afternoons watching the water go by, fishing, wishing I could spend every day here with no concerns about anything. I was becoming a real loner; I didn't have many friends. I knew lots of kids, but they all seemed to like others better. I would play with one group of kid's one day, then the next day, a different group. It bothered me somewhat, but I dreamed of a time when I would meet the love of my life.

I started looking for that special girl to share my life with. I knew that a lot of people thought I was way too young to start thinking of having a girl friend, but it was what I longed for as long as I could remember. I wasn't going to any of the meetings that the Sather sisters were having, and I didn't have time to go meet with Mrs. Cook's people. I was still reading and learning about things, because I wanted to know the truth. I needed to learn how to beat the demons in this town and make it safe.

Weekends were always the same for my parents. They would go out with their friends, dancing and stuff. They were part of a group of about eight different couples that spent weekends together. Some of the time, the group of adults and their kids would all go out together. It was fun. We went swimming in the summer and sledding in the winter. The rest of the time, the adults went out alone. One night when my mom and dad came home, they were fighting and yelling at each other. I was scared when that happened. I couldn't sleep so I lie very still trying to hear what was being said. My mom left their bedroom and went to the living room and started sobbing. I got up, went and sat next to my mom, and asked her why she was crying. She couldn't stop her tears, so I told her to go back to bed. I told her everything would be better in the morning. I was wondering why my dad didn't come out and try to comfort her. If I was ever married, I thought I wouldn't let my wife cry alone. I would be there, to hold her, and make her feel right. I went back to bed and fell asleep.

The next couple of weeks were quite strange. All of my parent's friends were switching husbands and wives, and a lot of the kids I knew had new dads or moms. Mrs. Lasson was now living with Mr. Hommer. Mr. Staple was living with his wife's sister, who used to be Mrs. Evans. It was like one big swap meet. I felt sorry for my friends who had to get used to having a new mom or a new dad. I was so glad that my mom and dad didn't switch. I didn't understand why it happened. I accepted it as part of life. I figured it was happening everywhere in the world—why should Clear Lake be any different? Seven different couples switched partners, and they all stopped doing things together, I guess someone was mad at someone, it didn't make any sense to me.

Thinking about all these people switching partners made me remember last summer when I went to the beach with Mrs. Hommer, Mrs. Staple, and Mrs. Lasson. I sometimes played with Tony and Diana Hommer and that day they invited me along. Tony was three years younger than I was, and his sister Diana was a year younger than I was. I knew she had a big crush on me; she had my name written all over her wall. When we got to the beach, all of us kids took off for the water. The ladies stayed back in the trees and sat down to sun themselves and visit.

After a while I got tired of swimming and decided to go see about lunch. I was walking back towards the ladies and they were all on their stomachs, tanning their backs. I didn't want to bother them so I sat down behind a big log to wait for them to wake up. They didn't know I was there, I was being real quiet, and I heard them talking. Mrs. Lasson was asking how old I was. Mrs. Hommer said I was a young man. Mrs. Lasson said that I was a good looking boy and that she wouldn't mind bedding me when I was a little older. I didn't know what bedding meant, but I was sure it had to do with sex. Mrs. Staple said, "if you ask Luke, I bet he would be able to satisfy you now."

They all started to laugh. I was feeling kind of good. It was nice to know that older women thought I was good looking. I sat there awhile listening to them talk about different things. Mrs. Hommer said to Mrs. Lasson, "I know why you want to do that Mills kid. Your husband isn't that good of a lover. He needs to learn how to make a woman feel good, not just himself."

They all started laughing again. Mrs. Staple said, "I agree with that. I have only been with him one time, and it was the fastest sex I ever had."

They all started laughing again. A bug landed on my arm and bit me. I slapped it. I heard the women ask if someone was there. I stood up.

They were sitting on their blankets with no tops on, their breasts were right in front of my eyes; it was the first time I remember getting excited about seeing someone naked. Mrs. Hommer asked, "how long have you been there."

I lied as I said, "I just got here." She asked me to turn around so they could put their tops on.

I was glad my parents were above switching partners. I didn't know what I would do if I had a new mom or a new dad. It wasn't a thought I liked to think about. I sometimes didn't want parents at all. I really didn't want to have to deal with a new mom and new dad. I would rather live by myself.

The mornings I had school, I walked across the field to the Clarks house to catch the school bus. I often left home early enough to spend time with the Clarks. I never knew what I was going to see. Leanna would be yelling at all of the kids and the kids would all be fighting over who was taking too long in the bathroom. There were nine kids going to school and living at the Clarks house. With only one bathroom, it was a funny sight to watch, if they wanted to shower before they went to school they had to get up early or chance not getting one. Whenever I walked into their house, I could never predict who would be sleeping with whom. Seeing some of them in bed together, I wondered when would be the first time I was actually going to have sex with a girl.

It was time to go stand down by the road and wait for the bus to show up. I hated riding the bus to school. We had to share the bus with some high school kids and some of them were not very nice. I got on the bus and made my way to the back seat. I liked sitting back there because I could see everyone and no one could bug me from behind. I took my seat and waited for the bus to take me to school. When the last kids were on the bus, an older boy came and sat right in front of me. I knew him. His name was Bob Sands. He lived around town and I had seen him down at the A-frame.

He turned around and smiled at me. I smiled back. I didn't think I had much to be concerned about, because there were too many other people around. The kids on the bus seemed to be in a rowdy mood and it was noisy. Bob turned around to look at me again, and I said, "hi."

He smiled and said, "you have not been doing what you should be doing."

I was looking at him, trying to understand what he meant. He raised his hand and pointed something at me and I heard a pop and felt pain in my eye. I reached with my hand to cover my eye and felt something sharp and painful. Bob looked at me and said, "next time, when you're told to be somewhere, you had better be there. If you don't want to see what your life can really be like in the light, you can try not seeing at all. And if you tell anyone who did this to you, I will make sure you die, and no one will know about it."

The bus was pulling into the high school and he got off. I was still covering my eye and could feel some kind of liquid coming through my hands. No one seemed to notice that I had been shot in the eye. When I got to the junior high school, I went to class. My teacher looked at me and started screaming. She grabbed me and took me to the office. The school nurse came, looked at my eye, and said, "we have to get this boy to the hospital."

Mr. Stiles came and sat next to me and asked, "Luke how did this happen?"

"I got shot in the eye on the bus."

"Tell me who did this, he is in big trouble."

"I don't know who did it. I was sitting in my seat and my eye started to hurt."

"I don't believe you. You had better tell me who shot you, now!"

I preferred being grounded or spanked to dying, so I answered, "I don't know who did it."

The nurse came out and said she had called my mom and my mom was going to meet us at the hospital. In the hospital the doctor took a piece of metal out of my eye. He said I had lost a lot of fluid out of my eye, and it would take a long time for it to heal. He said I had to wear a patch over my eye, and I would have trouble with my other eye adjusting to having to do all the work. He said I needed to wear the patch for at least six months. The police or sheriff didn't come to ask who shot me in the eye. I was allowed to go home later that day and my mom said I wouldn't be going to school for a while. I was happy about that, because I hated school. I hated the people there and knew I would have much more fun at home by myself.

I spent the next three months at home. I rarely wandered outside. I spent a lot of time sitting in my room and listening to music on the radio. One of my favorite songs, by the Group America, was "A horse with no name." I also liked the song "Sandman." I felt like it was the story of my life. I read comic books and worked at keeping the plants I had saved out of the woods growing. Sometimes I would sleep, or daydream about all the places I wanted to travel with the girl of my dreams.

It was the middle of February and it had been cold for almost three weeks. I was tired of being inside so I asked my mom if I could do outside to play. She told me, "yes, as long as you don't go down to Mud Lake and play on the ice." She was afraid I would fall though and drown. I told her I wouldn't go on the ice and headed out to play. I wandered down towards Mud Lake and a lot of my friends were on the lake playing and ice-skating. I went out on the ice and was playing with them. Mud Lake was on the edge of the old swamp where I had shot Shane. It was a weird feeling running on the ice, thinking that the water beneath was water that had the blood of Shane in it. I was wondering if his body had long since disappeared or if it was still in one piece, I didn't know for sure. I would look down through the ice to see if I could see some part of his body, the thought scared me. I played for most of the day on the ice. I didn't know why my mom was so worried about me falling through. When I got home that evening she asked me if I had been playing on the ice?

I lied and told her, "no. I went down there, but I was watching."

The next day I stayed in my room reading and listening to music. Late in the afternoon my mom came into my room and asked me if I had played on the ice yesterday. I lied again and said I hadn't. She held up the newspaper and showed me the front page. Looking at me she said, "if you didn't play on the ice yesterday, than whom would this young man be who looks like you and has the same coat as you?"

I looked closely at the picture—I was caught. I didn't know the newspaper reporter had been there. I told mom I was sorry for lying, and she said that I should never lie to her again. I lied and said I would never lie to her again, I knew that at some time, I would lie again. Besides, my parents lied all the time.

She left the paper sitting there so I picked it up and started reading the article beneath the picture. It said that a man from Seattle was doing some ice fishing and had caught a big old bass. When he was cleaning the fish, he found a ring and parts of a human finger in its belly. My heart sank a mile. Maybe they would begin a search of the whole lake and swamp and find more. The story went on to say that the man had planted the ring and was making up the story to draw attention. He was a black man, and I thought it was sad, if he had been white they would have believed him. I knew the truth, because the day I shot Shane he was wearing a ring on his middle finger. I wanted so much to tell someone that the stranger from Seattle wasn't lying, but telling the truth, but they would ask me how I knew. It was safer to live the lie.

It was spring and I went back to school. I had missed most of the year. I looked forward to seeing the kids that were nice. When I arrived at Mrs. Cook's class our old teacher was at her desk. I thought I would never see Mrs. Cook again. I wondered what had happened to her and if she would ever teach here again.

My teacher wouldn't let me go to lunch until I had my work finished. One day I had to stay extra long, trying to finish the assignment. When I finally was ready to leave, some mean kids were holding the door shut from outside. I tried to force it open but I couldn't so I went back and sat down in my desk. I started to cry and my teacher came over and sat down next to me. She said he had been watching me awhile. She said I was a loner, and was headed the wrong direction in life. She told me how when she was younger, how she struggled with schoolwork. How she was called fatso, and other mean names, how she decided her fate was in her own hands, not in the hands of others, how she recognized she wasn't what others said she was. She looked at me and said, "you can be whatever you desire to be. Follow your dreams and don't let these other kids bring you down. Rise above them." She urged me to turn out for sports, because she said that would give me purpose. I told her, "I love football, but the coach doesn't like me."

"Give it another shot. Don't give up because you failed once."

The bell rang and it was time to go to the next class. I thanked her for taking the time to talk to me and told her I would give sports a try.

It was the end of the school year and Mr. Stiles called me into his office. I didn't know what for? I knew I hadn't done anything wrong. I was wondering why he wanted to talk to me. When I sat down in the familiar chair in front of his desk, he lifted his eyes from a paper he was reading and said, "Luke, I have something very important to talk to you about. I hope you can handle this like an adult."

I had handled thousands of things like an adult why not this? I was thinking, this must be something really bad. I wanted to know so I said, "OK."

"I've talked to your parents and your teachers and we all agree that you're not ready for the eighth grade."

I didn't disagree, I didn't have any friends in this class, and I had missed most of the school year after being shot in the eye. I really liked the idea of doing the seventh grade over again. It would be like a new start.

"Yes, I agree with you Mr. Stiles, I am not ready for the next grade. I missed too much school this year and maybe next year I will be able to do my work a lot better."

I think I surprised him, I was sure he thought I would be terribly upset.

"I'm glad you understand. I think you will have a much better time next year. I'll make sure you don't have any classes with any of the kids from Clear Lake, so no one will know that you're doing seventh grade over. And I hope you will make some effort to make some new friends."

I liked the idea of no one knowing I was doing the seventh grade over it would save me from being teased a lot. I left, happy that next year I would be having a brand new start. Things seemed to be going my way for the first time. The demons were slowly fading from sight

CHAPTER TWELVE

"The Skagit Club is an exclusive club for the men that manage and hold higher positions in the company. A man must be in good standing. No drunkards or thieves, or other men of questionable character."

Club Charter
January 1903

Mark returned home from the club last night and seemed upset over something. He said he was not at liberty to tell me, but that it wasn't good. The men that make up the club it seems to me are an unholy group."

The Journal of Victoria Southerland
June 1904

Summers were a busy time in Clear Lake. People came to visit family and friends or to camp, fish, and swim. Clear Lake was the most popular swimming area in the county and the beach was always busy. I noticed that during the day certain men would come park their cars in the parking lot, and watch everyone on the beach. They never got out of their cars as they sat and looked at people. Some of them had binoculars. I figured they were perverts. I started to keep an eye on them, every time a little boy or girl left the beach to walk home, I watched to make sure none of those men grabbed them. It made me mad that there were men like that hanging around Clear Lake.

One day down at the beach, in mid afternoon I saw a bunch of my friends running out of the men's changing room. I went over and asked Rocky Barret what was going on. He said, "some queer guy is in there playing with himself, asking if anyone wants to help him."

I was mad, so I went and told Mr. Mally, who was in charge of the lifeguards. Mr. Mally went into the changing room, but the man had left. I decided to go back out swimming. I saw some of my friends sitting on the edge of the dock, talking. I sat down by them and the guy from the changing room showed up and sat next to us. He looked at us and started playing with himself. We all jumped in the water and swam towards shore. Mr. Mally had seen what was happening and ran out and grabbed the man dragging him out of the swimming area. I could hear Mr. Mally yelling at the guy to never come back. I thought, somebody should take him away and shoot him, than he will never come back for sure. I wondered what would turn a person into that kind of pervert. It had to be the demons that made their home in Clear Lake.

I worked hard that summer putting hay in for all the local farmers. I liked working hard. I was strong, and in good shape. My dad had told me that if I worked hard and pleased the people I worked for I would always have work. I liked that idea. After work I usually ran down to the beach to swim and see my friends. From the swimming area I could see the A-frame. I often saw Mr. Banks fishing there with a couple of older men. It seemed odd to me that I never saw their mouths moving. I wondered if they talked when they were down at Ellens Tavern. It seemed like Mr. Banks had forgotten that I was alive, he never waved to me, and he hardly ever looked at me. Maybe he was afraid of dying.

After swimming one day I went up to the Marks house. I never asked why they didn't go to the beach, even though they only lived one mile from it. They were the most consistent people I knew. Every day, their meals consisted of the same foods, cold sweet cereal for breakfast, bologna or hot dogs for lunch, and hamburgers for dinner.

After every meal, they drove to town to buy food for the next meal, everyone in town knew you could count on them like clockwork. It seemed like every time you looked out at the road the Marks were going by. In all my 18 years in Clear Lake, I don't remember them ever missing a drive to town. They were very nice and I don't think most of the other people knew that. Most people thought of them as a little odd. Brian asked me if I wanted to spend the night. I always liked staying at their house for it was a lot of fun.

After dinner and driving to town, we were trying to decide what to do. The Marks lived right across the road from Mr. Banks. Brian came up with the idea of pulling the nails out of the rail of Mr. Banks' bridge. When he came home from the tavern drunk and leaned on the rail, it would break and he would fall in the creek. We thought it would sober him up real fast. I thought it was a good idea—I couldn't see that it would hurt anyone.

Later that night, we went over and pulled all but one nail out of the bridge rails. It was about 1 a.m. We heard his truck rumbling up the hill and we hid in some brush and waited. He pulled into his parking spot out by the road and started stumbling towards the bridge. He made his way onto the bridge and leaned on the rail. The only nail holding the rail popped out and we heard a big splash. It kind of scared us, because it had really worked. We listened, waiting to hear him pulling himself out of the creek. He crawled out cursing and cussing the old wooden bridge. He was climbing up the bank of the creek saying that he should have replaced that railing years ago. We almost laughed out loud. We waited until he went into his house, then ran, laughing, towards town.

We went down town to see if there was anything else that we could do to have fun. We met up with Jimmy Barret. He had four brothers and three sisters and had moved from Mississippi. He asked if he could hang out with us. I said, "sure," thinking it would be fun to show him the town.

I didn't want to go down to the A-frame, I was afraid I would run into the Sather sisters and I wanted to avoid them. I thought they had put Bob Sands up to shooting me in the eye. We were walking down by the fire hall when we heard really loud music coming from the blind man's house. He was about 40 years old, blind, and always had kids coming and going from his house. The neighbors were afraid of the rough looking kids that hung out there. Tonight he was having a party; it was loud enough to keep the neighbors awake. I recognized a few of the kids we could see through the windows. I told Brian and Jimmy that we should call the sheriff, and watch when they came to check out the party.

We went to the pay phone by the post office and called the sheriff. I said, "hi, I am calling from Clear Lake and there is a party going on by the fire hall and I can't sleep. I think that kids are doing drugs and having sex. Thank you. Bye."

We all started laughing when I hung up the phone. We ran to the railroad tracks to wait for the sheriff to come. After about 30 minutes, four sheriff cars came driving into town. They turned towards the fire hall and two of them shined lights into the blind man's house. It was like watching the movies, people ran out of the house, some were running towards their cars and some were running into the woods. It was a sight to see—it looked like a bunch of rats being hunted down by bigger faster cats. The sheriffs were running around arresting anyone they could catch on foot, and there were car chases around town. It was better than a movie, and Brian, Jimmy, and I had the best seats in the house.

The next day the paper had a story about the big raid that had taken place in Clear Lake. It said that a number of minors had been arrested for drinking and taking drugs. It said they had recovered drugs, and to the surprise of all, the sheriffs found pornographic books and movies of children having sex. I was glad we called the sheriff.

I knew I had a victory over the demons that had those people in their grasp. I was hoping I could do more of that. I decided that when I saw things that were bad, I was going to do what I could to get help for those who needed it. I also knew that by doing so I would create enemies even among some of the people that I knew and considered friends.

A few weeks later, I heard that Mr. Banks had died. It was a surprise to me. I wondered how it had happened? I wondered if the bad guys had gotten him. Maybe the demons that knew all informed the bad guys. Maybe they knew he had talked to me a couple of years back, and were now finally getting around to taking care of business. I needed to find out, because maybe I was next on their list. I went up to the Marks's house and sat in their driveway across from Mr. Bank's house. I was hoping to see someone I could talk to. There was a car from out of state parked in his parking place. I walked across the road to the bridge. The rail wasn't fixed. I walked up to the house and saw a lady inside. She was working packing things into boxes. I walked up to her and said, "hi."

She turned around kind of startled. She looked at me, smiled, and said, "hi," then continued working.

I watched her, wondering who she was. She seemed determined, as if she was on some kind of mission. I asked, "who are you?"

She smiled and said, "I'm Barbara Lee, I used to be Barbara Banks. And who are you young man?"

I smiled myself and said, "Luke. I didn't know Mr. Banks had kids."

She stopped working and walked towards me and asked, "did you know my dad?"

"Yes. We were kind of friends sometimes when he was in a good mood."

"Yes, I know he did have his moods. Did you visit with him often?"

"Sometimes. But he was always fishing, or he was at Ellens tavern."

"He didn't hurt you in any way, did he?"

"No, what do you mean by that?"

"I wanted to know if he ever tried to hurt you in any way?"

"No, we just talked a lot. He did say he had done some bad things in his life, and he wished that he could have changed them."

Her eyes lit up when I said that. Her smile seemed to get bigger and I knew I was saying things she wanted to hear. "When is the last time you saw my dad?"

"About a couple of weeks ago. How did he die anyway?"

"He died of pneumonia. He must have fallen in the creek and became sick and never recovered. I'm glad he is finally gone."

My heart sank. I had killed Mr. Banks, because I was responsible for making him fall in the creek. I couldn't believe I was so evil. I started to cry.

"Oh now Luke, you don't need to cry. I didn't mean that in a bad way. It's that I haven't seen my dad in almost 20 years. We didn't have the best of relationships, and I wish things would have been different."

I knew what she was talking about. I wasn't dumb. This was Clear Lake, and she was a girl, and her dad had done bad things. My heart went out to her. I could see that she was remembering everything. She told me to follow her, so I did. We walked towards the back of the house in to a bedroom.

"This used to be my room when I was growing up. I had all kinds of dolls and pictures of horses on the wall. And look, they are still all here, like the day I ran away."

"Are you going to take them home with you now?"

She didn't hear me. She was lost in thoughts and dreams of her childhood. It was like she was transformed into a little girl before my eyes. She went over and picked up a doll, and held it in her arms like it was alive. By looking at her it was like watching her life story being told through her eyes. It was clear to me she had found her peace. I told her I could help her pack things up if she wanted. She looked at me and smiled. For having her dad die, she didn't seem all that upset.

I figured she was happy that something had passed, and was no more, like an end to a bad dream. The feeling in the room is one I can't describe. I watched as she picked up the dolls and her old toys, and took the pictures off the wall. I was sure that every little thing had a story behind it. I watched her emotions change with each possession she put her hands on. She made little sounds as memories flooded her mind. I was hoping she was remembering all of the good things, and none of the bad things. I wanted to tell her it was my fault that her dad had caught pneumonia, but I couldn't bring myself to upset her in such a way. I wanted to know some things, so I decided to ask her. "Why did you run away from home?"

"Luke, this wasn't a pleasant place to grow up. I would like to forget those things, they are long gone now and I have a whole different life."

I smiled at her—I understood what she wanted. I wasn't going to pry into her life. I was going to let her put all the bad things to rest with the death of her father. I began to understand why Mr. Banks had been crabby and mean most of the time. He had not only lost his wife, but I knew if he had any heart at all, he missed his daughter very much. I could see how the pain and hurt slowly destroyed him. His own demons had brought his life to misery and despair. I thought to myself that I would never let that happen to me. I would work hard in my life to make sure I had peace with everyone. I didn't want to go through life knowing I had hurt someone so much they never wanted to be around me. I made a vow to myself to be the best father to the kids I would have that I could be. I helped Mrs. Lee pack things into her car. Her car was full and there were still boxes on the floor. She said she would be back next week, and asked if I would watch the place for her. I shook my head yes. I watched her drive down the road until she was out of sight, then I started walking home.

On my way home I was thinking about how Mr. Banks had died. I felt bad about the joke we had played on him, it was intended to be funny, we didn't mean to hurt him. I wanted to avoid doing something like that again. I hoped no one would find out what we had done. He was gone now, and nothing was going to change that. I wondered if it would bother my friends, I doubted it would. I thought, maybe I'll tell Mrs. Lee what I did when she returns to get the rest of the things. I felt it was the right thing to do. I knew she had a right to know the truth. Besides, it might not be long before I was found out anyway. I felt I was bad, and heading down the wrong road.

How much does it cost?
How many must be lost?
Life has been taken by my hand.
My life is like wind blown sand.
For to many people I have lied.
I have no place left to hide.

Those words kept running through my mind as I thought about telling Mrs. Lee what I had done. I tried to figure out why I wanted to tell her. Maybe I was starting to like her, and I wanted her to like me. Than again if she really knew me, she wouldn't like me. If she became mad and called the sheriff, I'd run away. I would live in the mountains, and never come back again.

I got home and called Kenny Sutton. He and I were doing lots of things together since we met putting in hay for a local farmer. He was nice, and seemed to be a loner like me. I told him to meet me down at the creek for I had something important to tell him. He came from a very large family for he had two sisters and four brothers. They had moved up from Seattle to get away from city life and I couldn't blame his parents for that. He told me many times that he wanted to run away.

We met down at the creek by our favorite fishing hole. It was half way between my house and his house. In the summer the fishing hole was only three feet deep. We were sitting on a cliff about 12 feet above the water. I said, "if I dive in the water from here would you give me fifty dollars?"

"If you dive in, I give you fifty dollars. If you don't, you give me fifty dollars."

I knew he didn't mean it, neither one of us had fifty dollars. I took off my shirt, walked to the edge, and dove in headfirst. I barely scraped the bottom and came up. Kenny was screaming that I was crazy, "you could have killed yourself!" I smiled and asked for my fifty dollars.

"I don't have fifty dollars. Guess I owe you."

"No, don't worry about it. Just run away with me to the mountains."

He looked at me, and smiled and said, "OK."

We talked the rest of the day, making plans. I told him we should work hard all summer and make lots of money, and then we could buy everything we needed. We already had shotguns, rifles, bows, arrows, traps, axes, and saws, but we needed to get a few extra things, including enough food to last for at least one month. We figured within a month we could gather enough berries, and collect enough meat from fishing and hunting, to last through the winter, after the snows came. We agreed not to see each other for the rest of the summer, in case someone would figure out what we were going to do, and tell on us. We would run away in the middle of August. We shook each other's hands, and went our separate ways. I knew we were going to go through with what we were planning.

When I wasn't working that summer, I would often hang out with Jimmy Barret. His dad had runaway, Jimmy had said that he had killed a man in Mississippi and the law was getting close to him so he left his family. Jimmy had three sisters and three brothers. He was the third oldest and the nicest of them all. Mrs. Barret went to the church on the hill. The boys never went with her, and neither did Karrie, who was only a year older than me. When Mr. Barret moved out, another man had moved in. He brought with him his son, Don, who was 19 or 20. Mrs. Barret waited on both of them hand and foot. I spent the night there often, and saw lots of strange things. Demons were in that house also.

The son of the man that had moved in lived down in the basement. Karrie slept upstairs. One night when I was over there a little bell rang in Karrie's bedroom. She walked out of her room and down to the basement.

After a while, she came back up. I asked Jimmy what was going on? He said that Don had hooked a bell to a wire that ran from the basement to her room, and when he wanted sex, he would ring her, and she would go down and give it to him. I was thinking that she is only fifteen years old! I wondered if Mrs. Barret knew what was going on? But like most people in town she knew no evil, saw no evil, but lived with a man who wasn't her husband.

I would look at that older boy and want to beat the hell out of him. Even if Karrie did like him, I thought he was taking advantage of a very young girl. I was a little jealous, because I wanted her to like me, not some 20-year-old pervert.

I would often go over to their place to listen to an eight-track tape that Karrie had. It was Led-Zeppelin, Houses of the Holy. I would play two songs over and over again. The first was, "Over the hills and far away," and the second was, "D'yer Mak'er."

The bell stayed up most of the summer, and when I would spend the night, and hear the bell, I would start to sing, "oh oh oh oh no you don't have to go, oh oh oh oh oh. Baby please don't go." I remember lying in bed, thinking of being over the hills and far away, off to dream land where everything was the way I wanted it to be.

If you ever had anything missing from your home, you could find it at the Barret house. The boys would steal anything that they could carry or drag home. I would often go there to get my dad's tools, before he found them missing. I thought it was because they were poor and didn't have a dad to discipline them if they did wrong. The man that was living with Mrs. Barret never paid any attention to the boys.

Mrs. Barret was a large woman. She was always nice, but not very attractive. I wondered why this man had moved in with her, but never wanted to marry her? I suspected he wanted to be waited on hand and foot and to be close to Jimmy's sisters. One time I walked in Jimmy's house and heard noises coming from the family room. I didn't see anyone. I walked around the corner, enough to see in the room without being seen. I saw the man that was living with Mrs. Barret on top of Jimmy's younger sister, who was only six. He was making sounds like a demon would. If I had my gun with me I would have shot him. I didn't know what to do, but run. I went home and told my dad what I had seen. He said he would take care of it, I was so glad I had a dad like him. I considered myself very lucky.

I wished my dad could set everyone straight in town, and stop all the rape and bad sex going on. I thought maybe my dad knew about the demons and could help me get rid of them. I knew the demons were thick in Clear Lake, but I didn't know how I could get them all out of town, and out of people's lives.

I told Jimmy what I had seen, and he didn't seem all that concerned. I wondered if his mom knew? I knew that if my mom ever had a man move in with us, and he was doing that to my sister, I would kill him. No questions asked. It was strange how I felt when I saw someone being abused or hurt. Anger would flare up in me, and I would want the one who was being bad to be dead. I knew it was a bad thing in me, and I knew I had to learn how to control it, before it controlled me.

It had been almost a week, and Mrs. Lee was up at her dad's house cleaning, and picking up the remaining things. I walked into the house and said, "hi." She smiled back. I watched as she threw some things away. They looked good to me. I wanted to tell her what I had done but I didn't know how. I thought I would say things that would make her happy. I asked, "when you grew up here did you ever play up at the frog pond?"

"Do you mean the old pond up on the hill in the woods?"

"Yes, I call it the frog pond. Lots of frogs live there."

"I used to play there almost every day as a little girl."

"Would you like to take a walk up and see it one more time?" To my surprise she said yes.

The sun was filtering through the trees, casting light down on the trail as we made our way up the hill. I told her that this was one of my favorite places in the world. She was looking around a lot. "Things sure have changed a lot in all these years, " she said. When we got to the pond she looked over at an old cedar stump that was hollow.

"I used to hide from my dad when I was a little girl. I would run up here and get in this old stump and he could never find me."

"I hide in the stump sometimes to get away from everything."

She looked around and told me how she used to bring her dolls up here and have tea and cookies with them by the pond. I could see she was having very fond memories of her childhood, it was time for me to tell her what I had done. "Mrs. Lee, I have something to tell you. Your dad died because I took the nails out of his rail on the bridge for a joke—that is how he fell in the creek and got sick. I didn't mean for him to die. I hope you're not mad."

I stood there waiting for her to start screaming and yelling at me. Tears started to come to her eyes and she said, "Luke, it was his time. You didn't kill him. He would have died soon because he was being eaten alive by guilt. He never said he was sorry for anything and I think it's good he is gone. I hope he is resting in peace now. So Luke, learn your lesson, but please don't think that you killed my dad."

I was trying to figure out why she wasn't mad at me. We sat quietly in the sun and watched the frogs swim across the pond. I felt like I was her best friend. "Mrs. Lee, do you have any kids of your own?"

"No, I never wanted to bring kids into this world. But after meeting you, I think I would like to have a son like you."

It made me feel good that she liked me. She started telling me about her mom and dad. She told me her dad did bad things to her, things that should never be done to anyone. "My mom knew, but never did anything to stop him."

I felt very sad. I didn't understand why a mom would let that happen and not save her child. Strange it was.

"When I was 15, I ran away from home to get away from my dad."

Even though she didn't mention the sex word, I knew that was what her dad had done to her. I wished it didn't happen to so many girls in Clear Lake. I asked, "where did you go when you ran away?"

"I was treated really nice by a lady at the bus depot in Seattle. I went with her to a home for girls. I ended up living at the home until I finished school."

We talked for what seemed like hours. She was sitting beside me and put her arm around me and gave me a hug. It felt really nice. I was happy for her. It was nice to see she turned out all right.

We got up and walked back to the house. I helped her put some things in her car and she reached and gave me a hug. She held on for a long time. "Thanks for all the help. I don't think I will ever be back this way again. The house is going to be sold by a real estate agent. I hope you get some nice neighbors. Take care of yourself, and don't think that you had anything to do with the death of my dad. It was his time. If you're ever down in the Portland area please look me up. Bye now."

She got in her car to drive away as she looked at me with tears running down her cheeks. I smiled at her and waved, hoping that someday I would see her again.

The summer was a hot one. We didn't have very much rain and things were dry. I spent as much time as possible down at the beach swimming and playing with my friends. I was glad I was putting hay in for local farmers, and not picking berries. Haying was better work, and a lot more money. My brother Collin and I saved up some money and bought a record player so we could listen to music. The first 45 record I bought was "No Mr. Nice guy" by Alice Cooper. I wasn't very nice anymore and the song made sense to me. The second was "Feeling stronger everyday" by Chicago, and I was getting stronger every day.

Our sister Liz gave us two pennies to help pay for the record player. Collin and I brought the record player home and listened to our new records. Liz came in and said she wanted to use the record player. Collin said, "no, not until we are finished."

She went and got dad. He came into our room and said, "I hear that Liz helped pay for the record player?"

"Yes, she gave us two cents."

"If she helped pay for it, she gets to use it half the time."

Collin and I sat there with our mouths open. This wasn't fair, but I knew we couldn't argue with dad, he would get mad, then want to hit us. We gave up our record player to Liz. I started to hate her for all the things she did—she was always telling on me, and getting me in trouble. I wanted her to go away from this place and leave me alone.

The other money I made, I was saving for what I called the big get away. I really thought that if I could live in the mountains the rest of my life I would be fine, no school, no rules, and no adults trying to tell me what to do. Demons didn't live in the mountains I thought and I would be safe up there. The only thing that concerned me was how am I going to find a wife? I thought I would come down to the city in a few years and pick one out, and take her back to live with me. I would find a woman who would love to live in a log cabin with a big fireplace. She could wake up every morning to either a sun filled meadow or crystal mounds of snow. It would be a life many women would die for, and if I had children, they would be safe with me. There would be no bad men or demons around to hurt them. It was my dream and I was on my way to having it come true.

CHAPTER THIRTEEN

"Ever since we have opened camp three on the side of Cultas Mountain we have experienced many unexplained problems. The men talk among themselves about the Indian legend. To me it is hogwash, but I do ask that any new workers you send be from Seattle."

Company memo from William Smith to
Company headquarters.
May 1911

In a small town, sometimes you get bored. That was the way it was in Clear Lake. I wonder if anyone can tell me why kids find the dumbest things to do when they're bored. One hot morning I was staying at Jimmy Barret's house and we decided we were bored. There could be a thousand different things to do but it was easy to be bored. We went down by the hill that overlooks the highway. We were sitting under a big old fir tree, watching cars go by. I picked up a pinecone and threw it at a car.

Jimmy and his brothers picked up a few pinecones and threw them at cars also. It was fun. It was like being in a shooting gallery. I didn't think the pinecones could hurt anything, because they were light and soft. No one who was driving could see where the pinecones were coming from.

One car was moving slowly as it came into Clear Lake and we all started throwing pinecones at it. The car sped up and swerved to the right and went in the ditch. We all looked at each other and started running. Jimmy and his brothers ran to their house, and I ran for mine. When I got home my mom asked why I was running so fast. I told her it was to get in shape.

About thirty minutes later I was watching television and mom asked why there were two sheriff cars pulling up into our driveway? I said, "I don't know."

I was lying. I was afraid I had caused someone to crash and die—it wasn't going to be my summer.

The sheriffs came to the front door and my mom answered it. I heard them asking for me. "Is Luke at home Mrs. Mills?"

"Yes. Is he in trouble?"

"He is one of four boys that were throwing pine cones at cars on the highway. They may have caused an older lady to have a heart attack. She crashed her car in the ditch and she has been taken to the hospital."

I could see my mom's eyes filling with anger. I could hear her voice start to rise as she yelled for me. "Luke, get your butt over here! Now!"

I thought, this is it, go to jail, do not pass go, and do not collect 200 dollars, go straight to jail, but this time it wasn't a game. I came to the door and looked in the cars parked in the driveway. In the front car were Jimmy, Ben, and Ricky, and I knew I was going to be in one also. I walked out to the back car, and the sheriff opened the back door and told me to get in. He, along with the other officers, took us down to see the car in the ditch. They had us all get out and look. One of them said, "I hope you boys are proud of yourselves, you could have killed someone with the prank you were playing."

I was feeling bad, because I never thought anyone would get hurt. Ben had a smirk on his face for he was proud. He asked if the old lady had died or not? I was thinking that he had better not make the sheriff mad. I knew what the sheriff was looking for—remorse. I spoke up, "sheriff sir, we are terribly sorry for what we have done."

"Sorry isn't going to be enough to make up for the damage that has been done." I knew I had heard those words before.

The sheriff had us all get back in the car and he drove us down to his office in Mount Vernon. He took us on a tour of the jail, I thought he was showing us where we were going to be living for the next few years. He took us back to his office and sat us down and lectured us on how if we kept doing little bad things it would lead to bigger and bigger things. Then we would be put in the biggest jail in the state.

I was scared, so was Jimmy, but Ben and Ricky were dazing off into space. The sheriff told us to go back out to the car and get in. I didn't know what was happening. I thought he was going to take us to the big jail.

When he started driving he headed towards Sedro Woolley. I knew that he thought we were crazy, and he was going to drop us off up at Northern State Mental Hospital. I had heard that some people who did bad things were crazy, and couldn't help themselves. People that I knew who went to church said that people who did bad things were demon possessed, and so were the people up at Northern State Hospital. A lot of people around town worked there, some as nurses and others as tough guys that kept the people in line. Those people always made comments that the patients at the hospital were demons.

I remembered some of the people I'd seen when we went there to play our little league baseball games as entertainment for the patients. They would stand behind the fence, that kept them in, and watch us. Some of them were really scary looking. The women were kept on one side of the fence and the men on the other. Once when we were playing a game up there we saw a man and a woman having sex through the fence, and every once in a while a man or woman would show us kids their private parts when they thought no adults were looking. I thought they should put a fence around Clear Lake, because these people were no different from the people I knew. The scariest part was that the people in Clear Lake were allowed to have kids.

I wasn't looking forward to being sent to Northern State. Besides, it was up there that they would put wires on people's heads and give them shocks to heal their brains. I knew better. I had once tried to cook a hotdog using electricity. I took wires and hooked them up to nails and put a hotdog on the nails. When I plugged in the wires, the hotdog fried, so how could it not fry a brain? I was hoping our brains were not going to get fried.

When we were close to Sedro Woolley, the sheriff pulled in at United General Hospital. He told us we had to go in and tell the lady who crashed that we were sorry. Her name was Mrs. Hatfield. We walked into her room and she looked at us. She wasn't happy—for I could tell by the look on her face. We all said we were sorry and she lectured us awhile. She told us that we had better change our ways, or we would end up dying and going to hell. Ben and Ricky looked like they thought that was cool.

The sheriff told us to get back to the car. We got in and he took us back towards Clear Lake. He dropped the Barret boys off at their house and drove me to my house. Before I got out the sheriff said, "Luke, you have good parents, they care about you, not like those other boys. You should choose your friends better. I don't want to see you in trouble again or I will make sure you spend some time in jail."

I said, "yes sir."

I got out of the car, and the sheriff got out and talked to my mom and dad. I knew that once the sheriff was gone, I was going to get beat by my dad, I was an embarrassment to the family. When the sheriff left, dad told me to head out to the barn. I knew what was coming. I often imagined myself walking down death row as I made my way out to the barn, wondering if I would come back alive. I would try to get my mind set—ready for the lashes. I always tried to think of ways to avoid the pain.

Dad came out and took off his belt, for it was his favorite weapon of choice. I reached out to grab the rail post as he started swinging the leather down on my butt. I was going to try and not cry this time. I clenched my teeth every time I was hit. My arms tightened and my fingernails dug into the wood. I was thinking of the mountains, the meadows, the streams, high mountain lakes, there I would find peace. I smiled as he continued to swing his belt for I wasn't going to feel the pain. I knew I would never have to go through this again, because I was leaving home in a week. When he was finished he told me I was grounded for the rest of the summer, and I couldn't see the Barret boys until school started. I stayed in the barn until he was gone. I started talking to the chickens.

Because of the hot weather, they weren't laying any eggs. I decided that since they weren't laying eggs, they should be executed. I went to the house and got my 22-caliber rifle. I went back to the barn and held a trial. All the chickens were found guilty of crimes against mankind for not giving enough food, so I shot every one of them.

I pretended they were bad people in town, I pretended one was my dad. I don't know what possessed me—there were over twenty chickens lying on the ground all without life. I started to cry—I fell on my knees and sobbed and sobbed for the longest time. What had I become? I knew I was one of the worst persons in the town of Clear Lake. I was following in the steps of those before me. I was a demon, maybe even the devil. I had lost the fight with them, they had me, and I didn't even know it until now. I was evil, just plain evil, and there was no hope for me. I knew it was best for me to leave town and live in the mountains where I couldn't hurt anyone anymore.

Both Kenny and I were ready to go. We had done our shopping and had everything we needed. My backpack was full and heavy. It was a sunny morning when we left. I had my bow and arrows, my shotgun, and my rifle. I am sure we looked really funny walking out of town. We followed the creek up the mountain. It took us all day, but we reached paradise. It was a place called Split Rock. On the south side of the big split rock was a big meadow with nine ponds and a small stream running from pond to pond. On the north side was a big cave. We built our cabin right by the mouth of it. No one would be able to find us because it was the perfect place. The creeks were full of fish and animals were everywhere. The mountain was covered with berries and wild roots to eat. I knew, from reading, which roots were good and bad. My grandfather had taught me about berries—he gave me a simple rule to follow. White berries never, red berries sometimes, and blue or black berries always. I knew we would never starve to death.

It was exciting being in the mountains. If we wanted to we could walk about three miles and see the whole valley. We could look right down on the town of Clear Lake, 4000 feet below. During the next week we built our cabin and fished and picked berries. When it was warm enough, we swam in one of the ponds. Kenny and I explored all over the mountain. We saw deer, elk, and bear. One day I was out looking for a place to pan for gold. I thought if I found some gold, I could take it down to town and get some supplies when spring came. As I was walking a small stream, I felt that something was watching me. I turned around to find a cougar had been stalking me. I had always loved cougars. They were animals that lived by themselves. They were strong, full of courage, smart, independent, everything I wanted to be. I didn't want to kill him but I was glad I had my rifle with me. I was hoping that shooting close to him would scare him off. I raised my gun towards him and squeezed off a round. The blast scared him and he ran off. From then on I always watched for any sign of cougars in the area, I didn't want to become their dinner.

At night Kenny and I would sit by a warm fire and talk about life, and girls, and our parents. I knew we both were homesick, but neither one of us wanted to back out of the deal we had made. Sometimes, I walked up to the top of the mountain before sunset. From the top of Cultas Mountain you could see all the islands in Puget Sound.

On a clear night you could look south and see the lights of Seattle, you could look north and see the lights of Vancouver and to the west, Victoria. The sunsets were beautiful for there were so many colors. As the night grew dark and the stars came out, the house lights would materialize from every city, town, and the countryside.

I would sit there and wonder what was going on in every home? Were the people laughing? Were they crying? Was there love or hate? What kind of shows were they watching on television? I would see everything in my mind as I looked at the lights.

Up on the mountain, not a sound could be heard. It was silence—complete silence. It was a neat feeling to experience. It was one of the only times you could actually hear lonely. My heart would want to reach out to every child that was hurting that night and make it safe for them. For everyone that was crying, I wanted to dry their tears with the warm summer wind. Watching this would give me a powerful sense that I was meant to be a great healer in the land. How could I help when I was such an evil person?

Have you ever heard the sound of lonely?

Sitting by yourself on a mountain top.

Seeing millions of hurting people below.

Wanting to reach out and make their tears stop.

Listening, but hearing only the silence grow.

I never knew it could be so quiet on the earth. The stars would come out and I would watch them awhile. Some would fall towards the earth. As the night drew on, lights would slowly go off in the valley. There were always a few lights left on in Clear Lake. I would wonder what my parents were thinking. Did they miss me? Would they ever want me back home? Did my brother and sister miss me? I would pray that every thing was OK with them. I would go back to the cabin and fall asleep. I spent three weeks up on the mountain with Kenny. We had so much fun, I knew I could live that way for the rest of my life, as long as I found a girl to share it with me.

I finished setting my trap line; it was very hard work. I chopped some wood and sat down to cook up something to eat. Kenny wasn't his usual self. I asked him what was wrong. He said he thought maybe we should go back home, he was missing his mom and dad very much. I told him I knew the feeling. I was trying to understand how we could miss people that didn't treat us right all the time? The love of a child for his parents is a powerful emotion. Kenny's dad was a nice man, but when he became mad he would beat Kenny. It was the same with my dad, but I still missed him. I missed clean clothes, and someone doing my cooking. I missed my friends. I told Kenny we would pack up and head back in the morning. Thoughts ran through my mind, what was going to happen when we got home? I knew I was going to be beat, but it didn't change my mind, I knew I'd get over my punishment.

I went to bed and fell asleep. Some time during the night I started to dream. I dreamt that I was running through the forest, being chased by a big old bear. I was running, as fast as I could, but every time I thought I was getting ahead my feet would slow way down. The teeth of the bear would be right at my back. I would speed up enough for the bear to miss me. I was thinking of turning and facing the bear, thinking maybe he would stop, but I kept running. I ran for miles until I came to a very large crevice that was a thousand feet deep. I knew the bear was going to get me if I didn't find away across it. There was an old log across the crevice but I knew it would break if I walked on it. I looked back and could see the bear coming towards me. I looked across the crevice and saw Marie on the other side. She was dressed in white and looking at me. I yelled for Marie to help me. She smiled and said, "just fly Luke, just fly."

I yelled at her, telling her that she knew I couldn't fly. She smiled and said, "yes you can."

She started to fly towards me and when she was close to me she said, "Luke, take my hand.

As she took my hand I began to fly with her. The bear ran and jumped to get us but missed and fell into the crevice to its death. Marie put me back down on the side of the crevice I had been on, but I said I wanted to be on the side she was on. She said, "not yet Luke, you have lots of things left to do. It's not time for you to be with me. Now get your things and go back home."

I watched as she flew away into the sky towards the sun. I screamed for her to come back.

"Luke! Wake up! You're having a bad dream!"

It was Kenny yelling at me to wake up. I must have been talking in my sleep as I often did when I dreamed. When my eyes opened the dream seemed so real I could remember everything.

Late the next morning, Kenny and I made our way back towards Clear Lake. It was dark when we finally made it back to the edge of town. I liked it that way because I didn't want to talk to anybody before I got home. At the highway Kenny started off to his house and I started walking up the hill to mine. When I got close I could see my mom and dad sitting in the living room watching television. I went to the back door, put my things down, and walked inside. I went straight to the living room and said, "hi mom, hi dad."

They didn't look surprised at all. Dad asked, "did you run out of food?"

"No, why do you ask that?"

"Because we knew where you were the whole time, we were wondering how much longer it would be before you came home."

"How did you know where I was?"

"Everyone in town saw you and Kenny headed up into the mountains. The Forest Ranger saw some smoke one day and went to check it out and he saw you and Kenny. He called us and we told him to leave you there until you decided to come home."

"So you knew where we were all along?"

"Yes. We knew you would be back when it started to get colder at night. Both the Suttons and us knew that you and Kenny would be OK up there alone. We thought it best to let you work out whatever was in your system."

"Am I going to get a whipping?"

"No, I think you learned your lesson, I know it wasn't that easy to live on that mountain for three weeks. I think that's almost better than school. I am sure you learned a lot."

I was surprised, because I'd been prepared for anger, and a beating, and being grounded. I went into my bedroom and said hi to Collin. He was reading and didn't pay any attention to me. I put my things away and went and took a long, hot shower. It was nice to feel warm water running over my body for I was glad to be home.

The next day I made my way around town to see everyone I hadn't seen in a few weeks. It didn't feel like I'd been gone at all, every thing was the same except some new people had moved into the house next to the old church on the highway.

As I was walking down to Meekers store to get something to eat one day, I saw two girls sitting on the front porch of the house by the old church. I stopped and leaned over the fence and said, "hi. My name is Luke. I thought I would welcome you to Clear Lake."

They were doing girl things giggling and laughing, and they blushed as I talked to them. I wondered if they thought I was a little strange. They looked like sisters, but one was blonde and one brunette. I stood there, waiting for them to respond, but they got up and went in the house. I thought that wasn't nice. I wondered if there was something wrong with the way I looked. I walked to Meekers and looked at my reflection in the window—I thought I looked fine. I didn't know why the new girls wouldn't talk to me, but I told my self I would have them talking to me by the time Christmas came.

I decided to meet again with the Sather sisters. I wanted to know if anything had changed in the way they did things. I told my dad I was spending the night at a friend's house. He said, "OK, be home by Saturday at noon to help with some wood cutting."

All day at school I was really excited about the thought of learning something new this weekend. That night I went down to the old burner and waited for people to show up. When people started to show up I was watching every thing and every one, trying to figure out what was going to happen. For the next hour, there was a lot of chatter as many different people arrived. I was sitting listening to what people were saying. A bunch of people took what appeared to be their places around the burner.

They started speaking in strange words and calling on Satan to come fill the place. A weird feeling came across the area; it was like a very strong powerful feeling. After a few minutes a man asked for people that were having problems with other people. I perked up, this is what I was looking for, the power to deal with other people. I watched as a few people came forward towards the circle. One lady spoke up and said that she was having trouble with her boss and wanted her boss to become sick. The man in charge started speaking and calling up Satan to bring sickness to that lady's boss. I thought that wasn't nice, but maybe I didn't understand the whole situation. Others came forward and said things about people that they were having problems with. The man in charge cursed them all. I didn't like it all that much. Then the man asked if anyone wanted to have the help of Satan to bring prosperity. It seemed everyone came forward and told him how rich they wanted to be and the things they wanted to have.

I was thinking, who do they think Satan is? Santa Claus? I was laughing to myself. After all that was done, the man evoked someone named Iris. I was thinking I had never heard that name before. As I watched, everyone started taking off their clothes. I thought to myself—here we go again. The next thing I knew, every one was having sex with each other. I was watching and getting somewhat excited by what I was seeing.

A lady came up to me and started to touch me all over. I was watching her and she looked nice. She unzipped my pants and started to touch my penis. Shirley came over and started to watch. I was feeling uneasy about things but I didn't try to stop her. She asked if I wanted to have sex with her? I said, "not really, I have never done that before."

She said, "OK," and continued to touch me. When it was over she got up and went on to another. I had never felt that way before in my life. I liked it and wanted more I knew for sure. The meeting ended late in the night.

I didn't know what to think of everything I had done and seen, and I knew that I was changing inside and I was having mixed feelings about that. What happened to me made me feel good and I wanted more. I wished the lady that was doing things to me had been someone I loved. I wanted to know the full power of what those people thought that they had. I was determined to find the truth out for myself. I wanted to know more about sex and why it made me feel the way it did. I had felt the power that it gave me and I wanted to learn how I could control it. I was thinking of those things as I drifted off to sleep.

Sometime during the night I started to dream that I was in a boat drifting on the Skagit River. It was nice and sunny and the water was clear and warm. The salmon were running up the river to spawn, and eagles were gathering to feast on them. The river was nice and calm and I wanted to get out of the boat to swim. I thought it would feel so good to be in warm water. I took off my clothes and jumped out of the boat.

Every thing was going fine and it was a nice feeling being in the water. I was swimming back towards the boat when I started to feel the pull of the river. The current began to move faster and faster, getting rougher and forming whirlpools. I was trying to fight against the current but I wasn't strong enough for my arms wouldn't work. A whirlpool sucked me down and I started to be consumed by the salmon. They were biting at me and tearing the flesh from my bones. I was screaming for them to stop but my mouth was becoming full of water. I was drowning and I started to yell for help. I can't breathe—I am being consumed. A large eagle flew over and picked me up out of the water and brought me to shore. I thought I was safe but the eagles turned into demon birds and started picking at my flesh. I tried to run but my feet were not working. The demon birds were consuming my flesh and I was slowly disappearing. I started to scream for help but the birds had consumed my voice. I am dying.

I woke up and I was sweating so much my bed was wet. I sat up in my bed and was trying to figure out what my dream had meant. It was confusing to me. I didn't like the idea of being consumed by anything. I was trying to figure out why I had such weird dreams. I decided that I would find a book on the subject of dreams and try to learn what my dreams were saying. I figured if I knew what they meant, I could better control my life and those things around me. Maybe I could end up helping everyone that needed my help.

I never discussed with my friends at school what I believed or what I was doing. I didn't think they would understand. I was becoming a good friend with three other boys. It was the first time in my life that I was hanging around with the same kids.

Paul was becoming my best friend. He lived by Big Lake about ten miles south of my place. Rick lived up river near Concrete, and Kevin lived in the town of Sedro Woolley. What draws certain kids together? None of us had anything in common except that we all liked girls. I loved sports but the other three didn't play any sports. During every break we would hang out together and talk about many things, but never anything important. They seemed to like me for who I was, not because of what I had, or any of that popular stuff. It was a very nice feeling.

One afternoon on the way home from school, the bus was arriving in Clear Lake and I noticed a few sheriff cars at Hank Clossan's house. He was a few years younger than me and was always in trouble. I got off the bus in front of Meekers store and wandered down towards

Hank's house. A few people were standing around so I asked one of them what happened? He told me that Mr. Clossan had shot his wife with a shotgun. I asked if she was still alive? He said yes, then walked away. I saw Lenny standing over in front of the school. I walked over to talk to him because he was a cousin of Hank. I asked, "do you know what happened?"

"Yes, the bitch got shot. She was having sex with all the men down at Ellens."

"Well, is she alive?"

"Yes, Mr. Clossan didn't want to kill her, he wanted to make it so she could never have sex again, so he shot her in her crotch."

I was thinking, what an evil man—what would make a person do such a thing to someone they were supposed to love? Only demons I thought. Lenny went on to tell me the whole story.

"Yep, Mr. and Mrs. Clossan like to have sex with as many people as they can. I heard him and my dad talking about all the women they had been screwing. Mr. Clossan liked to watch his wife do it with other men. I guess she liked it so much that she started having sex with other men when Mr. Clossan was at work. He didn't like that at all, so he came home and showed that bitch he meant business. Yep, he shot her where it counts."

Lenny was laughing as he was telling me this. I thought it wasn't a funny matter. I looked into Lenny's eyes and saw he was enjoying all of what happened. I felt sorry for the woman that would someday be his wife.

I felt sorry for Hank, his mom was going to the hospital, and his dad was going to jail. He went to live with Lenny and I knew that wasn't such a great place to go live. My parents and Lenny's parents were together all the time. Lenny's parents were from a different world. Lenny's mom wasn't his real mom; she was a step mom. I don't think she liked Lenny all that much. Lenny was drinking a lot and was drunk most of the time when I saw him in town, but his mom and dad didn't seem to care all that much. I was glad that my dad and mom never wanted me to drink or do drugs, I knew that they cared for me. I never liked going over to Lenny's place after one time I had to stay the night over there.

I never understood why I was sent there to spend the night. My mom and dad weren't going anywhere but they told me I had to stay over at Lenny's house. There were demons in that house and I was having trouble sleeping, so I got up to go to the bathroom. I couldn't find the bathroom so I decided I would go outside, I always liked peeing outside, it was like being totally free. I heard noises' coming from the barn like something was trying to get the cows, so I thought I would go see what was happening. I thought that maybe someone was trying to steal some of the calves or chickens. I was walking slowly and moving softly so I couldn't be heard. I stopped at the door and peered through the crack.

Someone was after the calves' all right, Lenny's dad was standing in the calf pen with his pants down and a calf was sucking on his penis. I turned and ran for the house hoping that no one had noticed I had wandered outside. I was afraid he would come after me if he knew what I had seen. I knew for sure that Lenny's parents were from another planet. I didn't sleep the rest of the night; I was afraid that maybe I was next, and I was thinking of how I could get back out of the house and not get caught. It seemed that the night took forever. It seemed like a full year before light started coming in the window. I heard some noise downstairs and got up to tell them I was going home. I didn't see anyone so I walked out the door and made my way home.

As I walked I wondered what made men want to do things to animals when they had a perfectly good wife at home? I couldn't understand how anyone could get excited enough to have any kind of sex with an animal. I thought the best thing we could do for such people were to shoot them. I knew for sure that demons had taken total control of the lives of so many people in Clear Lake. I wanted sex, but with girls, not animals.

I continued on towards home, walking past the white witch's house. She was outside, working in her yard. She glared at me as I walked by. I walked on past towards Meekers store. The new girls were both sitting on their front porch again and I stopped and said, "hi." They started laughing again, I thought maybe I had something on my face, I smiled and asked, "where are you girls from?"

The oldest one, she was blonde, said, "we are from the Big Lake area."

"Do you like it here in Clear Lake?"

"It's OK, nothing special." I was thinking well now you met me and I am special. I asked, "do you girls ever leave your house?"

"No, our dad says we can't go outside of the yard. If we do, we will get in trouble."

I was thinking it was good that their dad didn't let them leave the yard. Sometimes bad things happened in Clear Lake and it was safest to stay home. The demons wouldn't be able to get them in their house with their parent's home. I didn't want to wear out my welcome so I told them it was nice talking to them and walked on towards home.

CHAPTER FOURTEEN

"One of the objectives of the Woman's Society is to make sure that the Clear Lake cemetery be kept in good condition. For this purpose we will raise funds to hire men to keep the grass down and the trees pruned."

Charter for the Woman's Society
May 1903

I was going over to the Clarks house a lot. So was my dad's first cousin, Dave Davis. He liked Sis and wanted to date her. She was ten years younger than he was and she didn't want to have anything to do with him. He didn't have a job and he was over there all day. He had two daughters and a son, Karen was my age, Trisha was three years younger, and the boy was a year younger than I was. They lived more with their grandma and grandpa than they did with their dad. Karen was a real big girl, and every one teased her. She would eat all day. I tried to be friends with her but she told me she hated boys and men. I never asked why their mom left—it seemed to be a common occurrence in Clear Lake.

A lot of people in Clear Lake seemed unhappy, I wondered why they didn't see how great life was, living in such a great place was reason enough to enjoy everything. I wanted to learn how to help people, then maybe everyone would truly be happy.

I was still thinking that my life was the best in the world, living and growing up around Clear Lake couldn't be matched anywhere else. I believed that if people would think like I did, they would be happy also, life was so wonderful and free. After school I would go exploring up on the hills, and walk the streams, looking at how beautiful nature was. I thought that no matter where I live in my life, I wanted my backyard to mirror the mountains that surrounded Clear Lake. I would dream of being a football player for the San Francisco forty-niners. I would come and build a house on top of Cultas Mountain, and I would have big dinners for everyone that wanted to come visit me.

On Saturdays and Sundays I would go down to the schoolyard and play tackle football with all of the older high school kids. It was great fun for we would play four to five hours. Our parents told us we had to play flag football, but we never listened to them, it was much more fun playing the game the way it was meant to be played. Every once in a while someone would get hurt, we didn't have any gear to protect ourselves. One afternoon three boys had to go to the hospital, one of them in an ambulance. For a few weeks after that, we switched to flag football.

When I wasn't playing football, I hung out with Scott and another friend Dean Dardal. We would hunt up on the hill with our bows and arrows for grouse and deer.

We explored the rocks, and looked for old cabins in the mountains. It was always fun to find old things that people had left behind. Sometimes when we left Dean's house to play in the forest, Scott would stay behind; he acted like he didn't want to hang out with us. After a few weeks of not wanting to hang out with us, he stopped playing with us.

Scott lived up the road from my house and he wasn't riding the bus to school in the mornings anymore. I was wondering what was going on with him? His dad had died a couple of years back in a chemical accident, so I knew he was a sad kid. He had an older brother who was always in trouble and two sisters who were very nasty. I noticed that Dean's mom was picking up Scott in the morning and driving him to school, I thought that was nice of her. She was picking him up after school. He started sitting real close to her in her truck, it only took us a couple of weeks to figure out what was going on between the two of them, even though she was in her mid thirties and Scott was only 13. The demons had claimed another one of my friends. I needed to find these demons and stop them before they had everyone.

I tried to figure out what an older woman with three kids could see in a young boy the age of her oldest son? I wondered what Dean's dad thought, if he even knew. I didn't see how he couldn't know—everyone in town could see what was going on. It wasn't long before it was the talk of the whole town. To me it was a sad thing. Dean was never the same after that. He started taking drugs and drinking a lot. I felt sorry for him. I didn't know how it would feel to have a good friend of mine having sex with my mom. It made Scott grow up fast. I always wondered what Scott's mom would think about an older woman pursuing her son? After that fall, I didn't see Scott or Dean much, as with most of my friends, they faded off.

The grass in the cemetery lawn had almost stopped growing. It would only need mowing a few more times. Sometimes there would only be two or three of us mowing the lawn. A lot of the scouts didn't like how much work it took to keep the grass mowed. Whenever I mowed, I took time to stop and say hi to Sharon and Marie. Some of the others always thought I was crazy for doing that, but I knew that Sharon and Marie could hear me fine.

To help make time go faster when I was mowing I would read the headstones in the cemetery. It amazed me that so many people had died so young. Some families died at the same time. I wanted to know the story of the person beneath every stone. What were they like? What did they do? How did they die? I wished they could all come up from the dead and give me the answers I wanted. I thought that would be real power, the ability to talk to the dead. I remembered that the Sather girls came down to the cemetery sometimes, but I didn't know what for. I thought that the next time I saw them I would ask them if they could talk to the dead. I hoped that they could.

After mowing the lawn I headed down to the A-frame to see if I could find the Sather sisters. Nikki was down by the water as I walked up. She looked at me and said, "what are you doing down here?"

"I am looking for Shirley, have you seen her?"

"No, what do you want with her, she's been mad at you for a long time."

"Well, I didn't mean to make her mad at me. I don't like all this sex stuff with all these different people."

She laughed at me and stood up and said, "you don't know what you're missing Luke. Sex can be a great thing."

"Well, I would rather know if they can talk to the dead." Her eyes lit up.

"I can talk to the dead. I have an Ouja board at home and some of us get together to ask it questions and it tells us many things."

I didn't know whether to believe her or not, but I thought it was worth a try. "Do you think we could meet soon some night and talk to the dead people in the cemetery?"

"I don't see why not. I will tell some others and we can meet down there next Friday."

She left, taking the trail towards her house and I made my way up the trail towards the road. I was excited with the thought of being able to talk to the dead, because I thought I could find out every thing about Clear Lake.

Even though I knew lots of people, I felt as though I was a stranger to them all. No one really knew me. I would think those thoughts and get sad. When I was in those moods I would go sit and listen to the radio. Neil Young would be searching for a heart of gold, and Credence Clearwater Revival would be taking me up around the bend. It amazed me how music reflected my feelings about my life.

I felt sad as I walked home and turned on my music. Mom complained about the music I was listening to. "That music will ruin your mind."

I ignored her and she continued, "that music is full of hate and sex and things that are not good."

I replied, "yes I know, music is like life, it has good and bad all together."

Her concerns didn't make sense to me. Dad and mom had a record titled "May the Bird of Paradise Fly Up Your Nose." I thought, if that's not a violent thing, than I don't know what is. Why would anyone want a bird to fly up someone's nose? Maybe it was their music that was bad. I thought of having kids someday. Would I hate the music they would listen too? I decided I wouldn't.

It was Friday night and Nikki had told me to meet her and a few of her friends down at the cemetery at around eleven. I arrived a little early to take a look around. There were a few houses close to the cemetery, and the people that lived in them seemed a little weird. The house next to the cemetery was a big old white house. It was two floors high. The only one I ever saw come out of the house was a boy three years younger than me. His name was Ralph. He had told me that his dad didn't live at home, just his mom and him. Sometimes I would see something move inside the house that didn't look big enough to be Ralph or his mom. I would ask Ralph about it, but he would say I was seeing things. I thought that maybe it was a ghost or something like that.

I walked around the cemetery, looking at the head stones and waiting for Nikki to show up. It was a warm night and a few clouds were passing overhead. I heard the sound of a lone car on the highway as a dog barked in the distance. I found a place to sit and was waiting when I saw a light come on in the old white house. Someone was walking around in the bedroom; they came towards the window and stood behind the sheer curtain. The figure was small and looked like a girl. She stood there awhile like she was watching me. I knew she couldn't see me, but I started getting a creepy feeling, like she was piercing me with her eyes. I was thinking of moving closer to see better when I saw another figure in the room. It looked like Ralph's mom. Then the lights went out and I couldn't see a thing. I sat awhile longer, trying to figure out what I had seen. Maybe it was a ghost or even a demon. I didn't know for sure.

I heard a few people walking down the road towards me. It was Nikki and Shirley and a few other girls. There were no boys with them, but I didn't mind, I liked the idea of me being the only male there. Nikki walked up to me and said, "hi."

She sat down and said, "this looks like as good a place as any."

We were sitting under one of the big Douglas firs that were in the middle of the cemetery. She opened a long box and pulled out a game board. It was different from any game board I had ever seen. I smiled and said, "I want to talk to the dead, not play chutes and ladders."

Nikki smiled back and said, "just watch."

She put a hockey-like puck on the board and told me and Shirley and Michelle to put one hand each on the puck and to think hard and clear our minds. A weird feeling came over me. Nikki told me to ask a question, so I asked if anyone that was dead could hear us? The puck slowly started to move under our hands to the side of the board that had the word "Yes" written on it. I knew that my hand had not moved it.

I was getting really excited about what was happening. Shirley asked the next question. She asked whom we were talking too? The puck started moving from letter to letter, spelling out the name Victoria. Shirley asked Victoria how old she was when she died? She told us she was 13. I asked, "how did you die at so young an age?"

The puck moved and spelled out murder. We all looked at each other. Michelle asked if we were in danger? Victoria said yes. Michelle asked what kind of danger?

The puck moved and spelled out "Church man." I was trying to figure out, what was a churchman? Nikki said to everyone, "we came here so Luke could get some questions answered. So let him ask the questions."

I thought for a bit and asked, "how were you killed Victoria?"

The puck spelled out strangled. I asked, "Victoria, who did this to you?"

The puck started to move and the board started to shake as if the ground was moving underneath it. A few of the girls jumped back and I looked up to see a light coming toward us. The board flew up and landed a few feet from us. Someone was carrying a flashlight, walking towards us. I wondered if it was someone coming to join us? The large person was a man and he walked right up to us and said, "Nikki, I'm not going to let you do these things any more. Now get up! You're going home!"

It was Nikki's dad. Nikki got up off the ground and didn't say a thing. He said to us all, "you kids should be ashamed of yourselves for messing with the devil and evil things. You don't understand the power or the nature of Satan. This kind of thing will only lead you to early death. I would like to see you all in church Sunday morning. If you would like to come, you're welcome."

As he started to walk away Shirley yelled, "are you going to abuse your daughter now?"

He didn't even break stride. I knew he had heard, but he kept walking. Shirley yelled, "it's you who is going to burn in hell!"

I was upset that he had come and ruined our meeting; it seemed rather rude. Some of the other girls had taken off, and I figured they were afraid of being found out by their parents. Only Shirley and I were left. She said I should go to church on Sunday morning and ruin his meeting as he did ours. I thought it was a good idea. I asked Shirley if Nikki's dad abused her? She looked at me and laughed, saying, "no, I asked Nikki, and she says he doesn't. But I don't care, not letting someone do the things they want is abuse to me."

"Well I don't think it's very nice to say things about people that are not true."

"It doesn't matter what the truth is, he should have not come here and ruined our meeting."

"Well it still isn't nice to say."

"Shut up Luke! You're so stupid sometimes."

I walked away from her, I saw for the first time what she really was—a nasty, mean, demon filled girl. I wondered how she had become so mean? Why did she have such hate in her heart? What made her want to hurt people with the words she said? I wanted to get inside her brain to see if I could find the answers to my questions. Why couldn't she see the demons in her? I needed to find the head demon and destroy him to set my friends free.

As I was walking across the cemetery to go home I looked up and saw the girl standing in the window again. I stopped walking and stood and stared at her. I knew she could see me in the light of the moon shining around me. Once she saw that I was looking at her she ducked back down behind the curtains. I wondered who it was, and why I never saw her at school, and why Ralph didn't talk about her. I knew I wasn't seeing things. On my way home I was thinking that Victoria didn't like Nikki's dad coming around. Why else would the board shake, and fly through the air? Why would a man scare a dead person like that? I didn't understand.

That Sunday I went to the church on the hill. It was Sunday school. I thought a few of the people were kind of shocked to see me there. I sat down and listened to them sing some songs and listened to them talk to Jesus and God. They all got up and said it was time to go to our classes. I thought, how boring, just like regular school. I went with the kids the same age as me. When I got in the room I started to annoy everyone and talk out of turn to make the teacher mad. My teacher was a lady who I had seen around town. I wondered why she was teaching these kids about God; I had seen her doing some things that I knew were wrong. I thought I would have some fun with her. I asked her if she thought God was real? She said, "yes."

So I asked if she thought the bible was true? She said, "yes." I asked, "than why don't you believe it?"

She was taken back with my question and got a mad look on her face. She said, "what makes you think I don't believe the Bible?"

"Well, my mom says the bible says you shouldn't steal. And I saw you take a pack of gum from Meekers store one day without paying for it."

I was smiling, I had her, and she knew it. She didn't know what to say. Some of the kids were acting uneasy wiggling around in their chairs. "And besides that I know you're not supposed to cuss, and I hear you saying bad words all the time. I heard you tell Mrs. Johnson down at the beach that you wanted to be fucked good at least once. Now a church lady shouldn't talk like that."

With those words she was screaming mad. I could see that demons were in her. A few people came running and asked what the problem was? She said I was cussing in church so they asked me to leave. As I was walking out the door I turned to look at her and said, "you're just like me, the only difference is I know whom I serve and you don't."

It was the last day that the scouts had to mow the cemetery lawn. As usual, there were only three of us. We divided the lawn into thirds, and I think I got the largest third. I didn't mind because I liked mowing lawn. It was good exercise and I could sing and think about a lot of different things. I was mowing the east part of the cemetery and was almost finished when I saw the white witch walking towards us. I quickly moved to the far side of the cemetery, just in case I had to make a run for it. I watched her as she walked up to a few graves and placed a vase of flowers on one of them. Curiosity got the best of me, so I started walking towards her. I looked at her and smiled, and asked who she was leaving flowers for? She looked up at me and smiled. I was thinking—wow she can smile—the white witch can smile. She said to me, "I have seen you before around town. What is your name?"

"Luke Mills."

"I'm Nina, you're the boy that was being chased by those other bad boys aren't you? I hope you're not like them."

"I am not like them at all."

She smiled at me, and said, "you used to run by my house every time you had to go by, but now you don't, you must not be scared of me anymore."

"I was told that you eat little kids, that is why I ran past your house."

She laughed and said, "I hear that I do eat little kids. What do you think? Do I eat little kids?"

I looked her up and down and thought—she's a big woman she must be eating something to be that big. "Well, it looks like you eat very well, but I don't think you eat little kids."

She started to laugh again and I felt comfortable so I sat on the grass next to her. I loved the smell of fresh cut grass it was always so sweet. I asked, "who are these people that you're leaving flowers for?"

Her eyes turned to the mountains as she told me. "These are my parents. My dad died many years ago, and than my mom died soon after that."

I looked at the names and dates on the stones. They had lived a long time ago. Born all the way back in the 1800's. I asked, "where is your husband, buried?"

"I've never had a husband. My mom and dad used to fight all the time. I lived with them until they died; we lived in the same house I live in now. My mom never let any men come near me. When men came around, she would get the shotgun out and chase them off. Soon everyone knew that they were to leave me alone. Besides, I thought that if men were like my father I never wanted to have a husband."

I checked her eyes to make sure I wasn't upsetting her. I asked her what her dad was like?

"He drank all the time and would yell and fight with my mother. He would take after me with whips and hit me if I did something wrong. He would even chase other women and my mom would get so mad. All she would say to me is to stay away from men."

Her dad sounded like the demons had been in him also. I had to tell her that not all dads were like that. "My dad is nice. He may yell once in a while but I know he loves me. So not all men are like your dad."

She turned to look at me; I kept right on talking.

"Besides, I am going to be a man someday and I am not going to be like your dad. I am going to do everything right."

She smiled and got up and said, "it has been nice talking to you. Please do stop by my place sometime. I will show you all my flowers and plants. You seem like a nice boy. Please stay that way."

"OK I will, and I will come over sometime."

She walked towards her house. I thought how wrong I had been about her being a bad witch. I wondered why everyone called her the white witch, instead of calling her Nina. To me she seemed to be a different person than what I was taught from those in my community. I wondered how many other people had been labeled something bad, but didn't deserve it. I thought it was like people calling me retarded. I knew that I wasn't, but a lot of people thought I was. Nina and I had a lot in common. We both were labeled something we were not. I figured it was the people that others thought were nice, that might be the bad ones.

As I finished mowing the lawn I looked up to see the curtains in Ralph's house move. I couldn't see anyone but felt as though I was being watched. It gave me kind of a creepy feeling. My curiosity was starting to get the best of me. I wanted to know what or who was in the house with Ralph and his mom. I went over and knocked on the door, and Ralph's mom answered it. I said, "hi, I am here to see Ralph."

She looked me up and down and said, "he's busy right now. What's your name? I'll have him give you a call."

"My name is Luke—if he is busy can I brother you for a glass of water? I am really thirsty." I was trying to think of anything to get into her house and to find out what was upstairs.

"Wait right here and I will get you a glass of water."

I waited and she brought me a glass of water. She didn't invite me in. She wasn't friendly at all. I drank the water and told her thank you and headed off.

As I was walking back across the cemetery I looked up to see a girl standing in the window watching me. The minute she saw me looking at her, she disappeared. I went back to Ralph's house and knocked on the door again. Ralph's mom came and answered it and said, "I told you Ralph was busy!"

"I know, but do you know that there is a girl up in a bedroom in your house?"

Ralph's mom was getting really mad and uncomfortable with me being at their house.

"You're seeing things, now be gone, and don't come back again today. I will have Ralph call you."

I walked away wondering what that was all about. I knew I wasn't seeing things. I wandered back towards home, looking for something to do.

CHAPTER FIFTEEN

"We should consider giving the men some time off from our logging sites in order to evaluate our practices. In the last week I have lost six men to falling trees or flying cables. Please take the time to consider this."

Memo from camp three foreman William Smith
to Company Headquarters.
June 1911

"Mr. Smith, there will be no time off for the men or for any review of logging practices. Men are expendable, and time is short. If you feel that you cannot comply with this order you too can be replaced."

Memo from Company Headquarters to camp three
foreman William Smith.
June 1911

"We are sorry to announce the unexpected death of William Smith. He will be greatly missed."

Company News Letter
July 1911

That winter in Clear Lake the weather turned really cold. Everything was freezing, the lake, water pipes, and the roads. My dad was working a lot. He was gone most of the time. One morning, before school, I heard the fire alarm go off, I thought maybe someone's house was on fire. A few minutes later, our phone rang and mom answered it. Sometimes dad would call to tell us he was going to be a little late coming home from work. I was watching my mom as her face turned pale and she took off running for the door. I followed behind her, knowing something was wrong. She got outside and screamed, "dad was in a car accident!"

Our neighbor, Fred, came running over and told my mom to get in his car. I started to cry thinking my dad was dead. I thought it must have been Arlene, the town gossip, who called. Fred and my mom drove down towards the highway. Liz and I were crying and Collin was being his normal self for he didn't show much emotion. I didn't want my dad to be dead. I didn't want to be poor. I didn't want my mom to marry some guy that would be mean to my brother or sister or me. I was scared. I didn't feel like going to school, so Collin said we could stay home.

Fred came back and told us that our dad was hurt but that he would be OK. It didn't make me feel any better; I wanted him home.

Mom spent most of her time with him at the hospital, I thought she was so used to being there herself that it was like her second home. After a week dad came home, but he stayed in his bed for another week. It was nice having him home; I went into his room and told him that I missed him and that I was glad he was home and safe. He was back to work in a couple of weeks.

After the accident, my dad seemed to be a different man. He got a whole lot quieter and would hardly say a word to anyone. I wondered if he had seen God in his near death experience? I wished he would talk to me about things but he seemed to distance himself from all of us.

Maybe he was afraid that the demons wanted him dead. I didn't understand what was really going on.

I wanted to know about him, what it was like to grow up when he
was a boy, what he wanted out of life. I wanted to know things about my
dad before he died. I wanted him to give me answers to my problems,
and I wanted him to explain everything I was going to encounter in my
life. He didn't seem to know how to talk to me. I would look in his eyes
and saw that he was lonely. He hardly ever kissed my mom, and when he
did, it wasn't with the kind of passion I had seen others kiss with. I
thought when I was married I would kiss my wife with such passion
and fire that she would never want to kiss another. I would cherish and
adore her with every ounce of strength and love that I could ever have.
Maybe his dad never told him how to love. Maybe his dad didn't know
how to love my dad. Maybe his dad never showed him how to treat his
wife with love. Some men never learn those things. The demons loved
to keep people in the dark about such things.

Things were becoming clear in my mind. My time of innocence was
fading fast, as was my ignorance. By listening to the people around town
and the kids in school, I was fast learning what was right and wrong in
relationships between all kinds of people, yet I still believed most things
that people said. I did know that if you had knowledge you had power
and without knowledge you could get hurt. The goal in my life became
not to get hurt by anyone or anything. I still had much to learn as a
young boy.

In school everyone desires to be accepted. You want everyone to like
you, and to have your teachers like you. If your teachers like you, you
run the risk of being called a teachers pet. So in an effort to gain the
friendship of others I chose to be a pain to some of my teachers. It only
ended me up in trouble.

One day I didn't feel like doing my schoolwork. My teacher told me
to get started and I told her I would do it when I was good and ready.
That ended me up in the office. I was talking to a counselor and he

started asking me personal questions. It seemed odd to me that he wanted to know those things. Maybe the demons had him also. So I asked if he was a fucking pervert or what? That got me a three-day vacation from school.

When I got home dad was getting ready to leave for work. I walked into the kitchen and said, "dad, I said some bad things to a teacher today and I was kicked out of school for three days."

I was waiting for the beating and yelling to start, but he looked at me with cold eyes and said, "I don't have time to deal with this now. But in the morning you had better be up in the field digging drainage ditches. When I wake up after sleeping a while, I'll come out and talk to you."

I knew that I should be doing what he said. I was surprised he wasn't yelling. I didn't mind the thought of digging ditch all day. I thought I'd make it a game. I got up in the morning, had some cereal, and went out to dig the ditch. At about eleven, dad came walking out into the field. I looked at his face and saw he didn't have any anger in his eyes. He told me to sit down and asked, "what did you say?"

"I asked my counselor if he was a pervert. I mean a fucking pervert."

Dad took a deep puff off his cigarette and sat there looking at me. I was wondering what kind of punishment he was thinking of doing to me.

"Luke, I don't want to ever hear you tell someone those words again. For the next three days I expect to see every ditch in this field cleaned and dug out. You will learn if you don't go to school you will be digging ditches for the rest of your life."

I was thinking I had heard my dad say the F word many times. It didn't make any sense to me that he could say it and I got in trouble for saying it. He got up and walked back to the house.

I took the shovel and pick and continued digging. I would smile and think to myself that no one could dig ditch better than I could. I would make dams and let the water build up, then I would break the dam and pretend that the whole town was being washed away. In my mind I could hear people screaming and crying as the water washed them away. It kept me entertained the whole day. I thought it wouldn't be a horrible thing to be a ditch digger the rest of my life. At least I would be outside and not in some office or classroom.

When I returned to school everything was back too normal, my days were filled with laughing and talking with friends, hanging out, and playing sports, it was all great fun. I wanted to fit in and be popular, but I wasn't the best looking or the richest or the best at something. I wanted to draw attention to myself so people would notice me.

A lot of kids had tried to bring alcohol to school, but they had been caught. I tried to figure out how I could do it without being caught. My dad had whisky in the cabinet and my brother had hypodermic needles and syringes for his animals. One night I got some oranges, and using a syringe and a hypodermic needle, shot the whisky into the oranges. It worked really well. I filled twelve oranges full of whisky and put them in a bag.

The next day I took them to school. After lunch hour, when we were going into Mrs. Norbecks class, I handed out the oranges to a few kids and told them to taste them. They did and they were excited, they acted as if I was the coolest kid in school. They all sat in the back of the class and got drunk. I didn't have an orange; I had given them all away.

When the bell rang a couple of the kids were having a hard time walking out to the hall. We laughed as Mrs. Norbeck tried to figure out what was going on. She thought they were acting silly, so she told them to stop or she would go get Mr. Stiles. They said go ahead and started cussing at her. She went and got Mr. Stiles and he found a few of us in the hall. He was a smart man for he got close enough to them to smell their breath. He smelled the whisky and they told him I had brought it. It was a death sentence to me; I knew I would be kicked out of school again. I couldn't win. Mr. Stiles sent me home and dad sent me to the ditches.

I thought I was getting better at digging ditches than anyone in the whole world. A few more times of being kicked out of school and I would have enough ditch dug to reach around the world. I would take a radio up in the field and listen to music as I dug. Carol King would be singing "Sometimes you win, sometimes you lose. Sometimes the blues get a hold of you." Credence Clear Water Revival would be asking me if I had "ever seen the rain falling down on a sunny day?" I would always answer yes—I had seen the rain fall without a cloud in the sky. Rain would fall all the time. I would get thinking that I was so alone in the world. I was the only one who knew the truth about things and no one else cared. I would dig hard during the day, hoping that my father would come and see how much I had dug and be proud of me. It never happened. I figured he was too mad at the things I was doing to be kicked out of school.

When I got back to school things were the same. I had no new friends. I wondered why so many people only liked you awhile. I figured friends like that were not worth having. I would listen to kids talk about their friends. Some would say that this person or that person was worth knowing. Others would want to be friends with someone because of who their parents were or how they dressed. I thought, why couldn't someone want to be friends with someone simply because they were a nice person. It was strange to me. I liked my friends simply because they were nice, at least most of the time.

It was always fun when school was getting out. I would look forward to summer and the good times I was going to have. The only thing sad about school being out was you didn't see everyone.

I was looking forward to not having Liz around. My dad and mom had told Liz that since Collin and myself always made our own money for school clothes she would have to work this summer. It was about time she was treated like Collin and I. They found a baby-sitting job for her with my mom's cousin Joe in Seattle. Joe and his wife had a little boy age three, and both of them worked. I didn't know them all that well but

I didn't care, Liz was going to be gone for most of the summer and to me that was a good thing.

On the first day after school was out, mom and dad loaded Liz into the car and took her to Seattle. I smiled and waved good-bye to her as they left. I was free; she wouldn't be able to tattle on me from 60 miles away. She liked telling on me, and mom and dad usually believed every word she said. I was very happy she was gone.

Liz had been away for almost three weeks when she called one morning while both mom and dad were gone. I answered the phone, "hi."

"Luke this is Liz, is mom or dad there?" Her voice sounded a little strange. Maybe she did something wrong, I thought. "No, dad is at work and mom is shopping."

"I need to talk to them. I need to talk to them before Joe and Connie get home."

She had urgency in her voice, as if something was dreadfully wrong. I asked, "Liz is every thing OK?" She started to cry and sob; I felt bad for her.

"Liz, tell me what is going on."

"It's bad Luke, really bad." She hesitated for a minute, than in words full of tears she said, "Joe is doing weird things to me."

"What do you mean weird things? Is he hurting you? Hitting you?"

"No! He is touching me in my private areas."

"Well tell Connie, she will tell him to stop Liz."

"No, I can't, Connie knows. Joe begs Connie to let him fuck me every night. She says he can't fuck me, but that he can have me suck his penis, and touch me, and things like that, and he does. If he comes home before Connie, he brings his friends over to touch me also." Liz was too young to know the F word, and I was getting upset listening to her.

Anger was running through my blood. I couldn't believe what I was hearing. I had to do something to stop this. I had to get her away from those people controlled by the demons. My sister was only twelve years old. I had to get down there to save her, and kill those evil people. "Liz, do you ask Joe not to touch you?"

"Yes, and I cry, and he tells me to stop crying and enjoy it."

"Listen Liz, once mom and dad get home I'll tell them and we will come get you."

"Luke please don't hang up, I don't want to be alone here. Please don't hang up the phone."

"Liz I will make sure that you will be OK."

"Luke! Don't go!"

I said good bye to her and hung up the phone. I was mad. There were times I didn't like my sister, but I hated the thought of someone harming my little sister. There was no way I was going to let someone do those kinds of things to her. They had to pay for their crimes.

I met mom at the door when she came home and told her all that Liz had said. I told her that once dad got home we needed to drive to Seattle to get Liz. Mom didn't say much, I thought she was really upset with what was going on down in Seattle. When dad walked through the door, I told him that Joe was touching Liz and that Connie knew and approved and that we needed to go down and get Liz right away. I told dad that we should take the shotguns and if Joe gave us any problems we could shoot him. My dad looked at me kind of funny and said, "Luke shooting people never solved any problems." I knew better than that— the people whom I had shot never gave me any more problems. My problems with those people were resolved, it was pretty clear to me, but dad saw things differently. I said, "well we don't have to take the guns, we need to go get Liz before something bad happens."

Dad took a deep sigh and said, "it's all based on the word happen. I think, that Liz is scared and tired of working, and that she made this story up so she could get out of baby-sitting the rest of the summer, and nothing has happened."

I got mad and screamed, "damn it dad! We have to go get her!"

My dad reached out and slapped my face. I looked at him with anger. He said, "I will call down there. But don't you ever damn me again boy, or it will be the last time you damn someone!"

I was happy, I knew that when he talked to Liz we would be on our way to get her. I waited for dad to call there. He took his time getting cleaned up, we ate dinner, and then he finally called. I tried to listen to the conversation but could only hear bits and pieces of what dad was saying. Finally I heard him talking to Liz, and he told her to do a good job for Joe and Connie and told her she could come home at the end of summer as they had planned. I felt an angry emptiness as I asked, "why are we not going to go get Liz and bring her home? You and mom don't believe anything is happening? Do you?"

"No Luke, nothing is happening. So you had better stop talking about it now or you will be punished and sent to bed."

I couldn't understand what they were thinking? I knew Liz wasn't lying, I could tell by the way she cried that bad things were happening to her. I felt empty, I had promised her I would make sure she would be OK. I wished I were old enough to drive. I went to bed thinking of Liz and what she was going through. I felt bad for all the times I had been mean to her. I wished my mom and dad would believe that bad things could happen to children. Somehow the demons had blinded them so they could not see what was happening.

I fell asleep and started to dream that I heard some noise coming from our living room. I got up to see what it was and I heard crying and screaming. I turned down the hall so I could see into the living room and I saw my sister lying on the floor with my mom and dad and grandma and grandpa hitting and kicking her. I screamed for them to stop! They looked at me and turned into devils with horns coming out of their heads and slits of fire for their eyes and forked tongues. They hissed at me and started to come after me. I took off running out the door. I was running up to the Marks's house. I made it inside the Marks's porch and looked in the window at Mrs. Marks. She also was a devil. I took off running through Clear Lake. As I looked behind me all the people from the whole town were devils, chasing me. I started running for Sedro Woolley and I came to the bridge over the river. I started to go across and then I saw that there were some devils on the other side. I was trapped on the middle of the bridge—the devils are closing in on me—they are going to eat me. They're reaching for me, I fight, I am falling, and they have thrown me off the bridge. I am going to drown. I woke up screaming and breathing deeply.

The dream seemed so real, so I got out of bed and went to see if Liz was in her room or in the house, but she was still gone. It felt as I was being watched by something evil, it sent shivers up and down my spine. I looked around but no one was visible. I knew that the demons had been in my house making me dream bad things. I didn't like having these kinds of dreams, as they seemed to be getting more intense. I didn't know what to think of the things I was dreaming.

Every summer Clear Lake had many people moving into town and moving out. As I was walking through town I saw a moving truck in front of Nikki's house. She was standing outside watching the men load the truck. I went over and asked where she was going. She said they were moving to Oregon. I asked her why? She said her dad had a new job down there. She said that he didn't like this place and wanted to get as far away as possible. I told her that I hoped things would go well for her wherever she ended up. I said good-bye and headed off towards the swimming area.

When I arrived at the beach, the beach manager asked to talk to me. I wondered what he wanted? I was always good at the beach, always careful to stay out of trouble. He said, "Luke, I have been watching you for a few years now. You're a good kid and a very strong swimmer. I was wondering if you were interested in becoming a life guard?"

I was impressed with myself. I smiled and told him, "yes I would love to become a lifeguard."

He said, "you will start your training tomorrow morning at 11."

I was so excited I wanted to yell. Many kids wanted to be lifeguards, and I was the one that had been chosen.

Within two weeks I was life guarding down at the beach. It was like being God, you decided the rules and what you said had absolute power. If someone did something wrong you decided what kind of punishment they would have to serve. On the other hand, it was a big baby-sitting job. Mothers would drop off their kids and leave them for us lifeguards to watch all day. I had to be a mother, a father, a policeman, a doctor, and everything else these kids needed while their parents were gone. I treated every kid fair; I was the good shepherd. I would stand on the high life guard tower and watch the beach, the docks, and the water, knowing that the safety of all these children rested in my hands, and in my mind there was no one who could take better care of them than me. If only I could see the demons before they hurt the children, then I would be the best protector of all.

It was strange to me that once I became a life guard things changed for me. All the girls wanted to talk to me and hang out with me and I really enjoyed it. A few of the older guys were jealous and would try to cause me trouble, but I would remind them that if they wanted to stay in the swimming area they had to obey the rules, or they could leave. It kept them in line. It amazed me that someone would pay me to watch people swim.

On my breaks I would go swimming with a few of my friends. I was having the best summer of my life. My mom and dad were gone a lot and my brother was always working. It was like living alone and being able to do what I wanted, but at night, I didn't like being alone, I would be scared and would get out my shotgun and load it and keep it close. The loaded shotgun gave me courage and a feeling of power.

Some time in July some of the boys that were always drinking and taking drugs came into the swimming area and started causing trouble. I asked them nicely to behave and leave the other kids alone but they didn't listen. There were too many of them to fight so I went up and called the sheriff to come and remove them from the swimming area. When they found out that I had called the sheriff they all left. One of the kids walked over towards the A-frame to a point and started throwing rocks at me on the lifeguard stand. I then recognized him as the kid who had tried to drown me a couple of years before. I wondered why he still hated me so much. The sheriff took after him and he left running to hide in the woods. It didn't make any sense to me that people had to act like that. I knew that the demons in drink and drugs had them all.

I had been sitting in the sun too much all that week and I ended up being sick. I asked my brother if he would fill in for me at work so I could rest at home. It was sometime in the afternoon when I was in my room lying in bed when I heard a knock at the front door. Dad was home so he answered it and I heard him say, "Luke is in his room last door down the hall to the right."

I was thinking that one of my friends was coming to see me. I sat up in my bed and waited for whomever to come in my room. I looked up and saw the boy who was throwing rocks at me at the beach. The same kid whom had tried to drown me. He came towards me and said, "I am going to kill you."

He jumped at me with a knife and I wrestled him to the ground. I yelled for my dad and he came running into my room and watched as I struggled with the boy. I hit the boy a couple of times in the face, and my dad just stood and watched. He must have thought I could handle this boy on my own. The boy must have become scared and he jumped up and ran outside. I made it to the phone and called the sheriff and told them what was going on. I hung up the phone to find my dad outside talking to the boy. Dad came back inside and said everything would be ok. Then the boy stood on the street outside yelling obscenities and saying he was going to kill me someday. My dad didn't do anything to him. It was strange to me, because it was as though my dad was a friend with this boy. If the roles were changed with my father that boy wouldn't be able to walk anywhere—I would have beat him to death. No one would ever assault my kids and live to tell about it. He took off down the road and I was hoping the sheriff would hurry up and come get him. My dad seemed upset that I had called the sheriff.

It was about thirty minutes later that the sheriff came driving up to our house with the boy in the back seat of the car. The sheriff said he had found him peeing on my brother's car down at the beach and had arrested him. The sheriff asked a few questions and then took the boy to jail. I thought it was a fitting place for him.

The next day I felt better so I thought I would go for a run before I went to sit on the lifeguard stand all day. I was sure of myself and did not fear too much. I decided to run down on the trails that were by the lake. As I was running by the A-frame I ran into the boy who I thought had been taken to jail. I stopped and decided I didn't need to be down here. He saw me and started after me. I turned to face him and said, "I thought you went to jail yesterday?"

"I did, but my mom and dad got me out and dropped me off back here in Clear Lake."

"Why do you want to hurt me? I have never done anything to you?"

"You would be surprised to know who wants you dead." He said laughing. "I might tell you who wants you dead right before you take your last breath."

"The only one who wants me dead is you." I said shaking my head.

"Wrong you are—if you knew, it might kill you with just knowing." He was laughing harder and anger was starting to burn in my heart. The he said, "you interfered with me and my friends and I am going to kill you for that. Besides you think you that you are better than me—so I will show you who is better."

Well, he was right about that, I not only thought that I was better, I knew. He came at me and I could see his eyes were bloodshot from taking drugs. He looked like a demon. Maybe demons were in drugs just like whiskey. His ability to move was limited and it was easy to take him down. When we were wrestling some kind of drugs fell out of one of his pockets. He was still saying he was going to kill me. I grabbed the drugs that had fallen out his pocket and shoved them into his mouth. I put my hand over his mouth and waited for him to swallow. I got off him and said. "I hope you enjoy your drugs."

I got up and ran towards home. I figured he would be high awhile than be OK. I needed to get home and get ready for work.

Later that day as I was sitting on the life guard stand I saw a couple of sheriff cars parked next to the trail that lead to A-frame. I was wondering what was going on but didn't pay much attention. About an hour later Ben came up and said that someone had found a kid dead out by the A-frame from an overdose of drugs.

Fear struck my heart. What had I done? After a while I figured it was better him dead than him trying to kill me. It was better him to be dead so demons couldn't use him. Besides he should have not been taking drugs. I felt no real remorse for what I had done. It was my destiny to make things right and fair for people and to protect people, even myself.

It was August and mom and dad went and picked up Liz from Joe and Connie's place. When she got home I asked her how everything went. She said she never wanted to go back to that place. She said Joe was a creep, and so was his wife Connie. She started to cry and said, "you told me you were coming to get me Luke, and you never came."

I didn't know what to say. It was beyond my power to go and get her, and if I could have, I would have. I felt really bad and I wanted to make things right for her. I wondered how I could get back at Joe and Connie for what they had done to my sister. I thought of many things, I remembered that we would be having a family reunion at the end of summer and Joe and Connie would be there. I made my plans and went and talked to Collin. He agreed to help me take care of them.

The day of the reunion I got up early. I took a few things up to the frog pond, where I intended to trick Joe and Connie into walking into a trap. People started arriving at the house at about ten in the morning. It was nice to see all the family together. Joe and Connie were having a good time, laughing and talking to everyone. I saw him looking at my sister and I didn't like the way he was looking at her.

After dinner I started telling Joe and Connie about the neat things up in the forest. I told them that once I had seen a girl up there touching herself. I was trying to get him to ask me to take him up there and sex was my bait. I figured Joe and Connie were city people and didn't have a good sense about the woods, it would make it easy for me to do what I had to do. I knew I had made them both curious about the places I was talking about, finally they asked to see the frog pond area and I said I would be happy to show them everything up there. Collin saw me walking with Joe and Connie towards the road, he knew it was time to meet me at the frog pond. On the way up there, walking on the trail, I told them all about the woods, the names of the plants, the animals. I told them about Big Foot, and how he lived close by. I was trying to scare them a little.

We were almost to the frog pond and we had to walk through a vine maple thicket. I had set a snare and I was hoping Joe would walk right into it. He stepped in the loop that was hidden by leaves. My grandfather had taught me how to set snares. I had tried to catch animals in them but never got any. Now I finally had my first animal, and he was a big one. The rope wrapped around his leg and jerked him up towards the sky. Connie started to scream but I told her to shut up. Collin came up behind her and grabbed her and we tied her up and put tape on her mouth. Joe was screaming and cussing and saying he was going to kill us. I laughed and said, "I don't think you will be doing anything for sometime pervert."

He was hanging a few feet off the ground and trying to get loose. We tied him up and cut him down. We put him next to Connie and I walked up and kicked him in the groin. I said, "you treated my sister wrong and now you're going to have to pay for your crimes."

I told Collin to take the tape off their mouths and told them if they wanted to live they had better be quiet or the tape would go back on.

Connie was crying and Joe was begging to be let go. I looked at them and said, "my sister cried herself to sleep every night. She begged you not to touch her. She looked to you, Connie, to protect her, but you didn't. So shut up both of you!"

I was really getting angry and I could see that Collin was thinking I was getting out of control. I told Collin to take Joe's pants off. He did, and Collin and I threw Joe over an old downed log with his butt sticking up in the air. I took a baseball bat that I had taken up there earlier and walked in front of Connie and Joe so they could see it. I said, "so you think it's fun to screw little girls? Well we will see how fun it is when I take this baseball bat and shove it up your fat ass!"

Joe was crying, begging for mercy. I walked behind him and swung the bat down as hard as I could onto his butt. He let out a yell and I raised the bat and hit him again. It felt good. I was enjoying this. I hit him four times.

Collin was standing there looking scared—maybe he was thinking I had gone crazy. I said, "I told my sister I would come get her and save her, but my mom and dad wouldn't believe me. I hate you two for that."

I looked over at Connie as she was shaking and sobbing. I walked over to her and yelled, "now you know how Liz felt! Do you like it? Tell me bitch! Do you like it?

She was shaking her head no, and I looked her in the eyes and spit on her face. Collin said, "Luke, I think they have had enough, we should let them go now."

"No! Not yet—I am not finished."

Collin sat down and didn't say another word. I told Joe that I was going to leave him here all night so Big Foot could come have his way with him, I thought what I said was rather funny. I told Collin to get my gun out from behind the old hollow stump. Joe started screaming so I took the bat and hit him again hard and that shut him up. Collin brought me my gun and I told him to take Joe and put him by Connie. I told them, "I am not into raping people, I don't believe in rape so I won't shove this bat up your asses, but I do get a great feeling about shooting people and I think that is what I am going to do."

Fear came across their eyes. Joe started begging to be let go as he said he would never touch a child again. Connie was sobbing and shaking. I asked Joe, "how many kids have you touched?"

He didn't respond. Collin was getting really nervous for he didn't know what I was going to do. He asked, "you're not going to shoot them, are you Luke?"

"You bet your last dollar I am. I am going to shoot them right now!"

I took my gun and pointed it at Joe's head and pulled the trigger and said, "bang!"

I didn't have a shell in the chamber. Connie passed out and Joe was shaking violently. I was having great fun. I said, "thought you were going to die there didn't you?"

I let out a laugh, then I pulled out a knife and said, "I don't want to kill you that easy. I think I will cut your penis off and let you bleed to death."

I started waving my knife around by Joe's face. Connie had regained consciousness and I thought I had made my point, I knew I couldn't kill them and get away with it. I got right down in their faces and said in as mean a voice as I could, "I am going to let you two live, but if you tell anyone what I have done, I will hunt you down and I will, and I mean, I will kill you! Someday when you least expect it I will cut your throat or shoot you. So you keep it to yourselves. If you tell the sheriff, I will tell him every thing that you have done, so if I were you, I would keep my mouth shut. One more thing, I don't ever want to see you here again. I don't want to see you even close to me. If I do, I will kill you!"

Collin and I untied them and I gave both of them a couple of kicks and walked back on home. Everyone was too busy to notice we had been gone, and no one noticed that Joe and Connie were not around. About thirty minutes later, they came walking back into the yard. My

Uncle Ted said, "by the looks of you two, it looks like you've been having too much fun together."

Everyone around started to laugh; I looked at Joe and Connie and smiled. Everyone thought they were up having sex somewhere. They said they had to get going and I watched them get in their car and drive away. I never saw them again. I remember hearing my mom commenting on how Joe and Connie never came around any more. When I heard that I smiled to myself, never again would they hurt my sister.

I didn't think what I had done was wrong. I was getting lost in my mind; I was the one who would bring justice to this world. I felt as though I was superior to everyone. I knew it was a matter of time before I had all the demons chased out of Clear Lake. I was over six feet tall—I was athletic and strong. In my mind, there wasn't a thing I couldn't do or anyone I couldn't take. I didn't walk around and pick on people, but rather I was the defender of those who couldn't defend themselves. I felt like the king of Clear Lake.

On the first day of my freshman year, as I walked up the front steps of the school towards a group of seniors, one of them jabbed his coke can at me and splashed coke all over the front of my pants. There were seven boys standing there, laughing and making fun of me, saying I had wet my pants. I picked out the biggest kid, walked right up to him, and took my fist and smashed it against his nose. It shocked them all. I looked at them and said, "who is next?"

They all backed off and started to walk away. The football coach came running from across the street and yelled at me to get my attention. I thought I was in trouble. He came up to me and said, "I want to shake your hand. You're the fourth kid they poured coke on this morning, and you're the first to fight back. If you can hit like that on the field I want you on the football team. I expect to see you in the locker room this afternoon." I smiled, I wanted to play football and the coach had noticed me, it was going to be a great year.

CHAPTER SIXTEEN

"There seems to be two different groups of people in town. It is just hard to tell which people are in which group."

Journal of Victoria Southerland
December 1923

The church down town had a youth group that met every Sunday night. All the good-looking girls in town went to that church. I went to a meeting the second week of September. I think a lot of people were surprised to see me there, I was getting a reputation as being kind of a wild kid. The leaders of the youth group were horrified; they had heard from others about some of the activities I had been involved in. I wasn't there to cause complete trouble; I planned to slowly gain the trust of everyone. I wanted to know how their power compared to the power of others.

I started going every week and on my way I would stop and invite the Brooks girls. They always told me that their dad would never let them go to church. I didn't know why? I thought that every parent should be willing and happy if their kids wanted to go to church.

I had a big crush on Bev Brooks; she was a brunette with big blue eyes and a pretty smile. I would walk by her house, hoping she would be on her porch so we could talk. I knew she liked me because if she saw me coming she would run outside to talk to me. I would lean against her fence and sometimes talk for over an hour. Bev and I became an item of conversation around town.

After about two weeks of talking to her I asked, "Bev why don't you invite me into your yard to sit on your porch, or into your house?"

She put her head down and said, "my dad would get really mad, and he might hurt you or something like that."

I was thinking her dad sounded really strange. I asked, "why would your dad do something like that?"

"He doesn't like boys, he is afraid that boys are going to hurt us. And he drinks a lot and gets mad and hates everything. He even got his gun out once and shot the television because we were watching a show with a black man in it. We have to have dinner fixed for him when he gets home, that is why I always tell you I have to go in at four o'clock."

"But doesn't your mom cook dinner?"

"Yes, but we have to help, or we will get in trouble." Her house sounded more like a slave camp than a home to me. Her and her sisters should be out having fun not waiting on their dad all the time.

One day I was standing talking to Bev by the fence as her dad came driving home. He looked at me and looked really mad. He got out of his truck and slammed the door and yelled at Bev to get away from me. Something about him gave me the creeps. I could see that demons were in him also.

Bev would tell me when her and her sister would be baby-sitting so I could come over and visit them. It was the only way I could be with her and not have her dad get mad. They baby-sat often for the Veeringas, who lived down by the post office. I didn't know the Veeringas first names because they didn't live there very long.

One night when I went over there, Tam and Bev told me I had to hear one of the Veeringa's tapes. I asked what the tape was about? Bev said, "just listen."

They put the tape in and two women were talking about having some boy delivering groceries and they hoped he didn't forget the bananas. On the tape they ended up having sex with the bananas. I laughed for it did seem kind of funny and Tam and Bev were laughing also. They showed me stacks of girlie books and books on sexual positions; these people had everything. We put the books away and talked awhile and they told me I had better go before the people came home.

I went outside on the porch and Bev went with me. I took her in my arms and started kissing her. It felt so nice having her in my arms. I took my hand and reached up her shirt. She stopped kissing me back and looked into my eyes and said, "why do boys always want to do that?"

I didn't know what to say, so I said the first thing that came to my mind. "Because it's there."

I felt like a complete fool. She said we had to think about what we were doing before we went any further. Bev was the first girl I had made any sexual advance towards, I liked her, and something inside me wanted to do more than kiss her. On the way home I thought I would slow things down and show Bev that I loved her and she would want me to do more than kiss her.

I would go to youth group and listen to what the leaders said. I would argue and ask questions to challenge their faith. I wanted to see how far I could push them. The new preacher would sometimes come into the meetings and sit next to me. I was afraid of the man, and for what I didn't know. He seemed to like me and that bothered me. He should have hated me for trying to upset his people. It was strange to me. He would always treat me kindly, even when I would cuss. Nothing I cared to do would get the man upset at me.

I was falling in love with Bev. I was spending as much time with her as I possibly could. We went for a walk up on the mountain one afternoon. We were holding hands, talking and laughing. It was a wonderful day. My heart was rushing with excitement being with her. Songs were running through my mind as we walked up to the meadow overlooking the lake. I turned towards her and our lips met as we kissed passionately, holding each other tightly together. I looked into her eyes and could see that she had a love for me. We sat down in the sun and continued to kiss.

Our hearts were beating loud and I could feel my pulse when our hands would touch. My hands were exploring every thing about her. I had worked her pants down to her knees, when she looked at me with tears in her eyes and asked, "why do you boys always want to do that? Why can't you just kiss and hold me and not want to have sex with me?"

I was confused for I thought she wanted me to make love to her. I thought that was what people did when they were in love. "Bev, I don't want to hurt you, I want to show you how much I love you."

She started crying even more. I told her to pull her pants back up and tell me what was wrong. We sat in silence for over thirty minutes. She looked at me with tears falling, forming streams of sorrow down her face and said, "Luke, at night when my dad comes home from the tavern, he gets Tam—or me—or one of my other three sisters and takes us to the couch on the back porch. I never know when it's going to be my turn to go out to the porch."

I didn't know what to say. I started to cry with her. I understood what was happening. "Luke, my dad always tells me that he doesn't want to hurt me, he says he is showing me how much he loves me."

My heart sank a mile. I felt like running and throwing myself off the cliff. I was doing the very thing, to someone I loved, that I hated other men for doing. Here I thought I was being so loving, so kind. Yet to Bev, I was just another man doing things to her that were not of the loving kind. Inside I was mad at her dad for taking something so wonderful away from her. He had taken something that could never be replaced. I asked her if her mom knew what her dad did?

"Yes, she does, and she comes and comforts us after dad is done. She says she wishes she could stop it, but says dad would kill her. We have no other place to go, and who would want my mom with five daughters?"

It didn't make any sense to me that a mom would let that happen to any of her children. Was her mom blind? Did the demons have her also? I just couldn't figure it out.

We sat there awhile and watched the clouds roll by, casting their shadows on the lake and town below us. When the shadows were on the lake the water would be almost black. No longer could you see to the bottom, but only contorted reflections of the trees on the hills. That was Bev and her sisters, to her my love was contorted, not real, not deep, only shallow and hurtful. I wondered how I could help her and her sisters. I didn't say much to her. I let the silence surround us and let our minds take us to places that were free and safe.

We were back at her home, talking over the fence when her dad pulled into the driveway and yelled at Bev to get in the house. I reached out and took her hand, and told her not to go. She let go of my hand, and with a cold hard look walked into her house. I wondered why she didn't fight at all? I wanted to run in there and beat her dad to a pulp. I wanted to make him feel the pain he was inflicting on his daughters. I couldn't understand why someone would do such a thing to their children. I wanted to kill him because he was stealing his daughters' life.

On my way home I knew I couldn't sit back and let this happen to Bev. I knew the right thing to do was to tell my parents what was going on. My dad could help me make it so their father wouldn't rape Bev and her sisters any more. I ran the rest of the way home. I went into the kitchen and mom and dad were sitting at the table. I said, "Bev's dad is raping her and her sisters, we have to do something about it. We need to call the sheriff."

Dad looked at me like I was crazy and mom kind of shrugged her shoulders and said, "what makes you think that?"

"Bev told me, she said that he does it a lot. It's up to us to help them."

Dad looked at me and said, "I don't know what we can do, the sheriff won't help at all, and if Bev's dad is doing something, he isn't a man you would want to mess with. He runs moonshine and is involved in some shady things."

"Is he one of the bad guys that used to come here?"

"No, he isn't one of the bad guys, there are no bad guys."

"If there are no bad guys, than who did I shoot?"

"Luke, this is no time for arguments. You need to learn how to keep your nose in your own business. It makes life a lot better when you keep your nose in your own things."

I walked away. I didn't know what to do. I thought about shooting Bev's dad, thought about making him pay somehow, I didn't want to sit back and let Bev and her sisters go through more abuse. The demons had won again.

I went to bed that night thinking that it must be a normal thing for dads to want to have sex with their daughters. Something inside me told me it was very wrong, but no one else seemed to care all that much. I thought what was wrong with the world. I was thinking of all the girls that I knew who had dads or grandpas or uncles that would want to be touching them sexually. It was a very sad thing for them and I was wishing I could make it all end for them. The demons had a powerful hold in this town I called home.

I slowly forgot about those things and I stopped talking to Bev and Tam. I would say hi to them, but I didn't stand out by the fence and talk for hours like I had done before. I accepted all the sexual activity as a part of life that we all had to live through. The demons had won, they were in control of the town, and there wasn't a thing I could do to stop them.

I have searched for love
In the depths below and far above
No love can be found
I am but dirt from the ground
For dirt can not love

It is what I am made of
To run and hide from all the pain
Or face it and become insane
To close my eyes and no more cry
My heart is hard and that is how I will die.

I went to sleep that night and dreamt that I was sitting down in the middle of town looking at all the green hills surrounding Clear Lake. It was so beautiful with big tall trees swaying in the wind. They were majestic, standing like warriors protecting their strong holds. Their arms were raised toward heaven, and their needles looked like arrows set to strike your heart.

The trees formed a carpet of green, covering the scars of the hill making it appear soft and smooth. Calling for people to rest in the presence of the fortress. A strong warm Chinook wind started to blow, picking up speed as it made its way across the valley. It started to blow the trees over. One tree after another kept falling and the hills became bare, and all the ugly scars became visible and it was no longer nice to view.

A fire started and the wind made it grow big and fast. It swept across the hills and left them charred and more exposed. No one else in town saw what was happening to the trees. An old man appeared—he had hair white as snow and he came towards me. He looked like Mr. Woodchopper. He knew my name and said, "Luke, come here."

I did and when I got close to him I asked if he had seen the trees blow over and burn? He said yes. I asked him if he understood what it meant? He said yes, but it wasn't time to tell me yet. I became very sad as he said, "soon Luke, soon."

I took my eyes off him and he was gone. The fire was getting closer to town so I started running for the fire station to tell them the town was in danger. I couldn't run for my legs wouldn't work. I saw the fire coming closer—I am getting hot—I am burning.

I sat up in my bed with sweat running down my body. I got up and walked to the living room to look out at the hills. There was no fire, and every thing was as dark as when I went to sleep. I made my way back to bed and thought about everything I was doing. I couldn't go back to sleep. Nothing in my life seemed to make any sense. Where I was going? What I was going to be? I wanted to be someone that made a difference in this world, but I couldn't see how I was going to do that. I lie in my bed, wishing I could travel the stars and get as far away from here as possible.

I was searching for life. I wanted to know about everything that would give me power to do the things I wanted. It was Saturday night and I went down to the A-frame to see if anyone was meeting there. A few people were gathered at the old burner. I walked up and watched awhile. This time they were not practicing sex. They had a big pot of some kind in the center of the old burner. They were putting all kinds of things into it. I thought it must be some kind of magic potion they were making. All of the people got into a line and started putting their hands into the pot and eating whatever they had taken out. I got in line and waited my turn to see what it was they were eating. I got up to the pot and looked inside—it looked really gross. I was going to pass, when a man told me to take some and eat it. He said it would make me really powerful. I thought, well, if it will make me powerful, I can fight my way through the grossness. I took some and ate it—it tasted really bad. I could hardly swallow it. After eating it I didn't feel any more powerful than before.

I watched the rest of the night and nothing great happened. They were just a bunch of people doing things they were thinking were bad. I was beginning to see that they were like people going to church, they practiced their religion with no real power. I was thinking I would have to start my own religion.

A few days after the meeting I began to feel kind of sick. I stopped eating things because it was painful to swallow. I was losing weight fast and after a week of being sick my mom and dad took me to the doctor. The doctor checked me out, took some blood, and had me put into the hospital. I didn't know what was happening, I didn't think anything was really all that wrong. They told me that I was very sick and needed to be operated on in the morning. They asked me if I had eaten anything like raw pork, or any bad food. I didn't even think of the stuff in the pot, and told them no. My mom was crying, for what, I didn't know. She was acting like I was going to die or something. I was thinking it was the demons that had made me sick.

All I knew was that I was hungry and I couldn't eat any solid food. It was nice being waited on hand and foot by pretty nurses. The next morning the doctor came in and told me what he was going to do. He said I would have to be put to sleep for the operation, that kind of scared me, we put animals to sleep all the time, and they never woke up, but the doctor assured me I would wake up. They wheeled me down the hall into a big room, inside was a man with all kinds of needles. He said, "hi Luke."

He was a neighbor of mine. I didn't know him all that well. All I could think of was that he had put up new siding on his house. It was aluminum. I was playing baseball in my friends' yard and hit the ball so far over the road that it hit his house and dented it. He was the only man in town who had a dented house. He had come outside and started yelling at me. I had told him to take a chill pill and we all laughed. Now this man was putting me to sleep. He looked at me with a big smile that seemed to be out of place. I thought, what if he wants to put me to sleep forever? He told me to count backwards from ten to one. I started counting and I remembered no more.

I woke up and things looked scary. I could hardly see and nothing made any sense. There were nurses walking around in the room and one came and held my hand and told me it would be OK. I was fighting trying to get up and the nurse told me to relax and be still. I couldn't talk, or even swallow.

After a while my mom came in with a doctor, she was crying and he was talking to her. I knew something was wrong. The doctor looked at my chart, then walked out. Mom said some friends of mine were waiting back at my room. They wheeled me to my room and some of the boys I played football with were standing there. They had a football with them, and said the coach had told them before the game that I was maybe not going to make it, so they played hard and won the game for me and brought me the game football. I looked at my mom and asked, "what do they mean, I am not going to make it?"

My mom looked at me and started to cry. She said, "the doctors don't know if you will make it through this sickness Luke." I didn't know what to think. My mom always made things bigger than they were. The boys made their way out of the room, wishing me luck as they left.

I received many cards and flowers; it was nice, I didn't know there were so many people that cared about me. I didn't like the idea that I might not make it, I had so many things to do, but as each hour passed I could feel myself getting weaker. They had lines hooked up to me and said they were giving me food through the lines. I told them I couldn't taste it—they all laughed. I was scared, as I didn't know where I was going. It was strange to me.

It was late at night and my family wasn't around. I had been sleeping most of the day, and getting weaker every minute. I could barely open my eyes. A tall man walked in my room, up to my bed. I thought maybe I was dreaming, but I felt his hand take mine. I tried to see through my half-closed eyes and saw that it was the preacher. He smiled at me and said, "Luke, may I pray for you?"

I wondered why he would want to pray for me, I had done nothing but bad things to him and to those who went to his church. I had cussed him and said bad things to him. I had teased his kids, and here he wanted to pray for me—it didn't make sense. I shook my head yes that he could pray for me. He prayed for God and Jesus to heal me. He let go of my hand and left.

I fell back asleep. I started to dream that I was climbing a big tall mountain. A few of my friends were with me and it was taking a long time to get to the top. I knew on top of the mountain were answers to every question I ever had about life. The path up the mountain was straight, and very steep, so I was looking for an easier route. I saw one and started walking and climbing that way. My friends were yelling at me that I was going the wrong way but I didn't care. I finally made it to the top and I wasn't where the answers were. There was a big crevice between me and my friends who had made it the right way. I was on top but not in the right place, I was very sad, so I was trying to think of a way that I could get over to the other side. My friends couldn't see me or hear me. I looked for the way I came up so I could go back down and start up the right way, but the sides of the mountain were so steep that if I stepped off, I would fall to my death. I tried anyway and started to fall. I felt myself falling towards the rocks below, screaming, crying.

I woke up and the sun was shinning in my window. I felt like a new boy, My throat didn't hurt anymore, nor did the rest of my body. I asked the nurse for something to eat and she yelled for the doctor. He came running in and checked me over. He was shaking his head over and over again. He said it looked like I had fully recovered overnight. I told him that the preacher had been in last night and prayed for me. The nurse said that no one had been in to visit me all night. I thought that was kind of strange, all I knew was I was feeling better and I was hungry. I thought that if I was suppose to die, and the preacher came and prayed for me, than he must have more power than anyone else I knew.

The next day the doctor told me I could go home. My mom came and got me. On the way home I asked if we could stop and get a hamburger and a milkshake. It was the best hamburger I ever had. I was happy to be alive and well. The demons didn't get me this time. I started going to church on Sunday mornings to hear the preacher. I wanted to find out where his power came from and if I could also have it. I would sit in the back of church and not really talk to anyone. I knew a lot of the people that were attending and had seen things that they did around town. I could tell by the looks on the faces of a few ladies that they didn't like the idea of me being there. I didn't want to cause trouble anymore; I wanted to find the power.

I kept going to youth group and decided that if I wanted to have the power I would find if faster if I was the leader. When it came time for elections, I ran for president of the youth group. Most of the boys were afraid to oppose me and most of the girls liked me so I got voted in. I overheard a leader of the youth group saying I shouldn't be president because I wasn't a Christian, I asked him if the Bible said that, and he said, "no."

I told him he wasn't being very Christian-like. He got mad, and I smiled at him. I tried to talk all the other kids in town into coming to youth group and a lot of them did, but even after all that, I still didn't have the power I was looking for.

CHAPTER SEVENTEEN

"The new minister has started a new club for the children in town. It is called the Indian Scout Club. The kids all dress as Indians and the minister takes them on trips into the hills to teach them things about nature. It is one of the better things going for children in town."

Clear Lake News
April 1913

Things in Clear Lake were changing fast. New homes were being built and strangers were moving in; I always tried to meet them. I wanted to know if they had any kids, especially girls. One day I saw a big black car drive into town. I was on my bike and followed them up the hill. They stopped at some property on the top of the hill, and I watched as the men got out and walked around. They looked like really important men. I rode over by them and asked if they were going to buy the property? They looked at me like I was intruding and said they didn't know for sure. They got back in their car and drove off.

A few weeks later I saw a bulldozer there, clearing a spot for a house. It looked like it was going to be a big house. There were a lot of signs that said "No Trespassing" and "Keep Out."

I thought that was odd, no one around Clear Lake had ever put up those kinds of signs before. At nights after the construction crews left, I would sneak inside and look around. A few days later they hired a watchman. I was walking around, looking at all the forms they had set up when I heard a mean loud voice say, "what are you doing in here?"

I had to think fast so I said, "I am looking for a job, I would like to make some extra money cleaning up this place, are you the one I talk too?"

"No, and can't you read? The sign says keep out!"

"OK, sorry I will be going."

On my way home I was thinking that when someone put up no trespassing signs it was an invitation for kids. All the signs meant was that there was something that we all needed to see inside.

The house was being built like a fortress. The next day I showed up and asked the man at the gate for a job, working on the weekends, cleaning up. He said he would have to ask Mr. Vendetii if it would be all right. He was gone for a few minutes, and then he came back towards me with an older man with gray hair. He introduced himself as Mr. Vendetii. He said, "so you want to work for me?"

"Yes, I need to make some money for school things."

"You look like a strong young man, here are the rules, you come here and work hard. Keep to the jobs you're given and don't ask a lot of questions."

Most of the people that I had worked for wanted me to ask lots of questions, but I figured he just didn't want to be bothered. "OK Mr. Vendetii, I will do that."

"Then you're hired."

"Where are you from Mr. Vendetii?"

He laughed and said, "I told you no questions, now didn't I?"

"Yes, but that isn't a bad question."

"You're right, it's not a bad question. I'm from Chicago."

"That is a long ways from here, why did you choose to live in Clear Lake."

"It seems like a nice place to retire. Now move along and we will see you next weekend."

I jumped on my bike and headed home. I was thinking, why would a man pick a small town like Clear Lake to come build a big house like a castle when he was from Chicago? It didn't make any sense to me. I thought it was interesting that he always had men around him that didn't do anything but watch, just like on television. The men looked like big old dumb goons, they always had suits on but looked unshaven. Mr. Vendetii never drove, as he would have someone drive for him. He must have been a really important man.

He had a big motor home at his property that he said used to belong to one of his friends. He said in a laughing way that his friend would be coming to his place for a long much needed rest. I never did see his friend show up. To me it was all very strange.

I wanted to find out the answers to all my questions, and him telling me not to ask any questions made me want to ask them more. I worked there for a couple of weeks and watched as they were building lots of things. They were always talking among themselves about things. I would try to listen but only heard bits and pieces. They kept talking about some friend of theirs coming to rest at this house.

It was a Saturday and I was looking forward to work because they said they would be pouring concrete. When I arrived at the gate I was told by one of the goons that my services wouldn't be needed today. I didn't see any other workers up at the job site; all I could see were Mr. Vendetii's goons, in their suits, trying to pour concrete. I thought it's about time that they got off their lazy butts and did something.

The more I thought of it, something didn't seem right to me, so I rode down the road and put my bike in the ditch and made my way up through the woods to watch from a distance. I could see a big box in the center of the forms, and they were pouring concrete around it. I wondered what was in the box, and why they wanted to cover it up. I thought maybe it was money, or gold, or something else worth a lot of money. I watched awhile. I heard a branch break behind me. I took off running, not wanting to look back. I made my way back to my bike and rode home. I was afraid to go back to work up at his house, so the next weekend I went by on my bike and left a note saying that I couldn't work for him any more.

A few nights later I dreamed I was walking up on the hill behind Mr. Vendetii's house. I came to a big pile of rocks on the very top of the hill. I thought it was strange that these rocks were piled up there. I started to pick rocks off the pile to see what was underneath them. I was working hard and fast when Mr. Vendetii came up behind me and asked what I was doing? I told him I was moving rocks because I thought something good was buried underneath them. He told me there wasn't anything underneath them and for me to leave. I went away and waited for him to leave. He left and I went back to finish moving the rocks, they were heavy and it was taking a long time. I finally had most of them moved when I saw what appeared to be a hand. I kept moving the rocks and I saw a face. It was no one I had seen before. He looked at me but his eyes had no life. Mr. Vendetii came back with his goons and started chasing me. I took off running and made it back home safely.

I woke up the next morning and remembered my dream. I thought it was nice that for the first time the bad guys didn't catch me. I liked dreams like that. I hoped that all the rest of my dreams would be that way.

It wasn't long before Mr. Vendetii's house was finished and he moved in. He had a landscaper come in and plant big trees all around his house so no one could see in. He also had a surveillance camera set up so he could see who was coming up to his house, and he had his goons walking the property all the time.

I thought maybe he was friends with the demons and was providing a place for them to hide. Mr. Vendetii had threatened to kill a few of the town's people every once in a while. He even pulled guns out on them. He was a different man.

Rumors started to be spread around town that Mr. Vendetii was a good friend once with a man named Jimmy Hoffa. People were saying that Jimmy Hoffa was buried under Mr. Vendetii's house. To me it explained why he didn't have anyone help with the concrete that day. It made sense about all the talk of a friend of his coming to rest at his place. Besides who would look for a Jimmy Hoffa in Clear Lake? If I had to hide someone I had killed, Clear Lake would be one of the best places to do such a thing. I knew that bodies sometimes are never found. We had no police, no mayor, and most of the people in town heard no evil, saw no evil, but most did some evil.

School still was as hard as it had always been—I didn't like it and would wish I didn't have to go. The only classes I was passing were history and PE. In English, we had to spend a week writing poems, I thought that was a good time to show the teacher everything I had been writing for the last year. When our grades came back I received a "D." I was mad, I thought I deserved at least a "B." I went and asked my teacher why I received such a bad grade. She said she thought I had copied my poems from someone else. I told her, "no, I wrote them myself."

She didn't believe me. I looked at her and said, "you wouldn't know an original poem if it jumped up and bit you on your fat butt."

I shouldn't have said anything to her. She looked back at me and said, "Luke, you're so uncouth."

"What does uncouth mean?" She told me to go look it up. I walked over to the dictionary and looked it up.

Uncouth: Barbaric, uncivilized, animal like.

I read that and thought—I am not barbaric, I am civilized. So I said, "if I am uncouth, that must make you a bitch, and you can look that up in the dictionary."

It was the wrong thing to do. She screamed at me to get out of her class and go to the office. I left and went and sat outside awhile. I thought about what kind of trouble I was going to be in. I was thinking of what my dad was going to do to me. I was thinking—why was I being so mean to people? I decided I needed to go back and apologize to my English teacher.

After school was out I went into her room and told her I was sorry for calling her a bitch. I told her I would become a model student and not cause any more trouble in class if she wouldn't tell anyone what had happened. She sat there awhile, then said that if I would bring my grade up and work hard, she would forgive me and let me stay in her class. I was so relieved that my dad wasn't going to find out what I had said. My grades slowly improved after that. Some of the kids were kind of surprised that I could actually do some of the schoolwork.

I was still going to church on Sundays, trying to figure out what kind of power this preacher had. I would hear some of the people talk about me. They were trying to figure out why I was there; only a couple of them ever came up to talk to me. Lily and Ron Carter were an older couple that had lived in Clear Lake most of their lives. They invited me over for dinner one day after church, so I went. They fed me a really good meal and afterwards we went into the living room to talk. I felt like an old person, as it was strange to me that after dinner every old person would go to the living room to talk. Mr. Carter asked my why I was going to church? I told him I wanted to have the power to heal people, like the preacher healed me. He smiled at me and I knew he found my thinking interesting. He told me if I searched really hard, and with all my heart, that I would find the truth. I asked him how do you search with all your heart? He said, "you're a good swimmer Luke, what if I held your head underwater for a long time?"

"I would drown, I wouldn't be able to breathe."

"But would you fight to try and get air?"

"Yes I would fight as hard as I could, I would tear and beat and claw my way to the air."

He looked at me with eyes that pierced right through mine and said, "Luke, when you want the truth as much as you would want air in that situation, then you will find it. That is what it's like to search and seek with all your heart. You have to put your whole being into it."

I understood what he was saying. It made perfect sense to me. Mrs. Carter came out of the kitchen with some pie. She sat down and said it was nice seeing me in church every Sunday morning, but that she would appreciate it if I would clean up my mouth. She said that a lot of the other ladies would never let me date their daughters until I cleaned up my mouth. That was good enough incentive for me. I told her I would quit cussing. I became good friend of the Carter's; I enjoyed being around them. For people in Clear Lake, the Carter's were about the only normal ones left. Everyone else had a demon or more in their closet.

That spring we got a new Boy Scout leader. His name was Mr. Webber, he acted very nice and he worked as a substitute teacher for the school, but I didn't trust him. He didn't have a wife and when I asked him where he had moved from he didn't give me a straight answer. He did not have good intent in his eyes, and I judged him right away as a pervert. I had read somewhere that demons entered people either in their mouths or eyes so I always watched the eyes of people.

It seemed to me that Clear Lake attracted perverts and I wondered why that was? A lot of people around the valley called Clear Lake, queer lake. I hated those words, but it made sense.

I wanted to keep my eyes on Mr. Webber when he was around the scouts; I made sure I was at every meeting. Sometimes he would put his arm around one of the younger scouts. I didn't like the way he looked at some of them, and I wanted them to be safe.

On the outside, I was looking more and more like a model teenager, I went to Boy Scouts, church, and was in school all the time. Inside my mind and body and soul I was having the biggest struggles of my life. I wanted sex, and from every thing I had been taught and seen sex was love.

In the youth group there were some really nice looking girls and I set my mind to get them to have sex with me. I wanted to date them, take them out for dinner, show them how nice I could be, then they would want to have sex with me.

I set my eyes on a girl named Jennifer. On our first date we went to a high school dance. I knew she kind of liked me but she was acting real nervous and kind of scared. Before we went inside I leaned over and gave her a kiss. Then I gave her another kiss. She looked at me and told me, "I'm sorry, but I don't want to kiss you any more."

I said, "that is OK."

I thought I'd honor her wishes, at least for now. I took her home after the dance and told her I hoped we could go out again. She said that she wouldn't go out with me unless I became a Christian. I told her I was a Christian. She said, "no, you're not."

I told her to look up Christian in the dictionary. She walked into her house and came back with the dictionary. It said Christian: civilized, etc.

I said, "see, I am a Christian." She said that I wasn't a real one. I said good night and went and got in my car and drove home. I thought that if she wanted me to become a Christian I would become one.

The next Sunday, after church, I asked the preacher, "how do you become a Christian?"

He asked me to come to his office, and had me sit down in front of his desk. Then he asked, "why do you want to become a Christian Luke?"

"Because if I want to date Jennifer again, she said I have to be a Christian."

"That's not too good of a reason to become one." I was trying to think fast, to impress him, so he could tell me how to become a Christian. I said, "I also want to become a Christian so I can have the same power that you have to help people."

I thought I had said the right thing. I thought that for sure he would show me right away how to become a Christian. He leaned back in his chair and asked, "Luke, do you know what sin is?"

"Yes, it's when Christians do bad things. I think I have seen almost everyone in your church sin."

He said, "all people sin, and deserve to die."

I figured he was right, everyone I knew had done bad things, except maybe the Carter's. He went on to say, "Luke, you have to become a Christian for the right reasons. You have to confess that you have sinned and need God to save you or you will die and go to hell."

I didn't like the idea of going to hell, and I had committed many sins, I had lied, cheated, stolen, cussed, I had seen so many acts of sex, I had wanted to have sex, and most of all, I had killed. I didn't think God could forgive me for all those things. I asked, "do I have to tell all my sins?"

"No you just have to admit that you have sinned, and God will forgive you."

"Good, there isn't enough time in a week for me to tell you all the things I have done wrong."

He asked me to pray with him and ask Jesus into my heart. I did, and he said, "Luke, you're a new person now, all the old things have passed, and your life is new. You now have the power of God on your side."

I liked the idea of the power of God on my side. I believed what the preacher had told me, I believed I was a new person, and to prove it to everyone in church, I was going to learn as much about the Bible as I could. When I got home I started reading the Bible. Over the next couple of months I read the whole thing. I was amazed that it talked about the very things I had seen growing up. It said there were demons and witches and devils. It showed me how I was supposed to live and treat people. The only thing I couldn't figure out was why if all these people went to church, that they didn't really believe what the Bible said. It confused me somewhat.

Walking down to the school one day to shoot some baskets I saw Nina working in her yard. I said hello to her and she said hi back. She asked me if I wanted to come see her garden? I thought it would be nice, because I always liked plants and trees. She showed me around her yard and invited me into her house for some tea. The walls in her house looked old, they had never been painted. In each room was a wood stove, for heat in the winter.

On the wall were old pictures of people that I assumed were her mom and dad. I looked around while she made the tea. She walked into her living room and asked me to come and sit down. The chairs were all old like in the movies. She didn't have a television or radio; I wondered what she did to keep from getting bored? I sat in her chair waiting to see what we were going to talk about. I asked, "what did your dad do for a work?"

"He was the town butcher, he would cut up everyone's meat for them. And when the mill was here, before it burned down, he would supply all the logging camps with meat."

"Did you ever work?"

She smiled and said, "yes I had to work every day, helping my mom and dad, but no, I never worked for someone. Some of the girls that I went to school with became dancers at certain halls in town. My mom would tell me to never become like those girls. Some of them were forced into dancing to make money for their families. They would tell me that they had to do horrible things sometimes, like what happened to you in the back alley."

Her voice turned sad as she was telling me these things. I was wondering where she was going with what she was saying, she started to cry and said, "I am sorry for not helping you that day Luke, I was so afraid of those boys and I didn't know what to do. I am so sorry."

"Oh, that is OK Nina, those boys never bothered me again, besides, if you had tried to stop them they might have hurt you."

She smiled at me, and kept on talking like she hadn't talked to anyone in years.

"When I was your age Luke, Clear Lake was one of the biggest towns in the county. We had a theater, dance halls, and many social clubs.

Clear Lake had electricity long before Mount Vernon. The mill would supply it for everyone. We had a hospital and even a train depot. It was a town going places. Things happened that changed all that."

I was getting a history lesson and loving it. I asked, "what changed for the worse?"

She took a deep breath like she was telling me things I shouldn't know. "Things got totally out of hand in town. Men became greedy and evil increased. There were rumors of a group of men that were sent out to do bad things to families that didn't comply with the wishes of those in power. I knew it to be more than a rumor for I had seen them once. Evil men they were."

I was getting scared listening to her. She kept on talking. "When I saw those boys doing those things to you it brought back bad memories of those bad guys and what they did to some. I have heard over the years that those men pass their evils from generation to generation. And when I saw what had happened to you, I knew that it was true and my will was broken. I, like many people in town chose not to remember those things."

In her voice was sadness, I wanted to reach out to hold her and tell her that every thing was going to be OK. She kept right on talking. "Like I told you before, my mom never let any boys come around me. She told me they were nothing but evil. She would always run them off with her shotgun and they would never come back. I learned after my mother died that not all men are evil, but I could never bring myself to court one, I am so terribly afraid of men. I have watched you for the last few years and you always treat the people you meet really nice and kind. When you came to talk to me in the cemetery, I realized you were a good boy. You used to run by my house all the time, but now you walk ever since those boys hurt you. You're like a lot of my friends, you grew up real fast that day."

She stopped and took a deep sigh as she looked for words to say. "My mother loved me, she never wanted anything bad to happen to me. She

wanted me to grow up a little girl, and stay that way, young and innocent. You lost your innocence that day Luke and I do wish I had tried to
stop that. What impressed me the most was you didn't run and hide,
you still walked down town all the time as if you had no fear. You always
smile, you look so nice when you smile."

I was blushing a little when she told me that. I understood what she
was saying. I felt sorry for her. She had lived her whole life alone. Her
parents had died back in the thirties, so for almost 40 years she had lived
by herself. She asked if I would come and visit again some time? I told
her I would like to visit again and learn more about the early days of
Clear Lake. I said good bye and made my way to the school.

I finally understood why she had left me alone when I was being
attacked by Shane and Bud. I was beginning to understand that a lot of
people in Clear Lake lived in fear of those they didn't trust. I had to find
out who the bad guys were and destroy them. I had to destroy my own
fears and make things safe. I had my fears also—my biggest fear was of
things that could come after me in the dark, it seemed that most bad
things happen in the dark.

Demons came in the dark, and devils and witches. It seemed that
people that wanted to do bad things always did so in secret. I wanted to
do things in the light, so that the other people in town would see me as
good and not a bad person. I thought that the power to lift headstones,
or the power to heal people, wasn't as prevalent as the powers that
caused people to do things in the privacy of their homes. I had been
looking for a power to make the world my world, but I saw there was
more power in the still small voice inside me that urged me to smile
back at someone instead of lashing out at them.

I was taking religion seriously. I believed what the preacher said. He
was a man who lived what he spoke; I hadn't seen too many people
like him. The only other people who I thought were close to living
what they believed were the Carter's. I had cleaned up my mouth, I

was working at doing everything right but I couldn't get my mind off sex. I always knew the demons were close behind me.

I would pray to God for hours and read the Bible for hours, trying to keep my mind from thinking about sex. I would feel really guilty, and sometimes give up hope. I thought if I did good things for God, maybe he would overlook my sin, so I would go out of my way to tell people about Jesus. I appeared to be on fire for God, but I knew if people could see inside me, they would see what kind of an evil person I really was. I stopped going out with girls from the church, I thought if I dated non-Christian girls than God wouldn't be mad at me if I tried to make sexual advances towards them. I told everyone I was trying to witness to the girls. I had become a deceiver.

I could put on the biggest show for the people at church, and most of them believed what they saw. I would fight for hours over how I felt about myself, I wanted to do things right, but it seemed impossible. I figured I was heading to hell but I wasn't going to give up, I was still going to try to live somewhat right. Even in all of this the demons had gained a stronger foothold.

One Sunday the preacher got up to give the message. He started talking, "I have something very hard to say this morning. Over the last few months many of the people in our church have died."

I was thinking, yes, that is true, many of the older people had been passing on, a couple of them were only in their fifties. He went on to say, "it says in the Bible that many of you sleep because you take and eat of the Lords supper in an unworthy manner. This church is full of people who are carnal to their very hearts. Do you believe you can live in sin and not anger God? If you continue this way, many more of you will be taken."

I thought, wow! I had never heard such a strong message. I was looking around to see how the people were reacting to what he was saying and there seemed to be a lot of mad people sitting in church that morning. He went on, "many of the people of this church are involved in sexual sin, and it's destroying your sons and daughters. You come in here and sit and listen to God's word, afterwards, you go out and sin like you have no fear. This isn't right."

I knew he was talking to me, but I wasn't mad, I knew I was wrong, but I found it impossible to stop. The preacher spoke awhile longer and ended by telling everyone, "God is a forgiving God to all of us who turn from our sins."

I always asked God to forgive me, and I believed He did, over and over again. I wished I could be worthy.

After church the preacher took his family and went straight home. People were talking as I listened to what they had to say and I couldn't believe my ears. Some were saying they wanted to get rid of the preacher, he was saying things they didn't like to hear. Someone said we needed to have the preacher come before a special meeting, to explain his views. It didn't make any sense to me. What the preacher had said was true. Not only was I living a lie, but also so many other people were living the same lie. The Carter's and a couple of others left without saying a thing. I gained even more respect for them because they lived the life.

On my way home I walked to the preacher's house. I looked in the window and saw him and his family seated for a meal, holding hands and praying, it's an image I will never forget, they were a family that loved each other and were happy to be together.

I thought when I grew up and married I would want my family to be like that. I sat on their front steps waiting for them to finish eating so I could talk to the preacher. When they were finished, I knocked on the door. The preacher answered it and asked me to come inside. I said I would rather sit outside and talk. He came outside and sat down next to me. I said, "you were right this morning, and I want you to know I am not mad at you for saying those things. I want you to know that people are going to be against you because of what you said."

"I know, people don't want to hear what is right and true. Luke, I know you're having many struggles of your own. Pay close attention to your own life, lest it slip away from you. I won't be here long; people's hearts in this town are hard towards God. They love the way of sin and there is a powerful spirit here that has control of the people."

"What do you mean? Are you talking about demons?"

"Luke you may not understand, but I believe that there are spirits that have a firm grip on this town. Someone or a group of people let those spirits into this town a long time ago and they have built a strong hold here and it will take a mighty act of God to bind them."

"Can you bind the spirits? I know that when I was sick you came and prayed for me and I became better. I know that you have power that others don't."

"It was the power of God that healed you Luke. I am but a vessel for his use. I don't know how to bind and chase these spirits out of this town without the help of others who believe strongly in God."

I could see on his face a great concern for Clear Lake. He looked very troubled. I could see he didn't know how to attack and defeat these evil spirits. I was feeling good, at least someone else knew there were demons doing bad things to people in this town. I no longer felt alone in the way I thought about things. I knew I had been right all along. "I know there are demons here in Clear Lake. I know people who worship Satan and practice witchcraft. I used to be somewhat a part of it."

The preacher looked at me as I was telling him these things and said, "Luke, these are not things to be dealt with lightly, our enemy is very strong and powerful, so you must be right with God if you're going to do battle with Satan and his demons. That is why it's so hard here, not many people in this church even think that this kind of thing exists, they think it went out with the dark ages."

"Well I believe they are here, and I believe you."

He smiled at me, put his hand on my shoulder and prayed, "God, protect Luke, and help him live a life to you."

He said he had to go back and spend time with his family since it was Sunday. I understood, and told him thanks for his time.

I made my way towards home thinking of all the things we had talked about. I could see how the spirits had control of the town. I thought of all the kids I had known over the years, and about their home life. I walked on past my house up towards the frog pond. I walked by Mr. Woodchopper's house. I missed talking to him. I found the hollow stump by the frog pond and sat down and kept on thinking about the evil spirits.

I believed they had killed Marie and Sharon, and had prompted Shane to rape me. They had caused Rich and Rick to want to have anal sex with each other and they had control of Bev's dad. They had compelled me to beat Uncle Joe with a bat here at the frog pond. The spirits hid themselves well. I wished they could be killed with guns and rifles. I wished they would leave me alone and quit trying to use me. Sometimes I could feel them inside of me. It scared me.

I knew what I had to do. I had to tell everyone in town about the spirits and then they would help me chase the spirits out of town, or even better yet, destroy them.

I waited for the next Saturday that people would be meeting down at the old burner. I went down there at around midnight and walked right into the meeting. Everyone was looking at me. I knew most of them had heard about me spending lots of time at church and reading my Bible. I looked around at everyone and said, "I have come to warn you of the spirits that are trying to take you over and destroy this town. You must stop serving this false god of yours. Satan is deceiving you into believing a lie. Please come and hear the truth Sunday morning."

A large piece of concrete came flying by my head. I ducked as it went by, I had no idea where it came from. Then a large black cloud rose out of the fire in the center of the burner. A man fell on the ground and went into convulsions. He slivered like a snake, then stood to his feet and said, "you of all people should be talking. You yourself are full of me, and I am lust, so now face your death."

"I have changed my ways and now I serve the true and living God, the blood of Jesus is protecting me and you can't touch me."

"If you have changed, than why do you lust in your heart after all your neighbor's wives?"

My body started to shake. How could this man know what I was doing in my thoughts and heart? It was true, I would often think about having sex with the women who lived in town, and he knew, I was in over my head. I looked to my right and saw that the alder trees had grown tall enough to hold my weight. I needed to get out of there fast. I took off running for the wall. I jumped and grabbed onto the limbs of the tree and it started to bend towards the ground. I landed on my feet and started to run for the highway. I looked back to see a few men chasing me. I ran as fast as I could as I was thanking God that he had given me speed and strength.

I ran all the way home, fearing for my life. No one was home when I got there so I locked all the doors grabbed my rifle and put in a thirty round clip. I thought that if I went down to them again, I should take weapons, because that is something they would probably understand. I waited for them to come walking up the hill but they never showed up. I figured I would have to be careful if I went out at night, I knew that during the day they wouldn't try anything.

It was late when my parents finally came home and found me asleep on the couch with my rifle by my side. They woke me up and sent me to bed. My dad said, "you had better be careful with that gun, you might hurt someone."

I told him I was afraid of the dark and went to my room.

Things were busy in my life. I was always finding things to do and keep my mind full but I never let my mind rest on how to get the demons out of Clear Lake. I would often think when I was doing my work or walking places. I had lots of time to think when I was mowing the cemetery lawn. As I was mowing the cemetery lawn I saw some movement in Ralph's house again. I had seen the figure of the girl standing there a few times this summer.

More of the scouts were helping this year and Mr. Webber always came along. He would watch us all walk back and forth. A few of us were wearing shorts and he seemed to like watching us walk by. His facial expressions would change and bad intent would show in his eyes. I had seen that look on different men's faces before as they were watching kids down at the beach, so I started watching him all the time. I wondered if I was the only one seeing this? I asked Gary what he thought of the things I was seeing and he agreed with me. I thought that if he made any kind of move towards any of the boys in the scout troop I was going to make him pay the price.

When a bunch of us stopped to rest for a bit and have a pop, I asked my friends if they had seen anything up in that house before? Nobody had. I told them to watch the window and they would see a figure of a girl. Gary stood up and pointed at the window and said, "I see a big fat naked woman standing in the window."

We all looked as Gary was laughing. We all saw Ralph's mom standing on the porch listening to us. She went back in the house and slammed the door. I felt kind of bad. I didn't want her to think we were making fun of her. We all finished our pops and went back to our mowing.

The grass always smelled so sweet after it was cut, it smelled almost good enough to eat. The next time I came to mow the lawn there was a big sheet of plywood over the window on the house. Ralph was outside playing so as I mowed along the fence that separated their yard from the cemetery. I asked Ralph why there was plywood over the window? He said he had broken the window and his mom couldn't afford to fix it. I smiled and went back to my mowing.

Not long after that I saw the preacher and his family packing things into a moving van. I walked over and asked where they were going. The preacher said, "Luke I am going to a different church down in the southern part of the state. This town is full of evil spirits. I am no longer welcome here."

"Well, I don't mind you being here, I kind of wish you could stay."

"That's nice of you Luke, a few people feel that way but the majority of the people in church have asked me to leave. A man cannot effectively minister to people that have no respect for the Lord or his servant."

I was sad to see him going. I wondered what had happened to make him want to leave. His wife looked like she was happy to be leaving. Only the Carter's showed up to help them load the truck. It made me wonder about the charity of the people in town; the people in Clear Lake were becoming stranger to me all the time. The preacher and his family came to church the following Sunday but he didn't preach, he got up and said it had been nice being here for the time he was, and that he would always pray for the people in this church. After the service he came and had a picture taken with the entire youth group, we were going to miss him.

CHAPTER EIGHTEEN

"Virginia Wasserman was laid to rest on Tuesday. She was twelve years old. The whole community turned out to pay their last respects. It truly is a sad day for out town."

Clear Lake News
June 1925

Teri was only 13 and wasn't old enough to be in the youth group, but I would let her come. She was a good kid, Denise was her older sister and Teri had an older brother. Her dad and mom owned the resort on the lake where I kept my boat. Denise and I had been good friends ever since I started going to church. I was finally good people. Denise worked in the cafe all summer with her mom. Teri and her best friend Ruby often came out and sat with me while I life guarded. Teri was in puppy love with the other lifeguard, Josh, and Ruby was in puppy love with me. Josh and I would tease them all the time telling them we were madly in love with them. Whenever we wanted anything to eat they would go to the cafe and get it for us.

Sitting on the lifeguard stand all day was sometimes a boring job. I would take my radio out with me and listen to music on KJR as I watched the water. Disco was coming on the scene and the movie "Jaws" was playing. Every once in a while Josh or I would call out a shark warning, for fun. Even though we were in a lake, mothers would start screaming for their kids to get out of the water. We would laugh and laugh. Some people were so gullible.

One evening, a young couple from Norway came down to the beach; they were on their honeymoon. I thought they sure picked a nice place to take a honeymoon. She was swimming and he was walking around the dock taking pictures of the blooming lily pads. He looked up and asked me if there were any sharks in the Lake. I couldn't resist. I smiled and said, "yes, real big sharks, but they usually hang out on the other side of the lake."

His bride heard what I said and jumped up on the dock with a terrified look on her face. I laughed and told her that there were no sharks in this lake, only in the ocean. No matter what I said, she wouldn't get back in the water. I learned that most people would believe anything. They had no knowledge of what was real.

I listened to a lot of songs that summer; they made the days on the stand go faster. "More, more, more, how do you like it? How do you like it? More, more, more, how do you like your love?" Wings would be singing "Band on the Run." It seemed, no matter what the song it somehow spoke to me and to where I was at in every different situation that came up. I thought music was a wonderful thing.

The people in the church asked me if I wanted to sit on the board to help select a new preacher. I thought it would be a fun thing to do. I didn't know why they asked me to be on the board, I thought they were trying to make me forget about the old preacher, they knew I liked him a lot. I was young and I thought I knew everything about anything. One thing I knew for sure was that there were demons in Clear Lake that needed to be destroyed, so whenever a man came to be interviewed for the job of preacher, I would always ask if he believed in real demons. The others on the board would always roll their eyes when I asked. Sometimes I got a halfhearted reply and other times no response at all. I stopped going to the meetings; the men in charge were going to what they wanted regardless of anything I had to offer. I thought maybe even the church was controlled by demons. Nothing made much sense.

In September we ended up getting a new preacher right out of seminary. I always called it cemetery, partly in fun and partly because I thought it limited individuality. I was convinced I would never have to go to seminary because I learned from God, not from men. Besides I knew that I had way more knowledge than the new minister.

The new preacher let the Boy Scouts use the church building for their meetings. I thought that was a good idea, because our old meeting place was getting run down. One night I showed up to our scout meeting early and walked inside to help set up. I was the senior patrol leader and wanted to be a good example for the rest of the younger scouts. Mr. Webber wasn't in the main meeting room but his car was outside. I heard noise down the long hall and went to see if he was down there. I went into the men's room and caught Mr. Webber touching Kevin Manor's penis. He looked at me really surprised and said, "don't you knock before you come in a room?"

"Not when I think there is a pervert in the room. I usually open the door and shoot the shit out of them."

"Kevin here was having some trouble with his zipper and I was helping him, so I expect an apology for calling me a pervert." I looked at Kevin's face and his eyes had tears in them. He could have been crying for getting his penis caught in his zipper but why would a 14-year-old boy ask another man to help?

"Kevin is this true what Mr. Webber is saying?" Mr. Webber started to speak, but I said, "let Kevin answer!" He looked at me, then back at Mr. Webber and very slowly tried to talk, but he started stuttering.

"I, I, I, do, don, do, don't li, li, like wh, wh, what he, he is do, do, doing to me."

Mr. Webber reached for me and I grabbed his arm in an arm drag. I threw him on the ground and yelled for Kevin to run. I stepped over the top of Mr. Webber and looked down at him. He seemed surprised that I had so easily put him on the floor. I said, "do you know I was raped once? And do you know what happened to the guy that did it?"

Mr. Webber shook his head no.

"Well I killed him. And that is what I should do to you now. But see I have become a Christian and I don't think God would like me killing you, but than again, it says that perverts should die. What do you think?"

He didn't say a word. He got up and headed out the door. I followed him to his car. As he was getting in I said, "if I were you I would keep driving and never come back, because I am going to tell every one what you did and what you are. And I do promise you that I will make you pay for your sins."

He drove off down the road. I never saw him again.

A week later the new preacher told me he had received a letter from Mr. Webber. He said Mr. Webber had left for a family emergency and wouldn't be back any time soon, I smiled, knowing we were all safe again.

The new preacher came to our next scout meeting and said there would be no more Boy Scouts in Clear Lake. He was looking right at me as he gave us the news; I wondered what else had been written in that letter.

I was getting bolder. I thought I was one of the prophets of the last days. I wanted people to listen to me, and I wanted them to understand all the fascinating thoughts I had about life. I was glad God had chosen me for special knowledge. I believed it was up to me to bring deliverance to Clear Lake, I felt I would move on to larger tasks after that. I felt bad for the people in Clear Lake when they didn't respond to me, but I knew a prophet was often without honor in his hometown.

Life was good. I felt like I was on top of the world, and anything I wanted to do, I could accomplish. No bad people were trying to get me, I was making good money, and I was becoming very popular. My mom and dad were not interfering in my life for I could basically come and go and do, as I wanted. My older brother Collin had graduated from high school and had joined the Marine corps.

The minute Collin left for the Marines, I was in the room moving his things out into the attic and arranging the room to suit me. I sat down and thought about Collin being gone. I realized I didn't really know my brother at all. I felt like I was the older one of us, even though he was two years older, I was a sophomore when he was a senior.

When guys picked fights with him, I would come and fight for him; many times I saved him from being made a fool. He was really smart when it came to books and math and things like that, but his lack of common sense would get him in trouble.

I hated it when people picked on him and made fun of him. I had grown bigger than he had. I would always tell him it was because I stood in the cow manure and he didn't. It bothered me that in all the years I was with him I didn't really know him. I didn't know his dreams, what he wanted to become in life. I didn't know what he liked in women. All I really knew was that he was my brother, and in my own way I loved him, but never knew how to tell him.

I sat there and started to cry because it felt like I would maybe never see him again. I remembered the beatings I took in his place to keep him from getting in trouble. I remembered letting him win, so he wouldn't get mad and try to beat me up. If he took after me, I would run from him because I was much faster, he would always cool off and forget it. I thought about all the fun times we had and smiled, hoping that he would find his way in life and be happy.

Sitting in church one Sunday morning, listening to the new preacher, I saw a beautiful new girl. She was sitting with her parents in the front pew and she had a full head of red hair and blue eyes. After church I asked if she wanted to come to youth group in the evening? She said, "yes," and my heart soared.

Her dad was a new high school teacher and they had built a new house up on the hill over looking the lake, right below where Sharon had been killed. At youth group that night I asked Caroline if she wanted to work with me on a project for the youth group? She said she would like to. I made arrangements to go over to her house Friday night to work on it together, I think she knew that I wanted to be with her. I couldn't wait for Friday to come, Fleetwood Mac was telling me "Don't stop thinking about tomorrow," and I wasn't.

That Friday night when I arrived at Caroline's house her parents were out for the evening. I had my Bible with me and we sat on the couch in the living room and started talking. We never opened the Bible at all, but talked and talked. I finally looked in her eyes and leaned forward and kissed her. She put her arms around me and kissed me back. We spent the next hour kissing, and I had never experienced anything like that before. I thought I must be in love for the hundredth time. I was wishing the night would never come to an end. After a while we heard her parents driving up the driveway. They came inside and saw Caroline and I sitting on the couch with the Bible open. I left for home thinking I had finally found the love of my life.

I went to see Caroline every day after that, and on the weekends I spent as much time with her as I could. Her parents left us alone for hours and I was always ready to kiss her, but I never touched her anywhere else, I was determined to treat her right. It seemed like a perfect relationship. I started to spend all of my free time at her house. I ate there and took naps there. People around town said that I had worn a path a mile deep between her house and mine. We went for motorcycle rides in the mountains and had picnics, and then we would lay around and kiss. We would dream of what kind of life we were going to have and how many kids we were going to have, how I was going to be a professional football player, and how after that I would become a minister.

It was my junior year in high school and things were going great. I was voted to the all league football team, lead the league in receptions, and started on both offense and defense. My schoolwork was going fine, I was no A student, but I was passing my classes. In the winter I wrestled to keep in shape for football. It was a fun sport and I was good at it. I went to state and won the state championship at one hundred seventy-eight pounds. I had lots of close friends and everyone seemed to like me, I don't think I really had any enemies. I knew there were bad things still going on in Clear Lake but I didn't think about them much. Most of the kids I had gone to grade school with had dropped out and were taking drugs and drinking too much beer. It was sad to see. Their lives seemed so messed up, and I wondered why I'd been spared the same fate?

Of twenty-four kids from my sixth grade class, only ten were still in school. I smiled whenever I thought about what some of my grade school teachers had said about me. Some of the brightest kids had dropped out and were on drugs and I was one of what they called the dumbest and I would be graduating in a year. I knew that if any teacher ever told me that any of my kids were retarded, they would get my full wrath. I think I learned differently than other kids.

I was in love with Caroline. I was with her all the time, at school, home, and at church. We weren't bashful about holding each other and kissing, because it didn't matter to us where we were. I was proud of myself because we weren't having sex. A lot of people thought we were, but at that time in our relationship, we weren't. Her mom and dad would bring her to watch me at my different sporting events all over the state. It was like being married without sleeping together.

I met her grandma who lived up river. She was a strange old lady. She believed in weird things. I enjoyed her company even though she was from a different world. I thought there was much that I could learn from many different kinds of people.

Hanging around Caroline and her parents I was getting to know them pretty well. I watched how Caroline's mom acted around her husband Bill and around other men. She liked to be noticed. Bill was kind of a jealous man for he would often get mad it seemed for no reason at all. He liked me, and so did Caroline's mom. They started getting more

comfortable with me and telling me things that had happened to them
at various times in their lives. I was beginning to see that they were no
different from other people in Clear Lake.

One day I heard Caroline's mom talking to a friend of hers. She was
telling her about her boss at work and how she knew he was interested
in her, how they had come close to kissing. I didn't like what I was hearing. She was supposed to love Bill and not be interested in other men. I
told Bill what I'd heard and he didn't seem to mind all that much. I did-
n't understand that at all. I was a very jealous man when it came to
Caroline. I didn't want her to think of any other boy at all, just me. I
guess I was being very selfish. Caroline was also very jealous towards
me. She would get mad if any other girl even so much as looked at me; I
liked it though, knowing she loved me so much.

One night Caroline's folks came home from dinner and Caroline's
mom was holding some magazine papers in her hand. She walked up to
Caroline and myself and showed us the papers. They were pictures of
naked people having sex. Caroline came unglued and I was blushing
trying to imagine why she was showing us the pictures. Caroline was
screaming at her mom and her mom was laughing. I tried to ignore
what was happening, but I couldn't understand why she would show us
such things. I wished that people who went to church wouldn't do such
things. If Caroline's parents didn't want Caroline and I to have sex, they
were sending the wrong message by showing us those pictures.

I was about to turn eighteen years old. I thought I had every thing
together in my life. I wanted to go to college but I knew if I didn't
receive a scholarship, I wouldn't be able to afford to attend. I decided I
wouldn't lifeguard this summer, but work in the woods logging. A logging company up river hired me. It was hard but fun work and in 1978
I was making ten dollars an hour, twice what I had made life guarding. I
would get up at four a.m. After ten hours of work in the woods, I'd
come home about seven, get cleaned up, and go visit Caroline before I
went back to bed to sleep and start all over again.

There were several times I almost died logging. With all the swinging cables and falling trees, it was a dangerous job. After a couple of months in the woods I knew for sure that I didn't want to be a logger. It was fun to do awhile, but not a lifetime.

In July I came home one evening to find Caroline sitting on my front porch crying. She had tears in her eyes and I knew something terrible had happened. I got out of my car and walked over to her. She got up and gave me a hug and told me that Teri had been killed in an accident that morning. We had recently attended a Spring Concert at Teri's school upon her request. She had a beautiful voice and had soloed on the Credence Clearwater song "Who'll Stop the Rain."

Now she was dead. Caroline said that Teri had been riding her bike down towards the highway and rode right into traffic. I didn't say a thing as I started to cry. The next day at work all I thought about was death. I was afraid to die, because I hated the thought of not being there for the people I love. I thought about Teri being so young. I asked God over and over again, "why her?"

She was so pure, so innocent. Why didn't God take the life of someone evil and bad? Teri didn't swear, or cheat, or have sex, or any of those types of things, but yet she was now gone. Someone like myself, that had done so many bad things in life, was still here breathing air. Life wasn't fair, and I knew it never would be. The demons liked bad people alive, but wanted to take the life of every good person in town.

Teri's mom asked me to be a pallbearer at the funeral. I felt honored. Caroline was having a hard time with the death of Teri. She cried at the slightest thing. Caroline and Teri had become good friends at church and Caroline missed her greatly. I knew what it was like, to lose a close friend to death. At night I would sit out on the hill over looking Clear Lake holding Caroline close and not saying much. I knew she could feel my love for her by being close to her. There was much comfort in the touch of our hands. We would watch the sunset over Puget Sound. The clouds would let rays of colorful light shine through them back towards us. Even though the clouds were dark, the rays of light shone on us. At those times I would feel as though every thing was right in the world.

The preacher at Teri's funeral tried to make sense of the tragic death, but words couldn't heal the hurt that everyone was feeling. He told us to take comfort that she was with God. I thought, well, that's OK, but I want her to be with her mom and dad and all of us. Just because she was with God didn't make me feel any better. Someone I cared about was gone and nothing was going to change the way I felt. The preacher kept speaking about the love of God and the grace of God. I knew that God loved, but I didn't know if I would ever understand why someone so young and pure would have to be asked to leave this world. I wished that I could show God a list of people that should be taken and not those who I thought didn't deserve it.

It was cloudy and raining lightly when we arrived at the cemetery. Some people were holding umbrellas. We carried Teri over to the hole that had been dug for her; it was only ten feet away from where Marie was buried. It was then that all the emotions inside me started to give way. I started shaking so bad I nearly collapsed. Josh, another pallbearer, grabbed me and kept me from falling. Teri's mom and dad and brother and sister came up to the grave and the casket was lowered into the hole. I wanted to scream and run forever but I stood in silence.

We all went back to the church to have some things to drink and eat. I thought it was weird that the family was expected to feed everyone on a day like this. Caroline was staying close to me and I thought about never wanting her to die or go away from me. On our way home the radio was playing a song by Billy Joel, "Only the good die young." I listened to the words and wondered if Teri had been bad, would she have lived? I thought about the kids who had died in my life and thought that truly the good do die young and the bad kids live. My thinking was totally warped.

When we arrived at Caroline's house we went for a walk up in the woods. We stopped and talked about life and love and we started to kiss.

I wanted to make love to Caroline. I asked and she said, "no, I don't want to."

I said, "what if you or I die tomorrow than we would never have had the chance to become one by making love."

It made sense to me. I kept saying, "I don't want to go through my life thinking I never had the chance to show you my love for you."

I kept asking and told her that it was OK because I was going to marry her after she graduated from high school. She gave in to my longings and we went back to her house and went in her bedroom and made love.

I thought I was ready for a sexual relationship and everything that went with it. We started having sex every time we were together. Her parents trusted us and they left us alone all the time. I often thought that I would never leave my kids alone when they were my age because of the things I was doing. I think that Caroline's parents knew something was going on but they chose to live in a land of naiveté. It confirmed my belief that those who don't know are the ones who get hurt. Knowledge is power.

Other than sex, everything was going pretty normally in our lives until one night when we went up to Skagit River woods to have sex in her parents camping trailer. We had been swimming in the pool and we got out to go take showers. I was standing in the shower when a little boy about eight years old came up and opened the curtain and pointed his finger at me and said, "I know what you're doing and it won't be long before you're all mine."

I looked at him and thought, what in the world does he mean? He was only eight years old, how could he know what I was thinking of doing? I told him to get lost and leave me alone.

I continued to take my shower and then I heard Caroline scream. I grabbed my shorts and ran over to the women's shower to see what was wrong. Caroline was inside, hysterical, saying that some boy had been in her shower, saying nasty things to her and saying he was from the devil.

I asked her what he looked like and she described the same boy that was in my shower room. I told her to get her clothes on and I would be outside waiting for her to come out and we could go to the trailer.

She came out and we walked back towards where the trailer was. Out of nowhere the boy appeared and started walking behind us telling us he knew what we were going to do. We tried to ignore him but he got louder and nastier. I'd had enough—I turned around to tell him to get lost. When I looked back he was gone, and I didn't think much of it.

When we got in the trailer, Caroline and I started kissing and then we started having sex. Then, out in the woods, where no cars could drive, came lights shinning into the trailer. I looked outside to see if maybe someone was out there with flashlights. The lights floated up about twenty feet, then floated back down and became more intense. I knew that God was upset with me so I fell on my knees and started praying to God to forgive me for sinning. Caroline looked at me funny like nothing was wrong. Then a car pulled into the camping site and shined its lights inside the trailer. I crawled on the floor to the window to try to see what kind of car it was. I was thinking that maybe Caroline's parents had caught us having sex. It wasn't their car and it looked like no one was inside the car. I was really scared, wondering who was watching us? I told Caroline to get dressed and we got in my car and I drove her home. Things were getting pretty strange being around Caroline.

A week later my house caught on fire and burned most of the dinning room and my bedroom. My mom and dad asked Caroline's parents if I could spend the night at their house until they had a place fixed up for me to stay. I was happy that I would get to stay with Caroline all night, even though we would be in different beds. I wanted to be with her.

That night, after watching television for the evening, we all went to bed. I was sleeping upstairs next door to Caroline's parents' room. Early in the morning I heard Caroline's mom scream for help in a weak voice. I went running into her bedroom and Bill had turned on the light. Joy was lying on the bed and an unseen force was pushing in her neck. It was like something was trying to strangle her. I grabbed her to help her sit up and something threw me back against the wall. I stood up and looked at Joy and her face was turning blue. Then whatever was choking her let go and she sucked in some air. Bill told me to go back to sleep that it wasn't a thing.

I walked back to bed and was thinking it was something, I didn't know what, but it was something. I started hearing something banging on the outside of the walls of the house. It was like someone was walking around the house hitting the siding with a small sledgehammer. It was loud and Caroline and her brother came running upstairs. Bill and Joy came out of their bedroom and Bill looked out the windows to see if he could tell what was making the noise. I was beginning to think some wicked spirit haunted the house. I thought it odd that Bill and Joy didn't seem all that concerned about what has going on. I asked Bill if he had a gun in the house? He said, "only a shotgun."

I asked him to get it for me so I could go outside and see who was making the noise. He didn't get me the gun. I was thinking it was weird, if this was my place and my family, I wouldn't be afraid to confront whoever or whatever was doing these things. The noise stopped and we all went back to bed. I laid there thinking about how close they had built their house to where Sharon had been killed as I fell asleep with that in my mind.

I started to dream that I was in this beautiful place. There were mountains and waterfalls and beautiful plants of all sorts. The fragrance was overwhelming my senses. I saw Caroline walking towards me and I reached out to hold her hand, just as I did it was no longer Caroline it was Sharon. She looked in my eyes and said, "Luke this isn't your love." I was confused by what she was saying. I followed her down the path and things started to change. Every thing was becoming gross and black. Sharon said, "this is your life Luke, flee from it." I let go of her hand and started running, the darkness was closing in on me and I couldn't escapee. I was struggling to get free but I was being over taken by it.

I woke up with sweat running all over my body. I looked out side and light was coming in the windows. I got up and went to the kitchen to get a glass of water.

At breakfast nothing was said about what had happened the night before. I was thinking that it was demons trying to get me. Why else would my house burn and it just be my bedroom? Then when I come up to stay with Caroline they come looking for me here. Was I ever going to be safe anywhere? When Caroline walked into the kitchen, all my thoughts turned towards her. She was so beautiful. I forgot everything except my love for her.

I spent every free moment I had with Caroline. It was amazing to me that her parents didn't know we were having sex together. I thought they were really out of touch with their kids. I felt somewhat bad about the things I was doing, but sex had a hold on me, it consumed my thoughts, my actions, and my life.

A lot of things were happening when I was with Caroline that didn't make much sense. One night as I was riding my bike up to go see her, it was really dark out and I was taking my time so I wouldn't get hit or ride off the road. The cloud cover was thick and I could only see the outline of the trees against the clouds. As I was riding I felt a hand grab me. I pulled away and started riding as fast as I could, trying to put distance between me and whoever it was. I could hear footsteps running after me as I started to climb the hill that led up to Caroline's house. My heart was beating fast, I wished I could see who was chasing me. At Caroline's house I ran inside and told her what had happened. She didn't act like she believed me so I let it drop. I was wondering if the Sather sisters were sending people and things after me? My fears about the dark were growing.

Caroline's parents were gone and we had to watch her little brother. We had sent her brother to bed and I was downstairs in the family room. Caroline was upstairs making something to eat when I felt something really bad coming down the hall from where Doug and Caroline's bedrooms were. I could actually feel something in my body, like my hairs standing up and a real sense of fear on my skin. I looked down the hall towards the bedrooms and saw a black blob floating in mid air. It came flying down the hall, past me, and right on out the window. I didn't know whether to believe my eyes or not. I was trying to figure out what it was, wishing that I wouldn't have been the only one to see it. When Caroline came downstairs I told her what I had seen. She looked at me like I was crazy and was seeing things. Maybe I was loosing it some. I had seen too much to let myself believe that. I at once knew the demons were living in Caroline's house.

Doug was crying in his room. I opened the door and he said the devil was sitting on his bed. I went into his room and felt a very evil presence—it felt stronger than what I had felt before. I told Doug he could go upstairs and lie down on the couch in the living room and watch television.

Caroline didn't seem all that concerned about the things that were happening. I tried telling her about the things that I had seen and what Doug had told me. She started kissing me and told me to not worry about such things. Her kisses took my mind off those things.

I started thinking about evil while riding my bike home. All of this demon activity with Caroline was starting to scare me. Caroline and her parents told me I had an over working mind. I knew what I had seen and it wasn't my imagination. Maybe the devil was still chasing me even after all this time I had been going to church. I didn't like that thought at all.

I rode my bike past the cemetery but was too scared to stop. I rode past the old church that had recently been bought by some people from out of town. They were turning it into some kind of church themselves. It was almost midnight when I went ridding by and I saw a bunch of cars parked outside and one man was standing on the front steps. I thought I should go to church to pray, maybe that would stop all this demon activity. I stopped and got off my bike and walked up to him and asked, "are you people having church to night?"

"We are having a meeting, I guess you would call it church."

"Do you mind if I go in and check it out?"

"I don't think you can do that, the meeting tonight is for the Order."

"OK, thanks."

"If you want you may check out the meeting on Sunday morning."

"I will sometime—have a nice night."

I rode off down the road until I was out of sight. I was curious about what was going on in the old church. It seemed to me that anyone should be able to go to church any time that they wanted. So I was going to sneak around and try to find out what they were doing.

I put my bike in some bushes and made my way through people's back yards until I came to the old church. I could see the man still standing on the outside of the church on the steps. I looked over the cars to see if I could recognize any of them. I made my way down over an old concrete wall and looked into the basement of the old church. I saw a bunch of people standing in a circle with white robes on. They looked different from the people who met in the old burner. At the old burner, everyone had worn black. I watched awhile, hoping I wouldn't be seen. They seemed to be praying or talking to someone, probably, I thought, to the god they worshipped. I had seen those kinds of robes before on television. The people who hated black people wore them and called themselves the Ku Klux Klan.

I had heard of this group being up in this part of the valley. At high school a few friends of mine, including Dale and Racie, had given me some papers on the KKK. I always thought Racie was an odd name.

One day in eighth grade Racie was saying, yeah to everything Dale said as he was talking about hating people for their skin color, and she would say, "I hate niggers."

She said I was a nigger lover because I had once gone out with Nancy who was a Korean girl. I smiled and said, "yes, I love all people."

I told her Nancy was a very nice person who never once did anything mean to anyone. Racie said Nancy's skin was a different color and she had no right to live in the same area as us. I wondered, how could anyone feel that way about any body? What if all the blonde hair people treated the brown hair people that way? What if we took all the fat people in town and made them move and called them names because they were not like us? What if we took every family that was poor and raped their children and took what they did have and killed them all? Wouldn't Racie herself fit into one of those categories? It didn't make sense to me to hate someone because they looked different, or acted different.

The people in the white robes started to walk out of the room so I ran to the other side of the church so I could see more of what they were doing. As I started to get settled into position by a window, car lights shown right on me. I took off running towards the lake, through the yards and over fences. Some men were chasing me on foot and I could hear cars driving fast, trying to cut me off from crossing the roads. I made my way towards the A-frame and back towards the highway. I was happy I was in such good shape. I knew no one would ever catch me on foot. When I crossed the highway they saw me in the lights of their car. I ran up past the old preacher's house and up past the Barret's house into the thick woods. I had forgotten my bike and when I finally thought of it—it was too late to go back and get it.

I rested in some tall brush and listened awhile to make sure no one was around before I came out and crossed the road and made my way to my house. I was trying to think of what they didn't want me to see? As far as I could tell they were not doing anything illegal. I wondered what they would do to me if they caught me? It didn't seem to me that they were worshipping the devil or anything like that. It was after two in the morning when I got home. I fell asleep and started to dream.

I dreamt that I was riding my motor cycle up on the mountain with Caroline holding on to the back of me. It was warm and I felt such love for her. We made it to the top of the mountain and started watching the sun set. It was beautiful. The sky became full of colors, from pink to purple to red. I started to long for more love in my heart as the sight of the sun setting was pulling me towards it. I felt myself starting to lift off the earth and I reached out to grab Caroline to take her with me. She didn't reach for my hand but shook her head no she wasn't going to go with me. I became very sad and asked her why she didn't want to go with me on such a beautiful journey? As I was watching her she started to change colors. Her red hair started to turn darker and her face became tan. She started to look like Sharon and she said to me, "Luke, I can't go because I belong to someone else."

My heart started to sink and my body with it. I started to fall and I couldn't stop, I yelled for Caroline to help me but she waved good-bye and walked off. I was falling fast almost ready to hit the ground when I woke up.

I sat up, then lay back down and went back to sleep. When I woke it was Sunday morning and I got up and showered and made my way towards church. I found my bike where I had left it and rode it to church. After church I started home to get my car to go up to Caroline's. I rode past the old church and stopped and looked at the people who attended there. They all seemed to be in their twenties and thirties and looked like they were still trying to be hippies. A lot of the women looked like they were pregnant but I didn't see any little kids running around. I rode home thinking I would find out more about those people in the next few weeks.

I spent my afternoons and evenings at Caroline's. I ate more meals there than at home. I wasn't very close to my parents but I knew they loved me and cared for me, they never missed a sporting event of mine anywhere in the state. They were proud of me for being All League in football and a State-wrestling champ. I wanted to be my own person so I didn't do much with them.

Right before school started I came home one night after football practice and dad told me to move my things out of my bedroom. I looked at him with a puzzled look on my face and asked why? He said that there was a girl that needed a home to stay in and my room was the biggest so Liz and this new girl were going to move into my room and I was going to get Liz's room. I didn't care because I was never at home most of the time. I asked who the girl was? Dad said, "Tammy Wolkins."

I wondered why she was moving from the people's house where she had been staying. She was a pretty girl and when Caroline found out she was moving into my house she became really mad. She asked me if I was going to take an interest in Tammy and stop seeing her. I told her no, that I loved her and had no intentions to leave her for another. When all of my friends at school found out that Tammy was staying with me they all thought I was a lucky boy. I would smile and think that I had no intentions of having any kind of romantic relationship with Tammy. She was going to be like a sister to me and I was going to treat her that way.

School was going well and I was looking forward to being done with it all. My weekends were spent hanging around with Caroline. One Sunday I went down to check out the strange new church. They called themselves the church of Guadeloupe. I didn't know what it meant.

I wasn't treated very friendly when I went inside to sit down. A guy looked at some candles that were burning and made the flames move with his eyes. I figured the man was moving his eyes with the breeze that was blowing back and forth through the old church. Some people seemed greatly impressed but I knew I could do the same thing as he did.

The preacher had a short message about the world being over taken by someone called Zog. He said people had to get prepared to fight a war against the evil ones who wanted to enslave us. I wanted to talk to the man who spoke so after the service I walked up to him and introduced myself. "Hi, I am Luke Mills."

He looked me up and down like he was sizing me up for something. "Hi, my name is Jim Matthew's, but people just call me Matthew's."

He was a man about thirty years old. He had a beard and his eyes were dark and deeply recessed in his head. He said, "I thought you would come back here someday."

"What do you mean?"

"You were the boy that was spying on us a while back." I was caught and decided not to lie about the spying. "I am sorry for that. I wanted to know what you were doing and the man on the steps wouldn't let me in."

He looked at me sternly and said, "don't ever spy on me again."

I knew he meant what he was saying. He didn't look like the kind of man you wanted to have mad at you. I said, "OK, I won't but I do want to learn more about what you were talking about this morning."

He told me in due time, if I committed myself to attending here and proved myself faithful, I could learn from him. I knew I wouldn't be attending their church very often in the near future. I did like what he said about having to fight a war with the evil ones, because I was in that war already and I thought that maybe he knew of the demons that had picked Clear Lake as their home.

Later that afternoon Caroline asked me why I hadn't been in church? I explained to her about visiting the weird church. She didn't like the idea of me attending some other church. She didn't seem to understand that I wanted to know the truth. To get her mind off the subject of churches I took her for a ride out towards Beaver Lake.

We parked at the fishing area and went for a walk up on the hill. When we found a nice place to sit and talk we started having sex. After we were done we started walking back to our car. When we got to the road and were walking to the parking lot, a car pulled in behind us and moved slowly. It wouldn't pass us but stayed right behind Caroline and I. We dropped over the edge of a hill to get to my car and I looked back to see who was in the car. I could see the outline of people but they didn't have any faces. It scared me. I yelled for Caroline to get in the car. I jumped in and started the car and pulled out to follow the car that was watching us. The other car took off down towards town. I followed it down the road to a corner, the car went around the corner out into the open flat and when I came around the corner the car was nowhere to be seen. I looked at Caroline, looking for confirmation on what I had seen. It was as though it had vanished into the fields. There was no place for it to hide or park without me seeing it. These happenings were starting to bother me more. I wondered who was so interested in what we were doing.

CHAPTER NINETEEN

"The hate of some people in town runs deep in their souls. Since so many of our young men have been sent off to fight the war in Europe the mill has hired Chinese men to work. The mill won't let them stay in the company houses or camps, but have made them a make shift tent camp to the south of town. If one of them comes to town alone he is likely to be attacked and beat. It truly shows the nature of this town."

Journal of Victoria Southerland
October 1918

That winter I worked on a dairy farm outside town. One of the men I worked with was twenty-seven years old, married, with two kids. He often told me about how he loved his wife and kids. He met his wife in high school and they were married right after graduation. She worked at a grocery store in one of the towns. She had been working there for a long time and she was an assistant manager. He would always complain that she spent too much time at work and not with him. I thought I could tell that he loved her very much. I was hoping that Caroline and I would have the same love for each other all of our lives. One weekend when he came to work he looked really sad. I asked,

"Why do you look so sad?"

"Because my wife was offered to manage a store over east of the mountains."

"Why does that make you sad? You should be happy, that will pay really good, and you can get a nice house and nice things."

"I don't want to move, she can stay here with me." He had anger in his voice that scared me somewhat. "Why don't you want to move?"

"I like it here, she told me that if I don't go, she is going with out me."

"Do you have a problem with her making more money than you?"

It was the wrong question to ask. He became mad and started cussing and telling me to shut up. He stomped out of the barn and got in his truck and drove off. He came back a while later and was being really quiet. It wasn't like him to be that way. I asked him some more questions.

"So what is the real reason that you don't want to move to the east side of the mountains?"

"Luke, I love that woman and I'm not going to let her do this to me or the kids."

He was talking in a way that I had never heard him talk before. I kept asking more questions to find out why he felt the way he did. "Isn't she trying to make a better life for you and the boys? Real love would say that you would do anything for your wife."

"There are things that you don't understand, believe me that I am not going to let this happen. She will be sorry if she carries on."

He had reached a higher point of anger and his face was turning red. I was seeing that what he was calling love was more of a control thing. Why, if you loved someone would you want to make them feel bad for trying to make a better life for their family? It didn't make much sense to me.

I could see that maybe he wanted to stay because this was where he grew up, or I could see it could be because his family was here. His family could always visit them where they were going it was only a three or four hour drive. If it were me, I would want my wife to be happy and as successful as she could be. I looked at him and said, "if you love your wife like you say, than you would support her and go with her to Eastern Washington."

He jumped at me and grabbed me and pushed me down in the cow manure and yelled, "Luke you had better watch what you say or I'll beat the shit out of you!"

I apologized and he walked off with his head hanging. I didn't understand his problem with the whole situation.

Driving home from school a few weeks later I recognized a man who was hitch hiking. It was cold so I thought I would give him a ride. I was driving an orange 1975 Chevy Vega that I had bought with my logging money. My friends made fun of the car and me, but it was paid for and I had bought it myself with no help. I did kind of wish it was a Celica Toyota and I could always pretend. The hitchhiker looked really rough, he was unshaven and dirty looking and I had seen him in the weird Matthew's church. When he got in the car we started talking. "Hi, my name is Luke."

"I am Otis."

He didn't seem all that friendly. I smiled at him and asked him where he was going? He said, "just into Clear Lake, up on the hill above the lake. Do you live up there? I have seen you driving up there a lot."

"No, but my girl friend lives up there and I visit her a lot."

I had seen a few of the people that attended that church up by Caroline's place. I figured they lived back in the hills somewhere. He said, "thanks for the ride, I am getting back from a retreat over in Idaho and my car broke down."

"That is a long way to go for a retreat. Did the whole church go that you belong too?"

"Not every one that attends there are believers."

"What do you mean by that? They all go to your church don't they?"

"Yes, but there is a higher level for people that understand who we are."

I didn't have a clue what he was talking about. He seemed to be way out in left field with his back turned to the plate. I was thinking that maybe he had done too many drugs or something like that. I wanted to try to understand what he was saying. "I know who I am. I am Luke."

He smiled and said, "but do you know you're God's chosen one?"

"Yes I know that."

"I don't think you understand what I am saying. In the world we are the minority, if the people that rule have their way we will be no more before the end of the century."

"We are not the minority, there are more white people here than any other kind of people."

"You have a lot to learn Luke. You have been fed a bunch of lies by the mainstream and you need to learn the truth."

I thought for a moment then said, "everyone says they have the truth. And I do want to know the truth and I am seeking for it."

"Listen to what Matthew's says, he knows a lot about all of this. We were back in Idaho preparing for the race wars that are going to happen in the next ten years. You had better be ready Luke or you will become one of the dead white guys."

He had me thinking—I had never heard this kind of teaching before and it interested me. I wanted to know more about what he had to say. He was serious about what he believed and wanted to take action. It was more than most people were doing in the church I went to. I looked at it as kind of a challenge to what I knew to be true. I believed that God loved everyone no matter what color of skin you had or where you were born and raised. I wasn't afraid to have my faith tested by these people.

About a month after the night Jimmy pushed me down in the cow manure, Caroline met me at her door crying. In her sobbing voice she told me, "Jimmy killed himself and his two boys up on the old logging road this morning."

I couldn't believe what she was telling me. I started to cry, not for Jimmy but for his boys, and for his wife who loved those boys with all her heart. I couldn't believe it—I had worked with him the day before. I had seen his boys out playing in their yard, with their mom was pushing them in the swing that Jimmy had built for them.

Why? Why would a man kill his own kids? Go ahead and kill yourself, but your kids? I couldn't stop crying. What kind of evil possessed a man to do such things? I knew the demons had a hold of Jim. I could see it in his eyes but didn't realize it until now. Caroline put her arms around me and said, "it was awful Luke. He shot them in the head, one at a time, then shot himself."

I screamed out, thinking how could anyone do such a thing to his own children? I could understand shooting someone bad, but to shoot your own kids was more than I could handle. I didn't know that he was so warped in his thinking. I knew he didn't want to move to the east side of the mountains. He could get a divorce and let his wife go, but no he has to make her pay—so he kills not only himself but also his kids. I sat down and tried to figure out his mind. This man had no love in him. How could he?

He told me that he loved his wife and kids but to do what he did showed me that he didn't even have love for himself. It wasn't in him to love anyone. What he had was pure selfishness and that's what he called love. It became clear to me that many men thought they had love but to look at it in reality it was selfishness.

Caroline and I sat there for a long time watching the clouds go rolling by. I asked, "who found them?"

"Your boss did. Jimmy didn't show up to work but Larry had seen him drive by the farm heading up the hill. So after a few hours he went looking for him thinking maybe Jimmy had got stuck four wheeling. He found them in the front seat of the truck with the gun sitting on Jimmy's lap."

I sat in silence, thinking it must have been an awful thing to find them that way. I felt sorry for Cindy. What was going threw her mind? What did she do to deserve something like this? I put my arms around Caroline and held her tight, wanting all the sorrow and pain to disappear.

The boys were buried in Mount Vernon and Jimmy was buried in Sedro Woolley. The funerals were at the same time. There were a few hundred people at the boy's funeral but only Jimmy's parents and a few of his family and friends at his. His wife didn't attend his at all. I could understand how she felt about him. I always wondered if she ever went to his grave and had a talk with him about the way she felt about what he had done? I could see her doing that. I could see so many things left unsaid, left undone for her to have to wrestle with the rest of her life. For me, death had taken on a new meaning. Even though someone was dead, so much was still left to be taken care of. I wanted to make sure that Caroline would know how much I truly cared for her and loved her. Those were words I never wanted to leave unspoken.

A lot of the people around town didn't seem to think much about the terrible things that had taken place. If they did think about it, they weren't talking about it. Maybe they couldn't comprehend how someone would actually do something like kill their own kids. Maybe they wanted to forget that it even happened. I thought the minister would talk about it on Sunday, but he also chose to ignore the subject.

Our new minister was fresh out of seminary. He was from the East Coast and he didn't believe like the minister that preceded him. I had a hard time listening to him. He didn't believe the Bible was all of the word of God, so whenever he spoke about the Bible, it always sounded like he was referring to a good story, good in the sense of Huck Finn or Moby Dick.

I loved to argue with him. I asked, "Mr. Devon, if the Bible isn't all the word of God than is it wrong to steal?"

"Regardless of what the Bible says it's wrong to steal."

"Well if there is no hell, than why do anything right?"

"Luke you have to accept that you will never know every thing in this world. Men have tried to understand God their whole lives but never came to the same conclusion. So we can not go and believe that the Bible is the ultimate word of God."

I didn't believe him. I knew he was so wrong in his thinking. If things were not true, than why spend your time being a minister? I could think of a hundred different things to do besides telling people stories every Sunday. Besides, Mr. Devon didn't believe that demons were real, and because he believed that way didn't mean that the demons didn't exist. I knew what I had seen and experienced and to me that spoke louder than anything some man who didn't have such knowledge could say to try to convince me otherwise. Again it told me that knowledge was power, he that knows, does not get hurt.

I was in my last year of High School and I was having lots of fun. I was in social studies class with the smartest kids in school. We had to do a team report on any currant topic. We had to work within groups. I had been getting an A all year, but I didn't brag about it, most of the kids wondered what I was even doing in this class because it was considered to be one of the hardest in school.

When Mr. Williamson put me in a group of five girls, they all went nuts, saying that they would surely not get a good grade with me in their group. These girls were five of the top ten students in our senior class. I could understand how they felt about me being in their group. They all thought I was stupid and I let them believe that. We would all go to the library to study for out report and I would sit at the table with them and daydream about being in the mountains fishing or hiking.

They had chosen euthanasia for our report. I didn't have to study for that because I already knew what I believed to be true about that subject. The girls would be in deep talk and thought. I would sit back and listen to them and dream about every thing else. Once when they asked me what I thought about what they were discussing, I told them.

"This time of year the meadows are full of melting snow and flowers are starting to pop their heads up to welcome the warm spring sun. The streams are filling up with clear cold water, so pure that even if it was a mile deep you could still see through it like it was glass. I told them that the Silver Firs and Mountain Hemlocks were starting to bud out, showing their new growth so fresh smelling, so bright, so soft. Even though the trees were hundreds of years old there was always something new about them. Isn't life like the mountains? Constantly changing and being changed by the years of weather. It could be snow, rain, or sun making things grow, while slowly eroding the mountain away. Some day my mountain will be no more, but all washed out to sea. That does not mean that I am going to go out there and take heavy equipment and tear my mountain down before its time. I will let time have its course, and so should it be with life. I don't want someone to decide it's time for me to leave this world and say Luke you have lived to 65 and now it's time for you to be put to sleep. That isn't right, no man or group of men should decide who should live and who should not live. As for me, I will live on my mountain until I die."

They all sat there looking shocked. First of all, that I could probably talk and second that I could actually think. I smiled at them, knowing they were seeing me in a different light. I could tell by the expressions on their faces that they didn't see me as a stupid person. Sarah said, "Luke your mind sure does work in different ways. How long have you pretended to know nothing? If you would have applied yourself you could be sitting with us in the top ten row at graduation."

"I have no desire to sit in the top ten row. I would rather sit up on my mountain and watch the valley below and know that my family and friends are safe."

They all looked at me like, where in the world is Luke going now? They all started to laugh. Julie asked, "Luke, does your mind ever stay on one subject for more than a minute?"

I looked at her and smiled and said, "once in a great while."

We finished our project, or I should say they finished their project. I did help with the presentation of our report. They all agreed with me that people should not be put to death for getting old. Our group received an A+ for our report and the girls were happy. After we received our grade the girls came up to Sarah and me said, "we are sorry Luke for judging you about how smart you were. It was really a lot of fun spending the last couple of weeks with you. It wasn't as bad as we thought it was going to be."

"Well thank you very much. It was great fun to work with such cute girls."

They all started blushing and smiling, and I knew I had made them all feel good. I turned around to head to the gym and Caroline was right behind me. She had a mad look on her face. I asked, "what is wrong with you?"

"I don't like it when you flirt with all these girls, I don't like you talking to any girls but me."

I looked at her and thought she had nothing to worry about. I loved her, not them, and I couldn't go through my life without having a woman to talk to once in a while. She was going to have to get over this jealous thing really fast.

Graduation was approaching and I was getting offers to go play football and wrestle at many different colleges. I had my heart set on going to school to become a minister and I was looking for a school that would offer sports and religion. I thought I had the whole world by the tail, swinging it around at my will. I believed I was going to make a difference in the world someday. I wanted to be a great help to mankind and make the world a better place for everyone to live. I didn't want other kids to have to see some of the things I'd seen or experience things that had happened to me or to those I knew. Maybe someday I would be president and pass laws to make everyone safe. I wanted to defeat the demons.

The last month of school I noticed that my second cousin was getting kind of fat. She was only fifteen years old and she was the daughter of Dave Davis. Her older sister in my class weighed about three hundred pounds. I felt sorry for her because every one teased her all the time.

Her younger sister was very good looking and skinny. Her name was Trisha. She seemed to be really sad lately. Her dad, Dave, had moved in with Mrs. Clark and his kids were living with his parents who were my Great Aunt and Uncle. I thought she might be sad because her dad had left to live with Mrs. Clark. I decided to talk to her to try to help her feel better about herself.

After school one day I drove up to where she lived and went and knocked on the door and asked her if she wanted to go have a coke in town. She said yes and we drove into town and went to the SideWalk Cafe. I asked, "how are things going?"

She looked at me confused, why was I asking this question? Then she answered, "not so good Luke. Life isn't fair."

"No it's not fair sometimes. You have to look every thing in the face and go on."

She sat there drinking her coke staring off into space. Her eyes looked like a war field, as they were all red and baggy. I asked, "you seem to be sad a lot, and you're not looking like yourself lately, can you tell me why?"

"So you noticed that I have put on some weight."

She started to cry and said, "Luke I am pregnant."

She asked to go so no one would see her crying. We walked out and got in my car and started to drive back to Clear Lake. As we were driving I asked, "I didn't know you had a boy friend, who is the father?"

It was the wrong thing to ask. She started to cry even more. She leaned over and put her hands in her face. I was quiet and didn't ask any more questions. After a while she lifted her head and said, "the father is my dad."

I didn't have any thing to say. I felt bad for her. All I could think was—it was time to go through the whole town of Clear Lake and kill all the perverts. Take no prisoners. My heart became full of hate for the men and women in town that knew these kinds of things were going on and did nothing to stop it. Trisha had stopped crying and said, "my dad used to have sex with Karen, she didn't like it so she made herself fat so he would leave her alone. She told me when I was eight years old that I should get fat because dad didn't like fat girls. I should have listened to her, then maybe my dad wouldn't want to have sex with me."

"Trisha, no father should want to do things like that to their daughters. It makes me mad that your dad did this to you. Does your grandma know who did this to you?"

"She doesn't even know I am pregnant."

"What are you going to do?"

"My dad says he is going to send me to live with my mom. She left him because she says he is a sick man and he said if she left she couldn't have us kids. So she left us here and I believe she knew what he would be doing to us. I hate her for that. She never loved me or my brother or sister, if she did, she would have taken us to live with her. She hated my dad so much that she didn't want anyone around that reminded her of him."

What she was saying brought tears to my eyes. All I could think of was what the hell was wrong with everyone in Clear Lake? "If you want Trisha, I can kill him for you."

She looked at me like I was insane. I was thinking of how I could kill him and not get caught. "I am serious Trisha, I can do that if you would like."

"Luke you're crazy. I don't want my dad dead, I love him and I just don't want him to touch me any more."

"Well OK, I won't kill him, I will cut his balls off."

"Luke stop talking like that! And don't you dare do anything to my dad."

"Well I want to help you somehow."

"Just be my friend, that is all I want." I smiled at her and told her I would be her friend.

I dropped her off at her grandma's, then drove over to Caroline's house. When I walked in her house she was standing there with a mad look on her face. I already knew what was coming.

"Who was the girl you were driving around town with?"

"It was my cousin Trisha."

"Why are you driving her around? Are you interested in her?"

"Caroline she is my cousin, and I wanted to talk to her about her home life. And no, I have no interest in her romantically. You need to stop being so jealous."

She walked away from me, into the living room, and sat on the couch. I didn't know what to think—things in our relationship were not going well. We had been going out for almost two years and we were starting to act like married couples I had seen around town. I didn't like it. Maybe she was getting worried that I was going off to college somewhere and she was still going to be in high school. I hoped that she understood that I was in love and she had nothing to worry about.

I was dropping by the weird church every once in a while to see what they were doing. Every time I was there Matthew's would watch me really close. I wanted to find out more about what they were doing because things didn't seem normal to me. Even though they called themselves a church, they didn't act like normal church people. They cussed a lot and acted like weird people most of the time. I didn't trust them at all. They seemed to be doing something secret all the time. Maybe they were the men that helped the demons? There were rooms in the church that I wasn't allowed to go in. I thought if a church had rooms that they didn't what people in—they had to be hiding something. Whenever I saw a "keep out" sign I read it as enter here. I had to somehow get into those rooms.

I chose Thursday night to break into the church because that seemed like the only night people weren't routinely there. Thursday night I walked to the tracks across the highway from the building. I laid down on the tracks and watched the church awhile to make sure no one was inside. I made my way to the back of the church, broke a window, and crawled inside. I had a flashlight with me and went straight to the door of a room I wasn't supposed to be in. The door was locked so I kicked it in. I started looking for papers and anything that could tell me who these people were. I found some papers and put them in my pack. I went to the other room and kicked the door in and walked inside. I opened a big closet and saw more money than I had ever seen. It was all neatly piled, almost to the ceiling. Where did these people get all this money? It was more than Mr. Woodchopper had ever dreamed of having. I was tempted to take some but everyone would want to know where I got all my money. There were some white sheets hanging in the closet. They looked like the ones that I saw them wearing the night I had been spying on them. I opened another closet door and found at least twenty rifles and stacks of ammunition. They had the three G's—God, Gold and Guns. I put some papers and a few books in my pack.

I went out the same window I had come in and across the highway up to my house. When I got to my room I sat down at my desk and started going threw the papers I had taken. I didn't feel bad for what I was doing because I felt like I was looking for the truth.

There was a swastika printed on the top of the first paper I read. They were planning to create a white homeland in the Pacific Northwest that would be free from all other races. That didn't set right with me, I believed God had created everyone on earth and every one had the same right to choose to live where they wanted regardless of who else was living there. Their literature was full of hate and I started to think I was in over my head. I was hoping that I could look these people in the eye and have them not see that I knew all about them.

The next morning when I awoke, I ate breakfast and burned all the papers and books I had taken. I was tense in school all day fearing I was about to be found out as the one who had broken into the church. After school I called the town gossip, Arlene, to see if she had heard of any sheriffs being dispatched to Clear Lake. She said no and wanted to know why I wanted to know. I told her that some kids at school had been talking about a big drug deal that was happening in town. I was smiling as I drove up to Caroline's house, I had given Arlene something to spread all around town, and she would be busy for quite some time. I was confident that nobody from the weird church would call the sheriff. With the things that were in the church, they would be fools to do that, but a lot of people that were criminals were fools. I had to play it cool when I was around them again. If I didn't go back around them they would know for sure it was me who broken into their church.

On graduation night I was kind of glad that I would be going away from Clear Lake for a few years. After the party that my parents had for me, I left with Caroline. We went to her house because her parents were at my house. We went to her room and had sex. It seemed our relationship had only one purpose anymore, and that was for both of us to get pleasure from each other through sex. I started to question my love for her. If she stopped having sex with me would I still want to be with her? I would always say yes in my mind but I was always catching myself looking and thinking about what it would be like to have sex with some other girl. Our time together every day consisted of having sex four to eight times. It was like I could never get enough. The battle between serving God and giving in to my desires was ending with me feeding my flesh to the fullest amount. Then the day that I feared second to only one came.

It was a Saturday in July when I called Caroline and her dad answered the phone and said Caroline wouldn't be able to see me that day. He said he needed to have a talk with me and Caroline and his wife. He told me to come for dinner after church on Sunday morning. I wasn't looking forward to the talk.

I knew what he wanted to talk about. Caroline had missed her period and both her and I thought she was pregnant. She had gone to the doctor on Friday and her mom told me she was sick that night, so I had not had a chance to talk to her. I wasn't ready to be a father. I was scared and alone. I couldn't talk to my parents because my mom and dad would come unglued.

I went for a walk and talked to God and told Him I was sorry for the things I had been doing. I told Him if He made it so that Caroline wasn't pregnant I would never have sex again until I was married. I cried and asked for God to forgive me. I told Him I was weak and that I needed help in overcoming my sin.

That night I dreamt I was with Caroline and we were on the highway walking towards Sedro Woolley. The sky had a very strange look, like a dull fire was burning in the clouds. A van full of bad things pulled up along side of us and I got scared and started to run and told Caroline to run also. She stood there asking me not to run. I was getting mad at her because she wouldn't come with me, so I went back to make her come with me, but then she grabbed me and tried to put me in the van. I fought my way free and ran down towards the river. I came to the bridge and stopped and looked across to the other side. It was safe there but I couldn't bring myself to cross the bridge. The van was getting closer and my heart was starting to beat faster and faster. I started across the bridge and it started to fall apart. I fell into the green water and started sinking fast. I was trying to swim for shore but arms with no bodies were dragging me under. I couldn't breathe. I am dying. I'm screaming for help, but no sound will come out.

I sat up in bed and reached for the wall to make sure I was in my bedroom. I was soaking wet and I got up to get a towel to dry myself off. I sat on the edge of my bed and thought about how my life was turning out. The very things that I hated in other people were the very things I was becoming. I felt like dying—I truly was worthless—I was a very evil person. I lie down and cried myself to sleep.

The next morning I sat next to Caroline and her parents in church. I wasn't looking forward to being at her house. After church Caroline's parents didn't let her ride with me. I drove to her house and went in and they sent Doug outside awhile. We sat down in the living room. Caroline's dad started to talk. "Luke we trusted you with our daughter and you have broken our trust. We are very disappointed in you.

You're nineteen and Caroline is only seventeen. We could have you arrested for rape."

I couldn't believe he was talking about having me arrested. He went on, "we thought Caroline might have something wrong with her and when the doctor did his check up he told us that she wasn't a virgin and that she had been having sex."

I was thinking he should have known that a year ago. "You're not going to be allowed to see Caroline any more. Thank God she isn't pregnant. You should think about your life and where you're going, you're headed down the wrong road right now and I'm not going to let you drag my daughter down with you."

There were tears in my eyes and in Caroline's eyes. What was I going to do without her in my life? I was also thinking about the gift that Caroline's parents had given my dad for his birthday. It was a pair of pantyhose with an extra slip for a penis. Here they were telling me of the wrong I was doing and they had given a gift like that to my dad. Who were they trying to fool? I was wrong in what I was doing but they were as wrong. Caroline's mom spoke up, "Luke we believed in you. We don't have any other choice. We are going to encourage Caroline to date other boys. You should go away for a few days and do some thinking. We are not going to press charges against you, but like Bill said, 'you will not be seeing Caroline.' We can't believe you did this."

I didn't say anything, but thought—well you better believe it, because we did have sex. And do you think she won't be having sex with others? Saying that would just cause more pain than what everyone was already going through.

Bill told me it was time for me to leave. As I left I looked at Caroline, hoping she would tell her parents she was going to go with me, but she was a good daughter and headed off to her room without looking at me. Hurt filled my heart.

No one was home when I arrived there so I packed a few things and headed off for my mountain. Back in the car the radio was playing

"Lonesome loser" by the Little River Band. Truly I was a loser. I drove as far up the logging road as I could and hiked up to the upper meadows. I pitched my tent and went and sat on a rock where I could see the whole valley. I remembered being up there before with Kenny. I remembered feeling so alone. Maybe I was destined to be alone. Moses was alone and he saw a burning bush. There was no burning bush on this mountain. I figured this was an unholy mountain because I had walked on it. It was Cultas Mountain—Cultas the Indian word for bad. Maybe the Indians knew something that the whites didn't.

I watched as the sun went down and saw all the lights come on. I could make out the skyscrapers in Seattle, 70 miles away. The lights of Victoria, British Columbia danced off the water of the Straight of Juan de Fuca. In all the thousands of lights that I was looking at—there must be someone out there that is just for me. Something inside told me that I would no longer be seeing Caroline. I thought I should put renewed effort into being a good Christian. God had heard my prayer and Caroline wasn't pregnant and I had promised Him I would do right. I thought I had better keep my promise, or die.

I stayed up on the mountain for three nights. It was kind of like being exiled. I explored and fished and dreamed all day. I wished my life could be so simple all the time. At night I could feel the visitors come. They just watched me, as I would pray for them to leave. After three nights I had enough and headed back home.

The next Sunday I went to my old church and got up and told all the people about what I had dreamt a few nights before.

"I dreamed that all the kids in Sunday school were sitting in the pews and that the new minister was taking garbage cans and dumping garbage on all of their heads. I tried to stop him from doing that but all you people were laughing and not helping. The garbage was words that came out of the minister's mouth, and you people are the ones who encourage him on." The whole place was in an up roar.

I walked out of church, planning to never return. I was going to free myself. I was going to leave and never return to Clear Lake. I was going to leave the demons behind. Within a week I had arranged to start session at a Christian college in Chicago.

CHAPTER TWENTY

"Sometimes I feel as though I have made an entire mess of my life.
Since the death of Mark I have not been able to find happiness. I
wonder if I am one of those souls created for eternal loneliness. The
only thing that keeps me going is my love for my daughters."

Journal of Victoria Southerland
December 1915

On the morning of my scheduled flight, I said good-bye to my mom
and dad and drove down the road. I saw Mr. Carter working in his yard
and he waved for me to stop. I stopped and got out and walked over to
him and asked what he wanted. He told me to sit down and relax. He
said, "Luke, what you said in church last Sunday was right. God has
given you an incredible gift and you should use it for his glory."

"I plan too, I am going to go to college and become a minister and
help people. I want to get away from this town. It's so full of evil and sin.
I don't understand why. It's like a host of evil spirits has chosen to live
here and not leave."

Mr. Carter came over to me and sat down. "Let me tell you a story
Luke. Maybe this will help you understand why Clear Lake is like it is.
Not too many people know the real history of this town. They all know
how this town was once the biggest town in the county. It was the

largest sawmill in the world during its hay day. It produced ten million board feet of lumber a year. This town was going places until the people chose to make a deal with the devil.

There were over two thousand men employed by the mill. The mill controlled the bank in town. Every business in town was solely dependent on the mill. The mill could make you or break you. The mill constantly needed more men for their operations and for the logging camps in the mountains. They would offer good pay and good living conditions and good food. A lot of men would come, but they wouldn't stay because a lot of them longed for female companionship. So the mill was losing men every day because there were only about seventy-five to a hundred women in the town and most of them were married. The mill somehow organized a secret group of men to terrorize certain people in town. The purpose of this group of men was to force women of any age into the houses of ill repute to perform sex with the men at the mill to keep them here to work. These men even went after young girls and young boys. If any families tried to fight them, the bank wouldn't let them borrow any money and they couldn't shop in the stores in town. No one would ever talk about what was happening, they would all try to ignore it, hoping that it would go away. The group was so secret that most of the people in town didn't know about them.

If you were to take a walk through the cemetery you would see a lot of the people died young. One young girl killed herself because of the things that were happening to her. The bad men even went so far as to burn up a house with the family inside because they wouldn't do as they were told. No one dared go to any authority at the county seat for fear of dying. The mill had complete control of the town and its people.

There were churches in town but the mill made sure that the ministers were kept in ignorance. If a minister got out of hand and started to tell the truth and saw the evil and demons that had taken over this town they would organize a movement to get rid of him. Clear Lake was in a beautiful setting but the people that came here had hearts as dark as the ashes at the bottom of the old burner. Greed was at the center of their lives and the mill would go to any lengths to add wealth to its self even if it meant rape, murder and lying. They would rape the hills and rape the children. They would take the lives of the men that worked for them and the lives of those who they used to achieve their purpose. It was as though the devil himself was running the mill. They were bent on taking everything good from the people and the land.

There was a family that moved here in 1897 and homesteaded up on the big hill about where Caroline lives. They had 140 acres of beautiful land. It was full of some of the biggest trees in the world. They cleared a small part for a farm to raise cattle and a crop for themselves. They saved about a hundred acres that they wanted to make into a park so people could see the big trees forever. It was a nice thing they were doing.

When the mill was running out of trees and having to go back farther and farther into the mountains they went to this family and asked to buy the trees from them. The family said no, that the trees would be saved so their grandchildren and their great grandchildren could see what the land was like before it was logged. The mill became very angry and one night the bad men went up and killed the father and raped the mother and daughters. They put them on a train the next morning and told them to never come back to this place. They clear-cut the whole property in less then a week. It was a very sad time for those of us who were afraid to do anything about what was happening. The people feared death over doing the right thing.

There was a certain young minister who came to town one year. He was full of fire for the Lord. The mill hated him. He would preach against the brothels, and the rape of the land, and the things that evil men were doing. A lot of people were going to his church. He had a beautiful daughter. Her name was Victoria. The mill warned him to stop preaching against sin in the town. They said that if he didn't stop that he would pay the price. He said he would never stop speaking what

God had put in his mouth. One night the bad men came and set the church on fire. Then they went to his house and took his daughter. He tried to fight but there were too many of them. He looked all night for her but couldn't find her. The next morning he found her body down on the edge of the lake. Most of the people thought she had drowned, but she had been raped and strangled.

The minister became filled with anger and went down to the mill and set fire to it. It burned most of the town down. It smoldered for days. You could see the black smoke for miles. The minister died in the fire. Some say he was trying to find the devil, trying to destroy the evil one in the flames. Those who live by the sword, die by the sword. The mill was damaged and would be rebuilt again but never saw the glory it once had. It finally went out of business in the 1920's.

That church was never rebuilt. There was a great exodus from Clear Lake. Only a few hundred people stayed behind, hoping to build a new life. I know that the demonic spirit was never dealt with and still makes its home here in this town and the surrounding hills. The bad men passed their work from generation to generation. I do know that they are still active to this very day hurting children and women in this town. I sure wish I knew who they are, I would stop them myself now. Luke, I believe in my heart that God will someday send another man to tell the truth to this town. I thought that maybe it was the last preacher we had. I know believe that God has shown me it's you. You have to know these things Luke. You have to understand and not turn from what God is calling you to do. You're the prophet for Clear Lake. You have to deal with that evil spirit Luke you have to defeat it. I will be praying for you."

I sat there trying to soak up everything he had told me. Every thing was making sense. The sexual abuse wasn't new. The bad guys had been around for almost a hundred years. All my dreams became clear in my mind, and I started to understand them. I understood why Nina's mom had never allowed any man to get close to her daughter. I understood the reason there was so much demon activity at Caroline's house. It was where evil had taken place and never been taken care of. My body was shaking, what I had been told seemed too awful to be real, but in my heart I knew it was the truth. I got up and thanked him for telling me the story and for the support he had pledged to me. I told him that when I was right with God, I would come back and deal with the demons in Clear Lake.

Instead of driving past the cemetery, I turned in to say one last good-bye to Sharon. I told her I was leaving town and wouldn't be back for a long time. I was standing by her grave when I saw that the window had been fixed over at Ralph's house. I walked over to the front door and opened it and ran up stairs. Ralph's mom yelled for him to not run up the stairs. I went down the hall to what I thought was the room that I had seen the girl in. There was a series of locks on the door; I opened them all and walked in the room. Inside was a bed and it smelled really bad. I looked to the corner and saw a skinny girl standing looking scared to death. She wasn't pretty, and she appeared to be retarded. Now I knew what they had been hiding. These people were ashamed of her. I smiled at her and told her in a soft voice that I wasn't going to hurt her. She looked at me and tried to smile but her face wouldn't work. Ralph's mom walked into the room and screamed, "what are you doing in here?"

"I wanted to see what you were hiding. And now I know."

"I'm calling the sheriff," she yelled.

"Go ahead. I am sure they would love to know how you treat your daughter."

"Get out of my house!" I'd seen enough so I walked out, got in my car and started for Seattle.

I didn't cry as I left the valley. I was happy I was out of there, my whole life was ahead of me, and what a great life it was going to be. I took all the hurt and pain and put in way deep inside me, hoping that it would never be found again. The more I could learn, the more knowledge I would have and the lest likely I would be hurt.

When I was at Sea Tac waiting for my plane I called the FBI and told them all I knew about the Order. I was sure that they would end up hurting too many innocent people. My flight left at 1:30 in the morning. It was the first time I was on a jet. It was fun and exciting. I was thinking about what Chicago was going to be like. I was thinking about Caroline and wishing that things had worked out differently.

When I arrived in Chicago I was lost. I had never been lost in the mountains but this was a jungle. I was told that I would be picked up under the United Airlines sign. I thought I had found it but when I looked down the isle there were over twenty United Airlines signs. Someone finally called my name and I was picked up and taken to the college. I truly felt like a bucket under a bull being in this big city.

I was expecting to see a campus with a nice clear river running through it, but when I saw the North Fork of the Chicago River it was just a drainage ditch with brown water. No sense in having my fishing pole here, there isn't a fish in the world that could live in that water. I laughed at what they called a river. They should come visit my home and I would show them what a real river is like.

I met a few of the teachers and a few of the students. I talked to a few of them about why they were here. We all had different reasons. A lot of those reasons didn't make any sense to me. I was kind of enjoying meeting everyone. I am sure a lot of people thought I was a little different from them. When I looked at myself I could see that I was way different.

On the first weekend I was in Chicago, I boarded the L to go see the museum of science and industry. When I first boarded the train there were lots of white people, but the deeper I got into Chicago there were more black people, until I was the only white person on the train. I was getting scared. An older black woman looked at me and said, "boy you look like you're scared to death."

"You would be scared if you were in Sedro Woolly where I come from."

"Where is Sedro Woolly?"

"In Washington State."

She smiled and said, "here is a word of advice. Just sit still, and don't look at anyone, and in about fifteen minutes you will be back in a safe area. And whatever you do don't get off of here until you're a long ways from here."

I thanked her and we talked about where I was from and what it was like in Washington. She was a very nice lady. I thought about people hating others because of their color, it still didn't make sense to me, but I wondered why I had been scared because everyone was black. I saw the way the men would look at me. They were like people I knew back home. They hated me because I was white. The world was truly a strange place.

I only lasted a few weeks in Chicago. I was having a hard time adjusting to living in the city and my professors didn't believe in the absolute authority of the Bible. I argued with them every class. Finally one day the Dean came to me and told me I should consider going to some other school that was more conservative. I thought that was a good idea and packed my things to head home.

I really missed my mountains. I didn't know why anyone wanted to live in a large city in the Midwest when they could live in such a beautiful place like the Pacific Northwest. I made my flight to Seattle and picked up my car at my cousins and headed back home. It was nice to see all the mountains again.

I moved in with a few of my friends that were in a bible study I had been a part of before moving to Chicago. Over the next year I gained insight into how to fight demons in the spirit world. I still wanted to be a minister but I no longer believed I needed schooling, I was going to learn from God, not men. I read in-depth about every religion I could find material on. I wasn't dating anyone, which was a good thing for me.

I was frequenting the Bible bookshop, and it was there that I met Leigh. She had such a cute smile whenever she talked to me. Her dark brown hair and green eyes and an easygoing manner that captivated me. Her father had been an active leader in the Reformed denomination and her family seemed so peaceful. We were married nine months after we met.

A couple of months later I was asked to be the minister of an independent church in the town of Arlington. I was flying high for the next few years, I was in a growing church and I thought that nothing could go wrong. I believed God was using me greatly. I didn't realize that my combination of youth, ego, role of leadership, and role of husband could turn explosive. Out first son was born and I blissfully added the role of father to my responsibilities. Thoughts of demons and my memories of Clear Lake were far from my mind.

One night while watching the news there was a story about Jim Matthew's and his followers called the Order. The FBI chased them to Whidbey Island and they were all killed in a shoot out with the FBI. I watched the news people talk about how they were white supremacist and that they were responsible for a number of robberies around the Northwest. I said, "I knew they would die fighting and for one another." My wife looked at me and asked, "why did you say that?"

"It's nothing, I was talking to myself, " I lied back.

I didn't want Leigh to know any thing about my past life. I knew if she found out things about me she would leave in a heart beat. I was feeling so empty and lost about who I was and where I was going. I stood for nothing I thought.

A few weeks later my wife left to visit her sister in California for two weeks. At the end of the two weeks she called and asked if she could stay a couple of more weeks. I wanted her home but I wasn't going to force the issue. Even though I said it was fine with me I felt rejected.

The next week I went to the elders of the church and told them that I wasn't right with God and that I was resigning from the pastor's job. I knew God couldn't work through an unclean vessel like myself. I was getting tired of living a lie. I wanted to find peace and rest.

I sat in my office cleaning things up and putting all my books away. I had failed my God, my wife, and my son. I was twenty-four years old and I still had not removed sin out of my life. The demons were still there. Again I thought of killing myself, but I wanted to be there for my son. I had failed and it seemed to me that I was trapped with no way out of the hole I was in. I still kept going on.

I questioned what kind of love was inside me? If I really loved God, would I do the things I did? If I really loved my wife like I was suppose to, would I have done the things I did? The only answer I could come up with was, no! I felt like I had lost all feeling in my heart. I was numb. I looked inside and all I saw was evil. Inside the secret chambers of my soul I had hidden things I didn't want anyone to ever see.

No one really knew the real Luke Mills, and if someone did know me completely they would hate me for sure. I had been hiding behind the minister role. I had been hiding behind my sports. If people could see what I had done they wouldn't believe what I really was like. My hiding places were slowly coming to an end. I was so afraid of not being loved that I never wanted anyone to see what was really inside me. In doing so I wasn't allowing myself to be loved.

I was hired to pick up garbage for the city. It was a fitting job for me. I was trash, I felt, and picking it up reassured me of that every day I went to work. The pay was good and so were the benefits but I never wanted to tell anyone what I was doing when they asked what I did for work.

It was great work—pick the can up—dump the can. Pick the can up—dump the can. It gave me a lot of time to think about things, some good, and some bad. The only thing bad about the job was the ass of a boss I had. He would call me every name under the sun, tell me my wife was a whore, pull my hair, put a knife to my throat and ask, "should I kill you now or later?"

He was a demon for sure. They had not given up on pursuing me. I hated it so one day I went and told the mayor every thing he was doing and the other men backed me up. He was demoted and sent home for a week. I never wanted to sue the city, it wasn't their fault the man was mean and insane. I had thought of killing him many times, but knew that would only end me up in jail. He just needed to learn proper social behavior.

In June of 1985 my wife and I had our second child. It was a girl. When she was born I was so proud. I held her in my arms and looked at her and said, "I promise you that with all my power I will never let anyone hurt or touch you in a bad way. If anyone does I will surely kill them."

My wife looked at me with a very puzzled look on her face. I handed the girl back to her and sat down and enjoyed being a new dad again.

Life was good. We were blessed with a new house in town and my kids were safe. I had certain things I was struggling with, but over all things were going well. I was getting along with my wife and with her parents. I didn't visit my parents much. I didn't like going to Clear Lake. There were too many memories there that I wanted to forget. Mom and dad always asked to see the kids but I was always busy and didn't have much time to take them over there. The last thing I was going to do was leave my kids in Clear Lake. There were still demons in that town, which I was sure, hated me with all their strength.

My brother married while he was in the Marines and had one daughter. He lived down south of Seattle with his wife. My sister married a Navy man and she lived on Whidbey Island about an hour away from the Valley. One week my brother called to see if we could watch his daughter for a few days while he went away with his wife. My wife said it would be no problem. He dropped his daughter off and she stayed with us for a few days. One afternoon after I got home from work my son was down stairs playing with Brenda. She was on top of him saying, "this is how you have sex." I peaked around the corner and saw what she was doing. She was saying things little girls that are eight years old shouldn't know. I told my wife what I had seen and I told her that I was afraid that my brother was sexually abusing his daughter. I went over to my parent's house that night and said to my dad, "dad I think that Collin is molesting his daughter, we need to get him help before it's too late."

My mom and dad looked at me like I was crazy.

"Well are you going to help me get Collin help or what?"

"Now Luke lets not jump to conclusions too fast."

I knew it was no use, they couldn't see things like this happened in life. I had to do this myself. I was going to have to face my brother and ask him myself.

When he came to get his daughter I asked if he had time to go golfing. He said he did. It was a nice sunny day and we were having a good game of golf. On the seventh hole I said, "Collin I have something I have to talk to you about."

He looked at me kind of funny and said, "go ahead and talk."

"Are you sexually molesting your daughter?"

He paused for a moment and said, "no, but someone is and I think it's someone in our neighborhood."

"I am sorry for having to ask this but I was worried maybe you were doing it and I wanted to get you help if you were."

"No, but we have her in counseling and I hope she tells us soon who is doing it."

"Well I hope you find out, and if you need any help taking care of them I will help you."

"Luke I would have thought you had gotten over wanting to punish people for doing those kinds of things. If you do something like that now you will go to jail."

"Well, those kind of people don't deserve to live. If anyone ever touches my kids, I will kill them."

"That isn't your choice to make. Now stop that kind of talk."

"What are you going to do? Tell mom?"

We both started to laugh. Asking my brother if he was doing such things to his daughter had been a hard thing to do, and I hoped I would never have to do it again.

In the winter of 1988 our third child was born. He was born early and had to have an emergency operation. He was sent down to children's hospital in Seattle. It was one of the hardest times on our marriage.

Facing the possibility of our son dying made me think of all the things I had done wrong and I figured that this was a punishment from God or that the demons were still after me and wanted to hurt my offspring. It was a confusing time for me.

Our son was in the hospital for three weeks before he was able to come home. I spent many hours on my knees asking God not to take him, but to take me. God was a gracious God and gave us our son back and brought Leigh and I closer to together.

To help pay for the medical bills I started a landscaping business. It was growing fast so I quit my city job and dedicated myself full-time to landscaping. It grew even faster and I was surprised how thoroughly I enjoyed it. Things seemed to be going pretty well in my life. I loved making settings that I had seen in the mountains in people's back yards. It truly was a wonderful thing.

My sister had distanced herself from the family. I didn't know why but I let her have her space. She was going through a divorce and I called her several times to see how she was doing. She would never return her calls and I hadn't seen her for over a year.

On Thanksgiving Day, after we had dinner my sister called me. I was excited because I hadn't talked to her in such a long time. She said she wanted to talk to me at her house. I asked if she wanted Leigh or the kids to come? She said, "no, just you." I told Leigh I would be gone visiting my sister and headed out the door.

I drove over to her house expecting to have a nice reunion with her. She met me at the door and asked me to come in and sit down. Her new husband was already sitting on the couch. I took a seat across from them and smiled and said, "how are you doing?"

They looked at me with hesitation and said, "Luke we have turned you in to the Sheriff's Department for molesting our son."

I couldn't believe what I'd heard. My heart was sinking and my pulse went up. "Why do you think that I did something like that Liz?"

"Mark says that he was touched and had semen put on him by someone that is tall, dark and has glasses."

I was thinking she had described half of the world's population. She went on.

"The time he describes is about the time he spent the night at your house. So this week we took him to a therapist and she had us contact the sheriff. And we wanted to tell you because you're going to be arrested when we go to press charges."

I didn't know what to say. I wanted to run—I wanted to scream. I had never touched a kid sexually in any way. I was being torn apart inside. I sat there listening to what they were saying. The demons were still after me to destroy me in any way they could. I wasn't going to make a defense for myself. I wasn't going to get into my innocence, because I felt my sister and her husband really believed I had done this. I asked, "did Mark name me?"

"No, just someone tall dark and with glasses."

"So you really believe I did this?"

"We are not sure, but we are not taking any chances."

I got up to leave and said, "I am sorry you feel this way. If you have any questions you may call and ask me but I will be going now."

I got in my car and drove towards home. I was scared, and again I felt so alone in the world. I started to cry thinking that my own sister would think I would do something so horrible to a child. I didn't know what to do. I wanted to go home and pack my things and my family up and move away from this whole valley. I pulled into my driveway and walked into the house.

Leigh asked me how the talk went. I looked at her and couldn't keep from crying. "Liz thinks I have sexually abused their son Mark."

She looked at me and asked, "did you? Do you like little girls and boys?"

She may as well have taken me outside and cut my heart out and threw it on the ground and stomped on it. Those words cut so deep, deeper than any words had ever cut before. I couldn't blame her though. I knew that she didn't know five percent of the things I had done in my life. She knew I had struggled with different things at times. How did she know if I was a pervert or not. Still those words hurt deeply. I looked at her and searched for words to say.

"Leigh I have never touched a child sexually in my life, I only like women who are over twenty and have breasts and pubic hair. That is what sexually excites me, not little boys or girls."

I called a lawyer friend at his house and told him what my sister had accused me of. He told me that if I was arrested before Monday, I should basically refuse to answer any questions. He warned me not to assume I was smart enough to understand the motives of any question they threw at me. He said he would call the sheriff on Monday and see what my status was with the investigation. I told him I wanted to run, he said that would only prove in people's minds that I was guilty. I hung up the phone and went to my room and lay down and cried myself to sleep. Every thought ran through my mind. I was trying to think of any time that I had done anything wrong to any child. I could think of none. The demons were winning again.

The rest of the weekend went slowly. Every car that drove up the driveway made me look to see if it was the sheriff. Things were very stressful between Leigh and myself. I was worried my kids would see me be arrested by the sheriff in front of them. Inside I wanted to strike out and kill every man that had ever touched a child in his life.

On Monday I went to my lawyer's office. He called the sheriff and they told him I was under investigation for first-degree child rape. Then he asked me if I had did it?

"No"

"Are you willing to take a lie detector test?"

"Yes I am."

"It won't be fun Luke, they are going to ask you lots of questions, it's going to be personal and it will get very ugly."

"I don't care, I want this to end."

He said that he would personally arrange and oversee a test and that the Sheriff Department wanted to do their own test. He recommended that I refuse to take the sheriff's test. I said I wanted too because I had nothing to hide.

A couple of days later I took the test arranged by my lawyer. It was like being tested to see if I was retarded all over again. Just this time the wires were to be hooked up to my heart instead of my brain. They hooked up the wires and said, "OK, we are going to start."

They went on for a long time asking all kinds of things. I told the truth. They had promised that none of the things they were asking was going to be made public unless I was found out to be lying. After the testing was over they took me into a separate room. My lawyer came in and said, "Luke you passed every question one hundred percent." I felt strongly relieved.

He said the Sheriff's test was going to be harder and they would really get nasty. He asked me if I was up for that. I told him I was.

In their test, the Sheriff asked about the same kind of questions. A lot of times when they were asking really personal things about my sex life I wanted to tell them to take a hike, but I knew that would be counterproductive. I wanted to ask the man asking the questions if he was getting off on my answers. I am sure they would have locked me up for that. I passed that lie detector test one hundred percent also. It was nice to have that out of the way.

I thought things were getting better for me until I heard from a friend of mine that my sister was going all over town telling every one I had sexually molested her son. I was broken. What could I do, I was labeled, everyone would look at me and think I was a pervert. The demons were relentless in their pursuit of me.

My friend said she had heard it at her work place and she had defended me. I thought about what good friends I had, but other friends that didn't know me well stopped coming over to see us. That hurt me, but I could understand they wanted to protect their kids and not socialize with a man who had been accused of sexual child abuse. I often contemplated killing myself. My high expectations for my life were not compatible with the degradation I was involved in. I couldn't understand how my sister would think and talk about me in such a way. It was I who would sleep at the foot of her bed when she would cry at nights. I was the one who had tried to keep her safe. Yet she didn't see any of that.

The Sheriff brought in a specialist from the university who interviewed Mark. He confessed that he was molested, but not by me. He wouldn't tell them who had done it. He said he was upset over his mom and dad getting a divorce and he didn't like his new dad all that much. My lawyer called me and gave me the news.

I was waiting for my sister to call me and tell me she was sorry. The call never came. I was hiding my hurt with all the anger I was displaying to those around me that I loved. I didn't understand myself at all or those who would want to keep hurting me. It seemed to me that the demons were winning.

Chapter Twenty-one

"I never thought I could love again. To find the love of my life is a dream come true. With my past now behind me I am able to live the rest of my life in the acceptance and love of another.

Journal of Victoria Southerland

May 1920

Leigh encouraged me to go see a counselor and talk about things I had gone through. I went to one and during our first meeting we had a talk about my life and other things. He said that by talking with me he sensed I had some serious problems with my father. I told him, "my father was a good man, he gave us a house to live in and food on the table. He attended all my sporting events. He did his job well in raising me." The counselor persisted, "no, he wasn't good to you." I looked at him and said, "if you keep talking like that about my dad, I will break your little neck."

He said he was right and that is why I was getting mad. I got up and walked out of his office. I wasn't going to go back to him and listen to his foolishness.

It was the summer of 1989 and every thing was going great. My family was healthy, my business was growing and my wife and I were enjoying each other. We sold our house in the city and had a house built for us out by my mountain. It was a beautiful setting to live.

I was putting shingles on my new roof when Cliff, the neighbor down the road, came running out of his house and hollered, "there's a phone call for you Luke. It's your wife and she says it's an emergency!"

My heart sank as I thought maybe something bad had happened to one of my kids. I ran for his house and he handed me the phone. "Hi, this is Luke."

"Luke, you have to come home now. Something terrible has happened."

"What?"

"I am not going to tell you over the phone, you just come home now."

"I am not leaving until you tell me." I pleaded with desperation.

"Luke, it's going to hurt you, you're not going to like it."

"Just tell me." I yelled.

"Your father raped your niece, Cindy, and your sister needs you now and the sheriff is headed out to arrest your dad."

I hung up the phone and walked towards my house where my truck was parked. I started to feel sick and I fell to the ground. I couldn't cry. I moaned like I was dying inside.

Thoughts from my childhood came flooding into my mind. I couldn't move. Cliff was looking at me asking what was wrong. Sorrow was flooding my soul. Things I had forgotten or didn't want to remember popped into my head. I now knew who the demons were. It became all clear to me. Had dad really raped me that night when my butt was so sore inside? I remembered my mom taking me by the hand and leading me down the hallway to the bathroom where my dad was waiting for me and being made to take a bath with him. I remembered being out in the forest and having things done to me, and being threatened that I would die if I told anyone. In my mind I had covered that up with seeing hundreds of rabbits running free in the woods, with my dad shooting at them and missing them all. I remember being chased by other men whom I was to be shared with. My dad and those others were my demons.

I remembered all the things that my mom had done to me as my father watched and participated. I remembered my sister crying at night because of the demons. Was it really dad? Did mom know all along? From my memory I was sure she did know and even help. Was my dad one of the bad guys and that is why he was never home when they came? I didn't want to believe those things but my heart knew them to be true. My own father who I had admired was the demon I had been seeking all along.

Cliff helped me up and I walked to my truck and got in and drove towards Clear Lake. I was going to my dad's house to kill him. I was going to make him feel the pain that I had felt so many times. I turned onto the road that led up the hill and pulled into the driveway. I got out and walked in the house. Mom and dad were sitting calmly on the couch. I said, "what did you do?" I had so much anger inside me.

"Luke I was trying to show Cindy I love her."

Anger built inside me. I screamed, "love! You have no concept of love. The Sheriff is on his way here to take you to jail. So get your butt outside so mom doesn't have to see this."

Mom started to cry and beg me not to do anything. I grabbed dad and threw him against the wall. He went to run outside and I kicked him as he ran out the door. He fell on the ground and I walked over to him as he shielded his face with his hands. I heard a car in the driveway and I got on top of him and raised my fist. I could see utter fear in his eyes, I wanted to kill him but he was my dad. A hand grabbed mine and pulled me up. It was the Sheriff. He knew me and said, "Luke you don't want to do that. We will take him in and he will get what he deserves for his crimes."

I looked at my dad and started to cry and said, "I loved you dad, I loved you."

My heart was totally broken. I looked at my mom and turned from her. Her eyes told me she knew everything. They put the handcuffs on my dad and put him in the car. Mom was telling me that she didn't know a thing, and I said, "right, and I am not your son." Did she think I was dumb enough to believe her?

I got in my truck and drove to the top of my mountain. I got out and walked to the top and sat down and watched. I didn't care about anything at that point in my life. Who would understand me? Who could love me? I couldn't even love myself. I sat up there all night thinking about everything. Maybe in the morning I would wake up and all of this would be one big dream and I would be four years old again. The thought made me smile.

Over the next few days I thought about a lot of things. I asked my sister why she had left her daughter at dad's house? She said that she didn't think dad could do the same thing to her kids as he had done to her. I had never left my kids at my parent's place, because something deep inside me had always told me to keep my kids with me. God had saved my kids. My sister went on to tell me that dad used to take her to other men's houses to be used sexually by them. She said that other girls were with her and shared by both adult male and females. That explained being baby-sat at different houses. She said that they did lots of mean and evil things. They would even threaten to kill them if they told. I myself remembered them being in meetings where they did evil things and I would try to stop them.

The faces of those people who hung around with my parents came to mind. These were the people who did the evil things to children. Both men and women preying on other people's children and even worse, their own.

My sister said that when dad was at Baker Lake throwing the dog in the water it was because he was telling her if she ever told anyone what he was doing he was going to drown her. She said, "Luke, why do you think we went through so many pets? Dad would shoot them in front of me or other kids and tell us 'you will be shot if you tell anyone.'"

She went on to say, "when you used to sleep at the foot of my bed, dad would come in and get mad at you and strip your clothes off and beat you till you passed out or went into a seizure. Mom and dad would lock you in your closet to keep you from interfering with what they wanted to do. Remember when we went out to that island and all those people were at that one yellow house? They were having sex with all of the children there, and you were fighting the men and women. They took you and locked you in a bathroom. We could hear you crying, saying you were going to kill them all someday. You escaped out a small window and ran to a house close by. But those people were evil also and they brought you back. I remember mom and dad beating you till you couldn't walk. You closed up and wouldn't talk for months. Why do you think everyone called you retarded? Mom and dad wanted you to be dumb because you never went along with their plans.

You would always fight and never do want they wanted. Even when mom or dad would want you to give them oral sex you would kick and hit and spit on them. You would get that look on your face like you were going to kill them someday. I do believe dad and mom are very scared of you to this day. They started to leave you alone when you were six. I think that is why you don't remember much, you chose to forget and live your own life. Luke they tried to kill you. Do you remember the time dad pushed you off the dock into the river? Or the time mom gave you something to eat and you passed out? The time dad held your head under water until mom started crying."

"Enough!" I wanted to hear no more. Those thoughts were unbelievable and all they did was hurt my heart.

I didn't know what to say. I did remember those things but I had chose to forget it all. All I could think was my poor sister had it far worse than I did. I understood why my sister was so explosive about our family. I could understand how she had felt betrayed by me. I had told her many times I would never let anyone hurt her. I had failed in keeping her safe and because of that her hate for me was great.

In my mind I had created the kind of family that I wanted to be a part of. I had a perfect stay at home mom. A dad who worked hard to give us kids everything. In my own world I had created the "Leave it to Beaver" world. But now that world was gone and reality was the only thing left.

A few days later my sister packed everything in her house and moved without telling me where she was going. Her next door neighbor called me and said that my sister wanted to leave me a message. She said that she was sorry for all the trouble she had caused me, and that I was the only family member that really cared for her and she knew I would never forgive her for what she had done to me. That was it. I wished she could have told me herself. I heard she moved to the East Coast.

With my sister gone and my brother living in Eastern Washington, I was left alone to deal with my mom and dad. I went to visit dad in jail and asked him where all his money was because mom had to pay some bills. He said he had no money. I asked him what did he do with it all? He lowered his head and cried. I asked him why he did the things he had done? He said he was trying to show how much he loved Cindy. I asked him about other things, but all he would do is cry. I felt like I was the father. It was a weird feeling. I told him he had no concept of what real love was.

When dad went to court for trial, I had a talk with him. I told him that he was wrong for what he had done. I told him that he had better plead guilty for his crimes. I told him that if it went to trial I would testify against him. I told him, "face your punishment. Remember how you used to say that to me? Well, it's your turn now."

The day of the sentencing I was handed a file full of papers. A man said, "Luke, you might want to look through this."

I went outside and started reading. It was an investigation of the things my dad had done and evidence taken from his sessions with different caseworkers. It said he had started having sex at age 11, with his sisters who were 15 and 16. He had homosexual sex with his best friend at age 13. When he was 15, he was having sex with his eight-year-old sister. He saw his dad have sex with his sisters often. He had sex with three of his grand kid's, Cindy, Brenda, and Mark.

The disgusting revelations went on and on, including the fact that he had another family in Seattle, which explained why he always worked so much on weekends and holidays. He confessed to contact with men that were like him but wouldn't give out their names. He was fearful of his own life, and if he told, they would kill him. I was convinced they were the bad guys. These men and women were still abusing children. The report said that he refused to answer many questions about unsolved crimes and incidents in and around Clear Lake. I wanted to know those things myself.

I was mad, I was hurt, it was he that had molested Mark and he let me take the blame. I wished him dead. This man was truly a sick man. To think that I came from him made me sick to my stomach. I put the report down and wondered what kind of man my dad's father had been? It seemed so true that the sins of the fathers were visited on the third and fourth generations. I said to myself that I had to break that cycle, and if it ever came up in myself I would kill myself before I hurt a child. I prayed that God would protect me from evil and demons.

I left the courthouse that day after the judge passed sentence on my father. I went by the cemetery and walked around looking at all the headstones. There were many people who had died young, and sometimes whole families lie next to each other with the same date of death. I prayed that one day the truth would set everyone free from the bondage of demons and their story would be told.

I still had a lot of questions. Who were the bad guys? I wanted to find them and eliminate them. Did dad have anything to do with the death of Sharon? What ever became of Mr. Anderson? Maybe it was him who was thrown into the lake that one night when I was young? Nina was long dead and buried and her story would never be told. I wondered if Mr. Woodchopper had a good life in Mexico? How many people had my dad, and the men he did evil with, hurt? Why did my mom go along with this sin for so long? Were not moms designed to protect their children? How many people in town knew about these things and did nothing? I wanted answers. I was sure my dad was one of the bad guys. It became very evident to me that the evil I feared most was the man I wanted the most approval from, my father. I had found the demons that had been haunting and chasing me all my life.

I made my way up to my mountain that day and sat down and put my hands in my face and cried like I had never cried before. After some time I lifted my head to look at the valley below. A thick layer of clouds and fog blocked my view. I thought about how my life was the same way—it seemed most of the time that my life was dark clouds and fog, never seeing clearly the direction I should go. As the heat from the sun dissipated the clouds and fog, I could see the town of Clear Lake sitting so peaceful. I pondered how its dark lies had affected the lives of those around me.

The Small brothers are both in jail. Two of the Barret boys are in jail, one of them for shooting a State Trooper. Bud Randahl has AIDS and is dying. Mr. Vendetii served time in jail in Chicago for various crimes— he was a big Mafia man. Mr. Hoffa still is beneath Vendetii's concrete on the hill. Caroline married a Luke and moved away. One of the Mark's boys is in a wheelchair, paralyzed from a driving accident. Lisa was molested by her dad and others and has lived for one sexual relation- ship after another. All of the Clark kids have been married and divorced, and have lives like their parents before them. The Mark's still run back and forth to town three or four times a day. Scott was gored by a bull and is mental. As for the Sather sisters, one is dead and the other is on heroin. Len and his dad became Christians and are leading good life's now. Jeff Mays died of a drug overdose. Bev's dad died of cancer but not before the state pulled her younger sisters out of his house. So many people were damaged.

Of all the kids I grew up with few remained in Clear Lake. Many were given a burned out torch from their parents and have never risen above the evil and sin that has them in bondage.

Others came to see that there is a better way to live, and became good mothers and fathers to their own children. Many of the people that I talked too didn't want to talk about the things that happened when they grew up. It was best they said to forget those things ever happened, but I could not ignore what had taken place. I knew I couldn't go through town and kill the people who had done the bad things. It wasn't right to make them pay for their crimes. "My Word is sharper than any two edged sword, cutting to the depths of a mans heart." So instead of guns or knifes, I chose to use the written word. More victories have been won with words than swords. There was so much more that I could have written about, but there wouldn't be enough pages to record the wrongs that took place. For so many people those events will haunt them for the rest of their lives until they chose to deal with the pain and the hurt. Only then can true healing come.

I came to understand from all the things that I had done and seen that I had a lot to learn about love. My own dark lies had truly hidden what I really desired. Real acceptance, and forgiveness, and most of all love. I had much to learn about real love, what it is and how it's expressed. I may never understand the reasons why behind everyone's actions, but I do know that I have a full life a head of me, and a chance to make things wonderful for my children. I had met my demons head on, and defeated them. They would haunt me no more. As I watched my kids playing outside in the creek on the side of my mountain I smiled greatly. I was finally seeing clear for the first time in my life.

I still drive through Clear Lake every once in a while. The remnants of the old mill are gone now. The A-frame is torn down, and the swimming area has all new docks. Except of a few new houses the town still looks about the same as it did thirty years ago. There are new faces mixed in with old faces. The people that knew the things that happened will deny them. Others will believe that such things never happened. Yet, we all know it is not what a person is on the outside, but what they are on the inside that counts. Some times, things are not as they appear to be.

So when you visit Clear Lake stop in and have a drink at Ellens. Stop and visit the postmaster and ask her where Jimmy Hoffa is buried. Go to the swimming area and listen for voices of children playing in the sun. Watch for the Marks to drive by on their way to town. Walk in the cemetery and read the headstones, and listen for small quiet voices from years gone by, telling you things you already know. The truth.

The End.

About the Author

Jeff McClelland lives in the Northwest. He spends his time with his children teaching them of the great outdoors. Spending his summers hiking and his winters skiing he finds time to write. Look for his next novel "Where Big Trees Fall".